D1526148

THE DEAD SAGA
ODIUM

By

USA Today Bestselling Author

Claire C. Riley

Odium The Dead Saga Series
Copyright ©2015 Claire C. Riley
Cover Design: Wilde Designs Elizabeth Constantopoulos
Editor: Amy Jackson
Formatting: Sarah Barton Book Obsessed Formatting

ALL RIGHTS RESERVED. This book contains material protected under
International and Federal Copyright Laws. Any unauthorized reprint or use of this
material is prohibited. No part of this book may be reproduced or transmitted in
any form by any means, electronic or mechanical, without express permission from
the author.

This is a work of fiction. Names, characters, places, and incidents are either the
product of the author's imagination or are used fictitiously, and any resemblance to
actual persons, living or dead, business establishments, events, or locales is entirely
coincidental.

LOVE FOR ODIUM. THE DEAD SAGA SERIES

"A MUST READ for fans of The Walking Dead."
Amazon Top 100 Reviewer

"A terrifying and exciting ride through a brutal post-apocalyptic landscape."
Goodreads Top 100 Reviewer.

"I cheered, I laughed with some very snarky characters, I saw some very original ideas, I got grossed out, scared, and happy. Claire C. Riley writes a pretty striking story, and hell, I'm still excited about it!"
Liz – Fictional Candy Book Blog

"This book is not about Happily-Ever-Afters. It's a suspenseful thriller full of action, sadness, angst, death and emotions!"
Lo - Crazies-R-Us Book Blog

"I would recommend Odium to anyone that isn't afraid of an accelerated heartbeat! I have never laughed so hard and been so scared all within the same breath!"
Liz-Crazies-R-Us Book Blog

DEDICATION.

For anyone who is prepared to stand up for the people with no voice. For those who are willing to fight for what they believe in, and to hell with the consequences. Because somebody *has* to believe that we can make a change in the world. After all, our humanity is what separates us from the *real monsters*.
Be real. Be truthful and be heard.

For my street team – Little Red's Deads.
Thank you for your constant encouragement, for your sweet and often equally hilarious messages, but mostly, thank you for being so fucking cool. I feel deeply privileged to know each and every one of you.

Thank you to all my beta readers, my editor and the amazing girls in my Bad Ass CP's writers group, you all rock so much, and I don't know what I would do without you all.

ONE

MIKEY

Life is crazy. It's unpredictable and confusing, but most of all it's hard. It's hard to lose people you love, and it's even harder to see them become monsters. But that's the way of the world now, what we've had to grow to accept. I don't think the world is ready for the apocalypse. It's never been ready. I know I'm not.

A great man once said that '*to fight evil, you must pluck it from its root*—to destroy that evil at its source, before it has time to grow and spread, killing or infecting everything around it. And when you've done that, life and love will spring free from where the bad once grew, and they will flourish.

That's the only way to survive this apocalypse.

We must end the evil—behead those demons, both alive and not—and let humanity breathe again. Because we're fucking suffocating right now.

There must be sacrifices—to save the ones we love, to protect those that need protecting. We must love freely, forgive quickly, and keep pushing onwards, because you never know when it will be too late.

There are some deaths that slip you by. Like the breath of air that leaves your lungs, they're gone before you even thought to realize it. Other deaths strike your soul. They gut you, stripping you bare of everything you ever were because of their profoundness.

You don't recover from those deaths.

You don't forget them, or move on.

These deaths stay with you, a part of you. Forever.

TWO

NINA

The crackling of the fire was seducing me, leading me to believe that we were safe. Staring into the flames, watching them dance and flicker, one would believe that there was nothing left to fear in this world. That the days and nights were as calm and peaceful as the sandy coast of an island.

But it was all a lie—a twisted illusion of reality—because in this life everything was to fear. Beneath those crystal blue waters lurked monsters and evil. You didn't always see the danger, but it was always there.

"Tell me something."

I glanced away from the flames with a heavy sigh and looked across at Nova. A cigarette was stuck firmly between her lips, and I raised an eyebrow to tell her to continue.

"Why did you really come on this suicide mission?"

I rolled my eyes at her but she pressed on. "I know you said all that caring bullshit," she waved a dismissive hand around, "but it's more than that. Who in their right mind would risk their life for people that they've never met and are more than likely dead?"

"You did," I said dryly and stared at her with conviction, but she only grinned slyly before pointing a finger at me.

"Listen, I did this for personal reasons. My sister caused all this shit, so it's my duty to sort her mess out." She shrugged and took a long drag on her cigarette, burning it right down to the butt. "I'm just doing my sisterly duties, bitch." She grinned again but it didn't reach her eyes.

"Oh come on." I snorted in irritation and shook my head. I stared back into the flames once more, throwing on another handful of small branches as I did. My argument was useless.

We were enclosed within a scrapyard on the outskirts of an old town. The place had been practically empty of the dead, which was lucky for us, because we were exhausted from traveling, fighting, and driving. We'd set off three days before from base camp to hunt out a woman named Hilary, who might or might not have been impregnated with deader spawn. Everything had been going well until we had to stop for gas and someone had tried to hijack us.

Of course those fools didn't know who they were messing with; they saw two women and assumed us both feeble and helpless, when we were anything but. It didn't matter now—they were dead and wouldn't be bothering anyone for a long while. However, our truck had been surrounded by the dead, and all of our gear with it.

We had hung back for a couple of hours, waiting for them to leave, but when the day turned to night and they were still there, we had to hightail it to somewhere more secure since the little garage was compromised, and there was no way I was staying in the woods after nightfall.

Thus bringing us to our current location. After walking miles and slashing and stabbing our way free from a large horde of deaders that took us by surprise, we found ourselves in an abandoned scrapyard. We cleared what little of the walking damned was here, and locked ourselves in for the night.

"Well?" she pressed, not giving up the discussion so easily.

I glanced back up at Nova, looking upon her dirty, pale face—a face scarred and grazed through the years of hell she had suffered through since this all began, yet beneath all the grime, her features were still sharp and beautiful. I huffed to show my unhappiness at answering the stupid question, but she shrugged again and took a swig of something alcoholic that she had found stashed in one of the office drawers. Her red hair hung low down her back, inch long roots and grease clinging to the long tresses.

"Back in the walled city, we were all terrified," I began, my stomach rolling at the memories. "Of the dead, of what would happen in the future, for our families, and selfishly, for ourselves. As time passed and we realized that this wasn't a small problem that was going to go away, not anytime soon, anyway—we grew to accept the new way of life." I swallowed down the lump in my throat and frowned. "I was mourning my husband and the loss of everything I had known—my entire life was gone. I was feeling lost and confused, but we were safe there—at least until the government or the army or someone ended the war with the dead. I mean, we were fed. And we felt relatively protected. But more people were turning up every day, and things were getting crowded. One day there was a small outbreak and someone turned, killing many of the people inside. Strict rules were quickly put in place, and when anyone new arrived they were stripped and checked for bites and diseases, any signs of illness. It was all going so well, considering, but I should have known when things starting getting like that. I should have known it was all going to go to shit."

I stood up and stretched out my back. Looking toward the tall iron-and-wood gate that we had locked shut, my hands now firmly shoved in my cargo pockets, I let out a heavy sigh. This place reminded me of the walled cities in a lot of ways: tall, protective fences, imposing gates. It was a false sanctuary.

I looked back to Nova and continued. "When things started to go wrong, and more and more rules were brought in to supposedly keep us safe, people started to be punished for things, whipped for not doing things correctly, or beaten for talking back. The first time we were all in shock, not quite believing what had just happened. I couldn't understand why no one was helping them or stopping what was happening—even me." I looked down at my feet. "I never knew that I would have so much fear," I murmured quietly, but I knew she had heard me.

Nova stood up but didn't do the typical girly thing and try to hug me. Neither of us were that type of woman, at least not anymore. Instead she thrust her bottle toward me. I took it, drinking down a quick swig—because the physical pain of burning alcohol in my gut was a far better one to handle than the pain of remembering.

I wiped my hand across my mouth. "We began to starve, slowly, but surely. The men in charge didn't care. Once people got so weak and at risk from dying, they were thrown over the walls. And there was nothing anyone could do then. It was too late to try to stop what had already begun. If you wanted to eat, you begged, borrowed, and bartered. Begging generally got you nowhere, borrowing was only good if you had a skillset, which I didn't, so I was left to barter for my food. Only problem was, I had nothing to barter with." I looked at her and this time it was my turn to shrug.

A deep frown etched across her forehead, and there was a silent understanding between us on what I bartered with. She shook her head and looked away as if embarrassed for me.

"Back behind the walls I was a nothing—a nobody. No one cared if I lived or died, no one stood up for me, no one ever tried to help me. It was like I was already dead," I stated simply.

I began to walk away; I needed space and air. My mind felt full of too many old memories that I'd sooner forget than remember. The memories haunted me. The screams that echoed in my mind late at night. The small bite mark on my inner thigh that still throbbed whenever I ran—and not a deader bite mark, a human one. It was all too much. What happened when I was captured by the Forgotten should have been worse. The experience was just as brutal but over a shorter period. But it wasn't worse, because by then I had hardened to brutality, adjusted and become able to blot it out—at least for the most part.

My time behind the walls would never leave me, though.

"You didn't answer my question," Nova said to my retreating back.

I turned to look at her. "I'm going on this suicide mission because I know I'm not nothing anymore. I'm not dead, and I won't let fear and cowardice stop me from living. Because I can't stand by and watch people die and do nothing about it anymore. If I die trying to save one person's life, then it's a better death than if I was dying for no other reason than fear."

Nova stalked toward me, and for a minute I thought that she was going to punch me in the face, but she didn't. She stopped, standing toe to toe with me, and she smiled. "Fear only wins if you let it rule your heart, darlin'." She gave me a small nod.

I gave her a crooked smile. "Exactly."

"When I met you I thought you were a total asshole," she said with a laugh.

"I was," I laughed back. "Hell, I still am. Don't go ruining my reputation." The dark atmosphere lifted as we chuckled, and I was glad that it was her that came with me on this stupid mission and not someone else. Mostly I was glad that I wasn't on my own.

"But seriously, you don't seem like the same person I met way back." She waves an arm around like we've known each other for years and years and not months. The apocalypse did that to you, each day seeming longer than they used to, making a week seem like a month.

It was my turn to shrug. "I guess I'm not. I came away from the city feeling angry, bitter, and full of hate. Like the world owed me something. I had to learn to adapt to the world again—to people that cared—and to start to care again. For three years I had only known pain and anger. You begin to get accustomed to that crap after a while. It gets in your head and it owns you, if you let it. But I feel better now—stronger, more emotionally and physically ready for this world. Let's just hope I live to experience some of it."

"You're still a moody bitch," she said with a laugh.

"Of course I am." I grinned. "Not all scars can heal so quickly. Plus, I guess some of the moodiness is just who I am."

She slapped me on the shoulder and smiled broadly. "I'm going to piss." She passed by me, and then it was her turn to stop and turn back around. "And Mikey?" she asked with a yawn. She was trying to be casual in her questioning, subtle almost, but she was about as subtle as a brick to the face.

I shook my head. "I don't know. I was just trying to help. Maybe I should have told him what happened with Rachael on our mission. But as much as I think your brother is an ass—because he is so very much of an ass—those people need him. I was too afraid if he left that if he left because of me, and anything happened that got people killed, that it would be my fault." I sighed, my heart feeling full. "I can't have another death on my conscience."

She nodded in agreement. "For the record, I thought you two were great together."

I pursed my lips. "Thanks, me too. But he didn't trust me, and this life is built on trust. If he can't trust me, then what's the point, you know?"

We lapsed back into silence as we both stared off into different directions, thinking our own morbid thoughts. When I looked back at her, she had started walking away again, and I shrugged and headed in a different direction to find more wood for the fire.

There wasn't much to burn—it was, after all, a junkyard full of old cars and trucks, all piled high, and all unusable. I heard a noise off to my left and immediately pulled out my katana. I stalked past a beat-up old Ford and crouched down low, and as I turned the corner I could see something moving in between the rows. From its jerky movements, I knew it was a deader we had missed.

THREE

My heartbeat picked up as I followed after it as quietly as I could. I came to the end of the row and saw it following blindly after a small, bony deer. My heartbeat went from quick to a full-on thunderstorm at the sight of the frightened animal, and I crouched even lower. The deader reached forward and growled hungrily. The deer bleated and backed up another couple of steps. It was only small, probably just a baby, and my heart panged for it. It was like watching a weird game of cat and mouse, only with the deader following the deer and me following the deader—that was, until we all came to a dead end. It was only then that the deer began to cry loudly, realizing its mistake—that its own judgment was now closing in on it.

The deader shambled forward quicker, eager to sink its filthy teeth into the frightened beast. However, in its eagerness it didn't sense me, and before it could grab the deer, I slammed my katana into the back of its head, feeling the soft crunch of bone trembling through my wrist. It dropped instantly to its knees and I pulled out my knife as it started to fall forward onto its face. Black gunk sprayed out from around the hole in the deader's head, and it finally found its peace.

I looked at the deer, seeing its innocence, its vulnerability in this world without someone or something to protect it. How it made it this long, I didn't know. I held out my hand to it and smiled, making soothing noises like I was trying to get a cat to come toward me. It continued to cry, though not as loud as before, as if it somehow sensed that I was different from the other person that had been following it. It was still untrusting, still frightened, but it wasn't as panicked as before. I moved forward, uttering more soothing words to it, until it could not back any further away.

Even in the darkness, I could see its thin body trembling with fear, and my fingers gently stroked its soft fur. Its heartbeat frantically drummed at a hundred miles an hour under my fingertips, and I couldn't help but shed a tear for it. All it had ever known was death and fear. And for some reason that horrified me to my core.

Because we should know more than this—more than death and destruction. More than hate and murder. This world was once a beautiful place—which, granted, I never took much notice of at the time—but if I could go back, I'd be grateful for every little thing.

Perhaps that was the real reason I wanted to find this woman: Because the child she carried was all about new beginnings, and hope. Because perhaps with that child—with that hope—we could build a real safe place, somewhere that no deaders could get to, and we could build a future from this dead world.

I gripped the neck of the deer and pulled it toward me. It struggled and cried out, even as I hushed it and rubbed its ears in an attempt to calm it, and then before it could move away I dragged my katana across its throat. It kicked out with feeble, weak legs as its blood gushed from its neck, and I held it at arm's length so I didn't get the blood on me. Minutes passed as it bled out, and when it was completely dead I grabbed it around its middle and carried it back to our fire.

I stepped over the deer's mother, the carcass old and long rotten—even the flies had finished their meal on the body. I headed back to Nova, wondering how we had missed it the first time around. Its body had been torn open, its insides dragged out and devoured. Its black eyes stared emptily in front of it. Like the eyes on a teddy bear, they were cold and devoid of life. Its mouth hung open in a silent scream, its tongue lolling to one side. I moved away from it quickly, not wanting to see any more, and feeling guilty as hell that I'd just killed its baby.

If there were a mirror nearby, I knew I wouldn't be able to look at my own reflection. I felt shitty for killing this animal, though I shouldn't have. I mean, it's ridiculous that I felt any remorse for killing something that would sustain me, and keep both me and Nova alive. It was something that only a weak person would feel, but I couldn't help it. I couldn't stop the guilt that poured through me, the sadness that engulfed me as I carried the innocent animal back to camp, its weight a heavy burden on more than just my arms.

It had survived this long with its mother, and then between me and the rotting deader, we had wiped this entire family away. It broke my heart, but my stomach ached with the need for food, for the nutrients that this animal would give me. I knew I was being a total freaking girl over it, but I told myself that it was okay as long as no one knew. As long as everyone kept on believing the tough girl image that I projected, no one would ever know how weak I really was.

Nova stood when I came out of the shadows, confusion covering her face, which quickly turned into a wide smile as she clapped her hands together in delight.

"Well, darlin', I didn't know you were treating me to supper." She laughed and took the dead deer from me. "Skinny little thing, isn't it?" she said, poking its ribs.

"Better than nothing," I replied.

"True that." She opened her backpack and pulled out some plastic bags from our supplies. Who knew that these things that had once polluted so much of our world would in fact be insanely useful at the end of days?

I passed an upturned drum filled with dirty rainwater—not safe to drink, but it was hella good to wash up in. I sank my hands into the icy water and scrubbed away the blood.

"Do you know what to do with that thing?" I asked. Because I sure as hell didn't. I saw what Mikey did to the rabbit and I could possibly mimic that, but this was not a rabbit.

"Just leave it to me," she said, and lay it down on some tarp we had found earlier.

She pulled out one of her knives and began to slice away at it, and even though I had just killed it, I couldn't bring myself to watch her. I stood guard as she cut away at it, the sound of tearing flesh and fur, snapping bones, and the smell of the blood making my stomach churn. But it also made me hungry, and I turned around to see if the food was ready to be cooked yet.

Nova had the deer in several sections, and was still digging into it with her knife. She glanced up at me and chuckled. "Come bag these guts and bladder up, darlin', but we're cooking the liver and kidneys—plenty a' nutrients there for us."

I shook my head with a grimace. "Nope. I'll dispose of them, but I will literally vomit on my shoes if I have to scoop and bag any guts."

She laughed even louder, and despite me retching as she dangled a leg in the air, I managed a small laugh too.

"You have to learn how to do this sometime, you know," she said, but I turned away as she scooped up the insides and tipped them into one of the plastic bags. The sound of them sploshing together made me retch loudly. "Come and get em'."

I turned around and headed closer to her, reaching for the bag of guts. She swung the bag at me like a child dangling a worm in front of her younger sibling, and laughed and jumped away.

"Nova." I scowled, but she did it again anyway and laughed even more. "Stop that, that's disgusting." I finally snatched the bag from her and darted away, holding the bag as far in front of me as I could.

"You're such a baby sometimes, Nina. Get rid of that and see if you can find some more wood for the fire so we can cook us up some food." She began separating the body parts of the animal, and I headed back into the car graveyard to bury the insides somewhere that wouldn't attract any deaders. I passed the deer's mama again and made a mental note to go a different way on my way back out. Every time I saw her dead eyes, guilt traveled up my spine. I also wondered about moving her corpse in case her blood attracted any deaders. Deaders tend to stay away from anything that was already dead—as if there was something in the scent of the living that attracted them, and as soon as that little flash of life is extinguished, they were no longer interested.

But I didn't like taking chances.

I carefully climbed up onto the roof of a rusted out car and placed the gore and entrails inside, under the driver's seat and out of the way, and then I climbed back down. The air was cold, and I hurried back to Nova using a different route than previously, wanting the heat from the fire.

I stumbled upon a car that looked like someone had been living in it. Clothes and blankets covered the backseat, a couple of plastic bags filled with various items like half-empty water bottles and canned sardines. I wondered if all of this stuff was the deader's that I had killed only an hour ago—obviously before he was a deader—because if so, then this stuff was free for the taking. Yet a niggling feeling made me leave everything. It felt wrong taking any of the things, just in case it was somebody else's and they came back for it. Though if we had locked them out of the scrapyard for the night, they were going to be either killed or seriously pissed at us tomorrow morning regardless. Because by locking them out we had either sentenced them to death or given them a nightmare night of survival. I closed the door on the car without taking anything and continued back to Nova. We had food—fresh meat now—and supplies. I couldn't steal someone else's things when it could mean life or death to them. I wasn't a killer—well, not a human-killer, anyway. I did just kill my first deer, after all.

I bit into the meat, pulling away thick chunks of stringy flesh. It tasted so good, and I couldn't help but let out a low, satisfied moan as it slid hotly down my throat. I would be embarrassed if Nova wasn't having the same reaction as me. I dropped the bone into the pile at my feet and took another leg. I shivered because of both the cold night air and satisfaction from the food.

Surprisingly, for such a skinny animal, there was more than enough to feed us. It was possible that our stomachs had just shrunk due to the lack of food, but whatever—I was just glad to be feeling warm with food in my belly. I took another bite, the meat coming away easily. Though possibly a little overcooked, it was still oh-so-delicious.

"This is good, right?"

I looked up at Nova, who was sucking the marrow out of a bone, and I nodded but didn't speak through my mouthful of meat.

"I mean, this is really good. Not just good, but good-good." She threw her bone into the pile and grabbed the last leg. "I don't remember the last time I ate without being rationed on it. Or maybe it's because it's real meat, and not some freeze-dried crap of some sort." She took a chunk between her teeth and began to chew, grease sliding down her chin that she wiped away haphazardly with the back of her hand.

I swallowed what I was chewing and nodded again. "It's really good" was all I managed before I took another mouthful of deer. I hadn't realized quite how hungry I was until the deer had started cooking, and the scent of fresh meat had sent me almost insane with hunger.

We finished off most of the animal, for once not being careful to ration and just eating until we were full. I packaged up the leftovers into more plastic bags and put them into our backpacks for the following day. It felt oddly comforting to feel so full of food that I had a slight tummy-ache from it. Comforting and satisfying. My head was achy and tired, my eyes sore from the need to sleep.

I put out the fire and we climbed up and into one of the cars, both of us piling inside to sleep. After finding a wandering deader we'd agreed it was probably not safe enough to sleep on the ground, even if we were almost certain that there were no more lurking in the dark. It was just not worth taking the risk.

Nova took the passenger seat, laying it all the way back and stretching herself out, and I took the backseat. I sat up for a while, staring out of the dirty windows. It began to rain, slowly at first but eventually coming down harder. The sky was dark and thick with clouds, not a single star to be seen. Even the moon was hidden from me, and after a while I finally drifted off.

FOUR

I woke up early, jumping upright as my dreams still flashed before my eyes, the sound of screaming ringing in my ears, and the taste of blood in my mouth. Nova was snoring peacefully, unaware of my freak-out, and I was glad of that.

A light sweat covered my brow and I wiped it away with the sleeve of my sweater, embarrassed that the memories were still haunting me. How could something still affect me after so long? And when would they stop? They had stopped for a while, when I shared a bed with Mikey—as if his presence had soothed my fractured soul. But since we had been apart, they had started again, and with vigor.

It was early, by the looks of things, and I automatically looked at the watch on my wrist, though it was a fruitless exercise. My watch had stopped working six months or so back, yet I still wore the pointless item because it reminded me of home, and made things seem more bearable. You know, like, '*holy shit let's chop this disgusting zombie's head off before it eats us, but hey, let me check the time first.*' Whatever—it made me feel more grounded to wear it, even if it didn't work anymore.

I lay there staring up at the ceiling of the car, looking at the rust stains that covered the interior, and the spiderwebs that had been built into the dusty corners. I watched a fast-moving spider scurry in from the cold outside and run across the roof and into its web. I grimaced, and I swear to God it was staring down at me. I was so glad that I hadn't known it was the night before—otherwise I would never have been able to sleep. I sat up, not being able to stand the spider's constant staring any longer, plus I didn't trust the shifty little bastard not to jump down onto my face. It was huge and hairy and might have had fangs. Hell, it could have been venomous for all I knew. I didn't want to run the risk of falling back to sleep and it falling in my mouth!

I shuddered, the involuntary tremor running through my body and giving me the heebie-jeebies. I gave myself a mental shake and forced myself to calm the hell down. I looked out the window and saw that nothing had changed while we'd slept, in the world or in the scrapyard. It was still the same crappy place we went to sleep in, and the same zombie-infested world as yesterday. Not like I had expected it to be any different, of course, but one day—you never know—maybe we would wake up and all of this would be a dream. But I suppose "nightmare" would be a better analogy.

I sometimes fantasized about that: waking up and it all have been something my crazy mind had created. I imagined that Ben was still alive and we still lived in our little house with the brown fence. That I still got to wear pretty shoes and makeup, and that if I was hungry I could just go to the refrigerator. I imagined the long bath I would take, with a face mask and bubbles and hair treatments, and our comfy bed that I would sleep in, curled next to my husband's warm body.

It was stupid and unfair to do it to myself, but sometimes it was hard not to. Sometimes the reality of this world was just so horrific that I needed to get away from it—to get lost in memories and imagination and think back to when things were good, and safe, and I didn't have to fight for my life every day. I never told anyone else I did this, mainly because I couldn't bear to voice these thoughts. They were mine, and they stayed inside me. No one else could have these thoughts and memories.

I wiped at my eyes, determined not to cry. The sun was shining today, though the air still felt cold and dampness clung to it. At least the sun was out—and that could only mean that winter was on its way out. Everything always seemed better when the sun was out. In such a dark and brutal world, a little sunshine could make everything seem…a little more hopeful, perhaps—for at least those thirty seconds when you could close your eyes, tilt your face up to the sky, and imagine that you were far, far away. And it made a good respite to the freezing temperatures we'd been traveling in.

From this position I could actually see over the fence and out of the yard. It looked pretty quiet out there, actually—no movements either near or far—and that was good. I was hoping that we could travel back to the truck and get moving again. Because we couldn't just leave it there full of all our gear. It had everything we needed to survive, and while I knew that Nova could handle herself and would no doubt be able to create some new style of weapon from some old rusty car parts if she had to, I would much prefer to have our nasty ration packs and weapons that we had brought along on the trip.

I yawned, a face-stretching, jaw-clicking yawn. My eyes watered and I stretched out my shoulders, pulling my arms across my body one at a time until I heard a satisfying click in each shoulder. I glanced back up at Mr. Skinny Legs. He was still sat there, watching me, and he continued to creep me the hell out.

"Nova," I whispered and nudged her shoulder.

Her snoring lightened but she didn't wake up, so I nudged her again.

"Nova!" I whispered a little louder, startling her awake. To my surprise, she jumped out of her seat and fell into the footwell of the car in two seconds flat. Her weapon was in hand as she stared up at me.

"What is it?" she whispered, peering up slowly out of the window to her right.

I held my hands up and tried to restrain my chuckle. "Whoa. Easy, tiger."

She looked back at me and scowled. "Everything's good?"

I shrugged. "I'd hardly class this as 'good,' but we survived the night, yes."

"Then what?" she hissed, still clearly confused as to why I had just woken her.

"I'm getting up. I'm hungry. I just didn't want you waking and being worried where I was." I shrugged again.

She climbed back up into her seat and lay down again. "Nina, you should never be allowed to wake people up. Ever."

I leaned over the back of her seat and stared down at her, but she already had her eyes closed again. "It's not my fault that you're wound up so tight. You're like a freaking cobra!" I whisper-shouted, though I had no idea why I was whispering, since she wasn't actually asleep anymore.

"You startled me," she said drolly, her eyes still firmly shut. "You should never startle a ninja."

"You are not a ninja," I snorted.

"I could be," she murmured already drifting back to sleep.

"Whatever," I replied tartly. "I'm going to look around. There's a huge spider back here and it's creeping me the hell out."

Before I could move, Nova was back on her feet and climbing out of the car. We were two cars high, and we precariously began to climb back down.

"Ninjas don't like spiders, then, I'm guessing," I said with a chuckle as I followed her down.

She met me at the base of the car, because apparently ninjas can climb quicker than me, and I grinned at her over the roof of the beat-up Ford that separated us. She ignored my amused stare, instead going through a quick inventory checklist of the items situated on and around her body. I'd do the same but I'd feel kinda stupid doing it. She was way more armed than me with several knives tucked into various sheaths from waist to ankle, and a shotgun strapped to her back. Satisfied that she had everything, she looked over and gave me a quick nod, and we headed back to where we'd had our campfire the previous night.

The telltale circle of rocks and burnt-out fire pit are still there, but any other sign that we were there was removed last night. Nova set about starting another fire for us, and I emptied the buckets that I'd cleaned out and left to fill with rainwater overnight.

Twenty minutes and we were sitting in front of a small fire with fresh water and some of the meat from last night. It was still delicious, and filled the empty hole in my stomach once again.

"So, the plan for today?" Nova asked, gnawing on a bone.

I threw my current bone into the fire and swallowed down my water. "We head back to the truck and hope the deaders have gone. They don't normally stick around for long once they sense there's no food source. If it hadn't been getting dark the night before, we could have easily waited them out."

"I just hope that it's still all there."

"It's still early." I checked my watch out of habit, though it still said ten to two, like it had for months. "If we set off now, we could be there in the next two hours." My head was beginning to throb, my sinuses feeling swollen, and I worried that I might be coming down with a cold. It was actually miraculous that I hadn't already, to be honest, what with how much time outside in the rain and cold I'd spent recently. Still, I hoped that it faded away without actually making me sick.

Nova nodded and began to pack our meager supplies away. I stamped out the fire and shouldered my backpack, and together we made our way to the gate. I climbed up to the top and looked down the road to check for any oncoming hordes of dead, but it seemed clear and I climbed back down.

Unlocking the gate, we left, making sure to lock it back up after us. You never knew when a safe place would be needed—for us or for others. We headed back down the road toward where we had left our truck stranded the previous night, a silence falling around us. Our footsteps were the only companions out there; not even a bird chirped in any nearby trees. That made me antsy, since birds only went quiet when there was trouble around. They always seemed to have the better sense to keep quiet when the dead were close. Not that the dead would really bother them. Deaders couldn't climb, which gave the flying species of this world a far better advantage than us humans.

I think back to my previous home within the trees and marvel once again at what a tragic loss it was. That place had been fantastic and had everything we needed. The Outdoor Activity Center had been useless, but the treetop homes had been safe above ground, a sanctuary within the trees. I missed that place—just as much as I missed the people that had lived there.

The army base where I lived now was great, no doubt—secured on all sides by six-foot-high fencing, large gates, and people who knew what the hell they were doing. But having two feet on the ground makes me nervous, plus, it was huge, far too big to really be watched by everyone. They had closed a lot of the base off, in the hopes that keeping it small and tight would make it safer, but I still didn't trust it. It would only take one weak spot in the fences to bring our world down. At least up in the trees I could always sleep safe in the knowledge that nothing could sneak up on me or break in while I was sleeping—at least nothing dead, anyway.

"You're quiet," Nova commented.

I yawned and swapped my katana from left to right, flexing my fingers out. "I think I'm coming down with a cold," I said, and as if on cue, I sneezed loudly.

"Bless you," she said helpfully. "You look thoughtful though."

I shrugged. "I'm always thoughtful." I smiled.

"Care to share?"

"Not really." I looked across at her. "Why so chatty today?"

"I'm not chatty, I want *you* to be. I don't really like the silence. The world is too silent these days. Still freaks me out. The world used to be noisy—cars, planes, laughing, talking, fighting, music." She bent down and grabbed a rock, pulled out her knife, and began sharpening it on the side of the rock.

The grinding slice of the metal on the rock was therapeutic, and I forgot that she had actually asked me a question.

"I hate the silence of everything, makes it hard to believe that we're not the only ones left," she added on after a moment.

"Can't disagree with that, I guess, but I kinda like the silence. It makes it easier to hear if a deader gets too close."

She sighed. "So? What were you thinking?"

I looked across at her again with a raised eyebrow. "Sorry, I'm not really the sharing type."

She snorted at me. "You shared last night."

I rolled my eyes. "I was feeling reflective last night. Today I'm not."

Nova huffed. "Come on, just talk about something mundane, then. I like noise. I need the noise." She put away her knife and swiftly pulled out a different one and began giving it the same treatment. "You could sing," she offered, and I barked out a laugh.

"No, that's not gonna happen."

She huffed and we continued our silent walk. Minutes passed by until the sound was broken up by Nova again. "Okay, so quick-fire round."

"What?"

"Ice cream or chocolate?"

"Again, what?" I raised an eyebrow at her again.

"Ice cream. Definitely ice cream. Okay, milk or fresh juice?"

"I'm not doing this." I scowled.

"Sure you are. Milk, but it has to be freezing cold, maybe even with a couple of ice cubes floating in it. Shit, I miss ice so bad! Okay, clean underwear or a new coat?"

"Underwear," I replied without any hesitance. "But I'm not doing this."

"Don't be so uptight, Nina." It was her turn to scowl now. She reached into her pocket and pulled out a cigarette. "You don't always have to be so teenage angst about things." She lit it and took a long drag. "I bet you listened to Nirvana your entire youth." She laughed.

"I am not teenage angst, thank you very much." I stared up at the road ahead of us. It seemed to go on for miles, this weird little scrapyard smack dab in the middle of nowhere, but I knew it was only another twenty minutes or so to the garage just outside the town, where we had left the truck. "We just need to pay attention. Besides, I never listened to Nirvana. I was more of a Jimi Hendrix fan."

"Really?" She looked across at me. "I never would have saw that comin'. I actually thought you would have been more of a boyband lover."

"Hell no!" I snapped, feeling offended at her misconception of me. "I was into classics like Jimi, Clapton, I loved Bob Marley." My thoughts drifted to a conversation I'd had with Emily and if there were rasta deaders. The thought soured my mood abruptly. I missed her already. And then I missed Mikey. And then I was pissed with myself for missing him. Stupid man.

"Sorry, Mom." She snorted out a laugh.

She chuckled, and I smiled and then we lapsed back into silence, just the sound of our boots on the lonely highway. Though the road was quiet, I checked back behind, as did Nova, there was nothing coming; however, the road up ahead of us held movement.

We both stopped and watched for a moment or two, noticing that the shadows of people were clumsy and uncoordinated, and we both continued to walk at the same time.

"Deaders," I said dryly.

"Yeah," she agreed.

We both mentally got our heads into the places they needed to be in order to kill these things—the zombies. Since they were in front of us, they clearly couldn't be ignored, which meant we had no choice but to fight them.

FIVE

"I'm so over all this shit, you know?" I huffed, my throat feeling sore and scratchy.

"Deaders are assholes," Nova chuckled. She finished her cigarette and threw it to the ground. "I definitely think you're getting sick, girl."

"I know," I grumbled.

There wasn't much wind, but what little there was typically worked against us and blew our scent in the direction of the deaders. We were closer now and could see that there were four of them. Scrap that—make it four and a half, since there was one on the ground. I couldn't tell if his legs were partially missing or completely missing, but I could see his little head bobbing up and down to get a better fix on the direction of our obviously delicious scent.

The four able-bodied deaders began to move in our direction, their groans being carried away in the wind. They were slow, as usual, but they didn't seem as rotten as the ones we'd encountered on the previous night, and that was worrying. In fact, as we got closer to them I realized that they seemed positively fresh.

I glanced nervously across to Nova, who seemed to have the same thought process as me. Her frown furrowed harder, her mouth set in a thin, determined line.

"They're new," I stated.

"Seems that way." She pulled out two long-handled knives and picked up her pace.

I didn't want to seem like the wimp in this situation, but I was not eager to get the killing over and done with. I wasn't a warrior or a fighter. In fact, I could quite happily go without ever killing another deader—or person—again. Unfortunately, the world being what it was, that was unlikely to ever happen. I didn't speed up, but I was ready for them regardless. I was always ready for them, even if I wasn't as eager as Nova.

I reached the first one, side-stepping as it stretched its one bony arm for me. The other arm was barely a nub of bone left jutting out of its socket, yet it still moved. I managed to get behind it and I raised my katana high, slamming it through the back of the deader's neck before it could turn around. The force of my blow knocked it to its knees but didn't cut it all the way through, and I grunted as I struggled to wrench the katana free from the thick flesh and bone of its neck. I pressed down, begging the sword not to snap.

Finally the blade cut right through and the head fell from its shoulders with a resounding *splat*. The body slumped forward with a *thud*, and thick black gore that smelled like rotten eggs and three-day-old sewage pumped slowly from out of the hole in its neck. The mouth of the head continued to snap, and I slammed my sword through the side of its temple to end the deader's eternal misery and then I moved on to the next one.

Nova was surrounded by two deaders and the ankle-biter, and I hurried across to help her. I jogged to her side, ignoring my own slow-moving deader, and I stabbed through the ankle-biter's skull. Ankle-biters were scary, because you never freaking saw them coming. I had drawn the attention of Nova's two deaders, but she stabbed one in the back of the skull before it could even take a step toward me, and the other followed swiftly afterwards.

I turned back to my one, sidestepping it and letting it follow me until its back was to Nova. She used both knives to hack either side of its neck in one swift movement, and the head popped up into the air like a jumping bean and landed on the ground with a small *thud*. It was still moving, jaws snapping away as it persistently tried to get to me, and I grimaced. It was possibly once a fairly attractive male. Cloudy blue eyes stared up at me hungrily, its teeth still relatively normal instead of broken and black. Even its skin, though pale and sallow, was still covering a full face, instead of having rotted away in parts, leaving us with a gory view of what lay underneath. I presumed this man had died from injuries other than the more standard facial bites, which were what usually got people killed.

Death brought on the zombie infection, not saliva or blood transference, and a chunk out of the face or neck was almost always a sure killer.

Nova's boot made contact with the head and sent it flying through the air and into the fields to the left of us. Black blood trailed through the sky in an arc and she whooped and fist-pumped the air.

"Touchdown!" she yelled ridiculously. She raised her hand in an attempt to high five me.

"That's not cool. You need to go find that head and end it." I bent down and wiped my blade across the now headless deader's body, cleaning it free of the gore.

"What? Why?" She bent down and cleaned her knives on a different deader's back. "You're just miserable. You're always miserable, especially when you're sick," she huffed.

"You don't know what I'm like when I'm sick."

Nova rolled her eyes. "Well you're sick now, and you're a moody and miserable, so looks like I was right."

"Whatever. You can't leave a dangerous head out in the wild like that. What if someone is walking through here and doesn't see it? What then? A dangerous head like that could kill someone." I scowled and stood back up, releasing a hearty sneeze. "Go find the damn head."

Nova stood back up, giving me a hard glare. "No, you go find the damn head if it's so important to you." She turned away and started looking through the pockets of another of the dead bodies at our feet, looking for anything useful. "No one would be stupid enough to walk through a field barefoot anyway. People wear shoes, Nina!" She pocketed several items, not bothering to show me what they were, which only pissed me off more, since we were supposed to be sharing everything.

"That's a dangerous head, Nova. Go kill it." I bent back down and started to fumble in my deader's pockets, finding some gum and a lighter, plus a picture of a pretty woman. The picture did nothing to temper my growing anger. "Do they not deserve any goddamn respect?" I muttered to myself more than her. So I was surprised when Nova replied.

"No, no they don't. I hate them all and they deserve to die a horrible death."

My eyes snapped to hers. "You're being a dick now."

"Since when did you become a union leader for the Undead Society? These aren't humans anymore," she snarled.

"I know that," I yelled and looked away, feeling my cheeks heat. What the hell was happening to me? A couple of months back in a real society and I'm turning soft. "Can you just go and get the damn head?" My voice softened. "Please."

She scowled at me but stormed off in the general vicinity of where the head had landed, and I continued looting through the pockets of the deaders.

I remembered watching an old black-and-white apocalyptic film with my husband, way back before the world ended, and I remembered wondering why they never searched the pockets of the dead. I mean sure, it's gross, but the whole world was gross now. Well, maybe not all of it. The world was actually quite beautiful now, without pollution and man destroying everything. Having been left to grow wild, Mother Nature had thrived and was truly excelling in her job description. But the rest of the world was ugly, and full of death and disease.

So a little looting from the dead? Pfft, that was nothing. If it meant living or dying then I'd gladly loot a hundred deaders. You never knew what crap people had previously carried with them, and on more than one occasion it had proved hugely beneficial. Unfortunately, every once in a while you found something utterly disgusting. Once I found shit in someone's pocket—actual shit! It was disgusting and I couldn't get rid of the smell from under my fingernails for days afterwards.

I slipped the photo of the beautiful woman back into the pocket of the headless deader and called it quits. Nova came back over, still scowling, but she had clearly done what I'd asked of her. I fell into step beside her and we continued our walk back to the truck in total silence.

SIX

Our truck was still there, with only a few remaining deaders nearby, thankfully. Enough that it was a pain in the ass, but not so many that it was a major problem for us. We killed the ones closest to the truck—well, Nova did most of the killing, since she was so damn quick about it—and we climbed in hastily before the others got close enough to eat our brains, and then we pulled out of the gas station.

"It never gets old, right?" She laughed, offering me her hand for a high-five.

I cocked an eyebrow at her and scowled.

"Come on! You know you want to bump this." She laughed even louder, but finally relented when I made no move to high five or fist-bump her. "You're always so serious, girl," she pouted. "You need to lighten up or this is going to be one seriously boring road trip."

"I just don't see any of this as funny or amusing, and I don't take it lightheartedly," I snapped. "And it's not a freaking road trip. It's a mission!"

I was tired of everyone thinking so badly of me, like I was the only bitch in the apocalypse. Like I was the only one that took any of this seriously. Day and night, we fought and clawed for survival—what's so funny about that? I typically wasn't one for self-pity, but lately I was beginning to feel something akin to it.

"You're right," Nova began, "it's not funny and nothing about this whole situation should be taken light-heartedly."

I frowned across at her, waiting for the punch line to her joke.

"The thing is, though, darlin', is this world is what we make it."

"But there's nothing left," I snarled.

"Of course there is, don't be so fucking depressive. There's a whole world out there. There's people to love, people to hate, and a future that we can build."

I scoffed at her words and she held a hand up to me.

"If you're always looking for the clouds, you'll never see the rainbows." She looked away, apparently done with her lecturing.

"Whatever," I mumbled.

We traveled in silence for a while, the only sounds being the truck's noisy engine and Nova humming to herself. She was still pissed that I had previously made her turn the CD off. She liked listening to music, but after the eighth time of listening to the same AC/DC album, I had called for a time-out. I loved music previously, any music really, yes, even Nirvana—not that I would tell Nova that. I loved the way so many different instruments could all come together to create one cohesive sound. It was fascinating and beautiful, and I loved getting lost inside it. But I also liked variety, and that's something you don't get in an apocalypse. I shuddered, pushing the thoughts away.

Raindrops began to fall, light at first, like a fine mist—the stupid sort of rain that is more of a spray, yet it drenches you from head to toe in seconds. Nova turned on the wipers and awkwardly lit a cigarette.

"I think we're coming up to where we left them," she says, glancing over at me nervously.

"Which means your camp is around here?" I asked tensely. I had known that we would be reaching both her camp and the place where they had left Hilary and Deacon to go off on their own. I just hadn't expected it so soon.

"It's a couple of miles southwest of here—close, but not close enough that we need to worry. Not unless things have changed since I left." She shrugged noncommittally, but I could see the anxiety at the corner of her mouth.

I bit my thumbnail and then silently cussed myself, realizing that I had picked up the filthy habit from Mikey. I was tense—tenser than usual. The thought of Mikey getting back to base camp and seeing me gone was driving me wild. Would he care? Would he be mad? Do I want him to care? I just didn't know anymore. We didn't have the most typical of relationships, though I guess no one ever did in this world anymore. Things weren't like they used to be. With my husband I used to worry about who would do the weekly grocery shopping and if we had enough cash for takeout on a Saturday night. With Mikey it was all about survival. Would he make it home from his next scouting mission? Would I come home after my next scavenging trip? Would I ever be any good with a gun? Would I ever stop being such a bitch? I sighed heavily.

Nova pulled the truck to an abrupt stop, the brakes squeaking loudly, and I was yanked back from my thoughts. I grabbed my katana automatically, poised for a fight. I looked out the window and then back to Nova with a frown. She was leaning forward in her seat, her eyes trained on the distance.

"What? What is it?" I asked.

Nova didn't reply, but pointed to the horizon; and I followed her finger, seeing nothing at first. Then I saw it: smoke. Gray tendrils of it lazily floating into the sky. The fire was old, not fresh, but it had also been big. And it was in the direction of where Nova's camp had been.

I turned to her, seeing the anxiety etched across her face. "What do you want to do?" I asked.

"I don't know, we should see what happened, right?" She looked at me, her eyes full of sincerity. "They could be in trouble."

I looked back toward the smoke. "I think it's too late to help them if they are in trouble." I looked down into my lap, not being able to meet her gaze. "Do we even want to help them? After what they did?"

She was quiet for a beat before she replied. "They weren't all bad. They just wanted to find a cure," she said, her words hard and unforgiving.

"But that poor woman, what they did to her—"

"That was all Rachael. We can't blame the majority for one person's mistake." I could tell it pained her to admit that, to say out loud that her sister had been seriously messed up in the head. But I didn't believe that it was all Rachael's fault.

I looked at her sharply. "Yet they all stood by and let it happen. How many more women, children, people have they harmed trying to find this cure?"

"You're so fucking high and mighty, Nina." Nova lit another cigarette, blowing the smoke out angrily. "What if it worked? What then? Surely the pain of a few is worth it for the cure?"

"You sound just as crazy as she was," I said angrily, my eyes burning vicious holes into her.

Her mouth opened and closed as she struggled to come back with an equally cruel retort, but there was nothing crueler than that, so she gave up, the air leaving her as if she had been deflated. And I felt lousy because I hadn't mean to hurt her; it was just that my stupid mouth making me say things before I really had time to think them through.

"Can we go see?" she asked quietly, almost as if she was afraid to ask.

I hated it when she did this to me, making me seem like the asshole if I said no to her. I mean, you can't say no to someone that pouts this much!

I watched the smoke rising in the distance, imagining the horror that might be waiting for us. The horror of all the people stuck there—trapped, held prisoner while they were tested on in the hopes of finding a cure for the disease which had ravaged this planet. But deep down I knew we had no choice. This place, this prison camp, is what we'd set out to find. Sure, we were looking for Hilary and Deacon, too, but it was this place that fascinated me the most. Me and my morbid curiosity.

"It's your call," I said quietly, knowing the answer before she gave it to me. Because we had to help as many people as we could. Surely that was the point of being strong—to help the weak, the people in need. Without that, what were we? Animals? Probably worse. We'd be more like the deaders. And that was why I had come on this trip to start with, right? To prove that I wasn't not bad—if only to myself.

Nova spun the truck around in the middle of the road, sending mud and dirt flying up around the wheels and then setting back off the way we had come. She eyed the road carefully, leaning forward as she drove and slowing down as she came to a thicket of trees. She turned down it, the long branches from overgrown brush scraping noisily down the side of the old truck. My stomach lurched and tumbled the further she drove, twisting in on itself in nervous anxiety. The road was overgrown and muddy as hell, and the rain had started to come down again—a light showering of pure freezing cold water that made Nova turn on the windshield wipers.

A mile or so down the road, she slowed down until we were practically creeping along at a snail's pace, every bump and knock to the truck noticeable. She wound her window down and leaned out as she drove, all the while muttering to herself.

I wound my own window down, hating the smell of the fire and smoke that lingered thickly in the air, it made my stomach ache with worry at the thought of what could have happened there. And of course, selfishly, the thought of possibly driving into something bad, something we might not come back from, always made me feel really freaking dandy! Cue eye-roll.

"Here," Nova said loudly, and I turned in my seat away from my open window and toward her as she pulled the truck down an even more overgrown path. We had almost missed it, it had been so hidden. "This isn't good," she said darkly. "No one has been down here in a long time. It wasn't like this before."

A chill ran down my spine at her words, but for once I kept my mouth shut. The truck bumped and shook as it went over the depressions in the ground and crunched over fallen branches. The rain was not making it any easier to see where we were going, and it was making the path slick with mud. I found myself biting down on my nail again, anxiety coursing through me, and when I looked at Nova I saw the same trepidation on her face.

She finally stopped the truck, putting it into park, and then looked at me with wide, worried eyes. "We're here, it's just around this bend." She jerked her head to the left.

The smell of burnt flesh wafted in to us even stronger than before, and my nose automatically wrinkled in disgust, but I ignored it and gave Nova a firm nod.

"You sure you're okay with this?" she asked.

"Not really, but I've got your back regardless," I said, clutching my katana harder.

Nova smiled at my words, and then when she noticed my hand firmly gripping my katana, she did a quick inventory of her weapons again before giving me a firm nod and winding her window back up. I did the same as she drove slowly forward.

She hadn't been lying, either, when she had said it was just around the bend. As the truck pulled around to the left, tall iron gates came into view, standing imposingly high in front of us. One of them hung loosely to one side, letting anyone or anything in. The wall surrounding what was left of the city reminded me of my own humble beginnings in the nightmare/walled city I lived in for several years. Which in turn left me with a distinctly bad taste in my mouth. My time behind the walls was not something I wanted to think about right then, and it certainly was not somewhere I'd envisioned ever coming again—yet there we were. I thought about what frightened me more, and decided it was the fact that I had just come face to face with my own nightmare. Nova had said that there were more walled cities, but I didn't truly believe her until this moment. But now, knowing that there were more of those places out there, more pain and humiliation, more suffering and starvation, I felt anger burning in my gut.

I swallowed it down, barely containing the heavy grinding noise my teeth were making as I looked at the gates in front of us. Like most structures left in the world, the walls were covered in flourishing plants; green ivy clung to the walls' surface, continually climbing ever higher. Mixed in with the ivy was some other unnamed plant, but one

I had seen several times before. It flowered in the summer, sprouting bright pink and yellow flowers that reminded me that there was still beauty left in the world.

The walls seemed smaller, yet built with more thought and care than mine ever had. And from our vantage point, they looked much stronger. Not that the walled city I had been in wasn't strong, because clearly it was—it had kept the dead out and the humans in for long enough—but there was something about this small city that spoke volumes in strength. I just couldn't pinpoint what exactly. Perhaps it was because I knew of the horrors that went on within the walls?

"Well that was not a good sign," Nova said darkly, referring to the broken gate.

"Nope," I replied.

"Well, we're here now, let's gate-crash this party."

We kept on driving, pulling through the open gate and into the city, carefully avoiding the debris in our path, and my eyes went wide as I took in the full horror. Nova gasped and pulled the truck to a stop before looking out of her window. I leaned over, looking out of my own window.

"Are they all...?" I didn't finish my sentence. I didn't need to. Nova knew what I was getting at.

"Dead-dead? Yep, looks that way," she said.

"And the people?" I asked, staring in stomach-turning dread at the human bodies scattered everywhere, limbs removed, insides devoured, and heads caved in.

"They either didn't turn or were put out of their misery by someone," she said, beginning to drive again. "At least that's what I'm guessing."

We passed a non-zombie body and I looked down out of the window, seeing the person's tortured expression. Most of their stomach was missing, a red and black gaping hole where their insides should have been. A single bullet-hole scarred the center of their forehead.

"But who did this?" I asked.

"Put them out of their misery? Or tore this city apart?" Nova asked, her voice devoid of emotion.

"Both," I replied.

SEVEN

I opened the door of the truck and jumped down, the thick mud splashing up my boots. The rain had started to come down harder, making it difficult to navigate through the mud and bodies. Not that it made any difference: there was no one there for us to help—at least, not anymore. All that was left was body after rotting body.

We were careful as we moved around the city, checking each tent and home for any signs of life; but barring the odd stray animal, which growled yet warily gave us a wide berth, everything was dead. Nova didn't say much. Her expression was hard as we moved around her old city. The only positive I found was that everything was still there—all the food and clothes, all the equipment, medicine, and weapons. It was a small miracle, really, that no one had stripped the place bare yet. Perhaps they knew it wasn't safe there, or perhaps there was no one left alive that knew about the place. I looked at one of the small wooden huts. The flames had been doused by the rainstorm, gray smoke had all but finished billowing, and I frowned.

This happened recently. Like, really recently.

I was about to voice my concerns to Nova when we came to a stop outside of a small wooden… house? Hut? It was clearly a home at one time, but it was tiny. Not that I was used to living in any sort of luxury or anything, but this was basically just a wooden shed made into a home. There were quite a few of those types of homes in that part of the city, and I was presuming they were better living arrangements than most.

I glanced at Nova. Her face was a blank canvas, but it was pretty obvious to me what this place was to her.

"This was where you lived," I stated cautiously.

"Yeah" was all she replied tightly, before pulling at the door and going inside.

The air was stale and cold, but it was made up nicely, with a bed made from wooden crates and straw, and a blanket thrown over the top. Another crate was turned upside down with a few meager belongings upon it, and pictures hung on the walls. Some of them looked like the stuff you used to find in art galleries, and they seemed so random and out of place here.

Nova made a weird noise in the back of her throat as she moved toward the far side of the hut, where bits of paper and photos were tacked to the wall haphazardly. She pried a photograph from the wall and looked down at it sadly before turning back to me, her eyes glistening.

"This is the only photo I had of us all," she said, her mouth turning up into a small smile. "I thought they would have given this place to someone else when I left." She looked around her and continued. "Or trashed it. I would have been seen as a traitor in their eyes for leaving."

I frowned at her, my shoulders feeling burdened with her guilt.

"You did the right thing, though."

"Did I?" Nova shook her head. "I should have helped these people. That was my fuckin' job, Nina. I'm as bad as the assholes that were in charge."

I looked at the photo in her hand and attempted a smile back as I looked upon the younger faces of Nova, Rachael, and Michael. They were young in the image, perhaps not more than thirteen to seventeen, their faces carefree and happy. Behind them were who I assumed were their parents. A man had a hand firmly on Michael's shoulder, a stern but warm smile on his face. And their mother—damn, she was pretty. I handed the photograph over to Nova, happy that she had it back. I know I would do anything to have some of my old photos back. To be able to see my husband's handsome face again. I closed my eyes and realized sadly that I could hardly even recall his smile anymore. The thought was chokingly sad.

"No, you're not," I said with more strength than I felt. My words seemed to have little effect, so I placed a hand on her arm. "I'll be outside, waiting for you," I said, and left hurriedly, knowing that she needed the moment to come to peace with her decision, and I needed the space to stop myself from crying at my own losses.

Back outside the rain was still coming down—the kind of fine drizzle that gets you completely drenched within minutes. My hair stuck to my face, and I didn't bother to push it away, but instead lifted my face to the sky and closed my eyes. I let the rain wash the dirt free from my cheeks, and I breathed in the freshness of it all. The pitter-patter of rain, the clean air, and the damp on my skin, with my eyes closed it felt surreal, as if being back in my old life.

"Fuckin' love the rain," Nova said as she came back outside.

I looked across at her and saw that she was all business again, her emotions raw and dark but under check, and her cocky smile back on her face. But I knew it was all a false pretense, and yet I let her have it, because we all have to put a mask on to cope with this world. Sometimes it was the only way to survive it.

"I could leave it." I shrugged, referring to the rain. I blinked away the rain that threatened to fall into my eyes. "It's just wet and cold." I sneezed again and wiped my nose on the back of my sleeve. It was gross, but what was a girl to do?

"Dude, it washes away the pain." She looked up to the sky, letting the rain fall on her face and I couldn't help but smile.

"I'd prefer a hot shower," I said with a grin. "And a shot of tequila to wash away my pain."

She looked down at me. "I'll drink to that," she laughed. "Let's get back to the truck, there's nothing here anymore. We'll grab some of the supplies and keep moving." She marched off, the muddy puddles splashing as she traipsed through them.

I followed her. Her mood was much darker than I'd ever seen on her. Not that I could blame her: she'd killed Rachael—her only sister— and there was a very real possibility that we might not make it back for her to see Michael ever again. It was a sad and very depressing thought as I realized that I wanted to make it back to base camp—that I wanted to see everyone again. Not just Emily-Rose, but Susan, Becky, James—even Mikey. Especially Mikey. Damn that man. Every one of them had a place inside of me now, and though it might not have been much, I would easily lay down my life for these people. I smiled to myself at how far I had come.

I caught up to Nova, walking by her side. "Are you okay?"

"Yeah." She smiled down at me. "I will be, anyway. It's just all bullshit, isn't it?" She didn't pose it as a question but more of a statement.

"It is," I agreed. "But things will get better. They have to."

She grinned at me again. "Well aren't you all buttercups and fuckin' roses today?"

I rolled my eyes. "Me? No, I'm still Miss Pessimistic, remember. I'm just trying to cheer my friend up."

She looked back across at me, her bright red hair plastered to her face, and she looked pale, malnourished, and cold, yet she was smiling insanely. "Nina, did you just say that we were friends?"

I looked away, a blush rising to my cheeks. She wrapped an arm heavily around the tops of my shoulders, making the damp from my clothes seep against my skin, and I shivered.

"Whatever." I smiled, pushing out from under her arm and feeling embarrassed. "It doesn't count for much, since you're my only friend, so don't let it go to your head or anything."

"There's the bitch I know and love," she laughed.

We fell back into silence as we passed through the deserted camp, only the sound of our footsteps and the rain coming down to keep us company. That and my now-raging headache. This place was much like every town that you passed through these days. Bodies lined the streets, the stench of the dead hung in the air, and it was hard to imagine what life used to be like pre-apocalypse.

"Do you think we'll ever get it all back?" I asked her seriously.

Nova looked up from her feet, glancing about us. "What? The world?"

"Yeah."

"No, I think that this is it now. Or at least for us. If we ever do make it back from this, it will be long after we're gone. Like our kids—or our kids' kids—will get to see the world for what it was again, but not us."

"Well that's depressing," I said sourly.

She chuckled, the sound being carried away in the rain. "Yeah, it is, but it's also realistic. That's why we have to do what we can now, so that the world can continue on after we're gone. However we may go."

"And how do you see yourself going out?" I asked. "I'm going die stupidly, I just know it. I'll more than likely trip over my own feet and shoot myself in the face with my own gun." I chuckled and she laughed back, but in reality it was a very real fear of mine.

"You know that there's total accuracy in that statement, don't you, Nina? I mean, I've seen you shoot, and it ain't for shit."

I opened my mouth to say something back, but there seemed little point when she was speaking the truth. Because the thing was, I could barely do anything; I somehow just always manage to scrape by through sheer luck and dogged determination. The little skills that I had learned along the way weren't nearly enough to keep me alive. Sure, they'd worked so far, but I needed to stop making it through things by the skin of my teeth and actually go into a situation knowing that I was going to come out of it alive. Or at least a little belief of that.

"Will you show me how to shoot?" I asked Nova.

"Of course I will. I need a new shooting partner now that I don't have Michael or Rachael." Her face fell at those words, the realization sinking in again.

"So, how are you going out?" I asked quickly, changing the subject.

"I'm going out in a blaze of glory—a hail of bullets and fire and the dead knocking on my door." She grinned widely. "I'll take as many of those fuckers out as I can before that day, though."

"Me too," I agreed.

"What, before you die from your total lack of coordination?"

I laughed and punched her in the arm. "Shut up!"

My words died on my lips as my eyes fell on our truck. I pushed Nova in the side to get her attention and then silently pointed to the truck.

"There's someone in it," I stated rather obviously.

Nova lifted up her gun and flicked off the safety. "Who are you? And what the fuck are you doing in my truck?" she shouted out loudly.

"*Our* truck," I sniped, raising my gun also—not that I could hit anyone from this distance, but they didn't know that. The person inside froze, their face looking at us through the dirty windshield.

"Well, it's more mine than yours, Nina," Nova said, her eyes never leaving the sight of her gun.

"Well not really," I said in annoyance. "It's ours, since you wouldn't be even doing this on your own, and since it was me that spoke to Zee and James and got them to agree to let us take it."

The person inside slowly backed out of the truck. Though we were close to whoever it was, it was too hard to make them out. The fine rain was coming down harder, creating a light mist between us. I thought it was a woman, and when she cackled like a real live Wicked Witch of the West, I knew it was a damn woman.

"She just cackled at us!" Nova snapped in annoyance. "Like a witch!" she said incredulously. "I hate witches."

"Well she *is* old," I offered to Nova.

And she was. Long, dark gray and white hair was held up high on her head in the form of a knotty bun, and her face held more wrinkles than a rumpled old blouse, yet I bet she was attractive once upon a time.

"That's kinda creepy!" I yelled to the woman, whose only response was to cackle again. I looked across at Nova and saw her grimace.

"If you do that again, I'm going to shoot you in the forehead!" Nova yelled to the woman. "And Nina?"

"Yeah?"

"It's totally my truck." She laughed and took off after the crazy, cackling woman who had just turned tail in the opposite direction.

I stared after Nova in annoyance before chasing after both her and the woman. My feet splashed through the mud, the dirty, freezing cold water soaking through to my socks.

"Goddamn it," I muttered to myself as I ran, feeling the water squelch between my toes. "Goddamn it!" I said louder as I slipped and almost fell on my ass. I realized I couldn't see Nova anymore and I slowed to a jog, looking around me at all the tents for movements or noise. We still hadn't checked out all of these, so for all we knew there could be deaders inside. I stopped running and turned in a full circle to check my surroundings fully.

"Nina, up here!"

I looked up, the rain pelting my face and dripping into my eyes, and I saw Nova climbing the steps to the top of the outer perimeter of the city. "Get your ass up here!" she yelled down to me with a gleeful whoop and carried on running.

This was Nova at her best—free and chasing some bad guy (or woman) down. This was what she lived for now.

I ran around the back of some of the old makeshift homes and found the steps before following her up the side. The steps were slippy from the rain and moss, which had started to cover them, and my own words came back to haunt me as I almost twisted my ankle and fell off the edge. I swear I heard Nova laugh at me and I cursed at her and everything else in this godforsaken world under my breath.

I reached the top and was grateful that the platform had a handrail going around the entire perimeter—not that it looked even vaguely sturdy, but it was safer than it not being there. Nova was off to my left, still following after the crazy cackler, who—lo and behold—was still cackling, like we were playing tag and it was all fun and games. I grumbled and followed them both.

I finally caught up to Nova, noticing that she wasn't even a little bit out of breath, where I was panting like I had been running for miles. She paid me no mind as her eyes stayed focused on the woman, but I heard the low chuckle in her throat.

"Fuck off," I sniped back. "I'm just a little out of shape is all."

"How is that even possible?" she murmured to me, her eyes staying focused down the barrel of her gun that she had aimed at the woman. "In these times, I mean. It's not like we don't have to run for our lives every single day, Nina."

"Blah blah, can you just shush your damn face and focus on the matter at hand, please."

"Someone's a little touchy today."

"I'm sick, okay?" I turned and glared at Nova, watching as her cheeks rose in a grin.

"What did you take from our truck, crazy pants?" Nova yelled to the old lady.

The old lady backed up until her feet found a gap in the fencing near the edge of the ledge. "I'm not crazy!" she said, actually sounding hugely offended. She burst out into her now-infamous cackle—well, infamous to us three, but whatever. I wasn't sure if her cackling outburst meant that she was agreeing with us on the crazy front or if she was even offended anymore. This chick was screwing with my head.

"Lady, there aren't enough cats in the world for your level of crazy!" I yelled back to her before sneezing into my hand.

Crazy Pants held up the key of the truck, dangling it in the air between us with a gleeful smile.

"Shit," I cursed, giving Nova a sidelong glance of annoyance. "You left the key in the ignition?"

I knew she felt my death stare but she didn't say anything about it.

Instead she chose to cock her gun as a warning to the woman. I didn't need to look at her to know that she was pointing it straight at the face of the crazy bitch.

"Give us the damn truck key," I snarled, "or she will shoot you."

The old lady cackled loudly again, baring her gummy mouth to me, and I couldn't contain the grimace from my face.

"Dude, that's just gross." Nova elbowed me in the rib and I nodded my agreement.

There were many downsides to the end of the world—obviously the whole life-and-death and constant perilous situations were always at the top of that list—but there were other things that I had never really considered before. One of them being dental care. Sure, we brushed our teeth as best we could—hell, I even carried my toothbrush and toothpaste tube around with me wherever I went like a damn health commercial. *Boys and girls, always brush twice a day, and in the event of an apocalypse remember to pack your essentials—gun, knife, tooth brush. Safety first kids, safety first.* However, I was way overdue for my six-month checkup at the dentist.

I looked at the woman's rotten, gummy mouth and felt a little nauseous. And a little sorry for her, truth be told. I was never a fan of the dentist, but if I would have known then what I knew now, I would never have eaten all that candy growing up. Or at least I like to believe that I would have been a touch more consistent on flossing. I had at least two fillings in my teeth, and I didn't know what I'd do if I ever needed any more. I'd met many people in the past four years, but never a dentist.

"Please," I said sincerely to the old lady.

She was clearly off her freaking rocker, but wouldn't anyone be if they were there all alone? After seeing what she'd most likely seen?

"Please give us the keys. You can come with us."

"Finders keepers, losers weepers." She cackled again, her eyes wild.

I sighed heavily, not wanting to hurt this woman, but it was getting to the point that we had little choice in the matter. We needed that key, regardless of what the consequences were to her, and Nova was quickly losing her patience. I sneezed again, pain shooting behind my eyes as I did.

"Actually, that's not how the saying goes," Nova offered.

The old lady looked confused for a minute, staring into space, and then put one of her bony fingers into her mouth as if chewing on a nail while she thought about it. She eventually called bullshit on Nova, and I couldn't blame her since that was definitely how the saying went.

"I'm serious," Nova continued. "The saying is, 'finders keepers, when I get my hands on you, I'm going to snap your scrawny neck!'" she growled out.

The rain was pouring down now and we were all getting completely soaked through, not to mention it was freezing. I was more than over the whole stupid conversation. My backpack was pressing into my back uncomfortably, my soaking wet clothes offering no padding against the weapons within it, so I could totally understand Nova's aggressiveness, yet I was still a little shocked by her lack of compassion. It was normally me that was the miserable bitch, and her the fun-loving one that enjoyed dancing in the rain and long walks on the beach. Could it be that my bad attitude was rubbing off on her?

The old lady backed up another step, dangling the keys in front of her some more. "Thanks for the vehicle, ladies." She took another step forward, until she was teetering on the edge.

The ruined city was decimated beyond repair, and I couldn't help but wonder if maybe she was crazy long before whatever went down at that place. That sort of crazy didn't happen overnight, no matter what you lived through. It was the sort of crazy that was born from seeing too much and living through too much. That sort of crazy came with years of practice.

She glanced over her shoulder and back to us, her eyes glinting with maniacal glee.

"Where are you going to go, Crazy Pants? There's only two ways out of here: down and to your death. Just give us the keys as you walk by," Nova said, and even without looking I could hear the smirk to her tone. "I won't even shoot you if you give up them up now."

I looked from Crazy Pants to Nova and back again, cogs turning as I pieced together a story of pain and desperation, and I gasped. Despite the cold rain beating on me, despite the chill that I felt all the way to my bones and the weariness I felt with life, I gasped, because some things just aren't right. And if my train of thought was accurate, then this was just plain wrong.

"What? That sounded like an important kinda gasp, Nina." Nova glanced at me with a fierce scowl.

"Do you think she was one of the people that were experimented on?" I asked darkly.

"Shit," Nova said immediately, lowering her gun, guilt washing over her features. "How long have you been here?" she asked.

Crazy pants scratched at an invisible beard on her chin while she thought. "Sixty-three years, three months, two weeks, one day, fifty-nine minutes, and six seconds, seven, eight," she cackled back.

"Well, I'm assuming that's her age." Nova rolled her eyes. "But I think we can assume that she was definitely here when the experimentations were happening, but I honestly don't remember her." She sighed.

"Eleven, twelve, thirteen." Crazy Pants kept on counting and Nova gave out a huff of annoyance.

"Christ, how do we make her stop counting?" I said with a grumble. "And give back our damn truck keys?"

"My aunt used to have the cutest kid," Nova said, and I frowned at her like *seriously? It's story time now?* "Bear with me," she continued. "She used to have the cutest kid. But that little shit was so naughty, and she would run everywhere just so that you would chase her." She looked at me seriously. "The only way to make that little kid stop running was to walk away from her."

I grumbled. "And that's why I never wanted kids. Kids are irritating."

"...Seventeen, eighteen, nineteen..."

"Really? Never?" Nova asked in all seriousness, to which I raised a sardonic eyebrow at her. She ignored me and continued. "I always wanted lots of kids. We came from a big family. I mean, I was one of three and we were the smallest. My dad had six brothers and two sisters, and they all had kids. Anyway, it seemed the obvious way to go. But life is what life is, and Mother Nature decided—"

"To start a damn apocalypse," I finished for her with a frown.

"No, she decided not to give me a womb that worked," Nova replied sadly.

I stared at her in both sadness and confusion. Crazy Pants's voice rang out behind us as she continued to count off the seconds. I couldn't imagine how horrible that must have been for Nova, but that moment was a completely inappropriate time to bring something like that up, plus I wasn't not emotionally capable of dealing with heavy news like that. I just wasn't made that way. I stared at her, my mouth opening and closing as I stumbled to find the right words and not come off as callous.

Nova shrugged and lowered her gun. "Fine, keep the damn keys.

We have a spare anyway."

I looked back at Crazy Pants, seeing the light go out of her eyes, and I took that as my cue to take a step backwards. Her smile dropped just as I started to turn my back on her. Both Nova and I kept on walking until we were back at the steps, and we started to make our way down cautiously.

"We do?" I asked, genuinely surprised. "Have a spare key, I mean."

"No," Nova said flatly, looking sideways at me as we carefully went down the slippery steps and making me feel like a dumbass for asking. As we reached the bottom step we heard the woman yell to us.

"Don't leave me." She sounded so sad and broken—defeated, almost—and I felt bad for a split second. Until I sneezed again.

I turned around, seeing her dejected face looking truly every one of her sixty-three years, three months, two weeks, one day, fifty-nine minutes, and however many seconds old she was now. Her eyes were miserable and lost, her mouth wrinkled and downturned, and she came down the stairs slowly, her arm outstretched with the keys clutched tightly in her palm. Her hair was plastered to her face, like long gray cattails, but she did nothing to brush it out of the way. Close up I could see how her body trembled, and I hoped that it was from the cold and not anything age-related.

"Please, don't leave me here," she pleaded sadly.

EIGHT

The tent was toasty warm, and the strong smell of damp and mildew hung thickly in the air. But that was a much better smell than the stench of death and festering bodies that had greeted on our arrival, so I wasn't complaining too much.

We all undressed once we double-and triple-checked the entire compound and secured the main entrance as best we could. There was no way, without lots of help, that we could get the gate back up and running, but there were plenty of trucks that we could park in front of the gate to stop any deaders from getting in. If other people stumbled upon this place, well…so be it, because there was no way to keep them out.

We had only found one stray deader trapped inside a laboratory, its arms pinned to an examination table by several knives, as if someone had turned it into their own tortured experiment. The deader growled up at me, its dull gray eyes following me as best they could. It wore a lab coat, and I couldn't help but think of the justification and badass karma that had come to seek its own revenge on this person. I had stabbed a knife through the back of its skull, putting it out of its eventual misery without hesitation or guilt.

We hung our older rain-soaked clothes over some string that we hung from one end of the room to the other, and dressed in some old combat gear that had been left behind: green camo pants, matching jacket with a long-sleeved tan T-shirt underneath, and of course my big black boots. I looked like I should have been in the army or something, and felt completely uncomfortable wearing the uniform, like an imposter of some kind. But I was hugely grateful for clean, dry clothes—especially since my cold now had me in its death grip. I coughed and sneezed, feeling like total shit as my eyes streamed.

Nova looked right at home—happy, even—despite the current circumstances. She tucked into one of the ration packs, a meat and potato concoction of some sort. I had eaten these cold previously, and they were vile, though of course I was always happy to have food in my stomach. This time, though, the food was warm—hot, even— and it tasted like a mouthful of heaven. Seriously. Like if heaven were something you could eat, it wouldn't be chocolate and marshmallows; it would be meat, potatoes, and thick, gloopy gravy. I slurped another mouthful in, knowing without even thinking about it that I would definitely be having another after I was done. It was the type of food I used to make whenever my husband was sick: meat and potatoes, to warm the soul and fight a cold. Okay, so soup was actually better at fighting colds, but meat and potato stew was a good second.

Crazy pants had fallen asleep right after changing into some dry clothes. She was barely coherent enough to tell us what the hell had happened. What little teeth she had left chattered so painfully that I wondered if they would smash.

Nova leaned back in her chair and lit a cigarette, slowly blowing smoke rings up toward the ceiling and humming something unfamiliar. I was tired, and felt nowhere closer to finding this Hilary woman and her husband or discovering their fate. It bothered me, the not knowing. This world was full of so many uncertainties, so many undiscovered evils that I needed to know the answer—for both my own sanity and to hopefully save Jessica.

It was hard to trust in anything or anyone when all you saw was the bad in the world. And right then all I saw was bad. I really needed a win for my team soon.

I threw my second empty packet to the side and leaned back in my own chair, closing my eyes and trying to let my body relax for five minutes. I wanted to sleep. Scratch that, I *needed* to sleep. It had been a stressful couple of days—hell, it had been a stressful couple of *years*. My thoughts felt wild, whirring around in my head and making my headache even worse. *What I wouldn't do for some painkillers right now,* I thought miserably. There were so many things to think about, so many possibilities and outcomes for Hilary, for the people back at the base like Jessica, and Nova and me.

Nova was humming louder, and I wondered if at any moment she'd break out into song. It wouldn't surprise me; nothing surprised me about that woman. She was entirely unpredictable, and most of the time amazingly uncomplicated—just the sort of person I needed in my life. Since what had happened with Rachael she had been different— more melancholy than was usual for her—but the further away from base we got, the more of herself I could see coming back. As if putting distance between herself and the place she'd killed Rachael was bringing her back to life. I had also noticed how much she clung to me now, seeing me as some sort of anchor for her, and I wondered if that was what Rachael had been to her…before she had to kill her, anyway.

Almost as predicted, Nova started to sing—quietly at first, eventually building into a full crescendo of out-of-tune warbling.

"Kill me now!" I yelled, covering my ears.

I heard Nova snicker but that didn't stop her from singing. In fact, I was almost certain that she got louder.

"Are you doing that on purpose?" I scowled, opening my eyes back up.

She grinned at me knowingly, right before her expression darkened and she quit with the show tunes. "Do you really think she could be alive? Hilary?"

I rolled my eyes, not wanting to answer that question. Did I think she could be alive? No. Did I think that the unborn child growing inside her could be the cure for everything? Hell no. In fact, I'd be surprised if there was anything inside her. Because surely her body would have just rejected the fetus. Fetus? Could it really be called a fetus? Surely "abomination" was more accurate a description.

"I don't know, Nova." I shrugged.

"None of us do, but what do you *think*?" she pressed.

"What do *you* think?" I retorted, throwing the ball back in her court. I didn't really want to tell her my dark thoughts. She seemed to need this, need the hope that this woman and child could possibly save the world from extinction. And didn't we all? But I didn't believe it.

"I think so," she said with a soft smile that made her look younger than she was. "I think the baby is okay, and it could help cure everyone— or at least prevent it from happening to anyone else."

Like a child still believing in Santa Claus or the tooth fairy, she was holding onto those hopes and dreams, and for once I didn't want to be the bitch that ruined it for her—to crush that dream with my own narcissistic yet wholly accurate reality. What would be the point in delivering the painful and brutal blow that I thought the whole trip was pointless?

Nova stared at me, waiting for my usual nasty snipe or gloating comeback, but I gave her neither. She grinned and then began to laugh, a low chuckle in the back of her throat that got louder and louder until small laughter tears formed in her eyes. I wanted to ask her what was so funny, but truthfully I knew it was because she saw me, she saw my lie in my silence. She shook her head, gave another grin to me and stubbed out her cigarette before standing up with a stretch.

"I'll do first watch" was all she said as she backed out of the tent, leaving me staring after her, dumbfounded.

She had known my thoughts without me even voicing them, and I was left feeling like the asshole once more. I looked over at Crazy Pants, seeing that her lids were half open with her eyes rolled back. Her mouth, however, was wide open with a thin trail of saliva trailing out of the corner of it. She was snoring, a choky, phlegmy sort of snore that made me gag and look away. I closed my eyes and let my head fall backwards as I yawned, but the knowledge that she was sleeping with her eyes partially open and staring right at me was enough to keep me awake.

I looked back at her, seeing that she hadn't moved, and once more tried to close my eyes and get some sleep. I was exhausted, my body worn down and aching from the trials of life and my stupid cold, but there was no chance of me sleeping right then. I opened my eyes again with a scowl and saw that Crazy Pants was now sitting up with a huge grin on her face, the dribble still trailing down her chin like a fat slug sliding down some lettuce. I yelped out a surprised scream and she cackled loudly, rocking back on her heels and clapping her hands.

"What the fuck is wrong with you?" I said loudly, jumping up.

"There's nothing wrong with me—nothing a good strong man couldn't put right," she whooped gleefully. "Am I right?"

"A man?" I asked with a confused frown.

When she licked her lips, a telltale sparkle to her eyes, I grimaced. "Oh my God, that's so gross," I said, feeling queasy.

Nova came back into the tent and looked across at me. "What's gross?"

I jerked a thumb across to Crazy Pants, and Nova followed my gaze. "Heeeeey, Crazy Pants, you're awake!" she said joyfully. "You know you have a little dribble." She pointed to her chin, her smile still in place as if it were perfectly normal to have a dribble trail down your chin. "It's dead out there, nothing moving," she said to me.

Nova sat back down in her chair and poured us all another hot brown drink. I want to say it was coffee, but it was too weak to be coffee, no matter how much Nova tried to convince me that it was, so let's just stick with "hot brown drink."

"So, how are you feeling after some rest? Do you want something to eat?" Nova handed out the drinks, directing her questions to Crazy Pants.

"I would love something to eat, and my name's Joan, not Crazy Pants." She smiled fondly at Nova while I slowly took my seat again. "I was just telling this one," she said, pointing in my direction, "that there isn't anything better than a good, strong man to make you feel right as rain, am I right?" She cackled and took a slurp of her hot drink.

Nova snorted out a laugh. "Firstly, quit with the cackling or me and you cannot be friends anymore. Seriously, that shit is creepy. And secondly, you are completely right on the man front, though it's hard to find one that isn't rotting and falling apart these days." She laughed and slapped her thigh like it was the funniest shit ever, and I rolled my eyes.

Joan laughed with her, all traces of her cackling days long gone, and even I couldn't help but grin and shake my head in amusement. What? Laughter was infectious. Nova really did bring the best out in people, and I was glad once again that we decided to do this trip together. I say "trip," but what I really mean is "suicide mission."

"My husband used to be a real man, all brawn and fighting talk. Went down like a real hero too," Joan said, slurping her drink again.

I looked away from her, not being able to bear the pained look on her face. I thought of Mikey and wondered, not for the first time, why I hadn't just told him the truth about Rachael being a nutjob and swear him to secrecy. Was my pride really that important to me? Wasn't he allowed to be a little distrustful of others and me after everything that had come to this world? I mean, I was one of the most distrustful people still alive, it's only fair that he would be too. I pinched between my eyes and took a heavy breath, feeling irritated about my decision, but more irritated that I still couldn't let go of the hurt that he didn't trust me. I guess my pride really was still important to me. After all, what did we really have left to hold onto in this world if we didn't have pride?

"Oh, I can bet he was," Nova said with another sharp laugh. "Joan, when did you get here? I used to live here a while back, and I don't remember you."

Joan's smile fell, her face looking haggard and aged again. "I wasn't here long before the dead got in," she said softly. "That was a sad day. It made me think back to when it all began, to when the dead first came."

My interest was even more piqued at the realization that she couldn't have been tested on if she'd only just arrived when this place fell to ruins. So she was just totally nuts then. Great.

"Do you know how they got in, Joan?" I asked carefully, not

wanting to startle her with my question and send her back in on herself again.

Joan's eyes looked up to meet mine. "The man let them in."

My eyes searched out Nova's, and I was glad to see that her frown matched my own.

"A man?" I asked carefully, seeing that she was barely clinging onto this moment. Her moments of lucidity seemed to be few and far between, and she was already beginning to slip away.

"Yes, the angry man." She looked across at us, and I noticed that her hands were shaking, the hot liquid spilling over the sides of her mug and over her bony fingers. It should have been burning her hand, but she didn't flinch, the horror of the past too alive in her mind in the moment to register anything. Her eyes were glazed and far away.

"He came while we were sleeping. It was dark, and people were running around and screaming, begging and pleading." She finally dropped her cup, the contents spilling out by her feet. "There was so much gunfire, I couldn't hear myself think." Her chin trembled as she looked over at Nova, coming back to the here and now. "He said he was delivering retribution for the sacrifices of the many."

I swallowed, my mouth feeling dry—pasty, almost—like I'd swallowed cement. "When was this?" I asked. Though the smoke that had brought us here told me when it was, I still needed to hear it, still needed to know for certain.

"Yesterday," she said quietly as she began rocking back and forth again, her eyes falling to the ground. "The angry man came yesterday, but it's okay, you'll meet him soon. He said he was coming back to burn this place to the ground." She blinked rapidly.

"When did he say he was coming back?" Nova looked across at me, her features hard and dark.

"Do we have any chocolate? I miss chocolate," Joan said, a wave of emotion crossing her face as she looked up at us brightly, all traces of her previous doom-and-gloom statement vanishing. "I used to love a hot cocoa right before bed, too."

"Joan, I need you to answer me," Nova said as softly as she could.

"With marshmallows in it! Cocoa with marshmallows was my favorite!" Her eyes shone, lighting up with excitement. "Oh, perhaps we could toast some marshmallows!" She stood up.

"Crazy Pants!" I yelled, drawing her attention to me.

"My name is Joan," she scowled.

"When did the angry man say he was coming back?" I snapped, and I could almost feel the glare of annoyance that Nova was giving the side of my face. Well, she could kiss it. There was no time to play the soft card. We'd just have to play good cop, bad cop. Of fucking course I'd be the bad cop. I always was, wasn't I?

Joan pouted. "You," she pointed a bony finger at me, "are a very rude young lady."

"Yes, she is," Nova snapped, "but it is important that you tell us."

"He said," Joan looked away from me with narrowed eyes and directed her answer to Nova, giving her a polite smile like they were the best of friends, "he was coming back today."

NINE

"**S**hit!" I yelled, standing up abruptly. "Nova, we need to load the truck and get the hell out of here."

She nodded and stood up without question.

"What? Why?" Joan replied, sounding worried. "I wanted marshmallows!" she wailed.

I spun to face her. "Because some crazy madman is on his way back here to burn this place to the ground!"

My breathing was becoming erratic, and I knew I was being bitchy when none of this was her fault. The woman barely understood what day it was. But what worried me—and as I looked across at Nova, I could see the same worry on her face—was what day this had really all happened? Could this man be on his way here now? Or would it be tomorrow? Joan had no concept for days—shit, she had no concept for anything, and she could be imagining the entire thing, but I wasn't about to take that risk.

"Nina, one man couldn't take this place out," Nova scoffed, though

I noticed that she continued packing all of our things. "I mean, this place is huge. Something else must have happened here."

I grabbed my damp clothes off the line hanging across the room and shoved them haphazardly into my bag. Sure they were filthy, but they were less threadbare than most of my things, and clothes like that were a huge commodity these days.

"Really? One person couldn't do this on their own? Even if they came at night and caught people unguarded? You're sure about that?" I snapped, feeling frantic.

How did I get myself into these situations? It was like I had some gravitational pull for bad luck. Joan yelled something about looking for marshmallows and left the tent, but I ignored her and continued to pack.

"No, they couldn't. Not unless they knew the run of this place," Nova said dismissively.

I glanced across at Nova, nodding ever so slightly as I thought about what she had said. Because in my head she was right, but in my heart I knew she was wrong. Joan had said something about retribution for the sacrifices of the many. That was a bold statement for anyone to say, and it sounded like someone with a grudge. Cogs slipped into place, and as I watched Nova, I saw the same realization cross her features also.

"It's someone that used to live here," she acknowledged softly.

I nodded. "Yep—someone that was tested on."

"Someone that had nothing and no one left to lose," she replied, her voice filled with dread.

I stood up, slinging my backpack over my shoulder. "Nova, do you think that we just found Deacon and Hilary?"

She watched me for several heartbeats, so many emotions crossing her face—guilt, anger, sadness. Because if this was Hilary and Deacon, then the deaths of all the people here now fell on Rachael's head. On Nova's head. Most people I couldn't give a shit about, but there were innocents here also—women, children, women like Joan, who had no one left to protect them and only wanted somewhere safe to stay.

"Or just Deacon," she said almost painfully. And she was right: Joan had said an angry *man*, , not a woman, had come back there. What hope did that hold for Jessica back at the base?

Nova finally stood up straight, her emotions in check. "Let's load everything up and take cover. If he's coming back, then we need to wait for him. We need to know what happened. If Hilary is okay and the baby…" Her words trailed off and she looked away shamefully.

I bit my lip, wanting to say something nasty about Rachael, wanting to cuss and yell and kick and scream and throw a hissy fit, because this whole shitstorm just got a whole lot shittier. But I didn't. It wouldn't help anyone or anything, so I bit my lip, swallowed my tongue, and pulled up my big girl panties.

"It might not even be them," I replied instead.

"Him." She looked up at me. "It's him. Grief makes you crazy—crazier than anything else can. This was Deacon's doing, all right. I remember him as we left, and he was so angry—furious, even. All he cared about was saving her. If she's dead, then…" She shook her head, not able to finish the sentence.

"All right." I said through a tight throat, nodding, the warm air inside the tent suddenly overwhelming. "It all seems too easy though, you know?"

"Because we've actually found what we were looking for? Or should I say who we were looking for?"

I nod. "Well, yeah. What are the chances of that?"

"When the world's population has been struck down to around twenty percent of what it originally was? I would say the chances are pretty fucking high actually." Nova looks at me like I'm an idiot, but I still have the uneasy feeling in my gut.

"I couldn't find any marshmallows," Joan whined as she came back into the tent looking sullen. "I tried everywhere." She slumped back down in her seat, her head lolling to one side, and began snoring almost immediately.

I blinked in surprise. "How the hell does she do that?" I mumbled.

I heard Nova chuckle. "What's there left to fear? She's not even really here half the time, and she has no clue what's going on."

"What do we do with her?" I asked as we made our way to the door.

Nova glanced back at Joan. Already a thin line of saliva was beginning to trail down her chin again and I looked away, my stomach feeling queasy at the sight.

"Leave her sleeping. She'll be more of a problem if she's awake and in the way." She shrugged and pushed out of the tent door. "Besides, there's no way we could keep her quiet."

"That's true," I agreed.

We loaded up the truck with as many supplies as we could fit in it—clothes, ammo, food, medicine. It was a haul and a half, and if we made it back to base I knew that Zee and James would be arranging another scavenging mission to recover anything else that was left behind. As I looked around at the rotting, half-eaten bodies, I realized that pretty much everything was left. Everything but life. Guilt like I haven't felt before embraced me. We'd left the base with good intentions—okay, and a little running away on my part—but with both Nova and I gone, and Mikey and Michael on a scavenge mission, the place didn't have nearly enough people to protect it. If anything happened to the people there while we were gone, I would feel that pain for the rest of my life—however short that might be.

We had been hiding for several hours on the top wall overlooking the gate. Night had quickly fallen, and the rain continued to do so as well. It was cold—colder than cold, actually—and I was beginning to wonder if Crazy Pants hadn't dreamt up the whole damn thing about an angry man coming back. Or maybe I was just hoping that she'd made it up so I could go get some rest somewhere. My teeth and jaw hurt from chattering so much. I was no superhero, and I really had no place being up there—especially since the noise my teeth were making was enough to wake the dead.

No, seriously—several deaders had already tried to come into the compound, and Nova was adamant that it was because of all the noise I was making. She hadn't even trusted me enough to go and kill them, since my hands didn't want to work properly, the cold having worked into their bones.

Another tremor of cold raked up and down my back until my body did a full-on convulsion. Nova turned to glare at me once more, but I ignored her stare since my eyelids felt frozen in place. She was like a machine: poised and still, frozen to the spot, her singular goal to stare into the horizon, waiting for whoever the hell it was coming back. Though my gut said Deacon, my heart hoped it wasn't. Nova didn't flinch or move when the rain began to come down, gradually growing more intense. She didn't even shiver as the wind whipped her red hair around her face. She crouched, waiting, persistent, and almost eager for the kill, her eyes narrowed, her hands poised.

"You can go inside, you know. You're not really doing any good being here," she hissed, and turned back to the front.

"If you're sticking it out, I'm t-t-totally sticking it out. We're a team," I quipped, trying to keep up my team spirit, but inside I died a little more as the wind howled across the back of my neck and I trembled in my boots.

"Yippee for me," she replied, sounding thoroughly pissed off about me staying. "It's not even that cold," she grumbled under her breath, but I heard her—though how was a mystery.

And she was right: it wasn't really that cold. I wasn't sure exactly what month it was anymore—January? February, perhaps. People stopped trying to work it out accurately a while back—but I knew that the worst of the winter was behind us. However, the damn rain was killing me. It was like pure ice drops pelting against my skin. And worse than that was how the cold that had been coming on had smacked me upside the head to say a big hello.

The backs of my eyes ached, and a low throb had begun to build in the base of my skull. Germs were what made you sick, but being cold and wet lowered your ability to fight the infection. The rain got into your clothes, soaking you right to the very bone until you slowly froze to death. As if on cue I shuddered again, clenching my jaw closed tight to stop my teeth smashing together. I clenched and unclenched my hands again, gritting my teeth and hoping to God that this asshole would show up soon so we could put him out of his goddamned misery and go inside and warm up by the fire.

Yes, people, my sympathy for Deacon and Hilary—if it was in fact Deacon and Hilary that had torn this place apart, had gone out of the proverbial fucking window. Screw these people and all their drama. I was freezing my ass off.

"Please go inside, I'm fuckin' begging you, Nina," Nova demanded, her voice laced with irritation. "You're not helping anyone by staying out here."

"F-f-f-uck you," I stammered back angrily, "I'm trying to be supportive and a g-good friend by staying with you."

She turned to roll her eyes at me. "Dude, do I look like I need any help from a chattering wreck like you?"

I stared across at her, feeling hugely hurt by her callousness, though I could see the immediate regret in her eyes as she'd said it. But it didn't matter. I felt like death, and now I had a whole bag of hurt to make me feel worse. I was trying to be sincere—trying to be a supportive friend, since that was what we supposedly were—and she'd basically just spat in my face. I blinked, wanting to cry and feeling annoyed with myself instantly that I had let her words hurt me, furious that my emotions were getting the better of me just because I had a freaking cold. Normally my skin was thicker than that, and I let comments roll down my back and into oblivion, but the sting of her words had cut me deep.

"Fine." I turned away from her, hoping that the single tear that had slipped out got lost in the rain that was still coming down and lashing my face.

"Dude, I didn't mean it like that," I heard her yell after me, but I continued back down the steps, ignoring her. "Come on, don't make me feel shitty!"

I had never felt so useless in all my damn life. I was cold, and feeling crappy and miserable, and the only people I had let get close to me were turning out to be royal assholes. I stomped off the last step, sniveling and barely holding back my self-pitying sobs. I knew I shouldn't give a shit what she thought of me—hell, what anyone thought of me—and perhaps I wouldn't under normal circumstances. Perhaps I would have laughed off her comment at any other time, but I was feeling mentally and physically drained. And this cold had just hit me like a ton of bricks. I needed some cold medicine fast, before I turned into a total girl about the situation.

I stormed through a puddle, biting my lip and refusing to cry as the rain soaked through my boots even more, and muttering to myself. Because really, I should have been glad to go inside, sit by the fire, drink hot non-coffee, and take a fucking nap, instead of crying about how useless Nova had just made me feel.

"Fuck her," I mumbled to myself, kicking a muddy puddle angrily and feeling like a spoiled brat. I sniffled miserably and looked up, my face slamming into the hard chest of a man.

I yelped and flinched backwards, narrowly missing the sharp blade that was directed at my head. Cold or not, I was not dying today, and I gripped the large, meaty arm of whoever was holding the weapon with one hand and slammed my elbow automatically into his ribs. A loud grunt issued forth and I repeated the action again until the blade finally fell free of his hands. I looked up into his face, shrouded in darkness and rain—a face full of anger and pity and grief. A face that crushed my soul and felt like a punch to the gut.

"You're not dead?" He spoke, his words gruff and full of red-hot anger.

"No thanks to you," I bit out. I held back my shivers of coldness, my body feeling suddenly alive and full of warmth, adrenaline giving me a new lease on life. I narrowed my eyes at him. "Who the hell are you and what the hell are you doing here?" I ranted, holding my katana out in front of me. I didn't even remember pulling it out, but clearly I had, and I held onto it with vicious courage.

"The question is," his voice rumbled through the wind and rain, "who are you?"

A loud clank echoed around us and the man dropped to his knees before falling face first into the mud. Behind him stood Crazy Pants—sorry, Joan. She held up a chunk of wood and cackled loudly before grabbing hold of the bottom of her skirt and beginning to dance around in circles, doing the can-can in a muddy puddle. I stared transfixed, somewhat in awe and somewhat in…what the hell is wrong with you?

I looked down, noticing that the man had fallen into a muddy puddle, his face fully submerged, and I quickly bent down and turned him over, watching in fascination as he coughed up mud and water and began to breathe again. Though his eyes remained shut, I still didn't trust him to be completely knocked out.

"Joan!" I yelled over to her.

She stopped dancing and came toward me with a smile as big as the Cheshire cat. "Yes?" Her eyes flitted down to the man in the mud. "Oh my, is he okay? What happened here?"

I rolled my eyes. Of course she'd forgotten already. "Go get Nova," I shouted instead of bothering to answer her question.

"Yes, will do." She began walking off, before turning back around to look at me. "Who's Nova?"

"Gah!" I threw my hands up. "The chick at the top of the wall—go get her."

Joan nodded and skipped off into the dark. Yes, skipped! I mused for a moment on whether she would forget where she was going and what she was supposed to do, but realized that I either had to stand guard or kill him, since I couldn't move this guy on my own. Adrenalin was still hot in my veins, but it was wearing off as fast as it had come, and my teeth began to chatter again only seconds later.

Minutes ticked by. I was beginning to believe that Joan had forgotten all about me, and I was deciding on what to do next when I heard the sound of boots splashing behind me.

I turned around to see Nova jogging toward me. "What happened here?" she said, drawing up beside me. "Did you do this?" she asked in genuine awed surprise.

I wanted to say yes, to take the small victory for my own. After all, Joan sure as shit wouldn't remember that she had knocked this guy out cold. However, it was too dishonest, and as much as I felt like I needed and wanted to prove myself to Nova, I couldn't lie about it. That was always my problem: I spoke the truth, most of the time when it wasn't really necessary, but there I was. Me and my big truthful mouth.

"No, this was all Joan. She's a tough old broad." I forced a smile. "I disarmed him and then she came up behind and knocked him out."

"Let's get him inside" was her only reply after a courteous nod of her head.

She grabbed an arm and I grabbed the other, dragging the guy through the mud and back into the tent that we had set up as our base. The warmth enveloped me as soon as we got inside, and I groaned in pleasure from it.

We pulled the now completely mud-soaked man to the far corner and used some rope to tie his hands behind his back. We then secured him to one of the main poles that were fixed into the ground and stood back, deciding if the ropes were tight enough.

I sat down heavily opposite him, feeling weary and exhausted. "Now what?" I said.

Nova sat next to me. "Now we wait for him to wake up."

"Is this him?" I asked.

Nova nodded. "Yeah, this is Deacon." Her words were heavy and full of resolve.

"So where is Hilary?" I asked.

Nova shook her head, her eyes looking lost for a moment. "He wouldn't have left her. Not ever, not unless…" Her words trailed off, and her head slumped on her shoulders until she was staring at her rain-soaked boots.

She didn't need to speak anymore. I knew what she was implying: he wouldn't leave her if she were alive—which meant that she was more than likely dead.

I thought back to the pained look on his face when I had first bumped into him. His face so full of grief, anger radiating from him like flames. Something bad had happened to him and Hilary. My thoughts, however, kept returning to the unborn child she had been carrying inside her. Had that been what had killed her? Or was the baby okay? Surely he wouldn't have left the baby alone? There were so many questions rolling around in my head, but all we could do was wait for him to wake up and hope that he would answer them. There felt so little hope in this world, yet I didn't realize until right then how much hope I had held out for this man and woman, how much hope I had put on the unborn child. Without that hope, I felt empty.

More than empty, I felt barren of anything.

"Where did Joan go?" I asked ,changing the subject but not taking my eyes off the man.

His entire face was caked in mud, a thin trail of blood dripping from what must have been a small head wound—but with not enough blood to cause me to panic, in case he died and went psycho zombie on us. The fact that the zombie virus hit you upon death and not fluid transference was both a blessing and a curse. The fact that your loved ones, at the end of their living days, would have to take a blade or bullet to the brain to stop them reanimating was even crueler than having to be the one to watch them turn.

"She yelled something to me about there being emergency back at the crow's nest and then ran off dancing," Nova laughed.

I wanted to laugh—the image alone was hilarious—but I couldn't laugh. I couldn't find any humor in the situation. And as I stared upon the muddy face of Deacon, I couldn't help but think that all of our hopes for the future had just been obliterated completely.

TEN

I woke with a terrified shudder and a loud sneeze. My dreams had been filled with my late husband Ben being torn apart by hundreds of tiny zombie babies with fanged teeth and wings upon their little crooked backs. I gagged at the memory of the dream, my mouth tasting like vinegar and bad applesauce, and I swallowed down the acidic substance that was loose in my throat.

My cold had worsened through the night, and I groggily looked around, seeing that Nova was still sleeping heavily. Joan had come back at some point during the night and was curled around Nova's feet like a cat. I looked across at the man—Deacon. He was still tied up, still slumped against the side of the tent, but I could tell he was sleeping now, rather than just knocked out cold.

I don't remember at what point I had fallen asleep, but I knew that I had slept for a good chunk of the night without moving, and my neck and back were now paying the price for it. My clothes were still damp and clung to my body like Saran Wrap, and I stood up, feeling my joints crack in retaliation. I stunk, too—not that I could smell too much with my swollen sinuses, but I could smell just enough to know that Nova would be throwing a fit when she woke up.

I dropped the damp blanket that had been wrapped around me, and was now subsequently soaked, onto my chair and grabbed some wood for the fire. The flames were low, but still giving off a little heat. The fire cracked and hissed as it came back to life, and when I looked around Nova had opened her eyes and was looking at me with a blank expression.

My throat burned in protest but I managed to clear my throat to speak. "Do we have any of the non-coffee left?" My voice sounded nasally and weird.

Nova nodded and sat upright, her eyes dropping down to her ankles where Joan was curled up, hugging Nova's boots like they were a teddy bear.

"When did that happen?" I asked with a raised eyebrow.

Nova shrugged. "I don't know. I think she just kinda slipped in here at some point. I haven't slept yet—been too busy watching our little guest."

"I thought you were sleeping," I mumbled.

Nova shook her head. "No. I didn't want to in case he tried something. I was just resting my eyes, as my mom used to say."

I looked back at Deacon with a frown. "What are we going to do about him?"

Nova didn't say anything, and I looked back at her to make sure that she had heard me. Clearly she had, going by the dark expression on her face. Instead of answering me, she reached into her pants pockets and pulled out her cigarettes, lighting one up and inhaling deeply. I noticed then that her clothes were completely dry.

76

"Are there more dry clothes?" I asked, eager to get out of my wet, stinky ones. Mud had caked around the bottom of the pants and was crumbling away as I walked, but I could feel it inside my boots, thick in my socks and between my toes. It was a horrible feeling, and every time I took a step I would grimace.

"Maybe in one of the other tents," Nova said, the butt of the cigarette never leaving her mouth as she reached down and tried to pry Joan away from her. She looked up at me with one eye closed to prevent the smoke getting in her eye. "You smell," she said without care. "Just so you know."

"I know!" I snapped, probably a little too loud, since Deacon then began to stir.

I turned back around to stare at him, noticing that although Nova had given up on trying to get Joan off of her, she had retrieved her handgun and was aiming it at him.

His eyes fluttered open and he groaned loudly, his look of pain turning to one of anger as he focused in on us. He was still covered in mud, though a lot of it had started to crumble away when it dried, leaving his face just looking dirty and gray. His dark expression was certainly helping with removing it.

"What am I doing here?" he asked, keeping his voice low and sounding deadly.

"You tell us," I retorted. "You're Deacon, right?"

I heard Nova huff next to me, and knew I had just given away our ace card too soon. I was eager, though, and clearly an idiot. His eyes narrowed into angry slits as he focused on me, eyes only once flitting to the gun that Nova held.

"How do you know me?" he snarled.

"Really? You don't remember me?" Nova grumbled from her

position next to me.

She still couldn't take a step toward him because of Joan at her feet. I watched as Deacon focused in on Nova, several expressions crossing his hardened features until he let out a heavy sigh.

"You helped Hilary and I escape." He spoke as if the words pained him, as if he were going back to a time he would rather not think about by admitting that he knew her.

"I did indeed. And where is she?" Nova said, getting right to the point.

I watched as Deacon visibly recoiled from the words, from us, shrinking in on himself before speaking. "You have to let me go. I need to get back to them."

My head whipped to the right to look at Nova, my eyes going wide at the revelation that she *and* the baby were alive. Nova looked just as freaked out as me by that point—her mouth hanging open, her cigarette stuck to her lip before she reached up and removed it. She threw it into the fire and looked back at him.

"Are you saying that Hilary is alive?" She spoke carefully.

Deacon hesitated briefly before answering. "Yes."

"H—o—l—y shit," I whispered.

"Will you help me? Please? You helped me before, will you help me again?" he asked, his voice sounding weak and fragile, his words desperate.

The strong man that had once sat there was now completely gone. I heard Nova swallow, the saliva in her mouth struggling to make its way down her throat as she swallowed again. I knew how she felt; I was having the same problem.

"You killed a lot of people here," I replied.

His eyes met mine. "These weren't people, they were animals. They tortured my poor Hilary. They deserved to die," he snarled through gritted teeth.

Nova snapped out of her trance, all care of poor Joan forgotten as she stepped toward Deacon. She got close enough to press the barrel of the gun to his forehead, and she glared down at him, her mouth twisted in disgust.

He jutted his chin out, his eyes boring into hers. "Go on then," he coaxed. "Do it!"

"What gave you the right to choose who lives and who dies?" She spoke almost breathlessly, her words heated and angry. And I couldn't help but worry she was about to blow his brains out in her next breath.

"I didn't choose anything," he ground out. "I think they should all die."

Nova snarled and pressed the gun harder against his skin as her rage matched his. Their eyes were connected, both of them staring venomously at one another. The air stilled around us, and I didn't dare move for fear of triggering something that I wouldn't be able to stop.

"There were innocent people here," she hissed.

"There are no innocents left in this world," he spat back.

Nova's arm shook with barely controlled rage, and equally Deacon wasn't backing down. His lips pulled back in an angry snarl and his body quivered with fury. My heart beat an unsteady rhythm in my chest, my headache hitting me full force and making me feel dizzy under the pressure. It was too early for this type of shit—for blood and guts and death. For killing and murder. For vengeance and rights. It would always be too early—or too late—for this type of thing. And perhaps I wasn't the monster that I had come to believe I was. Because I didn't want this—this bloodshed, this death—on my conscience.

"What about your child?" I asked softly in an attempt to reason with him and to talk Nova off the ledge. "Isn't your child an innocent? Doesn't that baby deserve better than this? Better than all this death?"

His eyes disconnected from Nova's and slowly slid across to look at me, and I noticed how dead they looked. His mouth quirked up in a gruesome smile and then he began to laugh. A loud, deep laugh that didn't sound like it held any amount of humor in it whatsoever. Joan had woken and sat up and she began to join in with his laughing, standing up to clap and dance in circles as her high-pitched laughter copied his deep, throaty, forced laughter as much as she could. She danced past me, her cold yet soft hands reaching out to clasp my face in her palms, and then releasing me and moving to Nova, who had lowered the gun and was staring at the ground.

Deacon stopped laughing abruptly, his laughter turning to tears, and loud sobs erupted from his mouth as his agony became raw and rough. His tears, in turn, set Joan off wailing and crying. She sat back down in the corner and drew her knees up to her chest, hugging them to her, and cried. And I think we all felt her pain right then.

Every cry.

Every sob.

Every body-wracking wail that left her mouth.

We all felt it. Deacon had stopped crying, his gaze now staring blankly at his feet as tears burned hot, silent tracks down his face, creating zebra streaks on his mud-caked skin. Joan continued to cry and wail. Deacon continued to cry silently. Nova continued to vibrate with rage, her gun hanging limply by her side. But I? I felt even emptier than I had the night before—as if a nothingness had drenched me to my very soul. I stared at him as he finally lifted his head up, his misery-filled eyes meeting mine.

"There's nothing innocent about that child," he said, his words sounding thick in his throat, as if it physically pained him to say it. "Nothing innocent at all."

ELEVEN

took a step backwards, my body slumping into my chair, the wind all but knocked out of me.

I had no idea what to say anymore. For once my words would not come. No witty comeback, no snarky remark. I was voiceless, as if the words had been dragged from my body, and my throat was nothing but an empty hole from which words could not escape. I thought of poor Jessica, of the unborn child that she carried inside of her. I thought of her joy at finding out that she was going to be a mother again, and I felt the pain that it would cause her to get rid of the tiny life that grew inside her. My stomach clenched. It wasn't a tiny speck of life inside her; it was death that grew within her.

"Where's Hilary?" Nova spoke and I looked up, seeing a calmness had come over her, her emotions finally under control.

Deacon looked up at her coldly and then spat in her direction. "Go to hell," he snarled, "all of you. You stay away from my family. You've done enough damage."

"Whatever has happened to you, whatever justification you think you have for killing these people, it's not good enough. It will never be good enough. There were children here. Families. And you killed them all," Nova ground out between tightly clenched teeth.

"They were already dead!" Deacon yelled angrily. "They just didn't know it yet."

"No, you killed them. You killed them in the worst possible way. You let in the dead and brought their worst nightmares to life. They fought the zombies, killing as many as they could, but in the end they all died." She shook her head as if the image of what he had done was alive in her mind—and maybe it was. She lifted her gun back up. "Nothing can excuse your guilt of that."

I realized how lucky we had been that the deaders that had been there—the ones that had attacked and killed the people that lived within the city—were gone. The thought of where they had gone would have to be analyzed some other time, because right then I knew that she was going to shoot him, and he deserved it. There was no excusing what he had done, yet I couldn't let her. No matter how much I wanted her to kill him. I couldn't allow her to. It was a stupid time to grow a conscience.

"Nova, wait!" I yelped, holding a shaking hand up to her. "Don't do this. You'll be as bad as him if you do, as bad as the people that tested on Hilary. Don't do this, you're better than this." I didn't know why I was trying to save him—he certainly didn't deserve it, not after killing so many innocent people—but one thing I was certain of was that she would struggle with this day for a long time to come, and killing him would only add to her internal misery.

"So what? He gets to go free?" Nova sneered angrily, her gaze never wandering from his.

My head was swimming, my thoughts muddled and confused. Everything seemed so screwed up, so wrong. I pulled out my katana and raised it before pressing it to his throat, looking at Nova and letting her know that I would take this for her, I would carry her burden. Because honestly, I didn't believe that she could carry any more on her shoulders. Not with all the horror of her sister and the damage she had done, the ball that she had set into motion. And Nova was needed in this world, where as I was not. I was nothing. Useless. A woman fighting for survival and coming out lucky every single time. I wasn't needed. I wasn't important. And so I would do this for her, for Nova. My friend.

"Where is Hilary? Where is the baby?" I asked Deacon.

"They're waiting for me," he said darkly, his gaze never leaving Nova's. "They're close by."

"Take us to them," I pleaded anxiously.

"No," he snapped. "I came here to torch this place to the ground and that's what I'm doing if it's the last thing I do. This place is evil. It needs to be destroyed."

I pinched between my eyes, my headache thumping mercilessly in my head. We couldn't allow him to burn the place down; there were too many valuable things there, too many things that could help people. Things that we needed—*I* needed. Yes, it was selfish, and yes the place deserved to burn for all the horror it held within its walls—much like all of the walled cities did. But we couldn't do that. Not when the things there could provide so much comfort and help to people.

"Deacon, this place was used for bad, but it doesn't have to always be that way. It could be made good again, it could become a home for people—other survivors. I can't let you burn this place down," I pleaded.

"Fuck this. He's not burning shit down, I'm killing him!" Nova yelled furiously.

"No," I yelled back, staring daggers at the side of her face. "No, you're not. I'll kill him if that's what's going to happen, not you."

"None of you are killing me!" Deacon roared angrily.

"Yes we are!" we both yelled back, looking at Deacon. Nova aimed her gun and I lifted my katana.

My breathing was ragged, my heartbeat ready to burst out of my chest, and I knew Nova was feeling the same way. She had the same crazy glint in her eye that I knew I probably had, the same look that Deacon had. We were at a stalemate.

"Please, no more death," Joan's soft voice whispered from behind us. And somehow through the beating of my ferocious heart and the rush of the blood in my ears, I heard her.

I turned slowly, seeing her cowering in the corner, silent tears tracing down her wrinkled cheeks. Her bottom lip trembled, her hands clasped together in front of her. I took a deep, shuddering breath and lowered my katana.

"No, no more death," I whispered to her with absolute certainty. "Not today, not like this."

She whimpered and crawled forward until she reached my feet, where she curled herself around my ankles like she had done previously with Nova. I reached down, clasping my hand around her arm, and helped her up to her feet, and then I folded her into my arms and let her sob against me. I glared over her shoulder at Nova and Deacon, feeling like the good guy for a change. Nova looked shamefully away, an angry blush rising in her cheeks. She glared down at Deacon but lowered her gun all the same.

All the while I continued to hush into Joan's ear to help calm her.

And I hated that I couldn't stop myself thinking it…but dear God she stunk. She stunk so bad it made my eyes water and I had to breathe through my mouth.

"Okay, we're done here." I peeled her frail, skinny body away from mine and took a step backwards, feeling nauseated by the snot bubble coming out of her left nostril. I turned away and looked at Deacon. "We are not blowing this place up, and you *will* take us to Hilary and your baby. It's important." I turned to Nova. "And you will not shoot this man. If you do, I'll shoot you. You got that?"

She looked at me deadpan before pulling out her cigarettes and lighting one. "What-the-fuck-ever," she said drolly.

"You don't understand," Deacon said, staring down at his feet. "If you understood then you'd want to burn this place too."

I stepped forward and crouched down in front of him. "I used to live in one of these cities. I do understand. They didn't test on me like they do here, but they stripped away everything that I was. They humiliated me, they hurt me…" I swallowed the lump in my throat. "They hurt everybody, so I do understand. And I don't blame you for believing what you do, but there are things here that could help people survive. You could make this work."

"You don't understand" was all he mumbled back, letting his head fall forward and his chin rest on his chest. "You just don't understand."

"So make us," I replied.

He looked up at me through his dark lashes, his eyes like liquid black. His full lips parted hesitantly, as if he were still deciding on how to reply to me. "Okay."

I stared dumbfounded for a moment before getting my act together and giving him a firm nod. "If I untie you, do you promise to behave?" I asked.

"Yes."

I looked over at Nova, who shrugged nonchalantly—though I knew she was anything but. "I've got this fool in my crosshairs, you don't even need to worry about that." Her eyes narrowed as she scowled down at Deacon. His lips quirked up at the edges into a sickly smile.

Well shit, these two were never going to play nice, I realized.

"Good," I snapped at Deacon, my mood darkening with the return of my thumping headache. "Nova, there must have been a medic tent here or something."

"Yeah, so?"

"See if there are any painkillers or some shit I can take for this flu. I swear my brain is trying to escape through my eyeballs. And we need something to clean his head wound. It's still bleeding and will attract deaders if we take him anywhere."

I took a step back and sat down in my chair feeling hot and sweaty. The adrenaline rush was wearing off and leaving me feeling especially shitty.

"It's just a cold, stop being such a baby," Nova said.

"It's the flu." I glared back.

She snorted back a reply and left the tent, hopefully in search of medicine for me. I'd suffered through several years in the apocalypse and I'd never felt so physically lousy from an illness. I'd fought off chest infections, knife wounds, sprained wrists, gunshots, beatings, and so much more, but this flu was kicking my ass.

I dozed in the chair until Nova came back. The room was hot—too hot—yet a cold chill still managed to run down my spine as the first signs of a fever began to hit. A cold sweat covered my body, and I knew that I must have looked like total crap when Nova frowned down at me.

"Don't go fuckin' dying on me, Nina," she said, and dropped a small white tub of what I assumed to be painkillers into my lap. I guess by the lack of tact, she was still pissed at me for not letting her kill Deacon.

I fumbled with the lid of the tub and shook out two white tablets before swallowing them down. I didn't even care about finding my water to get them down my dry throat, I just needed them inside my system as soon as physically possible. Thankfully, Nova let me rest for twenty minutes until the headache started to ease. The entire time she sat on the chair opposite Deacon, staring at him and smoking as if she had an endless supply and I wasn't in desperate need of some clean air to clear the fog from my head. However, I refused to tell her to quit chain-smoking in the room and risk looking like any more of a baby.

I stood up, feeling a little better. Though my body was still running hot and cold, at least I could think straight.

"Get up," I said, pointing my gun at Deacon.

He stood up without question, his jaw twitching in agitation, his dark eyes never leaving Nova's. I looked between them and shook my head. Nova was clearly provoking him as best she could, possibly in the hopes that he would do something stupid like try to run so she could shoot him. She was itching to, that much was obvious. And I was kind of surprised that she hadn't killed him anyway. There was no real reason to listen to me, and she knew I wouldn't ever shoot her. Yet I guessed that my opinion mattered to her, and my opinion of her was the only thing keeping this guy alive at the moment.

I went behind him and untied his hands, whispering in his ear not to try anything stupid as I struggled with Nova's crazy knots. After five minutes of struggling and grunting in annoyance I looked over his shoulder and caught the attention of Nova, who had miraculously gotten some bubble gum from somewhere and was chewing it noisily, all the while still eyeing Deacon with disdain.

"Dude? What the hell kind of knot is this? It's like some crazy ninja knot!" I huffed.

Nova snorted out a laugh but didn't move.

"Seriously, I can't undo this. There's some Harry Potter magic shit going on with these knots, I swear they're getting tighter the more I pull on them."

"Use a knife and cut them off him. My hands are busy." She raised her gun a little higher to show me—and possibly Deacon, though I doubt he had forgotten—that she still had him in the sights of her gun, and she smiled. If you could call it a smile.

I pulled my knife out and began to cut through the ropes until Deacon's hands finally fell to his sides. He pulled them up in front of him and rubbed the dry, red skin where the rope had scrubbed at the thin flesh on his wrists.

"Show-and-tell time," I said, coming to stand in front of him, my voice sounding harsher and crueler than I actually meant.

He sucked his bottom lip into his mouth, biting down on it as he weighed up his choices, his eyes flitting from me to Nova and back to me before finally nodding in agreement.

I walked by his side as we left the tent, Nova staying at the rear with her gun pointed at him.

"Yo, Crazy Pants, are you coming?" I heard her shout to Joan.

Outside the skies were clear for once: no dark rainclouds, no wind storms. The day was calm and mild, unlike my current thoughts, and I hoped that it was a sign of what I was walking toward.

My thoughts, however, continuously veered toward why I was even doing this. Deacon was a murderer. He had killed a lot of innocent people: women, children—and yes, evil scientists too, but in theory they were trying to save the world. While I couldn't condone what they did in any way, I also couldn't condone the murder of people so easily. An eye for an eye had never been my motto.

Plus, I pretty much knew from Deacon's reaction what I was going to see when we got to Hilary and the baby. Yet I couldn't stop myself. I *had* to see for myself. I had to prove to myself that there truly was no hope left in this world. No matter how much my heart had begun to believe that there was something good out there. That there was hope for mankind. For me. For everyone. What we were walking to would blow that theory away, and with it, my fractured soul would struggle to ever heal.

TWELVE

We drove in silence, Deacon tucked between me and Nova, and Crazy Pants—sorry—*Joan* in the back of the truck. Apparently she liked the fresh air. With each rev of the engine as we neared our destination, Deacon's body grew more rigid and taut with anxiety until his anxiety was almost something palpable. Something you could reach out and touch with the palm of your hand. I wanted to offer him some support, to tell him that it would be okay, but I couldn't. That would have been a lie. Because things would never be okay again. Things hadn't been okay for a long time now, and with each breaking dawn, when I thought I had seen the worst, a new horror seemed to arise from the ashes.

That's something I would never be able to get over. Something I would never become immune to. Because each day I was only shocked more than the last.

"Next left," Deacon said, his voice thick as he struggled to contain his emotions. His shoulder was pressed against mine in the small cab of the truck and I could feel him trembling, but chose not to comment or acknowledge it in any way.

Nova turned left, down a dirt track and past some trees that had grown wild in the years that had passed. We finally came to a stop in front of a small two-story farmhouse, and all the air seemed to leave Deacon's lungs in one quick gasp. The horror was clearly too much for him, the fresh agony of being here hitting him like a punch to the stomach. It couldn't be good, whatever awaited us, to garner such a reaction from him when he had seen whatever lay within already...

I looked away from his face, taking in our surroundings. The yard was overgrown, and what was once a small wooden fence surrounding the expanse of the house was now mostly broken down and rotten. The place had once been well-loved, with a vegetable garden and flower bed, the wooden exterior once a bright white, the roof a pretty red. However, now it was nothing more than a drab, broken home filled with unknown horrors.

I looked across at Nova as she turned the engine off and the cab of the truck fell into a thick silence. She was staring out of the windshield, her pale face a blank canvas, and in that moment all I could think to do was tell her to keep driving—to take us back to base camp and forget this crazy shit. We knew what was in there. We didn't need to see it.

Nova chose that moment to blow a giant bubble, letting it pop and making both Deacon and I jump.

"Let's do this shit." Nova looked across at us all, her stare cold, but her words even colder.

She reached for the handle on the door and pulled on it, letting the door swing wide before jumping out, her boots landing in the muddy earth with a resounding *splat*. I took a heavy breath and did the same, holding the door open for Deacon while he climbed out. I ordered Joan to stay in the truck—which, surprisingly, she did with no argument—and then we walked toward the door of the farmhouse. I looked around us as we walked, checking for deaders and traps and anything else that might be out of place.

I couldn't quite fathom why Deacon was just doing as we told him. I mean, sure, we had guns and knives, but he was no boy. He was a man with layer upon layer of muscle, broad shoulders, and strong hands that could easily snap my neck if he wanted to. Sure, Nova was badass, and yeah, I had a big-ass knife and a gun to boot, but it still didn't make any sense.

As we climbed the steps to the front porch, the wood creaking underfoot, I watched him carefully, waiting to see what trick he would pull on us. But then I saw it. The sag to his shoulders, the defeated look on his face. This man was broken, exhausted, and dead on the inside. He wasn't fighting us because he had given up already. He had nothing left to live for and didn't care what happened to him. He had given up already, and was now merely an empty shell for his soul to reside in.

Nova stopped in front of the door and turned back to look at him. "Should I knock?" she snarked with a grin. "Will the little lady come open up for us?"

Right in that moment I wanted to smack her around the face and tell her to stop being such a heartless bitch. I knew she was hurting, but weren't we all? Hadn't we all done things that were wrong, that were evil and cruel, and that we were ashamed of? Things that kept us awake at night, guilt eating away at our consciences? Or maybe that was just me.

Regardless, we had done what we had to do because we were trying to survive, just trying to make it through the day as best we could.

I couldn't—wouldn't ever—say it was okay for him to kill all those people, because it wasn't okay, and it never would be. He would pay for that crime, of that I had no doubt, but right there in that moment was what mattered. And right then, I knew that we were walking into his worst nightmare, and possibly our own.

Deacon stared at Nova with a deep-seated hatred, his eyes burning vicious holes into her, but she didn't care, and I couldn't help the disgust I felt for her in that moment. More so, I couldn't help but wonder if this was how people looked at me. I was heartless and selfish, I knew that, but to see yourself—your actions—reflected in another person was an entirely different thing. It was making me reevaluate my behavior. Because who I was seeing Nova be at the moment was not someone I wanted to be any longer.

She turned and twisted the handle on the door and swung it open. A smell wafted out to us—a musky, rotten smell that made my heart skip a heavy beat because I knew this smell, and I hated it. I held my katana against my chest, ready to use it if need be. I could feel the tension coming from Deacon as we stepped inside what I guess was his makeshift home, our footsteps sounding hollow and empty on the wooden flooring.

I looked around, noting that the house was relatively clean and tidy—a home against all odds—but something was off. Other than the smell, of course. I looked over at Deacon, who gestured with his head upstairs. His mouth was closed, his lips pulled thin, a grimace against his handsome and rugged face. We slowly climbed the stairs, each creak and knock of the aging wood making me cringe, my nerves tingling with the anticipation of what awaited us.

As we reached the landing I looked to Deacon again, but I didn't need to. A muffled sound at the end of the hallway caught all of our attention, and Nova moved out of position and toward the sound without waiting for me. Her steps were quick, her gait strong and filled with angry, nervous energy.

Deacon followed after her, his heavy steps loud as he rushed to catch up to her. She laid her hand on the door handle as she looked back at us and slowly opened it up, and then she turned her face away from me, looking inside the room and at the horrors I was envisioning it holding.

I stood at the foot of the stairs, somehow unable to make my legs move toward her or Deacon, who stood between the two of us as if unsure who he would need to react to first. His large frame blocked the hallway, and his arms hung limply by his sides in a sign of submission, yet his fists were curled up into solid forms, telling me a different story.

Nova's breath caught in her throat like the wind had been punched from her, and I looked up to her, watching as her shoulders sagged and she shook her head ever so slightly while she raised her gun.

"No!" Deacon roared, his body coming to life. He charged Nova, his footsteps echoing around the small space.

"Shit!" I yelled, running after him.

He hit her body sideways with his own, just as she was swinging her gun back around to shoot him. His shoulder slammed into hers, sending her sideways, and the two of them crashed into a heap together and began to fight. A shot went wide, and wood splintered next to my head, shards of what was once the banister sticking into my clothes, but thankfully none making it through the material and embedding themselves into my skin. I jumped, squealed, and maybe even peed in my pants a little. I had been shot before. It was not nice, at all. It felt like a hot blade slicing into your body, and I did not wish to go through that again.

I didn't have time to cuss up a storm, though, as Nova and Deacon, still on the floor, continued to fight over the gun in her hand. He hit her wrist repeatedly in the hopes of knocking the weapon free from her hand, but she kept it gripped in her palm despite his attempts.

I should have been more worried for their safety—one of them was going to shoot and kill the other after all—but at that moment, I had just reached the doorway after jumping over their writhing bodies on the floor, and as I looked in at the horror that the room held, the only thing I could think about was not throwing up on my boots.

My heart cracked, a thin splinter of it breaking away from the bloody pulp that beat within my chest, and I knew that it would never go back. I knew that I could never be healed from the atrocities that I was witnessing. I gagged on tears and bile, on heartbreak and fear.

I didn't notice that Nova and Deacon had stopped fighting, or that Nova was crying loudly.

I didn't notice that I was bent over, struggling to breathe through my own silent tears that burned hot paths down my cheeks.

I didn't notice anything but the blood and the bodies, and the groaning and the grunting, and the horror that was Hilary and her tiny writhing bloody baby still dangling between her thighs.

"No," I murmured to myself—to Deacon, to Nova. Hell, maybe even to Satan himself. Because this was too much. It was too much to see, to live, to breathe in. I would never be able to unsee this and forget it.

I couldn't do this anymore.

I staggered backwards, almost tripping over my own feet. Nova and Deacon stepped out of my way, making a path for me between their bodies. I continued walking backwards, my katana hanging loosely in my grip. I reached the stairs, looking back at Nova and

Deacon, listening to the growling coming from within, the smell of the room having followed me, and then I turned and ran down the stairs, taking them two at a time, almost falling as I hit the last step and stumbled outside, sucking in great lungfuls of air.

I collapsed to my knees, my body trembling as I tried to get rid of the image of Hilary and the bloody stain where her womb had once been. Of her tiny, perfectly formed baby and its tiny gray face with cold, dead eyes, gurgling from the back of its throat as it dangled upside down.

If this would have been a normal pregnancy—a normal birth—this baby wouldn't have lived, it was too young, and far too small to have survived. But this wasn't a normal birth, and this wasn't a normal baby. This was an abomination, a horror like no other. *It* had survived. *It* had lived, in a sense, though it was dead in every other sense of the word. *It* shouldn't have been living. *It* shouldn't have been moving around. *It* shouldn't have been there...

"This shouldn't have happened!" I screamed, the words exploding from my mouth before I could stop them. "This is wrong!"

A gunshot sounded out from the house, and I stumbled up to my feet and staggered back inside. Not wanting to go back *there.*

Not wanting to see *that.*

But I had to. For Nova.

THIRTEEN

I could barely hear anything beyond my own heartbeat as I reached the top of the stairs. I looked down the hallway and saw Nova fall backwards out of the doorway, her hands held up in front of her in defense. But I couldn't hear anything. Just my breath. It went in and it went out, the sound so crystal clear inside my own head. I could see Nova screaming, and I could see Deacon standing over her, angry tears covering his face and a shotgun pointed at her.

I was sure I was yelling at him, almost certain that I was begging at him to stop, but I couldn't hear myself speaking or shouting. All I could hear was the sound of the air inside of me.

And then it was like a balloon had popped and I was expelled back down onto the earth again.

POP!

Just like that. And I could hear, and see, and smell again.

"NO! Please, Deacon, please, no!" I ran toward him, my feet moving until I was standing over Nova, and the gun was pointed at me. I held my hands up in front of me in surrender like Nova had and pleaded for her life. "Please, Deacon, don't."

I couldn't see around him or over his shoulder—his body was blocking the doorway, filling the small space up entirely—but I had heard the gunshot, and I could see the grief written over his face. His body was shaking in anger, his face filled with rage, but it was in his eyes that I found his sorrow.

"Please, no," I begged again, reaching out carefully to touch the end of the shotgun and gently push it away from me.

Surprisingly, Deacon let me in, his breathing coming in ragged, choking gasps. Turning away from me, he leaned against the doorframe, allowing his body to slide down the length of it. Slumped on the floor, he let his shotgun clatter free from his hands, and as his face fell, he began to cry.

I glanced back at Nova, who still hadn't moved. She was looking at me like I was some sort of crazy person, and maybe I was. After all, I did just stand between her and a shotgun. Yeah, I was clearly fucking crazy. I shuddered as the realization hit me, and I stepped away from her and finally let my eyes look around the room again. I didn't want to. Not really. I wanted to leave this house—leave Deacon and his twisted, bloody little family and head back to the base. I had my answers now. I knew what needed to be done now for the sake of Jessica and her rapidly swelling belly. But I didn't leave. I turned to face the room, not finding Hilary or the baby.

I looked down at Deacon with a nervous frown, and I stepped over his legs. He didn't stop me, he just continued to cry into his hands as if the burden of this nightmare was finally over. Because now he was sharing it with us—other people that were alive. I stepped around the large bed that filled the majority of the room and saw Hilary's body sprawled on the floor, her ankle tied to the bed by some rope. Her head was a messy pulp of black blood and shattered skull bone, her body thin, almost skeletal. And beside her was the baby—if you could call it that.

I released the air that had been trapped in my lungs since I'd stepped inside the room. The dots in front of my eyes vanished as I pulled oxygen into my lungs, but with each breath I got a mouthful of the foul odor of the room. I took a small step forward, not wanting to get any closer to the bodies of the mother and child but needing to open a window, to let some of the deathly smell out of the room. The window was jammed, and I pushed on it once with the palm of my hand, and then again with both to get it to open, and I tripped as it finally opened. My foot slipped in the gore on the floor and I stumbled and nearly stood on the baby, my foot nudging the fragile body.

I looked down at its tiny face, seeing its pale eyes staring back up at me, and hearing the small, strangled growl coming from its tiny grey mouth. I gasped and staggered backwards, one hand going for my katana and the other covering my mouth to hold in the vomit that automatically rose up my throat.

Deacon came to life behind me, jumping up and pushing me out of the way as he charged past, reached down and sliced through the rotten umbilical cord, and then lifted the writhing bundle of death up in his arms. He pulled the tiny form against his body, his sobs deepening with every retched breath.

I wondered why he had left the baby attached all this time, why he hadn't cut that cord a long time ago. But then I guess the bigger question should actually be—why hadn't he put them both out of their misery, instead letting them both live—if you could call it that? I moved back out of the room, my brain wanting to shut down. I clutched the doorway as I exited, looking at a pale and forlorn Nova leaning against the balcony, smoking with shaking hands.

"I shot her," she said bluntly. "I couldn't let her live like that. Not that she was alive, but…" Her words trailed off. "What?" she said, frowning as she finally took in my expression. She lit another cigarette off the butt of the previous one and then crushed the old one underfoot. "Fuckin' hell, Nina, what is it?"

"The baby," I mumbled quietly.

"Baby?" Nova said just as quietly. Her face was a picture of confusion.

And I wondered how in the hell had she missed it when it had been all that I saw—a dead baby swinging from its cord, still attached to its mother. Her eyes drifted over my shoulder and I turned and flinched at the sight of Deacon coming out of the room carrying the baby.

"Oh my God, I didn't realize there was a baby!" She rushed past me to console Deacon. "I'm so sorry, no wonder you…" She reached out for the baby, pulling the thin wool blanket that Deacon had wrapped around it away from its face, and then she yelped and pulled her hand back like she had been burned.

She turned to me accusingly, as if I somehow had somehow this. But I couldn't speak, so I shook my head and swallowed, and tried not to cry. I closed my eyes to the pain and torment on Deacon's face and I thought about what he had said to us before we had left the town.

You'll understand why this place needs to burn if you see.

He's right: I do understand now. The place does need to burn. That place was a manufactured hell, and had no right being left standing. No one should ever live there again, because that place is pure evil.

Deacon passed us, both of us too numb to stop him. It took several minutes before I could think straight, before the stench coming from the room became too much and Nova finally turned back to me.

"Did I do that? Did I kill that baby?" She looked horrified, and I quickly consoled her that she wasn't the one who had done it.

"No, that…baby was dead already." I hadn't realized that she hadn't seen it. Her eyes must have been so drawn to Hilary coming toward her, not realizing that the woman was tied by her ankle and couldn't get to either of us. She must have shot Hilary, who fell backwards over the bed and dragged the baby with her.

"Are you sure?" She didn't sound or look like she believed me, and I knew the guilt would only last seconds if she believed that she'd killed that baby. Without a doubt, she'd turn her gun on herself—because that was too much for anyone to have on their conscience.

"Yes," I said, placing my hands on either of her shoulders. "Yes, it was already dead. You didn't do that."

Her chin quivered and she looked down to her feet. "God, why did he keep them like this?" she whispered.

"He couldn't let go, I guess." I shook my head. "We need to go find him and…" I looked away from her, not sure of what word to use. "We need to finish this for him if he can't."

"I don't think he'll let us," she replied.

"Then we'll make him. It needs to be put to rest."

Nova nodded in agreement and headed to find Deacon, both feeling shaky and unnerved. Outside we found him sat on the porch steps with the baby still in his arms. He heard us as we went approached—I knew this because he had been murmuring to it before we walked through the doorway. His deep voice had traveled into the house and up the stairs—soft, soothing whispers that a father gave to his child. He fell silent when he heard us behind him.

We walked down the steps, coming to stand directly in front of him.

"You're not hurting my baby," he said bluntly, his eyes locking with mine and filled with the familiar rage I had seen back at the walled city. "You're not hurting my child."

I kept my composure, even though inside I was screaming at him that this whole situation was wrong, that he was sick in the head for keeping his wife and baby alive, and that *thing* needed to die, to be put out of its misery. But I didn't say any of those things. Instead I nodded and held his gaze.

"Will you help me?" he asked, his words dripping with pity and sadness.

"Burn down the walled city?" I asked. "Destroy the place that did this to your family?"

"Yes," he choked out.

The bundle moved, the blanket stirring until I caught a glimpse of the dead baby in his arms. I gritted my teeth, breathing through flared nostrils. Both anger and hatred flared in me, disgust that this was what we resorted to as humans—killing our own. Wasn't there already enough to fear in this world?

"Hell yeah, I will," I said with strained words.

Deacon seemed satisfied by my answer, by the force of my words and my obvious conviction "Thank you," he mumbled, and looked away.

"That thing ain't riding in my truck," Nova fumed next to me.

"Yes, it is. He needs help," I said, not quite recognizing the woman that I was becoming.

"I ain't no damn shrink." Her nostrils flared.

"Good, because what we need is fire. Help me give him his vengeance," I pleaded. Because he deserved that much, at least.

Nova continued to stare at me. Eventually she slid her gaze across to Deacon. "You have to pay for what you did. But I'll help you get your vengeance, because she's right: you deserve that. Everyone deserves that—including the people you murdered."

I couldn't agree with her, and I guess neither could he, since he nodded and looked away. We all climbed into the truck, and after checking, I found Joan sleeping in the back, completely unaware of everything that had occurred in the last half hour, and by God I envied her ignorance to it all. Because I would do anything to go back half an hour and forget everything that I had just seen. I had thought it was bad when I thought Hilary had died, but for her to become a deader—for her own undead baby to have somehow eaten or clawed its way out of her, killing her and turning her into this monster—that was something else entirely.

As we trundled back down the muddied path, I watched the house fade away in the distance and I wondered if we should have also burnt it down. It was a house of horrors now, filled to the brim with only nightmares. Its walls were crawling with revulsions and pain. Deacon stared out the window silently, his arms still wrapped tightly around the moving baby as if he were protecting any normal newborn. The thought made me feel sick. Nova drove, her window open and a cigarette hanging from her lips, her face pale and deathly.

This was the most horrifying day I had ever experienced—possibly worse than when the outbreak had first begun, when I had no idea what was happening and it had seemed as if every nightmare was becoming a reality.

This day was worse than that. This had to be the lowest point, because I couldn't imagine anything worse than this, than what Deacon was going through at the moment, than what he carried in his arms. I promised myself silently that I would try and bring him some kind of peace.

He had killed so many people, and for that he would have to pay, because I finally agreed with Nova that he had to die. It was seeing his family, torn up and bloody, and knowing that he had truly lost it—that there was no coming back from this for him—that had convinced me. But first he deserved some sort of retribution for his own pain, and I would help him get that.

FOURTEEN

We piled our truck up with as much as it could possibly hold—clothes and blankets, food and medicine. It still seemed like such a damn shame and a waste to destroy everything, but I couldn't imagine letting this place stay in one piece, and there wasn't enough time to get back to base and get more trucks and get back here. It would take weeks to accomplish a full clear-out, and the longer it stood, the more my gut churned to destroy it. Because it couldn't be left standing. Not after everything that had occurred here. The scientists here, Rachael included, had supposedly been working on finding a cure, but as we went through the tents it seemed less and less likely that this had actually been the final outcome they'd had in mind.

Bodies had been experimented on, samples of blood and saliva taken and fed to non-infected humans. Through the brief notes that I forced myself to read, it became more and more apparent that the outcome had been to learn to control this disease for some reason. It was absurd and barbaric, and as I lit one of the tents on fire—one that contained dismembered bodies and brains in jars—and stepped away from the flames that licked up the side of it, I couldn't help but think that this was the very best outcome for the world. That by destroying this place we were actually helping to save mankind—because if anyone had gotten hold of those notes, we could all end up more doomed than we were already.

I chewed the inside of my cheeks in an attempt to stifle the scream that wanted to erupt from me. I tasted the metallic tang of my blood filling my mouth as I bit down harder. Thick smoke danced around the tent, and I stepped back away from it, not wanting to breathe in the toxicity of the fumes. I continued to frown and bite at my cheek, anger and sadness engulfing my heart and making me want to run and run and never look back.

What was wrong with people? Had we learned nothing in the years since the outbreak? Angry tears built in my eyes until the fiery tent was a blur, and I swallowed down the thick lump of hatred in my throat. A little piece of me had died and I knew it wouldn't come back. I felt like I was a continuously revolving door, a new emotion at each new turn.

Anger. Sadness. Hatred. Anger. Sadness. Hatred.

It wouldn't stop, and neither would mankind. We would always be trying to control others. Always trying to own and take what wasn't ours. What was the point in living if we were always trying to kill one another?

"Are you okay?" Nova spoke next to me, but I couldn't look away from the flames to acknowledge her. "This is all so much more fucked up than I thought possible," she mumbled.

I nodded in agreement, because she was right and I wanted—no, I *needed* her to know that she was right. That this was everything I hated about people, about life. The unfairness and cruelness of everything.

This was everything I hated about the walled cities and the Forgotten and all their craziness. Because I got it, okay? I fucking got it: The deaders weren't the disease. We were.

"You know he has to die, right?" Nova waited for my response, and when there wasn't one, she continued. "And that…thing, that has to die too. I'll make it quick for both of them."

I blinked, the tears falling from my eyes, and I nodded. Because this, too, was true. He had to pay for what he had done, he had to be made accountable for the blood on his hands, just like the Forgotten had to, but it would also kill me to do it. This man had already suffered so much and now he was going to die because of it. It all seemed so unfair and unjust, and I wondered if we were as bad as the scientists in this cheap laboratory, deciding who lived and who died.

"He's a sicko. How could he let them live like that? Ughhh, they weren't even alive, they were dead, and he could have ended that torment. But he didn't." Her words were a blur of rushed air, flowing into one another as she spoke.

I felt numb to it all. To him, her. To her hatred and the whole crazy, vile situation. I shook my head, barely registering what she was saying anymore. I couldn't do this. I couldn't be the god who decided who lived and who died. There was too much of that now. I opened my mouth to speak, my tongue feeling heavy in my mouth.

"I think we should let James and Zee decide that," I said through a throat thick with emotion.

"What? No! He has to die, now! And they won't let that thing anywhere near the base." Nova's hand gripped my shoulder and she spun me to face her.

I barely recognized the person that stood before me. Gone was the happy carefree woman that loved to dance in the rain, and standing

107

before me was a broken, distraught woman full of anger and bitterness. She had lost so much, and I hadn't realized how much she had been hoping that this trip would make things right—that the damage her sister had caused would somehow be justified if everyone had been okay. In her eyes I now saw how her hope had been to go home with a healthy woman, man, and a baby, and the very real possibility of a cure.

Instead we were returning with nightmares.

"It's not down to us to decide this—to decide his fate—and honestly, I don't want it to be." I wanted to be able to take this burden away from her—to kill this man and put her, and him, out of their misery, but I couldn't. I wasn't strong enough. Or maybe I *was* strong enough. Perhaps that was the problem. I wasn't just a hate-filled woman anymore. I was finally opening myself up and allowing other emotions to embrace my soul, and surely that was a good thing. Right? But if so, why did it feel so wrong?

Nova snarled angrily at me. "You're turning fuckin' weak, Nina."

"And you're turning cruel!" I retorted with an angry sob.

"I learned from the best." Nova glared at me.

"I won't let you do this."

"You can't stop me."

I closed my eyes, feeling the heavy thud of my headache behind my eyes. She was right: I couldn't stop her. There was nothing I could do. Because if it came down to this man or me, it would be me. I waited in silence, gathering my thoughts, deciding on my next move—my next plea.

"Please, Nova." I resorted to begging, because I couldn't win an argument against her. "Let's not do this. Let someone else decide. I don't think I could live with it."

For several moments she didn't say anything, and then she grunted out something indecipherable before turning and stomping away.

I sighed, my heart feeling too heavy and full, almost as if it couldn't possibly hold any more heartache. Nova was right: I was turning weak, and this weakness could get me killed, but it felt so hard right then to continue being strong. My walls had been breached and I was struggling with getting them back up. Between Emily and Mikey I was turning into a fluffy kitty-cat instead of the fierce lioness I used to be. Yet I couldn't ever regret letting these people into my life and my heart. Even if it did get me killed.

I watched the tent burning until the smoke began to sting my eyes and then I turned away from it and carried on the arduous task of setting everything else on fire also. Nova and Deacon had been busy while I had been standing watching that one tent burn. Most of the compound was on fire now, flames licking high into the sky.

Yesterday we had followed the smoke signals and arrived at this compound not knowing what we would be walking into. What we found was that everyone was dead and the bodies were burning to dust. Today we would leave this place and head back home, leaving behind yet more smoke in our wake, as this place burned to ashes. It felt almost poetic, and also like good karma in some way, to destroy what was once the destroyer.

The place was burning well, and thankfully the rain had stayed away. In one of the storage rooms we had found some gasoline, and we used some of it sparingly to help ignite the compound. Another wasteful act, but necessary if we wanted to ensure the full destruction of the place.

I headed back to the truck, stomping through the muddy earth and avoiding the decaying bodies that still littered the ground. I moved around a group of charred bodies, wincing as I saw that one of them was still moving—only fractionally, and not really enough to do any harm to someone unless they fell directly on top of it. Plus, this place would be gone in a few short hours—yet it seemed unjust to leave it like that, burnt to a crisp and almost mummified, buried under a pile of bodies. I drew my katana out and took another steadying breath before driving it through the deader's skull. There was almost no resistance from the weakened skull, and only a tiny *crunch* and *pop* as the blade met its mark and pierced the brain. Still, it made me feel sick to my stomach.

"Another one bites the dust," I muttered, pulling my katana back out.

I frowned down at the blade, noticing that the gunk on the end was tinged green instead of just the normal black gloop that was inside deaders' skulls. I lifted the blade to my nose and sniffed, feeling freaked out that it didn't smell of rot and decay. In fact, it didn't smell of anything at all.

I looked around me, feeling paranoid and worried. Had we just destroyed the cure? Or had we in fact eliminated a new type of deader? The heat was rising from the fires as they steadily grew and joined each of the smaller fires, so I hurried to the truck by the main entrance.

"Nova?" I yelled as I drew close.

She was standing beside the truck, smoking as usual, and looking wretched. Anger and sadness engulfed her. I could see it in her eyes, her stance—hell, I could almost see it emanating from her in waves of disgust. Deacon was sitting inside the truck, the bundle in his arms, his eyes flitting to Nova every once in a while.

"What?" she barked out as I got closer.

I scowled at her, wanting to rip into her with a nasty comment, but we were too alike. It wouldn't get us anywhere but into another argument.

"Look at this." I raised my katana to show her the deep green blood.

"What is that?" She frowned.

"Sniff it," I said, raising the blood up to face height.

"Fuck no! What is it? Is it shit? My shit goes a weird color if I eat too many beans. I'm not sniffing your shit, Nina."

I stared at her, dumbfounded, and then despite the panic and worry, despite the anger I felt for this situation and for her callousness toward Deacon, I laughed. And once I started, I couldn't stop. Nova glared at me, unimpressed.

"It's not funny, Nina. That's sick. There's something seriously fuckin' wrong with you."

I noticed the corner of her mouth quirk a fraction, and though she was pissed off and hurting, I knew that she thought it was funny. That I would actually make her sniff my crap.

I shook my head, still laughing, even though what I was about to say to her wasn't in the least bit funny.

"It's not my shit, asshole. I just killed a deader, and this was the stuff inside its head." I had stopped laughing but I still held a small smile at the idea. "And it doesn't smell. At all."

"What? Let me look at that."

I raised the katana up to her nose and she took a deep lungful of it.

"It *doesn't* smell," she mumbled.

"No. What does this mean, Nova?" I asked seriously.

She shook her head. "I honestly don't know. They either found a cure, or were getting close, or they created something much worse."

I could almost feel her burden grow heavier as she spoke.

"But there's nothing we can do now, we need to get out of here."

I nodded in agreement. The heat from the fire was growing steadily and the smoke was getting closer. I started to go around to my side of the truck, since Nova was driving.

"Nina."

I turned to look back at her quizzically. She held my gaze for several seconds, as if trying to order her words in her head and then she looked away.

"I can't sit next to that thing," she mumbled without looking at me.

I glanced over at Deacon. I didn't think he had heard her—not that it would have mattered if he had, but I was glad he hadn't all the same. Neither of us wanted to sit next to that baby. It was going to be a long trip back to base and I wasn't sure that James and Zee wouldn't just execute Deacon and his child on sight, making this whole situation pointless. But either way I couldn't be the one to kill him, or it, and I really didn't want to be around when it happened.

"I'll sit next to you," I said, not wanting to be stuck in the middle of Nova and Deacon but not wanting her to freak out at having to sit next to him either.

Plus, it was the least I could do since she had agreed not to kill him. Actually, she hadn't agreed, but he wasn't dead yet so I took it as an agreement, anyway. Joan had said she would go in the back of the truck with all the gear, though I wondered if she would be comfortable with so much back there. But as long as the temperature didn't drop too much, that would suit her and us just fine, since she smelled so bad and we really didn't have any other option. I found her splashing in a muddy puddle and gave her the heads-up on the plan, and thankfully she didn't seem to give a shit about where she sat and happily climbed into the back of the truck.

I moved past Nova and climbed into the truck through her door, squeezing myself into the middle seat. Deacon looked across at me sorrowfully, his eyes dark pits of despair. The sound of his dead child making all sorts of weird, creepy noises in his arms sent a shudder down my spine. I knew then that this would probably be one of the hardest journeys I would ever make. I looked away and tried not to listen to the noises, to not smell the foul stench that emanated from his arms, but it was almost impossible.

Nova climbed in next to me, glancing at me once with a look of appreciation before starting the truck. We pulled out of the compound and headed home, four people and one dead zombie baby, and a truckload of gear heavier. Yet the greatest weight would always be inside us.

FIFTEEN

"**N**inety-six bottles of beer on the wall, ninety-six bottles of beer. Take one down, pass it around, ninety-five bottles of beer on the wall! Ninety-five bottles of beer on the wall," Joan hollered loudly in the back of the truck, singing at the top of her voice.

If you could call it singing. It was more a deep, throaty screech that set my teeth on edge and made my stomach clench with the very urgent need to yell and scream at her to stop. She had been doing this off and on for the past couple of hours, and not for the first time that day, I was hugely grateful that she was in the back and not sitting next to me, where she would have been close enough to strangle. I didn't want her death on my conscience—not along with everything else. Yet as she reached ninety-three bottles of beer, I wondered if my conscience would be okay with her death. Because I was getting seriously close to losing it.

We had hoped that she would get bored and fall asleep, or at least run out of beer bottles, but when she had reached zero bottles and we had breathed a deep sigh of relief—even Deacon looked grateful—she had started from the top again. This was her fifth go-round, and I was feeling fidgety with the need to yell, or stab something. Or yell *and* stab something. Hell, I wanted to yell and stab and maim something, I was feeling so irritated with her out-of-tune singing.

"I'm going to stop the truck and kill her," Nova bit out, her nostrils flaring angrily. "I'm serious, Nina. I'm going to slit that wrinkly old throat of hers if she doesn't stop in a minute."

"You joined in before. She got to three bottles and you joined in! This time around is your damn fault!" I snapped back angrily.

"I thought it would help her shut the hell up if she realized that it was truly the end of the song," she grumbled back. "I even yelled the fuckin' end at the fuckin' end!"

"You encouraged her. She thought we were all having fun, asshole!"

"I did no such thing."

"Yes you did. You sang with her. Now she knows we can hear her and is doing it all the more. She thinks she's entertaining us when really she's signing her own death warrant!" My voice raised into an angry yell and I felt Deacon flinch next to me.

I ignored him, knowing that if I said anything at all to him about that it would be along the lines of something horrible. Between Joan's God-awful screeching and his zombie baby's stench and weird noises, I was officially finished with this trip. I wanted out. I needed a new truck. In fact, I was ready to line up Deacon, the zombie baby, and crazy Joan and execute every last one of them. Nice Nina had officially vanished, at least for the day.

Nova grumbled something under her breath and slammed on the brakes. The truck skidded to an abrupt stop, and she dragged the handbrake on and jumped out of the truck. I followed her out, both of us marching to the rear of the truck, where the warbling was coming from.

Nova opened the door and glared in. "SHUT UP! You shut up right now or I'll leave you here. Do you understand you, crazy fuckin' woman?"

I raised an eyebrow at her back. I think Nova needed to take a good long look in the mirror at who was actually the crazy one here, since she was the one screeching like a banshee.

Joan came further forward, her face leaving the shadows. She smiled down at us pleasantly. "Are we here?"

"No, we are not, and you will not be making it back to our base if you don't shut the hell up!" Nova continued to yell, her shoulders rising and falling with each panting heavy breathe.

"I'm sorry," Joan mumbled apologetically. "I didn't mean to."

Both Nova and I exhaled loudly, the anger leaving us in one great big gust. She was just a lonely, crazy old bat who needed a friend, not us yelling at her. I felt pity for her, because who knew? Maybe I'd be just like her one day soon.

"I'm glad that you're sorry," Nova said, and began to turn away.

"I pooped," Joan replied with a blink.

"You what?" Nova and I replied together.

"I pooped in the corner. Are we here?" Joan smiled at us again.

Nova turned back to look at me in disbelief. "She shit in the truck."

I had no words.

"Dude, she shit in my truck!" Nova pulled out her gun, flipping the safety off. "I'm shooting her."

I grabbed at her arm. "Do not shoot her!"

Clearly Crazy Pants was back and Joan had checked out for the night. This wasn't her fault—not that I wasn't seriously pissed that she had crapped in the corner of the truck and possibly defiled everything, because I was.

"Let's set up camp for the night. We could all do with the break." The smell from inside the truck wafted out to me and made me retch, and Nova glared at me even more.

"Fine, I won't kill her, but you're cleaning the damn truck out," Nova snapped and stomped away.

I looked back at Joan. She was like a naughty puppy, playful and mischievous and with no idea of the damage she had created or the havoc that she was wreaking around her. She smiled and blinked, and then her nose scrunched up and she hastily climbed out of the back of the truck.

"Something smells back there," she said as she passed me.

I ground my teeth together to stop myself from yelling at her. At the moment, the old me and the new me were fighting for supremacy. It would be easy to give in to the old me, but I really didn't want to be that asshole anymore. Besides, Crazy Pants wouldn't give a shit what I said anyway. So instead of cursing at her and saying all the horrible things I wanted to say, I took a deep breath, climbed into the back of the truck, and began searching for her crap.

And it was, just as she had said, in the corner.

The baby made all sorts of noises that I couldn't put words to. They weren't exactly growls or hissing, or gurgling, but a combination of all of them. It didn't seem to be rotting—not like a typical deader did— but by God, it stank. Between the demon baby and Crazy Pants, our little camp smelled bad and so did the truck, which was why we had all decided to sleep in the open. We had strung cans up around our camp to alert us of any deaders stumbling upon us, but in all honesty, the stench coming from the baby would automatically dismiss our location to deaders. They wouldn't smell our humanness above the smell of death that clung to that thing.

Still, first thing in the morning I was making at least Joan wash up in the small creek I could see on the map. I could and would get rid of her stench, even though I couldn't get rid of the baby's.

Earlier we had tucked into another meal of ration packs and the rest of the deer I had killed back at the scrapyard. The meat of the deer was dry and chewy but it was better than slurping all of our food down from a packet. We needed more meat now, though—fresh meat—and Nova had promised that when daylight hit she'd do some hunting.

She was great at it. She knew how to track and skin any animal, how to get the very most from every kill so that nothing went to waste. We hadn't starved so far on this trip, mainly thanks to her, because other than my deer kill, I couldn't see that I had done much to help with anything. Between me catching the flu and my newfound conscience, I had been pretty useless so far. My cold had abated a little with the help of the medicine Nova had found, but it was still there nonetheless. My head and muscles ached, my eyes stung, and my sinuses felt painfully swollen. I tried to ignore it and not mention how sick I felt after Nova's nasty comments at the compound about how weak I was, but now that we were settling in for the night and the day's adrenalin had worn off, I had to recognize how truly awful I felt.

I was on first watch while everyone but the zombie baby slept—because of course that thing wasn't sleeping. I stared at it for hours, its weird growls and stench getting in my head and making me feel haunted. The poor thing never stood a chance, and I think that was one of the things that I was struggling with the most. It was a monster, an abomination, but it should have been a sweet, chubby-cheeked baby. It was heartbreaking.

I sneezed again, and my brain felt like it was clanging around inside my head. I needed to get back to base so I could rest properly, and I needed to keep rehydrating if I was going to flush out this nasty flu anytime soon. Which meant I needed to pee more often because I was drinking so much. It wasn't just exhausting, it was hugely inconvenient.

I rested my head back on the tree I was leaning against and listened carefully to the noises of the forest. It was pretty quiet, with just the wind in the trees. No owls hooted; clearly they had learned long ago that noise drew the deaders to them. Nova snored—loudly, I might add. Joan was surprisingly quiet, a welcome respite after today's singing. *Perhaps she wore herself out with all the singing,* I thought, smirked to myself.

Deacon's breathing was even and calm, though I knew he wasn't truly asleep. I knew he didn't dare sleep for fear of what Nova would do to his dead spawn. Me, he somewhat trusted, but not Nova. And I couldn't blame him. Something had snapped inside her since we arrived at her old compound and seen the destruction there, and of course Deacon and his dead baby hadn't helped the situation. I understood why she'd changed, how she had adapted because of her warring emotions, but I was also surprised by it—by how broken she had allowed herself to be. Maybe that made me a judgmental asshole, but I was still surprised.

I tried to let my thoughts drift to things of unimportance, but of course everything held importance these days. The simple things that we used to take for granted, the things we used to waste—all of them now meant so much to us. Every little thing from the past meant something. Just like Nova's photograph of her family. Some things seemed useless, but they weren't. Not really.

Things could break us and make us in the blink of an eye. I wondered if that photo had broken Nova, if she could come back from this and be like the woman I had first met. I truly hoped so, because none of this was her fault, no matter how much she blamed herself for it. Only Rachael could be accountable for her actions, and that bitch was dead now, so I considered the slate clean.

I thought of Mikey and Emily-Rose, wondering what they would be doing right then. Would Mikey be safely back from their scavenge mission yet? Would they be sleeping, curled up comfortably in their beds, the duvets wrapped tightly around their bodies to shield them from the cold? Or perhaps Mikey was on guard duty. Did he miss me? Did he miss the space I used to occupy in his bed? Because I missed him.

I finally let myself feel the things I had been denying myself. I missed his warmth, and the way that his strong arms wrapped around me would force me closer to him, and the protection that he wanted to give to me regardless of whether I needed it. I loved his smell, the muskiness and sweat that always seemed to be on him. It was both manly and just plain Mikey. But most of all I missed his kisses. The way his full lips had owned me completely, making me forget to be a bitch and just become a woman again—a woman I had forgotten all about somewhere along the line. He made me feel complete. He made me feel feminine, and he took away the loneliness that had devoured me since this nightmare began.

But I had let him go. I had let my own stubbornness get in the way of whatever it was that was developing between us. I had been scared and anxious, and had masked all of that with the pretense of protecting everyone at the base because of Michael's threats. I had been a coward, to both my own heart and his. I could see that now, and I could finally admit my mistakes. I was an asshole.

For not the first time in twenty-four hours, I found my eyes filling up and I rubbed at them to stop the tears from falling. I wanted to believe that my tears were just because of the flu that continued to lay heavily on me and make me feel even more exhausted and therefore weepy, but I knew that was a lie. I scoffed at myself. I hated this part of the new me—this teary-eyed wreck of a woman. It was pathetic. *I* was pathetic. It's a good thing Mikey and I had split up, because we were never going to last anyway.

My heart still panged for him, though, and the loss was acutely harder when I didn't get to see him on a daily basis. It made me feel all the more weak and angry. Especially knowing Mikey had probably moved on to the next woman by now. Perhaps they were sharing his bed tonight, her keeping him warm and giving him the closeness he so desperately wanted—the one thing that I had found so hard. I bit down on my lip, sucking in a breath at that thought. But then I forced my chin up, refusing to be this pitiful sap that I seemed to become whenever I thought about Mikey. He made me weak. He made me believe that things would get better, that possibly I deserved better. But I didn't, and things would always be like this.

Mikey gave me false hope, and for that I wanted to hate him just as much as I cared for him. With his false hope he had set me free; he'd brought me back out into the world, kicking and screaming and fighting. I needed him to know how much I thought of him. How grateful I was for what he gave me without even realizing it. If I ever saw him again, I hoped I'd remember these things to tell him, because he deserved to know. No matter who he might be sharing his bed with now, he needed to know that he was right. And I was wrong.

Now I just had to pray that both he and I made it back from our separate destinations to see one another again.

SIXTEEN

Morning sun broke through the trees and woke me. Actually, the rain was what woke me—that and the nightmare of greedy hands tearing at my clothes to get to my warm skin underneath. I retched and sneezed as I woke, the feeling of thick fingers both imagined and not, still fresh in my mind. The rain pelted my face as it slipped between the leaves of the trees. It was icy cold and I gave a series of loud sneezes before I had even the chance to properly sit up.

"A-tissue, a-tissue, we all fall down!" Joan chirped next to me.

I righted myself. During the night that shall now only be called "The Night of Self-Loathing and Needing to Constantly Pee," Nova had come to sit with me. She still seemed like she had a fire up her ass, but she at least seemed calmer than she had all day. She'd sat with me and smoked for a while before I'd finally decided to get some sleep myself. But instead of retreating to the now-aired-out truck to get some shut-eye, I'd stayed by her side.

Maybe it was the way she had continued to glare at Deacon while he slept fitfully after exhaustion had finally sucked him under. Or maybe not. Because yeah, she was calmer, but her eyes still held their deadly intent. I trusted her less now than I had earlier. That realization made my heart hurt even more.

Joan sat down next to me, her expression sad and thoughtful, and I was brought back to the present.

"What's wrong?" I asked, stretching out my back.

Joan shook her head miserably. "Sometimes it comes back to me."

"What does?" I realized that this was Joan talking now, not Crazy Pants. I had come to the conclusion at some point yesterday that she wasn't totally crazy, but she also wasn't quite there anymore. I think trauma had taken a lot of her mind, which I couldn't blame her for. I was only surprised more people weren't like her. She was two people, and had purposefully fractured herself to cope with this world, and would flip from persona to persona depending on the desperation of the situation.

She was Crazy Pants who was stark raving bonkers and did whatever she pleased without worrying about the consequences. And then she was Joan, and this was the real her. She came in drips and drabs and mainly reminisced about the past, telling us tales of her husband and life before the infection. I somehow preferred Crazy Pants to Joan. At least Crazy Pants didn't make me feel so depressed.

I leaned in closer, breaching her personal space and getting nearer to her than I really wanted to. That sounds heartless, but she still smelled of actual shit, so judge me all you want. But still, the more compassionate side of me wanted to offer her what little comfort I could.

"Everything." She looked up at me, her expression distraught. "Everything comes back, Nina, and it hurts so much."

It was the first time she had used my name, and it sounded strange coming from her. Her eyes twinkled with unshed tears and I knew she was going to lean in for a hug. I braced myself for it—for the snot I could see starting to dribble from her nose, for the way her scent of shit and dirt would cling to my clothes. I opened my arms and waited for it because I was trying my hardest to not be a total bitch these days, and this would be an un-bitchy thing to do. She continued to stare at me for several moments, and just as I was about to tell her to give me a hug because I was feeling like an asshole with my arms opened wide like I was replicating some kind of biblical image, she stuck her tongue out at me and blew a raspberry. Spittle splattered my face, and I gagged as she stood up and moved off to squat behind a tree without another word.

I blinked uncertainly until I heard her grunting loudly.

"Oh for God's sake!" I hissed and stood up on shaky legs.

I looked around, not seeing Nova anywhere but finding Deacon sitting in the truck, his face looking down, still fixated on the baby in his arms. His mouth was a thin line of anger, frustration, and sadness. There was no way out of this shitty situation. I was trapped between a crazy woman who was endlessly shitting and a depressed man carrying around a zombie baby. I pinched the bridge of my nose, hoping for some relief, but the meaningless gesture brought me none.

A crack to the left of me had me drawing my katana and turning, only to find Nova coming out of the trees.

"Easy, tiger," she said without emotion. She held up a snake and something furry that I couldn't distinguish in her hands. "Breakfast." She grinned.

I forced out a smile. "I was sleeping and you left."

"I was close by. Besides, I gave Joan a signal to call me if there was trouble." Nova squatted down and began to build a fire.

"A signal?"

"Yeah, a signal."

"Dude, that's not cool. She doesn't even know what day it is—you can't rely on her to give you a signal. You should have woken me." I forced my voice to stay calm and not raise in anger. But it was hard.

Nova let out a frustrated breath. "You wanted meat, I brought you meat. Stop whining. Joan would have signaled me, trust her."

As if on cue, Joan came back from around the tree. I was unimpressed to see that she was sniffing her fingers.

"Joan, what was the signal to call if there was danger?" Nova yelled to her while simultaneously looking at me obnoxiously.

Joan stopped sniffing and looked at the ground for a moment before looking up with a smile. "I had to slide to the left, slide to the right, cha-cha-cha!"

She even did the dance.

I blinked at Nova, waiting to see if this was the signal she had given, but after an awkward five seconds Nova burst out laughing.

"Okay, okay, point taken!" She laughed harder and turned back to the fire. "She fuckin' cha-cha'd." She shook her head, her long, greasy red hair, dangling down her back in a matted ponytail, swayed from side to side.

"It's not funny," I chuckled back. And it wasn't funny. At all. I could have been eaten in my sleep! But hearing Nova laugh again, and seeing Joan cha-cha in the middle of the forest in this super tense weird ass situation was as bizarre as it was humorous, and I couldn't help a small smile from slipping out. "Wake me up in future, okay?"

"Okay," Nova replied, still laughing. "I promise."

I walked over to the truck, stepping over the deader alert traps we had set and opened the door. The smell hit me like a brick to the face.

The stench of death was getting stronger. Deacon's eyes met mine with angry force, almost daring me to say something about the smell of death. His eyes were shadowed by dark rings underneath, and the whites of them were red from lack of sleep. A light sweat covered his pale brow, but he stared me down defiantly. I swallowed down the bile in my throat and tried to breathe through my mouth, but I knew it was no good. There was no way that Nova was getting in this truck with that thing. I blinked uneasily, not sure what to say. Luckily, he broke the tension first.

"We'll get in the back," he said calmly, pre-empting what I was going to say to him but was struggling to find the words for.

I nodded awkwardly. "I think that would be best."

I held his gaze, trying not to let my eyes drift down to the wriggling bundle he held, but it was impossible. He looked away first, and together we looked upon the face of death in his arms.

The baby should have been a sweet, rosy-cheeked miracle, but instead its skin was gray and sallow, almost translucent in appearance, enabling us to see the dark lines of disease beneath its papery thin skin. Its hairless skull was misshapen, an odd angle to it, and its eyes stared back at me unblinking. Foggy and full of death, they were wide with hunger. It made the same noises it had been making all last night and yesterday, but upon seeing me it grew louder, as if it had grown accustomed to Deacon now, and knew that he was there to protect it. I, on the other hand, was food.

I gasped as it fought to free its arms from the tight blankets wrapped around it. Deacon stuck one of his dirty knuckles in its mouth, and it began to gnaw away at it with its rotting gums, much like a baby would do to a pacifier.

The messed-up thing was, Deacon was pacifying it, even though

126

we both knew that the baby was actually trying to eat him. It was only for its lack of teeth that he was safe.

I shuddered, but forced myself to calm. "Are you hungry?" I asked quietly.

Deacon shook his head no, though I knew he must be hungry by now. "I'll get in the back," he mumbled again.

"Okay," I replied tersely. I looked away. "You know this is wrong, right?" I looked back up and gestured toward the baby.

Deacon looked right back at me, his eyes full of fire. "This is my baby. The last part of my wife. There's nothing wrong with that," he growled.

"Deacon, that baby is—"

"Mine!" he cut me off. "This baby is mine. It didn't want to be this, it wasn't supposed to be like this, but it is what it is, and I love it just the same."

We stared at one another for a moment—me feeling confused by my total understanding of his emotions, but not wanting to accept it, either, and him hating me for making him question his own sanity. Because that's what it came down to: he had lost his damn mind, and the fact that I understood and sympathized with a murderer and someone that was carrying around a zombie baby was freaking me out.

"Stay away from my baby!" he yelled loudly, his voice gravelly with emotion, and I flinched from the force of his words.

Deacon opened his door, climbed out, and moved around the side of the truck to get in the back. It didn't go unnoticed that he left the door open to air it out. I turned around and saw Nova marching over toward us, her gun in her hand, her expression one of pure hatred.

"Nova, no!" I yelled at her.

But she didn't listen. Nova barged past me, though there was plenty of room for her to pass without nearly knocking me over.

"You're an asshole!" I yelled and ran after her. I grabbed her before she made it around the back of the truck. "Stop."

She shrugged out of my grip, but I grabbed her with my other hand and yanked her backwards, and she spun to meet me.

"What? He could have hurt you."

"No, it wasn't like that," I pleaded.

"We have to end this now, Nina," she yelled furiously back. "I won't let him hurt you or anyone else."

"Don't use me as the bait. Don't fucking do that."

"I'm not," she said with no conviction.

"Yes you are. It's not up to you to decide if he dies," I pleaded.

Nova pushed me and I stumbled backwards.

"And it's not up to you if he lives!"

We stared at each other, both of us panting in anger. We had come to a stalemate, because she was right, but so was I. It wasn't up to either of us to decide this.

"So then why don't we let him go?" I said cautiously, the thought still forming. "He's got his vengeance, and he has his punishment."

Her mouth twitched as if to say something, but she didn't speak. She put her gun in her waistband after flicking the safety back on. "What punishment? We can't just let him go—not after what he did, Nina."

Her words were raw and throaty while she spoke, and I knew she was right again, but then what? What was the point in dragging him across the state back to our base only for him to be killed there? I thought of the look in his eyes as he'd stared down at his little bundle of deathly joy. The smells and the sounds it emitted, the horror that he had to continually look upon. And for how long would he be able to do it? To keep it with him? To let it live this horrendous life?

"I think he's paying for what he did. He's been paying all along." I pleaded with her to understand my meaning, and I wondered whether I was being even crueler by suggesting we let him go.

Nova looked at me and swallowed so loudly I could hear it. "Fine. Let him go. See if I care. He doesn't get to take any of our gear, though. You send him on his way with the clothes on his back and that's it."

I thought about it for a moment. "We should at least give him a meal."

"You're pushing your luck," she retorted, to which I rolled my eyes. "Fine. One meal and then you get him out of my sight. One meal. After that he better be long gone before I change my mind and blow his brains out—his and that disgusting thing!" she huffed and stormed back over to finish breakfast, leaving me with the happy news of telling Deacon that he was free to go.

The thing was, I wasn't sure if he would want to leave. Sure, he was worried about what Nova would do, but let's be honest: we had barely trained a gun on him since setting the compound on fire. He could realistically have left whenever he wanted to. Yet he had stayed.

"Shit," I mumbled as I made my way to the back of the truck.

SEVENTEEN

Deacon was making himself and the dead baby more comfortable in the back when I looked in. His eyes immediately sought out mine, his hands instantly curling into fists as he pulled the baby closer to his chest.

"What?" he barked out.

I shifted from foot to foot, feeling massively uncomfortable and wishing that I would have kept my mouth shut.

I cleared my throat before I spoke. "You can go," I stated. This should have been good news to both him and us, yet I felt awful, and his glare did nothing to ease my guilt.

"Go?" he asked, sounding confused.

"Yes. I spoke to Nova and we agreed to let you go." I stepped back to allow him some room to exit the truck. "You can have some breakfast before you go. We have meat, sort of. Nova caught a snake and something fuzzy." I rambled on nervously, my words tumbling out faster and faster as I watched the confusion and hurt cross his face.

"I thought it was a rabbit, but when I think about it, I actually think it might be squirrel. Who the hell knows? In fact, it's probably best not to think about it and just eat it—"

"Where will we go?" he asked, cutting into my long ambling speech.

I stopped talking and took a deep breath. "I don't know, but you can't come back with us."

"Why?" he asked softly, his words almost a plea to me.

I looked away, feeling guilty and angry all at the same time. "Because they'll kill you and...and the baby if you come back with us." I looked back up to him.

His eyes were still pinned on me, and I watched as his Adam's apple bobbed up and down as he swallowed. "You have to pay for killing all those people, Deacon. But this is your one chance. While I don't agree in any way with what you did, I can understand the place you must have gotten to, to see that as your only option. I get it, but I can't condone it, and neither will anyone else."

A single tear dripped from the corner of his eye and he made no move to brush it away. "But look what they did to my family." His large chest heaved, each breath painful to him as he looked down at the baby in his arms and then held it out for me to see. I couldn't stop the painful pang in my chest as I looked at the dead baby's sallow face.

I agreed with him in some respect: they *did* need to pay. At least, the ones who did this needed to pay. But Deacon had made everyone pay—innocent people—and for that there could be no mercy. However, I wasn't going to be the one to dish out the punishment to this man, and I wasn't sure I could be around anyone who did. He had been through so much already...God, my head was so messed up with indecision. I hated it. I was used to making a decision and sticking to it, knowing my mind and not having anyone sway me from it. But recently, I didn't feel like myself. I felt…changed.

"Look, I'm just the messenger here. I'm just telling you how it is. If you come back with us, they will kill you. Of that I have no doubt. And after they kill you, they'll kill your baby. I'm trying to help you here."

He stared at me accusingly, as if he knew that only part of what I was saying was true. As if he knew that the other part of me wanted him and that thing far away from our truck, and my conscience. He would pay for his crime—by having to live. And I wouldn't have to watch the consequences unfold. Yeah, I was a coward. I wasn't ever going to deny that.

"And what if I won't leave?" he rumbled out.

I raised an eyebrow—mainly because I was surprised by how much he clearly didn't want to leave, but also because I hadn't counted on him just refusing to leave.

"Well, you have to," I snapped.

"But what if I won't?"

I huffed out a heavy breath and glared at him. I was doing everything I could to not lose my temper—counting backwards from ten, taking steadying breaths, putting myself in his shoes—but his shoes sucked and my sinuses were stuffy so it hurt to take a deep breath.

"You don't have a choice, Deacon. Nova will kill you and the baby if you don't go. Now come eat, and then we're leaving. Without you," I snapped before turning away from him and heading back for some breakfast.

I needed more medicine and something to eat. And coffee. And cupcakes. And possibly a weekend spa break with a sexy male masseuse. But since I wasn't likely to get any of those things in this lifetime, I guess I'd stick to snake meat and whatever the fuzzy thing was.

I stomped back over to the small fire, where Nova had speared the meat and was turning it above the flames. She glanced over at me questioningly.

"He doesn't want to leave," I stated. "He's not going to go without a fight, I'm almost sure of it." I rubbed a hand down my face.

Nova chuckled darkly. "You did good."

I raised an eyebrow at her. "I did?"

I couldn't quite figure out what she meant. Why had I done good? I'd just told her that Deacon had refused to leave and we were going to have to force him to. I couldn't see the good in any of that. In fact, it felt like things were about to go to hell again, and truthfully, I was sick of hell. Sick of the fighting and clawing for existence. I just wanted to eat breakfast and have a cup of coffee.

"You did." She grinned. "Did you tell him to come to breakfast?"

"Yeah." I frowned, not liking the tone of her voice. My heart raced, telling me that something wasn't quite right with her. "Nova?" I started to talk, but Deacon made his way over to the fire at that moment, closely followed by Joan, so I shut my trap and hoped for the best. Which really wasn't saying very much, since my best had always been to just not die. But whatever.

We ate in silence, only the sound of our chewing to keep us company. The rain had stopped, but every once in a while a freezing cold fat raindrop would drip down from the leaves and they always seemed to get me. I grumbled as another one hit the back of my neck and trailed slowly down my spine.

I looked up, seeing Deacon taking small bites of his food. He looked deep in thought, and that couldn't be a good thing. I looked across at Nova, seeing her eating a chunk of snake while she stared intently at Deacon. That also couldn't be a good thing. I had a feeling in the pit of my stomach that things were about to get seriously messed up between these two.

The sound of moaning had me jumping to my feet, my hands instantly dropping the small bone I was holding and reaching for my katana. Movement off in the trees to the right had me on full alert, yet Nova barely glanced up from her snake.

"Dude, deaders," I said in annoyance.

She gave a little shrug. "So go kill it."

I looked away from the movement in the trees to scowl at Nova. "That's your reply? Really?"

I wasn't too bothered about going off and killing deaders on my own; that wasn't really the point of my argument. I was more shocked by her lack of concern for them than anything else. For all she knew there was a horde.

Nova stopped snacking on the snake and looked up at me with a condescending grin. "Nina, do you want me to come kill the big bad scary zombie with you?" She punctuated each word and made me feel stupid. "I can hold your hand if it gets too dark. We could spoon tonight if you want."

I stared at her silently, feeling my cheeks flame with both anger and embarrassment. All the while she stared right back with an overly large grin on her face.

"No, that's not what I was saying. I meant maybe we could pack up before they reach us," I snapped. The noises were getting closer and unnerving me, and this was getting me nowhere. But she was right: it sounded like there was only one—two at the most—and the trees were so tightly packed together that a herd would have no chance of moving as a collective—not without making one hell of a noise.

"They need killing," Nova replied, sounding bored as she continued to eat. "I killed some this morning, these ones are yours. I'm not leaving until I've finished eating. Besides, it only sounds like one."

"Fine, I'll go kill it myself then, but if I get eaten, I'm blaming you." I began marching away.

"Nina?" Nova called after me.

"What?" I replied without turning around.

"What about the spooning? Can we still spoon?" I heard Nova laugh wickedly as I stormed away.

The trees were thick and overgrown, and branches stuck out at odd angles and scratched at my skin. I could see movement up ahead and I tried to be quiet, but it was damn near impossible given my surroundings. I glanced back once, unable to see even the smoke from the fire, and wondered whether this was actually pointless. Would the deaders even be able to hear us? They certainly couldn't have seen us, and I'm almost certain that the freaky zombie baby was masking our smell.

It was too late to back out now, though, as they had most certainly heard me.

I grumbled, taking note of my surroundings and realizing that there wasn't an awful lot of space to swing a big-assed katana around.

"Crap," I cursed under my breath.

I spied a deader heading my way and tried to focus on a way to kill it quickly, instead of focusing on what state of decomposition it was in. I kept on moving forward, hoping to find a small space to allow me some more room, and was greeted with a small opening in the thick of trees. There was a fresh deader kill already there, which must be the one Nova had said she had killed this morning. I was also surprised that I had actually doubted Nova's honesty when it came to it, but decided to assess my newfound trust issues with her later, when I wasn't about to kill a zombie.

A deader stepped into the clearing opposite me, its eyes wide and staring hungrily at me. I swallowed and tried to stem my fear as I always did. Because you never really stop fearing them. You would think that you would become immune to it after a while, that you would give up on the fear and just face the problem head-on with a stomach full of iron determination. And perhaps some people did. I certainly didn't, though. I still got goose bumps at the sound of their growling—which didn't say much when I still got scared of spiders, but whatever.

I stepped out from around the tree, careful about where I stood as I slashed out with my katana in the hopes of getting lucky. It didn't happen, and I blindly swung three times before stepping further into the clearing so I could get a better swing. I knew my stance was sloppy, my grip tight—too tight—and Mikey would be having a fit if he saw how careless I was being, but I couldn't seem to get it right as I stumbled around on the uneven ground, stepped over the dead zombie, and almost tripped. The deader was a gangly thing, with overly long arms and gnawed-down fingers, and its hair was styled into what was probably once an impressive fifties-style quaff. However, now it hung limply down the center of its forehead. Thankfully it didn't smell anymore, but its papery-thin skin sounded painful as it rubbed against the rough fabric of its once pristine suit. We moved in a tight circle, it constantly lunging for me and me constantly moving out of its way. I needed a clean shot, but couldn't quite get the arm reach. A quick jab to the stomach would send a normal man to his knees, but this wasn't a normal man, and it would only make things more difficult.

A growl from behind had my gut clenching as I realized my mistake too late: I had come full circle as me and the deader had continued to reach for each other. I hadn't bothered to check for more deaders after seeing the first one, and now, as I took a quick glance behind me, I saw at least two more coming up to take a bite.

EIGHTEEN

"O h shit!" I squealed—yes, squealed. Don't judge me.

A deader stumbled out of the clearing, its hands clasping hold of me as it brought its mouth down on my shoulder and I felt the first bite tear through my clothing. I flailed wildly while simultaneously being pulled backwards, and I fought to stay on my feet. If I went down, I was a goner—of that I was certain. All sense of reasoning and skill went out the window as panic overtook me and I fought to stay alive.

The first deader had gotten close enough in front of me to easily grab me, so I lifted my leg and kicked out as hard as I could. My boot slammed into its stomach, but instead of sending it flying backwards, my booted foot impaled the center of the deader's stomach cavity with a sickening *crunch*. It continued to reach for me, even while I stood on one leg like a flamingo, my other boot firmly implanted in its gut. The deader behind me was gnawing on my shoulder, its teeth finally breaking through the material of my clothing and I cried out in pure, painful panic as I felt the first scrape of its teeth against my flesh.

Another deader had moved around to my right side now, and it was almost too much to take in. My mind wasn't being able to fully wrap itself around what was happening, and was ready to close down.

This was it.

I was going to die.

I screamed loudly, which in hindsight was probably the stupidest thing I could have done, since it would alert any other deaders to my location. But I couldn't help it, and so hindsight could kiss my skinny ass. Teeth sunk into my skin, and when I felt a warm rush of blood spurt free from my shoulder, I panicked. I flailed, I kicked, I pulled, and I screamed some more, not wanting to die like this—alone in the woods, never being able to apologize for being a terrible human being to the people I cared about.

My mind registered the sound of a gunshot, but it wasn't close. Or perhaps it was and I was just losing it now. Or perhaps my screaming had attracted a horde to us and they were now descending upon Nova and the others. Oh God, what had I done? I had killed them. But what was I to do? Die quietly? Another gunshot sounded out just as the deader to my right reached for me, its hands clinging onto the material around my waist, and it buried its face into my clothing.

I could feel the rip of my jacket, the tear of my own flesh from my shoulder, and my own gut-wrenching screaming as I continued to fight them off. Their teeth were broken and jagged and this was all going to end quickly. At least I prayed it would. The urge to quit the fight—to let my sad and lonely life be obliterated was strong—but the thought of never returning back to Emily kept me fighting, giving me a fresh surge of energy.

Tears, hot and fresh, ran down my face, blood poured down my arm, and my left hand swung out blindly with my katana, eventually finding purchase in the side of the first deader's face. It wasn't enough to kill it, but it seemed to make it stagger as if I'd hit a cluster of nerves that made it somehow harder to control its limbs. It stumbled backwards and I barely held onto my katana as it did. There was a loud sucking sound as my foot left its stomach and my katana dislodged from its face at almost the same time. I placed both boots on the ground and pulled with everything I had to get free from the feeding deader's teeth. I took the risk of chopping my own body in half, deciding that this would be the better option than to be eaten alive, and I swung out with my katana, reaching across my own body and slamming the weapon into the head of the deader that was currently trying to eat my stomach.

It sunk into its skull, slicing right through until I felt the sharp edge of the blade touch my stomach. I gasped as the deader attached to my shoulder bit down and pulled at my muscle and sinew. The pain was excruciating. Red hot pokers sliced into me as it tried to tear me apart with its mouth. Its bony fingers dug painfully into me, and as it pulled backwards, my flesh firmly in its jaw, I gritted my teeth and pulled in the opposite direction.

My skin snapped free from its death-filled grip like stretchy meat, and my body sprang forward, almost into the waiting arms of the stumbling deader in front of me. Blood pumped from shoulder, and I realized with relief that the katana hadn't chopped me in half. It had cut me, though I couldn't be sure how bad. I could feel a hot, slow trickle running across my stomach. However, somewhere in the battle I had finally dropped my katana. So now I was weak, and weaponless.

I staggered to the left, panic making me feel dizzy and disoriented. My vision blurred, but the sight of two deaders coming closer to me was clear, and I knew I needed to run. I slammed into a tree, almost tripping over the branches and roots that scattered the ground. I placed a hand on my shoulder, attempting to press against the wound and stifle the blood flow. I slipped between two trees, the deaders close behind but thankfully just as clumsy as I was. I didn't know where I was running to. If there was a horde back at the truck, then I would be running from one danger straight into the middle of another. But I couldn't just stop. I couldn't give in. I had to keep going, keep trying.

These thoughts whirled through my mind as I pressed on, forcing my shaky legs to keep putting distance between myself and the chasing deaders as I staggered from tree to tree, and I prayed that I was heading back in the right direction. Through blurry eyes I saw a figure running toward me. It wasn't a deader, I was certain of that.

Nova got close, and I could focus on her face long enough to see the panic and worry etched across it.

"Shit, Nina!" she said, her eyes going wide as she saw the state of me. "Oh shit, I'm so sorry."

"Help," I whispered out as I stumbled toward her. She could keep her damn apology; that was no good to me now. What I needed was her to go kill the deaders trailing after me.

She swallowed nervously before speaking. "You're such a drama queen," she huffed, briefly examining the bite on my shoulder with a wince.

I knew she didn't mean it, it was just her way: add amusement to a scary situation and make it less scary. Still, if I'd had any decent hand-to-eye coordination right then, I would have punched her in the face.

She looked behind me, seeing my following friends, and she pulled out her knife and pressed a hard kiss on my forehead. Her eyes met mine seriously, and for the first time in almost a week, I saw Nova—

the real Nova—again.

"You wait here. Let me get rid of these fuckers for you, darlin'."

I didn't know if she was still trying to be funny with her "stay here" comment, but regardless, I was going nowhere. She stomped off behind me and I allowed myself to sink down to my knees. I didn't bother to turn back and look; I knew she would be able to handle them with no problem. Her knife was shorter than mine had been, so she didn't need the arms reach that I had needed. Besides, I had seen the fire in her eyes.

I listened to her yelling at the deaders behind me, and I almost wanted to laugh at the things she called them, the way she spoke to them like they had any clue what she was saying. But I didn't laugh. I gritted my teeth and caught my breath, thankful for Nova and the fact that she kicked ass so well.

"Stupid rot bags. I'll teach you to bite my friend," she mumbled, and the sound of her knife sticking in rotting meat followed closely after.

Moments passed before she came back around and stood in front of me. She tsked and reached down to pick me up, placing an arm around my waist to take the brunt of my weight as she walked me back to camp.

"Well you got yourself all fucked up again, didn't you?" She huffed out an annoyed breath. "Seriously, it's like you attract danger."

I tried to glare at her, but everything hurt and I couldn't get up the energy to do it. We headed straight to the truck, where she helped me up the steps and bundled me inside. She walked around the front and climbed in before starting the engine.

"Where's Joan?" I asked Nova, feeling incredibly tired.

"In the back," she replied as she turned the truck around and headed back to the road. "Everything is packed up and ready to go!" she said.

"Where's Deacon?" I asked, knowing that there wasn't enough room for everyone back there. My shoulder throbbed, the world going fuzzy. I had lost too much blood and I wanted to sleep, yet a deep, subconscious part of me knew that would be the wrong thing to do. *Sleep equals bad*, I told myself, forcing my eyes to stay open.

Nova didn't reply to my question, and I ground my teeth in annoyance. "Where is he?" I touched a hand to my stomach, and when I pulled it away, there was blood on my hand.

"Shit," Nova said as she gave me a quick once-over. "How are you? You still with me?"

I nodded, but my body slumped sideways as she screeched around a sharp bend. My head bounced off the glass and Nova mumbled out an apology but didn't ease up on the gas.

"Gotta put some distance between us and that place before I can pull over. I saw a herd on the road back there. Hold on for another mile or so, darlin', then I'll clean it and stitch you up. You'll be as good as new in no time."

I watched her mouth moving, her words seeming far away—as if they weren't coming from her mouth at all, but were words floating around in the air between us like a separate entity. She looked over at me, her eyes wide. And I could see her yelling at me, her words sounding distant to the throbbing in my ears. She reached a hand over and slapped me hard across the face, and all at once my hearing came back.

"Wake the fuck up!" she yelled at me furiously. "You do not sleep until I tell you to." She reached a hand back to slap me again.

"I'm awake!" I yelled back, feeling more alert. I should have thanked her for getting my adrenalin pumping again, but my stubbornness wouldn't let me.

She continued to hold her hand up, readying to slap me again, and I flinched.

"Dude, I'm okay!"

She grinned and put her hand back on the wheel. "'Atta girl," she said, paying attention to the road ahead. "I'm pulling over in a minute or two, so keep the pressure on."

I nodded, pressing my hand to the bite mark on my shoulder. I winced, but kept the force on it regardless. I needed to help myself if I was going to live. My head throbbed, my shoulder burned, my stomach stung—everything felt painful, and I was so grateful at the moment that I had Nova with me.

"This is all your fault," I said tartly.

"I know," she replied immediately. "I'm sorry." She was silent a moment before adding on: "If it's any consolation, it doesn't look all that bad."

I glared at her, and she at least had the decency to look guilty before looking away.

"Where's Deacon?" I asked, my throat feeling raw from all my previous screaming.

"He's gone. He left. Just like we told him to," she replied without emotion, her eyes staring straight ahead. "But seriously, that," she gestured to my neck, "really doesn't actually look too bad. I mean, it's bad, obviously, but you're not going to die from it, I don't think. I'm pretty sure you'd be dead now already if it had bitten something really important. Not that I'm a doctor or anything, but you know, I think your clothing protected you from the worst of it. But it still needs stitches. Just not right here. Keep pressing on it." She reached over next to her, where there was a bag of clothes, and fumbled around until she found an old T-shirt and handed it to me.

I pressed it against the wound with a wince, thinking over what she had said about Deacon, and I realized with worry that I didn't believe her. Her distraction had almost worked, my own pain almost canceling out the niggling thoughts that were now running rampant in my head.

"Pull over!" I ground out slowly.

"No, we need to get away from here. I need to get us to safety before I pull over, and then I need to stitch your shoulder." She turned to look at me, looking frustrated. "Screw him, Nina, and that thing!" she snarled.

"There are deaders back there, they could be in trouble," I pleaded, feeling awful for leaving him like that.

"I killed the ones after you. He had more than enough time to run, he'll be fine," she replied quietly. "Stop worrying about him and that fuckin' demon spawn."

I went silent, a sinking feeling hitting me. My teeth chattered noisily. I felt cold and panicked. The terror of nearly being eaten to death, of seeing my life flash before my eyes, and then the guilt of leaving Deacon and his baby in such a dangerous situation with no food or weapons lay heavy on my soul. I began to cry.

"Stop that," Nova said quietly. "No crying. You're stronger than that, Nina."

I shook my head in denial. "No, I'm not," I managed to get out between sobs. I wasn't sure if it was the comedown from my adrenaline high that was actually bringing on my waterworks or what, but a deep sadness was squeezing my heart and stopping me from thinking clearly.

"Yes, you are. Now get your shit together."

I wiped at my eyes and nose, stemming the tears and snot, and nodded. My shoulder hurt so badly, and every time I moved my stomach throbbed in pain. I was full of self-pity, a total emotional wreck. This journey had been a total waste of time. Hilary was dead, and now we had to go back and tell Jessica that she had to terminate her pregnancy. Had I ever really believed anything different? I knew without really acknowledging it that no, I didn't, but a part of me had prayed for a good outcome to this whole mess. Because I needed something good right then, I needed something positive to cling onto. In a world filled with so much misery and sadness, I had once again let myself hope.

Stupid hope was going to get me killed.

Nova fidgeted uncomfortably in her seat, finally pulling her knife out of one of her many pockets and her gun out of another. She stabbed the knife into the dashboard and threw the gun into one of the pockets in the door.

My eyes glanced across at the gun, and I took a heavy breath filled with relief. I was safe. I was in serious amounts of pain at the moment, but I was safe. She had saved me. And she was right, I needed to get my shit together, because I was alive and so many others weren't. For that I should be grateful. I took another steadying breath to calm myself.

I turned in my seat to look at her. "There were gunshots," I said.

"So?" Nova replied.

I frowned. "You said that there were no deaders at our camp."

Nova huffed out an annoyed breath. "So what? What's your point?"

"I heard gunshots. What did you shoot, if not deaders?" I looked at the side of her face as I spoke. The words left my mouth as I realized exactly what she had done. "No," I murmured. "Please, no, Nova," I begged her, but I knew it was pointless.

Her expression didn't change and she didn't flinch at my words. Her eyes left the road long enough to look me in the eye. "You know, in certain countries they kill babies that are born different. They kill them before the placenta is even delivered."

I stared at her open-mouthed, not sure what response she was looking for from me.

"That thing should have been killed when it was born, Nina. It had no right to live. He had no right to let it continue on in this world." She looked away from me. "We're trying to rid the world of this evil, after all. I just did my bit in ridding a little of it today."

My heart beat in my chest, the heavy thud of it making me feel dizzy and sick. There were no words to speak, nothing to describe what I felt for her or what I thought about her actions.

"You killed them?" I breathed out, the cab spinning.

She didn't reply, but I watched her hard features tense even more, her jaw grinding.

"How could you do that? They were leaving, Nova. They weren't our problem anymore."

"They did leave," she said harshly. "They left this mortal coil, and good fuckin' riddance to them." Her mouth puckered into an ugly shape, and I felt the bile rising in my throat. "We did him a favor. He'd thank me if he could."

"Who are you?" I asked, repeating her earlier sentiment. "This isn't you, Nova. You don't go around killing people. Not like this."

But when I thought about it, what did I really know about her? About her brother and sister? Her sister had infected God knows how many people and tried to kill me. Her brother was the biggest asshole ever, the silent brooding type that screamed "I'm a secret serial killer," and then there was Nova. I'd thought she was good, but she was just as messed up as the rest of them.

I turned in my seat, still clutching the bloody T-shirt to my wound. I couldn't stand to look at her anymore, and even though she had saved my life back there, I knew that I didn't trust her anymore. The sound of Joan's singing echoed forth to us as she suddenly began another rendition of "Ninety-Nine Bottles of Beer," and for once I was glad for it. Because there was nothing left to fill the ever-deepening void of silence between Nova and me.

"Giving me the silent treatment won't change anything. You have to know that what I did was for the best, Nina. You can't be that fuckin' stupid." Nova's voice had risen to an all time high, and I swallowed as I struggled to control my rising panic and worry. "Answer me!" she screamed, slamming on the brakes.

The sudden stop had me flying out of my seat and slamming my weak and broken body into the small footwell of the truck. I cried out, my hand slipping from my wound. Fresh blood began to pump from the bite mark. I looked up gasping as Nova glared down at me, her lips twisted in a vicious snarl.

"Look how far the high and mighty Nina has fallen," she growled out, clenching her knife so tight her knuckles went white. "You're so fuckin' self-righteous."

NINETEEN

MIKEY

"**Y**our snoring pisses me off."

I ignored Melanie's droll tone for what felt like the tenth time this morning. That woman didn't ever have a nice word come out of her mouth. She was beautiful, but goddamn she was a bitch. She made even Nina look like a saint.

Nina.

My frown deepened when I thought about her. I'd never met someone who frustrated me so much. She was stubborn, mean, grumpy, moody, she was untidy and hated to be told she was wrong—the list of her faults was endless. She had all the traits I disliked in a person, all the things that I normally ran from, yet, buried down deep, there was a softness to her.

This apocalypse, and all its shit had tried to destroy the person Nina had once been, but every now and then I would catch a glimpse of that woman, and goddamn she was anything but mean. This crazy, bitchy woman that refused to let me forget about her was so kind and generous she would have made Mother Teresa blush with shame. She just hated anyone seeing that side of her; she saw it as her weakness. There was something more to her than what she let everyone else see, something that I had forgotten about through these long years since the plague of zombies had risen. When I thought of Nina, I remembered to smile. I forgot the pain, and I began to believe that there could be a life for me after all—a life more than this, at least.

"I hate it when you bite your nails. It's disgusting."

I glanced sideways at Melanie, her words cutting through my thoughts. She wasn't even looking at me. She was staring out the windshield, watching the road ahead and listing off the reasons why she didn't like me.

Nice.

Bitch.

But I was glad for the distraction. Thinking about Nina was a one-way path of self-destruction. We were over, and she would never forgive the fact that I hadn't trusted her, because trust was everything to her.

I stopped biting my nails, noticing that they were shorter than they had been in a while. It was something that Nina had hated, too, and I'd tried to stop doing it. I guess since we weren't together anymore, I had restarted that old habit.

"You chew ridiculously noisily. It's like listening to a pack of wild animals eating a rotting carcass."

"A rotting carcass?" I said without humor.

Melanie mimicked what I think was supposed to be me eating, and I huffed out my annoyance and turned away from her, listening to her bitter laugh.

I grabbed my knife from my waist, my nostrils flaring, and began sharpening it in an effort to stem my irritation. It wasn't working.

"I hate that noise. It's annoying. Just like you."

I gritted my teeth and continued to scrape the blade against the rock over and over, intentionally being as loud as possible. I was a people person—everyone liked me. But not this bitch.

I had no idea why she disliked me so much. Granted, she hated everyone, but she had a particular distaste for me that she, for some reason, felt the need to vocalize.

"And I also hate—"

"All right! Enough, Melanie," Michael barked out. "We get it: you hate him."

Melanie huffed. "I hate you too, pretty boy, don't think you're any different." She closed her mouth, silencing her latest insult, and I stifled my laugh.

Michael had been more of a broody asshole on this scavenge trip also. He had barely said a handful of words to either Melanie or me for the whole day. Something had gotten up his ass recently, but I didn't know what. At first I had thought that it was because he felt awkward about me coming on this trip, considering I had thought he and Nina had had a thing while on their trip. But after first night confrontations I had learned that that wasn't the case. In fact, he had laughed at the mere suggestion of it.

"That bitch?" He had barked out a deep laugh that made me want to permanently make it so he could never laugh at another thing again. "No, man, just no. She's a special kind of crazy just for you. Besides, she hates my guts. I mean, really hates my guts." He held up his hands in mock defense, though the cut in his eyebrow that I'd just put there proved he shouldn't have been mocking me.

I didn't know what to think about that. Nina had refuted my

claims that she and Michael had had a thing, but I hadn't believed her. I knew she had been keeping something from me and I had jumped to a conclusion—the wrong conclusion. I had used my own moral standards on what could have been wrong instead of seeing the woman that she was. I was a cheating bastard, always had been—except with her. I had assumed that she was the same as me, with no moral compass, but she wasn't. She was better than me. She always had been.

As the days had gone on, I had felt shittier and shittier for the way I had spoken to her and the things I had accused her of. The image of hurt flashing across her features right before she slapped the shit out of me was one I couldn't forget. Yet my own stubbornness had me keeping my distance from her and treating her like an asshole to make sure she never wanted me back. She deserved better than me. I was just a street thief, someone who had killed hundreds of innocent people in one of the walled cities. I was scum. I was worse than scum—I was the shit that came out of scum.

I ran a hand along my scruffy beard, wondering if scum actually did shit.

"I hate it when you scrub your beard like that."

Melanie's irritated voice interrupted my thoughts, and a growl of annoyance left me before I could stop it. Up until now I had managed to nearly always ignore her pissy words and continuous bitching, when really what I wanted to do was put a knife to her throat. But I hadn't. Because my silence annoyed her more. Now I had risen to her bait and I could hear the satisfaction in her laugh.

"And I hate growling. You're not a dog, are you, Mikey?" She laughed without humor.

Anger built in my stomach, low and throbbing, and I breathed through it, struggling to keep ahold of my temper. I would not give in and give her the satisfaction of a response. But damn this bitch to hell. I had never hit a woman before, but at this point I had no problem with killing one. Besides, the jury was still out on if she was a woman or not. She was more like the spawn of Satan, and I had read once that they were hermaphrodites.

"I need to piss," I said instead, looking past Melanie toward Michael.

Her smug grin fell when she saw she wasn't getting under my skin—at least she thought she wasn't.

"Pull over."

"We can't stop here, we're coming up to the road of the damned. Those crazy bastards will kill you in a blink of an eye," Michael said seriously.

"'The road of the damned!'" I said over-dramatically. "Sounds serious."

"It is. They don't screw around. The last trip I took, they threw a woman in front of the truck to get us to stop."

I turned in my seat to look at Michael, but he didn't return my stare. "And we use this road because?" I prompted. Because clearly it was insane to keep traveling the same road that could get you killed. It was like making the same mistake over and over again, without learning anything from it.

"Because it's either this road or a twenty-mile detour to where we need to go," Melanie replied with a roll of her eyes, like I was the dumbest asshole to ever walk the planet.

"Here we go," Michael said. "Guns at the ready. And remember, we do not stop for anything."

I lifted my gun from my lap and stared out the window, seeing nothing but trees. The air was tense in the truck, but I couldn't see what they were afraid of. I looked back to Michael and Melanie, noting that they both were indeed looking quite worried, and I tried to have the same emotion about all of this. But for the most part, there seemed nothing to fear.

A small bang hit the roof of the truck and I flinched and raised my gun up to the ceiling. Another one hit shortly after, and a large rock rolled down the windshield and onto the hood.

"What the hell?" I mumbled.

"They're above us, Michael, get us out of here!" Melanie yelled as what sounded like a hundred angry fists began barraging the roof of the truck.

A rock hit the center of the glass, a large crack forming, and I prayed that it wouldn't implode on us. Michael had sped up, and I wound my window down and looked out and up, seeing that, sure enough, people were indeed in the trees, their arms laden down with rocks that continued to throw down on us. A heavy rock narrowly missed my head and I ducked back inside.

It was too dangerous to try and shoot them down, as rock after rock hit the truck, denting it and almost smashing the glass. Cars were rusting at the side of the road and I briefly wondered if these were the vehicles of past victims.

"Hold on," Michael yelled, as if knowing something we didn't.

Seconds later, what could only be described as a small boulder landed on the hood of the truck, and steam hissed up around the impact mark. If that did serious damage to the engine, we were royally screwed.

Michael didn't stop, he didn't slow, and he didn't bother to shoot at anything or anyone. He drove like a madman to get us the hell out of there, and I couldn't help but wonder if the extra twenty miles to get to our location would be worth it. Because this was madness.

The anger I felt as we passed them intensified as I realized what Nina had already gone through to not only get to the mall, but also get back from it. Shit, it was no wonder that she was quiet when she came back. No wonder she had seemed a little colder, a little emptier. I had accused her of cheating, when she'd only been disturbed by what she had seen.

Sometimes it was easy to forget that she had been in a walled city, protected—if you could call it that—from the horrors of this world. Her harshness, her meanness, was a perfect shield to deflect anyone from trying to hurt her again. Yet I knew I had done it—hurt her. I was an asshole. A total fucking asshole.

TWENTY

R otting zombies littered the mall parking lot—both alive and dead, though thankfully most seemed to be finally dead. We drove up to the access entrance around back, and Michael and I climbed from the truck, taking out the few zombies that were milling around the fence as if they were waiting for it to open so they could go to work. We pulled the fence out of the way, allowing Melanie to drive the truck through the opening, and we pulled it back closed behind her.

She shut the engine off and jumped out, her typical "keep the hell away from me" expression firmly planted on her bitchy little face.

"So, we piled a lot of the gear that we couldn't take with us last time right by the entrance. But it's still worth investigating other places," Michael said seriously, walking toward the employee entrance. "This place was hardly touched, so there's a lot of useful stuff."

"Dead inside?" Melanie asked, pulling out two guns.

"Not anymore. There was a large group of them, but we got rid of them last time." Michael looked at us both with a serious frown. "That being said, keep alert. There could be some trapped. I had one stumble out of a changing room last time." He shook his head. "Scared the crap out of me." He had the decency to smirk at that.

Michael was supposed to be the tough guy of the group—at least that was the image he liked to project to everyone: moody, broody, and untouchable—so it was nice to see a little humility from him.

"We're staying tonight, right?" I replied, following him as he made his way to the door.

"Yeah, no point heading back now, we'll be traveling in the dark. No sense in that. Shits dangerous enough out there."

"Good, I'm ready for some food and shut-eye now," I replied, rolling out my shoulders. My back was aching after being trapped in that truck for so many hours, my ears ringing from Melanie's shrill voice.

"Stop being such a Polly pissy pants," Melanie snapped, and stomped past me and Michael, her shoulder barging against mine. "There's no real men in this world anymore."

I had taken one step toward her retreating back, raising my knife, when Michael placed a hand on my chest.

"Don't give her the satisfaction," he said, and moved past me.

I knew he was right and I breathed out a heavy breath and followed them both to the door.

"No one else has been here since last time," I noted with a frown. "Do you think that's weird? I think it is."

Michael looked around, but I couldn't tell if he was frowning more than usual or just the same. His face generally just looked pissed off and irritated.

"No one had been here before us either," he noted. But his voice held some concern.

Melanie rolled her eyes. "There just aren't a lot of people left anymore," she said dramatically.

I thought to the group at the roadside, the desperate measures they went to in order to steal people's belongings. They murdered their own people, as well as others, for that crap. If there were places like this left untouched out there, then why did they go to the effort and loss and not just come here? It made no sense—unless there was more to them than we'd originally thought.

I stared hard at Michael, pouring my worries into him. He seemed to be thinking the same thing, but it was something we would have to consider some other time, when we weren't right out in the open like this.

The door had been held closed with piles of bricks, the lock clearly busted out, and we moved the rubble out of the way and made our way inside. It was quiet, the darkness oppressing as we made our way down a long corridor without windows. I was tense; the journey had been long and hard, thanks to Melanie's constant bitching and my own demons eating away at me. My katana was held firm in my grip as we came to the end of the first corridor and took a right, pushing open large double doors that led into the heart of the mall.

The roof was a dome made of glass, and the sunlight streamed in. The glass was all still intact, keeping the entire place airtight. Though cold in there, it was warmer than outside, and in the summer months, I bet it would be downright cozy.

The air was still and silent, and I looked around with another frown. Melanie moved straight off out into the open, a handgun in either palm. She cocked her head both left and right before she moved off to the left, passing the pile of gear that had been pre-gathered when Nina had been here. I took off to the right, still wary, but feeling more relaxed now with sunlight streaming in.

There was something about the dark in an apocalypse that freaked me out. Hell, it freaked everyone out. I had never been afraid of the dark, not even as a kid. All those times my father had locked me under the stairs for getting into trouble at school had taught me that there was nothing to fear in the dark but yourself. But after the apocalypse, there actually *was* something to fear in the dark: zombies. Those mean bastards thrived in the dark, and one wrong move could get you killed.

Everyone was afraid of the dark these days. The dark released its nightmares upon you.

Michael said this place should have been completely clear, but to be careful—and I couldn't agree more. I had seen it happen one too many times: a zombie hidden away and taking everyone by surprise, turning a whole group before you could even blink. That wasn't going to happen to me. If I was going to die, it was going to be somehow heroic. I had messed up every part of my life so far, and everyone else's that I had touched; the least I could do was die doing something right. Maybe if I died being the man my father had said I could never be, just maybe it would make up for everything I had screwed up.

I carefully made my way from one end of the mall to the other, passing shops filled with useless items that held no meaning in this world anymore. It was hard to believe that this used to be what made the world go 'round—money and the crap you bought with it. I had never worked retail, but I had a girlfriend who once worked in a clothes store in one of these big malls. She had loved the staff discount, but hated the pretentious assholes she had to serve all day. People that looked down their noses at her because they could afford the latest trends and she couldn't. People that stayed in five-thousand-dollar-a-night hotels and ate caviar like it was going out of fashion. People that thought they were better than everyone else. I'd hated people like that, which was how my hatred for the rich had begun. The stories that she had told me each day—how they had sneered at her or spoken down to her and there hadn't been a damn thing I could do about it—that's the part that frustrated me the most. I had been out of work at the time, scouting the jobs section every day, pounding the pavement, but there was nothing out there. And it killed me. I had wanted to tell her to tell them to stick their jobs up their fat asses, and that we didn't need their money, but we depended on her salary to live.

One day a rich woman wearing a fur coat and a diamond necklace got caught shoplifting by my girlfriend. My girlfriend had told me how she had seen her shoving a silk scarf into her handbag, and when confronted about it, the woman had kicked up such a fuss that she had to be dragged into a back room. Apparently she had been one of the store's best customers, and they didn't want to lose her business. They'd let her off for her theft, and my girlfriend had lost her job for embarrassing the customer. The thing that pissed me off the most was the thought that this stupid rich bitch could've afford whatever the hell she'd wanted. She didn't need to steal; she'd chosen to.

It had been the end of our relationship, and my girlfriend had moved back in with her parents a month later, leaving me with a large rent bill. I'd hated rich people even more from that day forward. They had ruined my life one way or another for as far back as I could remember.

I passed a jewelers and couldn't stop myself from looking inside. It was, after all, part of my nature: I was a thief—or at least I had been at one time—and a damn good one too. I had started out working jewelers like this, stealing five-thousand-dollar watches and diamond necklaces from people as they left the stores, hoping that one day, one of the women I'd stolen from would be the one that had ruined my life. It was like getting my revenge for what had happened to me and my ex. As my skills grew and my name moved among the underground, I had quickly moved on to actually breaking in and taking things myself. It saved time, and besides, I was damn good at it.

Surely it would be criminal to ignore such a skill.

Like a magpie, my eyes instantly landed on all the feminine jewelry—diamond tennis bracelets, pearl necklaces, and emerald earrings, each of them worth more than an average blue-collar worker had earned in a year. There was nothing more attractive than seeing a woman naked, barring a diamond necklace draped between a set of heavy breasts. Nina would look beautiful in something like this, but there was not a chance she'd wear it. Maybe before the infection she would have loved such an item, but not now. Shaking free from my memories, I went on back to find the others.

I found Melanie inside an outdoor goods store, where she was trying on various boots. I looked down at my own boots, deciding a new pair was a good idea. My current ones were a mess—old and a size too small. It would be good to find boots that fit me for a change.

Melanie huffed, mumbling something incoherent under her breath, and I turned to frown at her.

She looked up at me with a scowl. "Is there a problem?"

I chuckled at her bitchiness and shrugged. I had to give it her: her insults were creative. And I would have told her so if I thought she'd accept the compliment. I turned back to the rows of mismatched boots and ignored her grumbling. They didn't have the ones I wanted in my size, so I went to the back of the store and headed into the stockroom in the hopes of finding some there. The door had been busted in some time ago, the handle swinging uselessly, giving me the impression that the living had been here at one time or another.

It was dark with no lights on, and I propped the door open and began rummaging through shelves and shelves of boxes until I found the ones I wanted in the right size and carried them back into the main store where there was some light. I sat down, dragging my old stinking boots off my feet. They smelled so bad, even I grimaced and I threw them as far away from me as I could get them.

"Where did you get those?"

I looked up, eyeing Melanie and debating on whether to answer her or not. She was, after all, a bitch that had it in for me and didn't deserve being treated as anything more.

"You two still fighting?" Michael said as he came into the store. He looked like he was finally relaxing, which would be a new one for him.

"Fuck off," Melanie snapped.

Michael looked behind himself at the shelves of mismatched boots and then down at the matching ones I had. "Where did you get the boots?"

"Storeroom," I replied without missing a beat. I looked over at Melanie and grinned. Yes, it was childish, but I didn't care. She was a bitch, I was an asshole. We both knew our places, and I was happy to live up to my name.

"I fucking hate you," she said as she stood up and stormed off, and I laughed as she cussed me out over her shoulder.

Michael laughed and followed her while I pulled off my graying socks that were all but stuck to my dry and blistered feet. I had grown used to the uncomfortableness of dry, cracked skin and blisters, but that didn't mean I liked it. I snagged the socks off, threw them in the corner, and grabbed a clean pair from one of the racks. They were good, manly socks—thick yet soft—and I groaned a little as I slid them over my dirty feet.

"Damn," I breathed out. A man could easily forget how good new socks felt. "God damn, that's good." I wiggled my toes, letting the soft wool press between them. Yeah, new socks rocked!

I slipped my new boots on and tied them tightly before I went to look around the store for what else I could change into. I was dirty and sweaty, my clothes old and threadbare, and they stank like they had never been washed. Which wasn't actually true. I'm sure they had been washed at least once in the many months that I had been wearing them. It had been too long since I had bothered to change out of the stinking T-shirt and sweater I was currently wearing—another side effect of not being with Nina. She would tell me I stank and make me wash—not that I needed telling, of course. Because I knew when I stank, I just didn't care enough to do anything about it. None of us really did anymore. Especially Michael. Christ, he stank all the time. He worked out more than anyone I knew, and the constant smell of sweat clung to him.

"You're such an asshole. Go die somewhere," Melanie yelled as she stormed out of the stock room carrying a new pair of boots. She glared as she passed me, leaving the store without as much as a goodbye or a "kiss my ass."

A moment later and Michael came out grinning.

"What was that all about?" I asked, frowning. Michael tended to avoid confrontation. Though he never shied away from it, he wasn't one to instigate it, either.

He shook his head, a grin still on his face. "Nothing. Come on, let's go eat."

TWENTY-ONE

I followed Michael out and we made our way through the empty mall. This place gave me the heebie-jeebies. It reminded me how I used to feel when I was just a common thief going into one of these places, feeling every set of eyes on me, all of them accusing and knowing what I was there to do. At least, that's how my paranoia had made me feel. Wait, who was I kidding? I was still just a common thief, though now I had morals. Sort of. Well, mainly that there was just no reason to go around stealing stuff anymore, because money wasn't worth shit anymore.

Either way, I could sense the eyes of people staring out from their storefronts, even if those people were actually just in my imagination. We headed to what used to be the food court, stepping over several dead bodies on the way. In the center of the mall there was a huge hole blown into the concrete, and dead bodies—those of the zombie variety, anyway—were scattered everywhere. Body parts were scattered across the broken marble floor—arms, legs, heads, you name it. I was glad to see that everything was totally dead, though, and nothing even twitched as we moved among the ruins.

The restaurants were set out in a large circle, with the tables and chairs in the center of them all. Most of the furniture had been knocked over at some point, and dried blood was smeared across the floor and furniture. The stench of the dead was long since gone. Even the smell of rotten food no longer lingered, and my stomach growled both hungrily and happily.

Right outside what used to be a crappy burger bar was a group of four chairs around one table. Michael gestured us over, dropping his backpack next to the table, and I did the same.

My eyes moved across the table as I realized that this had probably been where they had all sat when they'd come here the first time. It made me feel strange thinking that—almost like I was spying on someone else's life.

I still remembered when I had gotten the stupid idea of going back home after I had first gotten away from the Forgotten. Memories had pulled me back to my old apartment, but as soon as I had stepped inside, I had known it had been a stupid mistake. It had been like being trapped inside a picture. Everything had stayed exactly the same as when I had left, as if stuck in time, back in the moment when I had first run from the zombies. I could almost hear the zombies outside my door, scraping and groaning, the people from the other apartments running and screaming, the children crying. All my clothes, my belongings—they didn't feel like mine anymore. They were someone else's, from someone else's life. Not the Mikey I had become, the Mikey who had killed and done whatever it took to survive. Yet who I had been previously hadn't been much better. At least now I felt at peace with who I was.

I hadn't even stayed the night there, choosing to stay in one of my neighbors' homes instead. I didn't take any photos or any clothes when I'd left the next day. The items weren't mine anymore, and I hadn't wanted to take that person with me. That person—that Mikey—had been angry and hateful, wanting to make people pay for everything they had done, even if the only thing that they had done was have more than me. This new Mikey, while being a killer, wasn't nearly as angry anymore. Because in this new world we were all equal, and that was all I had ever really wanted. I couldn't hate the rich anymore, because they were more than likely all dead, since they were such arrogant pricks, and those that were still alive were suffering just like the rest of us now. In some ways, karma had played a magnificent trick on the world. She had spun her web and canceled out everything that singled people out. Color and creed didn't matter, wealth and importance didn't matter. The zombies ate us all.

In many ways it was like the world had a fresh slate to start again, though it was far from clean. This world would never be clean again—not until every zombie was dead.

But, I knew that I couldn't be the angry Mikey from long ago, not when what I was angry about no longer existed in this world. I ran my hand over the top of a chair, wondering which one Nina had sat in, and then I shook my head when I realized that was actually an incredibly creepy thing to do. Great, new Mikey was a creepy bastard. Still, I guessed as long as I didn't start wearing her underwear and talking to myself in the mirror, acting out nonexistent conversations with her, creepy Mikey wasn't so bad.

"Whatsup?"

I glanced up and saw Michael watching me. "Nothing," I said in a hurry. "Why? What's up with you?" I arched an eyebrow.

He smiled. "You're still pussy-whipped."

Melanie scraped out a chair and opened her backpack, having found something to eat already. "You totally are," she laughed, pouring a small sachet of salt inside one of her ration packs.

"No, I'm not," I replied indignantly. "I was just thinking about shit, you know." I looked across at Michael, who was still smiling.

"Thinking?" he said, his voice tinged with humor. "About what?"

"Nothing important. Just stuff," I huffed, feeling completely pussy-whipped. Nina wouldn't leave me; even this distance I'd put between us wasn't far enough to get her out of my head. She was going to drive me insane at this rate, and she didn't even realize it. She still thought I couldn't give a shit about her, when the truth was I cared too much.

"Stuff?" Michael prompted with a smirk.

"Stuff and thangs," Melanie said with longing in her voice. "Stuff and thangs." She looked off into the distance.

Both Michael and I looked across at her and burst out laughing.

She shrugged and ducked her head, looking embarrassed. "Pussy-whipped asshole," she grumbled in response to my staring. "You deserve her, she's just as crazy about you. Like two peas from the same messed-up pod."

That actually might have been the nicest thing she'd ever said to me. Or anyone. Though I was certain it was supposed to be an insult, it had been just the thing I needed to hear.

I smiled obnoxiously. "I didn't know you cared so much."

"I don't," she grumbled, and turned her back to me.

This apocalypse changed people. Melanie, I had to assume, was just like this: bitch, born and bred. I could deal with that. I could even work with it, so long as I knew she had my back when the shit hit the fan. I was yet to find out if that were true; however, she hadn't made it this far, being this mean to people, without good reason. Besides,

Michael seemed to trust her, and now I knew he hadn't been after my girl, I was inclined to trust him.

Michael and I walked inside the burger bar. It didn't smell anymore, which was good, but I guessed at one point the smell must have been incredibly bad. Rotten food filled the freezer, dead flies and maggots everywhere, all the food almost unrecognizable now from its original form, just piles of mush. Though it wasn't hard to work out what it had once been, it certainly didn't whet my appetite for lunch.

We shut the door to the freezer and made our way around the kitchen, opening up boxes and quickly jumping out of the way when we disturbed rats' nests filled with tiny dead babies. I was glad they were dead, knowing for a fact that Michael would have been cooking them up on a fire if they weren't. Thank God for small miracles.

I was pleased to see that there were tons of ketchup packets, though. Damn, I had missed ketchup. Almost as much as I had missed new socks. I grabbed a packet and tore open the top, squirting it into my mouth and then humming in pleasure before opening up a second packet.

It wasn't a substantial meal by a long shot, but I could slurp down those little packets until my belly was filled, no problem.

"You'll get the shits eating all of those," Michael said as I tore open a fourth packet.

"It'll be worth it," I mumbled as I swallowed the flavorsome liquid down.

"No, it won't." he replied.

"Gimme a break, man." I tore the top of another packet off with my teeth and squirted it down my throat. "I've missed this shit so much."

I closed my eyes and said a small prayer of thanks. My feet were warm and comfy, and I had all the ketchup I could eat.

Today was a good day.

TWENTY-TWO

"**Y**ou're snoring again!" Melanie yelled across to me, just as something hard hit my bed. I jumped, almost falling out of bed.

"For fuck's sake, woman!" I grumbled back angrily. "Leave me alone before I shoot you."

I had been having the best dream: Nina and I on a desert island with all the beer and burgers you could eat and drink. She had just gone into the sea, and had been in the process of slowly taking off her coconut bikini. And now I was wide awake, in this shithole. With no Nina, no beer and burgers, and no coconut bikini. Just Melanie's shrill voice to keep me company. It was like a living, breathing nightmare, and one that every hour or so she woke me up to.

"Don't talk to me," she shouted back coldly, and I growled in response.

Michael continued to sleep undisturbed by our bickering, his hand still clutched tightly around his gun. It was still dark—the middle of the night, no doubt—and I was comfy for the first time in a long time. This had been the first time since Nina and I had split up that I had slept well without that woman in my bed.

Earlier, after eating, we had climbed into some of the display beds in the homeware section. They were kinda small for a dude, since they weren't ever meant for sleeping in, but man they were comfy—springy mattresses, soft duvets, and pillows that were clean and bouncy. My head had into the feather pillow like it was a marshmallow, and I had sighed loudly. Yet as soon as I had closed my eyes, my face burrowed into the softness of my pillow, I knew she had slept there. The smell of her sweat and her hair still clung to the material like she had been there only moments before. This was where Nina had slept. The thought was both comforting and awkward.

Michael and Melanie had been right: I was pussy-whipped. The woman was fucking haunting me, yet I had drifted into a blissful sleep regardless of my guilty conscience and self-realization at how lame I was being for pining after her after all these weeks—at least until Melanie had woken me. I would have understood her being pissy about my snoring, but she was on guard duty so it's not like I had even woken her up. I pulled the duvet back over my head and closed my eyes again, hoping for the island dream, but instead all that was there were the horrors of this world—the screaming, the murder, the blood, the death, the zombies, and the hurt on Nina's face when I had told her it was over. You don't latch onto people easily in this world, and you certainly don't come to depend on them, but she had with me, and I had messed it all up.

I sat up feeling furious with Melanie and ready to finally put an end to her nasty ways. She had been sitting by the entrance of the store, using an old metal trashcan filled with papers and wood alit with orange flames to keep herself warm. I stared at her silhouette for a while, my anger dissolving the longer I watched her. She was looking into the flames like she was hoping to find some form of peace there. Shadows played across her unusually calm features, and for once I saw a woman and not the she-devil persona that she liked to put out.

I lay back down again and closed my eyes, and began thinking about what the camp needed the most. Journeys like this wouldn't be able to continue for much longer. Not only was the fuel running out, but the assholes at the roadside were getting worse, according to Michael.

They were getting more dangerous, and would need to be taken out completely if they continued. Zee had been trying to get us to attack them for some time, to take them out, but so far we had all resisted. Who wanted to fight other humans when there were the dead to kill so frequently? But after this trip, I knew it would have to be done—no two ways about it. Another dirty job which I didn't want to do but would no doubt be enlisted for. I was going straight to hell after this life. Of that I was certain.

"This place is a gold mine," I said as we carried things over to the truck, dropping them by the back doors.

Melanie was in the back of it, stacking everything inside as orderly as possible to enable us to take back as much as we could.

"I mean, maybe we should all just move in here instead of keep carting it all the way back to the base." I wiped my forehead with the back of my arm and grunted as I lifted another box of toiletries and medicines. Things like these were small luxuries in this world—

deodorant and toothpaste, a highly sought after commodity that people fought for. Who would have ever believed that toothpaste would be more sought after than even the rarest of diamonds?

"Stay here?" Michael asked with a grunt as we passed by each other. His box was filled with clothes—mainly socks and underwear, pants and sweatshirts. The apocalypse had hit in the height of summer when shorts and T-shirts were the quickest-selling item. But they were not of much use to us now. However, socks and underwear were always a necessity.

I had known a man who'd killed someone else for a new pair of boxers. I shit you not. It was a gruesome and bloody murder, too. A man tearing apart another man over goddamned underwear, who the hell would have ever believed such a thing?

I had actually thought many times about driving to the coast and finding a shipping yard—one with all of those containers that came from oversees. They would be filled with so much useful shit—food and medicine and clothing. So far it had yet to be anything but a pipe dream, though. Just like my island dream.

I lifted up another box, its heaviness telling me it was either food or weapons. I trudged back over to the truck, dropping the box heavily just inside the doors of the truck so Melanie could slide it where she wanted to and not have to pick it up. She arched an eyebrow at me.

"It's heavy." I shrugged in response to her hostility.

"I'm not a princess," she retorted, and bent over and picked it up, grunting immediately.

She looked taken aback by the weight but tried not to show it, and I stayed where I was, watching her stagger to the back of the truck with difficulty. I should have walked away, been a gentlemen and not embarrassed her further. I should have, but I didn't, because I was an asshole and she was a bitch.

Michael sidled up beside me, dropping another heavy box where mine had just been. "Shit, that one's heavy," he breathed out. "We can't stay here. Besides, the base is just fine. It has everything we need," he grumbled and stormed away.

I followed after him. "I know you love that place, but we're having to travel further and further for supplies. How long do you think we can keep that up?"

It was a genuine question, one I had been wondering myself for a while now. I shrugged out of my jacket and threw it to the side. It might have been be freezing out, but I was boiling. All the moving of this crap had me sweating my ass off.

Michael dropped his current box to the ground and turned to me looking pissed off. "We'll sort something out," he snapped, taking his own jacket off.

"Like what?" I replied, rolling up my sleeves.

He looked exasperated. "I don't fucking know, Mikey. But we can't leave that place. People have made it their home. We can't just take that away from them."

"So they'll have to make a new home," I snapped back. His reluctance to see the bigger picture was beginning to piss me off. Something had to change, and maybe this wasn't the best solution, but we couldn't keep on much longer like we were.

"Most of those people wouldn't last the journey. And if we came up against trouble..." He shook his head, and I wasn't sure what stunned me more—his humanity or the fact that he seemed worried about coming in to trouble. "They're not fighters. They're old people and kids mostly. Do you really think they would have the stomach for some of the things we have to go up against? The things we have to do?" He ran his hands through his hair, looking even more frustrated. "Besides, the only thing really keeping those people mentally alive is the fact that they have a home. They wouldn't live a life on the road. They need walls and a roof, carpets and furniture. They need the normalcy of a life that once was."

I understood what he was saying: desperate people do desperate things. I'd seen more than my fair share of their desperation. There were risks, of course, but there were also advantages. In my eyes, the risks outweighed the advantages. The base had been a great place so far, but if the weather kept going much longer the way it was, we would all be screwed. Next year we would be more prepared—we could grow food and store for the winter—but right then, the people were freezing and starving to death. And the defenses of that place weren't that good anymore. We didn't have the manpower to cover it all. It was an illusion of safety, and one they had all grown comfortable with. Sure, most of the zombies had been kept away thanks to the booby traps surrounding the place, but if the Forgotten or someone equally organized found it, we would all be dead.

"I just worry," I began, but Michael cut me off.

"Well, don't. We've been holding this shit together since long before you showed up. If you want to leave, just leave. Don't use us as your get-out. Fucking own it if you want to leave." He stooped down, picked up another box of supplies, and stalked off.

I stared after him, half agreeing and understanding what he was saying, and half considering his suggestion of leaving. I looked up at the tall walls of the mall, and the fence protecting the access entrance. The place was secure, and there was plenty of stuff here. I knew our group wouldn't be making many trips back, so there would be more than enough to last me for a long time. Besides, I hated staying in one place for too long. There were too many risks associated with that. Maybe it was time to move on. A chill moved down my arms, the hairs standing to attention. I was getting cold now, since I had stopped working, and I reached over and pulled my hoody back on.

Michael stomped up beside me and I looked across at him. He was frowning more than usual, his mouth pulled into a hard, tight line. He bent down to retrieve another box, and when he stood back up he continued to stare at me for a moment as if he could read my mind. I started to speak, but he shook his head to silence me.

"This group needs you, Mikey," he said simply, and walked away.

TWENTY-THREE

We were back on the road again, the journey to the base seeming a long and futile one. The rain lashed down on the windows, making the roads muddy and the truck skid from side to side every now and then on rotten, sodden leaves. We drove slow, keeping the speed down, meaning we got to take more of the scenery in than we usually would.

Normally it was just a blur of trees and road, with broken vehicles and dead bodies littered across the blacktop. I avoided looking too closely; it was the same shit I had seen for the past couple of years, and I had no time for reliving that. But driving slowly, you got a true sense of not just the destruction, but the beauty hidden beneath. Below the devastation, nature was trying to flourish. It was a beautiful, heartbreaking thing, that even with all the death in this world, something was thriving. *Something* was thriving. I hated that it gave me hope for the future.

Would mankind ever rule this earth again? I doubted it. There would always be death, and I don't mean your grandpa dying at the ripe old age of seventy-eight. I mean, there would always be a zombie somewhere. There would always be one hiding somewhere, and people would always die, their bodies reanimating into a walking nightmare. I had heard enough about fake cures, and had given up on all that shit a long time ago. As long as people walked the earth, so would zombies. But to see nature still growing, still surviving, that definitely made me reconsider if there was hope for any of us. Because if Mother Nature could thrive after everything that had happened, then maybe we could to.

"You ready?" Michael asked, his voice thick with irritation.

"Always," I replied, winding my window down and holding my gun out of it ready to shoot any crazies that jumped out at us.

We were at the worst part of the journey: "the road of the damned," as Michael had named it. Anything could and likely would happen there, apparently, and Michael and Melanie had filled me in on enough horror stories of some of the shit these people had pulled to last me a lifetime. Apparently they would do anything to get a passing vehicle to stop, including throwing women and children into the road and to their deaths, or like what happened on our way to the mall—barraging us with rocks from above. The windshield had a large crack in it just to prove it. That was just another reason I didn't want to continue making the journey anymore: those people were crazy, and so far, their level of crazy hadn't paid off, but sooner or later it would. Sooner or later they would get lucky, and us not so much. Or sooner or later we would have to do something about them. Neither option rested easily on me.

Michael stepped on the gas, making the truck lurch forward and simultaneously slide to the side. Melanie muttered a curse under her breath but kept her eyes trained ahead. The air smelled damp and earthy, but underneath all that I could smell something else.

I stared into the tree line, seeing nothing moving and I frowned. Something wasn't right; it was too quiet, too still. There should have been something happening by then, but instead there was just silence.

"Michael?" I began.

"Thinking the same thing, man. Something's up," he called back.

I was relieved to know that it wasn't just me getting a bad vibe, and as the truck went around a sharp bend I spared myself a second to look away from my side of the truck and out of the windshield, toward the road. I sucked in a sharp breath. Now I knew something was really up.

"I don't think this is another trick," Melanie said, her words almost getting lost in the sound of the noisy truck engine, the rain, and the heavy beating of my heart. "I think this is for real."

I looked back out of my window, feeling the truck slowing down but thankfully not stopping. Bodies littered the road, the devastation something that I wouldn't be able to erase any time soon. Corpses literally torn in half. People, now reanimated, hanging from trees, their clothing the only thing stopping them falling as they reached hungrily for us. Water ran two inches deep on either side of the road, an outcome of the heavy downpour we were having. But it wasn't colored in mud and dirt; it didn't look like rainwater. It was red—small rivers of blood running parallel to each other.

I swallowed hard as a gust of wind caught the scent of death in its grips and fanned it toward me, the smell hitting me with force. I gagged, but felt better when a second later I heard both Melanie and Michael do the same.

"What the hell happened here?" Melanie asked, her usual acid-laced words missing, replaced by sad curiosity.

I shook my head, not knowing how to answer. This was a nightmare come true. Men, women, children—all of them were dead, their bodies torn apart, their blood flowing like a river.

"A horde," Michael offered, and I nodded, still feeling too numb to talk. "A big fucking horde took them out."

I had seen death, experienced death, I had even delivered a lot of death. But there was something about seeing this sort of destruction of a group that tore you up inside. These people deserved to die, no doubt—at least most of them did—but not like this. No one deserved to die like this. Certainly not children. I wouldn't even wish this on the Forgotten. My thoughts drifted to Nina and the scar across her cheek, the way she still flinched when I held her, and I knew that last part was a lie. I did wish this on the Forgotten. On Fallon.

I swallowed, gaining some composure. "If it was a horde, it had to be a huge one," I turned to look at my companions, "to take out this group."

They both nodded. I realized that Michael had stopped the truck. It idled in the road, the engine, the rain, and the faint groans of the dead the only noises to be heard. There were zombie bodies scattered around, and I was glad that this group had put up a fight, but something else was bothering me, something I couldn't quite figure out enough to put into words.

"At least we don't have to worry about being attacked by them anymore," Melanie said darkly, and I found myself nodding in agreement.

She was right: this eliminated most of my argument for moving us to the mall. If this road was now clear then it made the journey a helluva lot less dangerous. Michael started the truck again, and I put up my window. It didn't block out the images outside, but it at least stopped the rotten death smell that hung in the air. We started to drive again, leaving behind the death, when the rain suddenly stopped as quickly as it had started—as if God himself had turned off a tap—and I was at least thankful that something seemed to be going right. I wondered if it was an omen, a sign that things were about to turn for the better. Because it was about damn time.

No road of the damned to worry about. The rain had stopped. And I had come to the decision that I would—no, I *needed* to—speak to Nina, to at least explain and apologize. In the midst of all this death and destruction, it had solidified my resolve on the matter. She deserved better than me, but damn it, I loved her crazy ass, and I was not willing to let her go—not without a fight. Everything I had just seen had proved it to me. Life was too short—way too damn short. Every day was a danger, a risk we took when we stepped outside whatever walls or gates were supposedly protecting us. If I could risk my life every day to get food for people I hardly knew, then the least I could do for myself was risk getting my heart trampled on by telling Nina how much she meant to me.

It was ridiculous, really. In the middle of an apocalypse, surrounded by danger and death at every turn, and all I could think about was the crazy woman that haunted my dreams. The way she smiled when she thought I wasn't looking, the protective look she had when she was near Emily, and the soft feel of her skin against mine. What had started out as sex had grown into something much more. I had never believed in true love—that sort of crap was for books and movies, and I didn't have time for that shit in my life; but I'll be damned if I didn't love Nina with every part of me. She owned me. She completed me. She made me want to be more than I ever thought capable. Instead of running from my past, I wanted to turn and face it, to tell my past that I did have a future, and I damn well deserved to have one, because I was more than what everyone believed me to be.

I was a good man.

My heart sped up, a small quirk at the side of my mouth as I thought about her. She was going to give me so much shit, but it would be worth it if she would take me back. I had been an asshole, and she had been no saint, but for the first time in my life I loved someone, and I wanted to fight for them and for that love.

As soon as we got back to the base I would find her, and I would tell her, and she would likely kick my ass, but it would be worth it. And if she wouldn't listen to me, I would damn well make her.

"What are you grinning about?"

I looked across at Melanie, still grinning, still thinking about Nina, where she was and how embarrassed she would be when I declared how I felt about her in front of everyone. She would go red in the face. The sexy blush she got when she realized someone gave a shit about her had always been one of my favorite things. My smile froze and then slowly fell as the thought that had been niggling away at me finally revealed itself.

"I think he just realized that he loves his woman," Michael said with a dry laugh.

"Took him long enough," Melanie replied. "Did you hear me, asshole? It took you long enough."

I stared into Melanie's eyes, my words not coming out of my mouth.

"What the fuck is wrong with you? Stop staring at me, you pervert."

I looked across at Michael. "The base," I finally said, horror lacing my words.

Michael met my gaze, a deep frown cutting between his eyes. "What of it?" All humor was lost now as I watched the same dread-laced realization crawl across his own face.

"The horde," I gasped. "We haven't passed the horde."

"Shit!" he yelled out angrily and stepped on the gas.

The truck shot forward and I listened as things fell over in the back, but it didn't matter—nothing mattered at that moment except getting back to the base.

"What? What's wrong?" Melanie at least had the consideration to sound worried.

"The horde that took out the road of the damned—it's heading toward the base," I said, my eyes meeting hers.

Her eyes widened, her mouth tightening into a thin line. "Get us back there, Michael. They need us."

TWENTY-FOUR

"How much longer?" Melanie asked.

"An hour—two, tops, if I keep this speed and we don't hit any problems," Michael replied.

"They could be okay, right? I mean, the horde could be just around the next bend for all we know," she said, her words sounding forced and disbelieving.

"They could," I said as I stared grimly out the window.

"We'll be there soon. It will be fine. The horde will be slow, we'll catch up to them. Maybe we can take them out before they even get there," Michael replied without taking his eyes off the road, his sole concentration on stopping the truck from skidding and crashing into a tree.

"They're not helpless. They have help. Matty is there, he can shoot. Susan is a mean shot too." Melanie began checking her guns, though I knew it was more to keep her hands busy than anything else.

I felt the same; the restlessness that ran through my body—urging me to do something, to stop feeling so fucking helpless—was nauseating.

"They have Nina, she can fight," I said, wishing I had taken the time to show her more with the katana. Maybe show her how to shoot. Because she was great with a knife, a katana, a machete, but her shooting skills were terrible, and that would mean she was going to be in the thick of it. Hand-to-hand fighting. I swallowed hard, feeling even worse.

"Nova is there. Nothing will happen while Nova is there," Michael said matter-of-factly.

"And Zee, and James," I added.

It helped. It helped a lot. Listing off the people that would be useful in the fight, thinking of the weapons that they would use, the skills required. Of course there was still a hole in it all—and that hole was us. We weren't the superheroes of the group, but with a huge horde attack, our presence would be sorely missed. If we could get back and warn them, prepare them, they would be fine. The group had gotten lax with security; we were so far up and out of the way that it was easy to. The booby traps surrounding the place kept most of the zombies away from the fences, and the ones that did get close were easy to take out. But a huge horde would push through those small defenses easily.

"Can you not go any faster?" I asked, my voice filled with desperation.

"Hold on," Michael replied.

The truck moved quicker; the skidding it was doing was scary as shit, but I didn't care. The thought of Nina dying, of my friends being eaten alive, was scarier. I trusted Michael to control the truck. I trusted that he would get us there in time to help those people.

The base was a perfect place to hole up in an apocalypse—as long as there were enough people to man it. And there weren't, not by a long shot. Every trip out left a bigger and bigger hole. If one of us never made it back, or someone was injured, it affected everyone and everything. I felt sick. Worry drenched me from the inside and soaked me to my core. I didn't believe we were the saving grace of all plans, but we were three of the best fighters and we weren't there.

We drove in silence for over an hour, our thoughts consumed with worry and anxiety about what we would be greeted with. I knew that both Michael and Melanie were praying as much as I was, with every mile that passed, that we would run into the horde and overtake them. That we would get to the base before the inevitable attack hit. That there would be enough time to warn our friends and get everyone to safety, or at least be prepared for the slaughter. But with each mile that passed, and no signs of the horde, our hopes dwindled more and more.

As we came around the final bend toward the base, our hearts froze and we collectively held our breaths. The horde had definitely been there. The ground was stained with dried blood and gore, the slow trudge of their collective footsteps leaving a trail of grime behind. The muddy grass on either side of the road was trampled, a shoe or two left behind from a bumbling zombie. I wound down my window, and the smell of their rot hit me. They had been here recently, or maybe they were still there.

The silence that clung thickly in the air dashed my hopes for seeing anything good as we entered the base. We stopped outside the main guard post and sadness beat at me with a heavy hand. The insides of the windows were splashed with blood, and bloodied handprints smeared across the door that swung open and banged every once in a while against the side of the small hut. I wondered who had been on guard today. Who it was that we had lost to this attack? Had they had chance to radio up to the main base and warn them before they were swarmed?

We drove further into the base, the road covered with the same telltale stains leading up to the main gate. As we came up to the main drag and saw the metal gates collapsed and lying flat against the ground, we all knew that it was over. The air wasn't filled with gunshots or screams, the moans of zombies, or cries for help. It was silent, a slow breeze drifting across a quiet base filled with our nightmares.

Any hopes we had still clung to were crushed as we drove over the gate and pulled the truck to a stop in the center of the main square. We watched in silence as the horror that was now manifested into something real and visceral turned their heads to us, and our friends, now dead and reanimated growled and stumbled toward us.

"No," Melanie whispered as the woman that was Susan dropped the body part she had just been gnawing on and growled, baring bloodied and broken teeth. Her gait was staggering and clumsy as she kept her gaze fixed on us. "No," Melanie whispered again.

There weren't many there. Certainly no horde remained, just the destruction and devastation it had left, a stark reminder that nothing and no one was ever safe. People lay twitching as they let go and died; some zombies continued to eat, and others were hungry for fresh meat.

Michael turned off the truck, the few dead growling angrily at the sound of the brakes squeaking. "Single shots. Hand-to-hand, if you can. We can't waste anything. Once we've taken care of business, we search for any survivors."

His words were clipped and authoritarian, and I stared at him in envy. How could he keep it together when everyone we knew was most likely dead? He met my gaze, and I knew. I saw myself in his expression. Because he had been through this before. And we would go through this again. And again. And again. This was our life. This was the cycle. And it was never-ending. With that thought I gritted my teeth and swallowed down my fears. These people still needed our help, even if that help was simply giving them peace.

"Let's get to work," I said grimly, and opened the door.

Melanie climbed out after me, and together we moved toward what was once Susan. She took care of Susan without hesitation, a single stab to the forehead to put her down. Melanie closed Susan's lids and stood back up, her expression blank.

I listened as a shot rang out to my left, and I moved toward a body still twitching on the ground. I looked down upon Becky's tortured face, her mouth opening and closing in pain, blood trailing lazily out of the corner. Her eyes stared up at me, clouding over even as I watched, as the virus that tore through the dead engulfed her. Her mouth closed, and then snapped back open, and a low growl erupted from her throat right before I stabbed my blade into her forehead and put her at peace.

I looked up, noticing that Michael and Melanie were each dealing with their own deaders. Those zombies seemed older, more weather-worn even from this distance, and I was grateful that they weren't more people I knew. We were close to the hospital, and I prayed that Nina and Emily would be inside. Nina would find Emily at all costs; she wouldn't let anything happen to her, even at her own expense.

I gulped and moved toward the door, praying to find it locked. Sweat trickled down my face and stung my eyes, and I rubbed it away with my sleeve.

My hand rested upon the cold metal handle, and I looked back to find Michael and Melanie behind me, giving me cover. I saw in their eyes that they knew what I was praying for, knew what I was hoping to find when I pressed down upon that handle. And I saw their disappointment as the handle turned easily and the door swung open.

I turned back, looking inside and smelling the familiar stench of death and decay waft out to me. My gut churned and my heart sank, but I gritted my teeth and pulled out my handgun. Because I wouldn't let them suffer a moment longer than they needed to. But this was one job I wouldn't be able to deal with up close. I would not be able to put these people out of their misery with a knife. There needed to be distance put between what they had become, and what I would always remember them. But I would do it.

Our footsteps were almost silent as we moved along the darkened corridor. The lights blinked on and off every once in a while, and every time my nerves tensed as I waited for something or someone to jump out of the darkness. As we reached the main room, Michael moved ahead of me.

He pushed open the main door quietly, the long, whining sound of the hinges making us all tense simultaneously. The lights continued to blink, and the starkness of the white walls reflecting against the red splashed across them was startling. As a group we pushed inside, and my heart sank and my stomach burned with loss.

What used to be Alek looked up from what he was doing, his pale and unfocused eyes a huge contrast to his dark skin. He growled and moved toward us, his fingers still wrapped around the piece of bloody meat in his palm.

Meat—it was the only way to think of it now. Not flesh or human. Not friend or foe. But meat. Because if I considered it as anything else I might just lose it. He growled again, the noise sounding pained in the silence.

I stepped forward, moving around Michael. "I've got this."

I raised my gun and took a breath. I stared down the barrel, watching as my friend came closer to me, the look of hate and hunger on his face unnerving. I felt the guilt eating away at me. This was his nightmare, the one thing he feared more than anything, and I hadn't been here to help stop it. I had convinced him to leave the Forgotten and come with me, and this was where his journey had ended. It was all my fault.

"Mikey," Michael said cautiously as Alek got closer.

"I said I've got this." My voice sounded foreign to my ears. The words were mine, but I didn't recognize the voice. It was thick and choked, as if the words were being squeezed out of my too-tight throat. This wasn't me; I didn't let things like this bother me. I got on with the job.

I got things done.

Alek shambled closer, his head cocked to one side, and I saw the bite mark on his neck. The veins and muscle were shredded, a gaping hole left where something had been torn away. God, I hoped it hadn't been Emily that had done this to him. Nothing could be worse than being killed by someone you loved, being turned into what you feared most by the thing you loved most dearly. My stomach creased, feeling like it was folding in on itself.

"Mikey, man…"

I raised my chin, put my gun away, and pulled out my knife. I stepped forward, one hand gripping Alek's shirt, and I stared into his eyes as I plunged my knife through his forehead. The light went out immediately, his body becoming a dead weight in my arms. I pulled my knife back, ignoring the small gush of black blood that sprayed out, hitting me in the face, and I gently laid him on the ground.

"I'm sorry," I said to him, and stood back up.

I moved toward whatever he had been eating, my eyes staring down into the bloody mess that was once Emily. It took me a minute of searching to distinguish what was what, and then I collapsed to my knees with a loud groan.

I heard Michael and Melanie quickly come up behind me, their footsteps sounding far away, and I heard their gasps. Emily's innocent face stared up at me, one eye completely missing and the other pale, death-filled eye blinking. A quiet, breathy growl was coming from the place where a throat should have been. She was barely recognizable—her body, her face, her limbs. Her features were all but missing, just bone and gore remained; but as I stared into that one pale blinking eye and felt a hand reaching for me, grasping onto my clothing, I knew who it was.

Nina had to be dead, because she would never let anything happen to Emily-Rose.

I stood up, looking down on the young girl that Nina had protected so fiercely—the girl that Nina had risked her life for on so many occasions—and I staggered backwards, shaking my head, the knife clattering from my hands.

They were all gone. All of them.

"I've got this, Mikey," I heard Melanie say, only moments before the soft growls ceased.

TWENTY-FIVE

"How many?"

"Fifty-five so far," I said to Zee.

We had found both Matty and Zee trapped inside Zee's office. The door was solid metal and locked from the inside, with only a single barred window. They couldn't get out, but equally, nothing could get in.

He shook his head sadly, his gaze falling down to his leg. We'd found the odd survivor here and there, hidden in attics and basements or locked inside buildings. There weren't many, though. Most people had died fighting. Or running. A lot were still missing, and I hoped that meant that they had made it out alive and were on the run. Some were both lucky and unlucky—like Zee. He'd had his leg bitten into so many times it had been just a mess of pulp and bone. Lucky for him, Matty had been on hand to chop it off and stop the bleeding, leaving him with a bloody stub above the knee. He'd lost so much blood I was surprised he'd lasted, but the man was tough and he wasn't going down without a fight.

Jessica had been trapped in the attic of her small house. Zombies were still converged inside her living room, so she hadn't been able to get down. I noticed the small swell of her stomach, cringing at the thought of new life being born into this hateful world. I wanted to yell at her for being so irresponsible, but now wasn't the time. I still hadn't found Nina, and I couldn't decide whether I felt better for not knowing, or worse.

Matty stormed into the small room, his bow slung over his back, his clothes still bloody from his amputation of Zee's leg.

"The gate's back up, but if that horde comes back, we're completely screwed." He breathed through his nose hard, and it was obvious that his next words were not ones that anyone would want to hear. "I don't think we can stay here anymore. Not unless we get more manpower."

"That's not going to happen, is it?" Zee said, though he wasn't asking a question. "So how many are alive? And how many are travel-worthy?" He pushed himself up to a sitting position, his face pulled tight in pain.

"Twelve. Two aren't going to make it," Matty said darkly. His eyes flitted to me and then away.

"We still have people missing—Nina, Nova, James." I raised my chin in defiance of his silent accusation that they were all dead.

I sounded desperate and weak, but I couldn't help it. I couldn't accept that she was gone. Not yet. Nina was a survivor, and until I found her body I would continue to believe that she had made it out of this nightmare alive. I watched Zee's face twitch, and at first I assumed it was because he was in pain. Then he caught my gaze and looked away uncomfortably and I steadied my resolve to hear the worst.

"She's dead?" I asked quietly, my jaw grinding over and over until my teeth felt painful. "Did you see it for yourself?"

He looked back at me. "She's not here," he replied.

"Then where is she?"

"She and Nova..." He cleared his throat. "Take a seat, Mikey, this is going to take some explaining." He lay back down, the effort to stay sitting up too much.

But I couldn't sit down. My arms and legs were restless, energy bouncing through them. "Just tell me. Is she alive?" I ground out.

Matty stayed where he was, looking as frustrated as I was, and I was glad to see that this was all going to be news to him, too. I wasn't sure how I would react if everyone was in on some huge conspiracy.

"I can't be certain exactly where she is, but she left here with Nova and a truck full of weapons about the same time you did. She was alive the last time I saw her." He shook his head, his features pulling tight.

The room spun as I thought about what he was saying, but I couldn't get my words out.

"Where was she going?" Matty asked for me.

I decided right there and then that if she left because of me, because of how I had treated her, that I'd put a bullet through my head that very minute. I couldn't live with myself if she died because I was a total screwup.

Zee took a deep breath. "This is where it gets complicated."

"My whole fucking life is complicated, man. Now tell me." My hand twitched on my gun. If he didn't tell me this minute I was going to blow his damn brains out, consequences be damned.

"She went to find a pregnant woman by the name of Hilary. The woman is infected with..." he looked away, "...zombie sperm."

"Excuse me? Did you just say zombie sperm?" I asked slowly with a humorless grunt of laughter. I looked across at Matty and saw he had the same confused-as-hell expression on his face. And that was good, because it at least meant I wasn't the only insane person around here that had heard the words "zombie" and "sperm" in the same sentence.

Zee nodded and continued. "There's more. We don't know if the child growing within her is zombie or human, but Nina and Nova felt that they needed to find out before it was too late." Zee had composed himself enough that I could sense his own dissatisfaction with everything he was telling me.

I rubbed a hand across the back of my neck. "Before it was too late?" I narrowed my eyes at him, not quite grasping what he was telling me.

Footsteps in the hallway had me turning as a woman came in. She smiled shyly and moved around the side of Zee's bed, giving him a soft smile.

"I brought you some stronger meds," she said, and injected them straight into his vein without even bothering to ask.

My eyes traveled down to the small swell of her stomach, and she looked up from what she was doing and defiantly met my gaze head on.

"You?" I whispered out in accusation as the pieces began to slip together.

"Yes, Rachael implanted Jessica with zombie sperm, in the hopes that she would be able to have a child. Jessica can't have children anymore. She believed this was her only chance to have another," Zee said uneasily. "We don't know how the child will…be when it is born. Apparently Rachael had done this before and Nina went to find this other woman, to see what became of her and the child." Zee's words were strong and sure, yet his distaste for everything we were talking about was obvious.

Jessica had a hand covering her belly, and she wouldn't look at me or anyone else in the room. Her face was pale and sickly looking and her guilt was stark, but my relief that Nina hadn't been at the base when shit had gone down was starker, and more of a priority than this crazy bitch.

"So Nina will be back soon? She's okay?" I wasn't asking, I was confirming it to myself. A small smile rose on my face. She was okay. I knew it. I almost fist-bumped the air at the realization, but decided against it.

Matty's radio crackled to life, and he pressed the button to speak. "What is it?"

"Another one's gone. I've just put him . . . it, down for good," the voice spoke back solemnly.

"I'm on my way." Matty spoke into the radio and then tucked it back into the pocket of his cargo pants. "We've lost another person. I've got to go... Let me know if you need me, if I can help with anything," he said, sounding uncomfortable, and turned and left.

Matty was a good kid. He was barely twenty-one, but he took everything in his stride. He was alone in this world, had been since day one of the outbreak, but he always seemed so upbeat about everything. I liked the way he fought, and I liked the way he moved on with things quickly, as if this was all perfectly normal. But of course none of this was normal.

I finally slumped into the chair behind me, feeling speechless. There was so much that needed doing around there. So many bodies to burn, so much security that needed fixing. Yet my thoughts would only think about Nina. She was crazy and reckless, a total bitch for the most part, but she was also selfless and kind-hearted. The loss of Emily would kill her—that is, if she made it back here.

"Do you know where she was going?" I asked, looking up at Zee, ignoring the stare of Jessica.

"We need you here, Mikey," he said sternly, as if he'd read my mind.

I huffed out an annoyed and frustrated breath. "And she's all I have left now. She might need me too." I put my head in my hands, my thoughts conflicted.

"We need you," he said again.

He was right, they did need me here, but I needed *her* here. I was being selfish and reckless, but goddamn it I'd never forgive myself if she didn't make it back. If I never saw her face again. A stronger man would have listened to his conscience and stayed to help these people—people he had come to care about and see as his friends. But I was clearly not strong; I was weak, and I had to find her regardless of the consequences.

I stood up abruptly, and Zee sat up in his bed with a hiss of pain. He watched me with dark eyes, his mouth set in a grim line. He could give me the grim reaper speech all he wanted. I had made up my mind.

"I'm sorry," I said firmly, making sure he was fully aware that I wouldn't be swayed from this decision.

"You can't leave us," Jessica murmured. "We need help here."

"I suggest you keep your mouth shut. This is all your fault," I snapped, and I found some sick satisfaction in watching her flinch.

"I'm sorry," she said as she brushed past me and quickly left the room.

Zee nodded, accepting that I was going to find my girl regardless of the consequences.

"Does anyone else know?" I asked curiously.

"About?" Zee didn't meet my eye, so I waited in stony silence for his reply. He knew exactly what I was talking about, and I wasn't about to play this game with him anymore. He looked up at me, and I realized that I didn't see a leader anymore, but a coward. He had let

Nina and Nova go on the hunt for this woman, and he had kept it all a secret so he wouldn't be held accountable if anything went wrong. He huffed out an annoyed breath when I didn't respond.

"You mean about Jessica and the other pregnant woman? Just one other person knows." He spoke carefully, but he didn't need to. I finally understood exactly what Nina had been keeping from me.

I smiled tightly. "Michael."

Zee nodded, and I felt myself bristle with irritation. He had known all along what was going on. "Does he know that Nina went to find this other woman?" I ground out.

"No, he doesn't." He paused, sounding uncomfortable. "There's something else you should probably know: Nova is his sister. Rachael was too."

"They're all brother and sisters?" I said in surprise, and then watched the worry flick across Zee's face. "You don't want him to know that Nova left with Nina, in case he wants to go find her?"

"We need him here," Zee replied bluntly. "Just as much as we need you."

"And what about him? Does he not deserve to know what kind of sick bitch Rachael was? Does he not deserve to try and find his only family?" Irrational anger was pumping through me, but I couldn't stop it. There were so many secrets, people hiding things from one another, and that sort of shit was killing us all.

"Michael knew about Rachael. He was the one who told Nina that he'd leave if she told anyone else what happened. He didn't want anyone desecrating her memory." It was his turn to smile tightly now.

I presumed his words were meant to calm me, to quiet the raging storm that he could see building within me, but they had the opposite effect. I closed my eyes, counted to ten. Then I counted to twenty, then I counted backwards. Hell, I even counted sheep, and then I counted the angry thumping of my heart, but nothing would quiet the fury that I felt, the rage that built inside me until there was no more room and it exploded from me.

I stood up, my fists clenching and unclenching at my sides. This arrogant asshole—Michael—had destroyed the one good thing in my life, and now she had gone off on some ridiculous saints' mission to save some woman she didn't know. She had lost Emily, she had risked her life, and all because Michael had told her not to tell anyone about his family's dirty little secret.

I turned and stormed out of the room, letting the door crash harshly against the wall. Somewhere in the distance I heard Zee calling me back, but fuck him, and fuck this place. The corridor was a blur as I raced down it, my anger only growing as I searched for him.

I exited the building and headed toward the hangar where he normally parked all the trucks and stored the ammo. Zee must have called on his radio, because to my left I could see Matty and another man running toward me yelling and waving their hands, but I ignored them both. I entered the hangar and saw Michael right away. He was unloading the truck we had just come back in. He looked up at me, his eyes widening as he took in my angry expression.

"You okay, man?" he called out.

But I didn't hear what else he had to say as I charged him, knocking him flat on his back. The air left his lungs in a whoosh and I pinned him beneath me with my thighs and began planting fist after fist into his face.

"What…the…hell?" he yelled between each pound.

He bucked, trying to get me off him, and after the third attempt he managed it, throwing me to the side. He was up on his feet and kicking me in my ribs before I could stop it. I yelled out in pain as my body flew sideways and crashed into the wheel of the truck, the air leaving me in a great gust. I coughed, trying to draw air up into my lungs as he launched another kick and hit the same spot in my ribs, making me want to throw up.

"What the fuck is wrong with you?" He kicked again, this one going into my face, and I felt my teeth clash together and the copper taste of blood fill my mouth.

I groaned and rolled over, ignoring his yelling, and instead focusing on trying to get air into my lungs. My heart was pounding, and I sucked in gasps of stale air as the nausea abated. I rolled over onto my knees, staring down at the floor, spitting out blood and phlegm as he continued to yell obscenities at me.

"That woman has got you pussy-whipped, I told you. You've lost the plot. That crazy bitch has sent you over the edge."

His words were the nitrous oxide to my anger and I was back on my feet and barreling into him before he could finish his sentence. His body slammed up against the side of the truck and I landed a heavy punch in his gut, sending him curling in on himself with a groan. I reached out and grabbed a handful of his long, greasy hair, lifted his head up so he could look me in the eye, and then rammed my fist into his face.

TWENTY-SIX

Blood exploded from Michael's nose and splattered my face and clothes. His hands clawed at me, his legs kicking out—anything to throw me off him—so I planted another fist into his stomach hard enough to make him dry heave and gasp for air. I took a step back, and he had the dignity to stay on his feet, his hands clutched around his middle as he stared me down with blood dripping from his face.

Matty ran up beside us, pushing in between and placing a hand on each of our chests, his eyes wide with worry. "What are you doing?"

I didn't reply to Matty, but stared long and hard at Michael, the taste of blood still in my mouth. His threat had put us all in danger, and I hated the fact that he had risked Nina and everyone else for the sake of his sister's memory. *She* was the crazy bitch, and he knew it, yet he was more than willing to go flinging names and accusations at Nina, the woman who was off trying to sort out the mess his sister had left behind. My anger was so heavy I could almost taste it, and the urge to kill him was hard to resist.

I pushed Matty out of the way with one swoop of my hand and stepped into Michael's space, ignoring Matty as he stepped in close, one hand on my sweatshirt so that he was ready to pull me away from Michael if he needed to.

"I should kill you." Tension rippled through my body, my muscles straining to hit something.

"Go on then! Do it!" Michael roared back angrily, pushing his face into mine.

"Don't do it, Mikey." I faintly heard Matty's voice through the haze of blood rushing to my ears and I swallowed, the motion feeling almost choking. "We need him."

"You're not even worth it," I snarled at Michael and turned away.

"At least your bitch can't see what a pussy you really are now that she's dead, asshole."

I spat on the ground, the pool of saliva red with blood. I grinned and turned around, stepped back into his space, and head-butted him hard enough for us both to see stars. I staggered backwards and Matty gripped hold of me, trying to keep me on me on my feet. I slumped to my knees anyway.

"Easy, easy," Matty said. "Are you okay, man?"

I nodded, still not having the sense about me to vocalize that no, I was not okay. I was so far from the realm of being okay that I was in another country. That I wouldn't be okay until I knew that Nina was safe.

"You knocked him out cold. Either that or he's dead," Matty said. Strangely, he didn't sound particularly worried. "He an arrogant dick, so I'm sure he deserved that," he shrugged, "but we need him alive."

The room stopped spinning and a laugh bubbled its way up my throat. I looked across at Michael, seeing that his face was a mess of blood and bruises, and while I knew that I didn't look any better, I certainly *felt* better, and that was all that mattered right this second. The pounding in my chest had simmered, the blood previously as hot as acid running through my veins had cooled, and I could think clearly again.

I stood up, taking a deep breath as the room spun. I let Matty help me to my feet, and I shook my head to clear it of the remaining cobwebs before I stepped forward, gripped Michael by his collar, and dragged him away from the truck, not caring when his head bounced off the concrete floor.

"Easy, man. Like you said, he's not worth it." Matty spoke next to me, but had the good sense not to touch me.

Michael groaned and his eyes fluttered open as I leaned his still rousing body against one of the benches, and then I walked back to the truck, loading weapons and food inside it. Almost everything had been emptied from the truck and set up in piles ready to distribute to the rest of the base, and I grabbed items from each of them.

"What are you doing?" Michael yelled, his voice thick with irritation and anger yet still sounding groggy.

"I'm going to find Nina and your sister," I replied without turning to look at him. I noticed Matty had come to help me load up, anticipating things I would need as I spoke.

"Nova?"

"Yeah, Nova," I bit out, throwing a bag of knives into the back of the truck.

"I thought she was dead," he said quietly, clearly confused. "I thought she was here...when the horde attacked."

I finally turned to look at him, seeing a spark of something in his eye. Hope. But I didn't have an ounce of sympathy for him. "No, but they might be dead by now, thanks to you. She and Nina went to find the other woman that your other crazy-assed sister impregnated with zombie DNA. My crazy bitch of a girlfriend has gone to try and right your sister's fuckup," I snarled before turning back around. I looked for the keys to the truck and then realized he would have them.

I turned back to him, stalking forward, and stared down at him. He struggled to his feet, raising his chin as I got close.

"Give me the keys," I said, and held out my hand.

"Where are you going?" He looked into my face, realization dawning on him. "You're going to find them."

"Yes. Now give me the keys."

"They could be anywhere."

"They'll be wherever that damn woman is. Now give me the damn keys."

He fumbled in his pocket before holding them out to me. I reached out to take them and he grabbed my hand. My eyes glared into his, but he met my hate-filled stare with his own.

"You bring my sister back to me," he said quietly, his expression softening. "Please."

"I don't owe you anything."

"You don't, I agree, but I'm asking all the same. She had no idea about any of this, she's just trying to do the right thing." His voice was thick with emotion, and regardless of how much I hated him just then, I couldn't deny that his words affected me.

I stared at him for a long moment, a thousand insults and hurtful accusations racing through my mind, but what was the point? He felt like shit. I felt like shit. We had both lost so much and the damage was done now.

"You can't stay here now," I said instead. "This place is seriously compromised. That gate won't hold another breach."

He released my hand. "We'll be at the mall." He attempted a smile but it was more of a grimace. "I heard it was a good place to make a new home."

I ran a hand across the back of my neck and let out a deep breath. "Whoever told you that was one smart motherfucker, that's for sure."

Michael surprised me by barking out a sharp laugh, which turned into a wince as he grabbed his tender stomach. He met my gaze again, both of us somewhat calmer now.

"These people need me, Mikey. They won't make it there without my help. They're not made for this world."

I nodded in agreement.

"That woman, Hilary, and her husband… they were north of here the last time we saw them. Get me my map." Michael pointed over to his bag by the truck and Matty headed over to retrieve it.

"Our camp, our city, it was here." Michael circled a space on the map and then proceeded to circle two more locations. "That was where we left them," he said, pointing to an isolated spot, "and this was where they said they were heading." He handed the map over to me. "Bring Nova home to me, please. She's all I have left." He slapped a hand on my shoulder, holding it there a long minute until I nodded again.

I shrugged out from under his grip and walked away. I climbed in the truck and started the engine. I drove to the hanger door and looked out of my window, watching as Matty helped Michael walk toward a bench to sit down. They both looked up at me, Matty with his typical no-nonsense "let's get on with it" expression, and Michael with what was soon going to be two black eyes, judging from the dark shadows already forming underneath.

"You should put some ice on that," I called out with a dry laugh.

"Don't look so smug. There'll be a rematch, man," Michael snapped back.

"That's if I come back at all," I replied.

"You will. You're going to bring my sister home to me," he said seriously, all joking aside.

"I'll do my best."

"If you don't, I'll kick your ass. I won't go easy on you next time."

It was my turn to laugh now as I stuck my arm out of the open window and raised my middle finger. "Keep telling yourself that."

I turned away and drove out of the hanger, hoping that I could do like he asked. Not for his sake, but for Nova's.

TWENTY-SEVEN

NINA

"**I**'m going to take a look at your bite. You look too pale." Nova's voice cut through the hollowness of my dark thoughts.

"I'm fine," I replied, looking warily at the knife still held tightly in her palm.

"Don't be an asshole," Nova spat back as she lowered the knife. Reaching into her backpack, she pulled out a small first aid kit. "Come here."

I huffed and ignored her, turning to stare out the window and pretend that I hadn't just seen my life flash before my eyes. Twice. In less than half an hour. I think that was a new record even for me.

"Move your stupid ass over here now!" she yelled, making me jump.

I turned to glare at her angrily.

"Don't even fuckin' start with me, Nina, or I swear to God."

I opened my mouth to speak but closed it again as my slashed stomach and the bite wound on my neck ached painfully. They both needed cleaning and stitching or I actually would be in trouble. I hadn't died yet, so that was at least a little good news, but both my neck and stomach hurt every time I moved. Hey, at least my flu wasn't bothering me anymore. Cold. Whatever.

I shuffled over in my seat, avoiding eye contact with Nova. Joan had gone silent in the back but I hadn't heard her get out so I had to assume that she had fallen asleep, or she had fallen over when we had stopped abruptly and was knocked out cold. I couldn't help but be grateful for her silence at the moment, though, even if that did make me a total bitch.

"Take your jacket and T-shirt off," Nova said while arranging some cleaning fluid and gauze.

I did as she said, carefully stripping myself of my jacket and both T-shirts that I was wearing. I hissed as I lifted my arms over my head, biting down on my lower lip to stop the scream from escaping.

Nova glanced up, her eyes raking over the various bites and knife wounds covering me. "Jesus, why is it always you?" she said with a shake of her head.

"Just lucky I guess," I huffed out.

She was right: it *did* always seem to be me. I had gotten shot, I had gotten bitten, and I had gotten beaten and raped by the Forgotten— not to mention the horror of what went on behind the walls. It was always me. But I had survived all of that too. I was a survivor, not a victim. Plenty of my friends had died, and plenty more would have if they'd had to go through the things I had. With that thought I felt stronger and empowered.

"This is going to hurt," Nova said, and I finally met her eyes. "Like, a lot."

I bobbed my head and swallowed, my tough girl charade showing some cracks. "Whatever," I said in as bored a voice as I could get out.

"I mean, this shit is *really* going to hurt." Her eyes looked toward my neck. "I'm not kidding. I would totally cry if this were me."

"You would not."

"I totally would," she said with wide eyes.

"You're not helping," I said with a surprisingly steady voice.

"I just don't want you thinking that I'm about to kill you again."

I rolled my eyes but didn't reply.

"And I don't want you to feel bad when you cry like a little bitch," she laughed. "Because you're totally going to."

The bite had finally stopped bleeding, but I knew I had lost a lot of blood from it, which meant it was deep. I knew that there was a possibility that there would be nerve and muscle damage, but I could move my arm so I took that as a positive sign.

"I'll be fine." I rolled my eyes again, forcing my fear deep down into my gut, somewhere that I wouldn't have to be scared out of my mind.

"Do you want something to bite down on?" she asked.

"Just do it already," I snapped. Her words were making me feel worse.

Nova grinned a little and leaned closer. "Crazy bitch."

She held some gauze in one hand and the bottle of rubbing alcohol in the other. After a moment's hesitation, she shrugged and tipped some of the contents directly onto the wound.

It was only a second later that I screamed loud enough to attract every deader in a three-mile vicinity and passed out from the pain.

I woke to the sound of the truck moving and slowly rubbed the sleep from my eyes as I pried them open. We were on the road again, and the truck was filled with so much cigarette smoke that it made me cough, and then gasp in pain.

Nova looked across at me and smiled. "You're awake."

"No shit," I replied tersely, and sat up.

"How are you feeling?"

"Like I'm about to die from secondhand smoke," I said, opening a window.

At some point between me passing out and Nova stitching me back up, I had slumped down in my seat at an awkward angle. My bones clicked and cracked as I straightened myself up.

"So, how does it look, doc?" I asked cautiously.

"Oh, you know."

"No, I don't."

Nova grinned at me and opened her window, throwing her cigarette butt outside. More of the smoke cleared, escaping out the window and into the night air, and I could almost breathe properly again.

"It's nighttime," I commented, looking around in amazement. "How long was I out for?"

"Too long," she said, and patted the gun on her lap. "I wondered if I was going to have to make a little target practice of your forehead." She grinned.

"That's both creepy and insensitive." I scowled.

"I learned from the best," she chuckled. "Your shoulder was bad, darlin'—like really bad. *But*, it was just flesh. Nothing important eaten away. Just flesh and blood loss. Once I cleaned it out and stopped the bleeding, I knew it was going to be okay."

"Wow, thank you," I said, genuinely grateful. "I bet you've had a lot of practice, what with being in the field, right?"

Nova laughed. "Practice? Shit no, I hate the sight of blood. I vomited three times while sorting your shit out." She pointed to the floor and a stain of what must have been hastily cleaned up vomit. "But, when we get back to base, Becky can check out the damage and sort you out good and proper. My needlepoint will have to suffice for now."

I nodded, and then shook my head in amazement and possibly bewilderment. I was hungry, I realized. My stomach gurgled painfully, and I looked down and lifted up my top, seeing butterfly stitches across the center of my stomach.

"That wasn't too deep, thankfully. You really need to be more careful. You could have chopped yourself in half back there!" Nova glanced back over at me and laughed again. "Crazy bitch."

"Clearly I didn't do it on purpose," I replied sarcastically.

She chuckled and the truck lapsed back into silence. Well, apart from the singing I could hear coming from Joan in the back. Thankfully not another rendition of "Ninety-Nine Bottles of Beer" again, and not as loud either.

I rested my head back on the seat and stared out into the dark. Now that we were headed back to base, I wondered what it had all been for. Hilary was dead, and so were Deacon and the baby. I don't think I would ever look at Nova in the same way, but in a lot of ways, now that I had calmed down, I respected what she had done. I certainly couldn't do it. Deacon at least deserved some peace. And so did that child. And though Nova hadn't done it for the right reasons, she had ended their misery. Perhaps now they could all be together again. If there really was a heaven, anyway. Of that I still wasn't totally sold. If there was a heaven, then that meant that there was a God, and if there was a God, what the hell was he thinking letting zombies walk the earth? This was a messed-up game he was playing.

But while I respected what Nova did, I also couldn't forgive it.

"So, what now?" Nova asked, her voice cutting through my dark and morbid thoughts.

"I don't know. We head back to base and tell Jessica the bad news. We'll need to terminate the pregnancy as soon as possible, and hope that it's not too late." My words sounded sad, even to my own ears.

"I meant between us," Nova replied, sounding as equally sad.

I turn to look at her. "There is no us," I murmured.

"We were friends. I saved your life," she says with a scowl.

"I don't trust you anymore. You lied to me."

"I did what I thought was best for everyone," she huffed out.

I shook my head. "No, you did what you thought was best for you."

"Nina!"

"I don't want to fight with you, Nova. It's not you, it's me, blah blah. I'm a judgmental asshole, et cetera, et cetera. Say what you want about me, I won't deny it. I'm no good with people, I push everyone away, don't take it personally. It's just better this way." And I truly believed that.

I had pushed everyone away. Everyone but Emily. And at the moment, she was the only reason I was heading back to the base. If it weren't for her, I'd be heading as far and as fast in the opposite direction. Away from Mikey and Nova, away from the base and all the people there. I wanted to be on my own. I was tired of losing people. I was tired of learning to care for someone only to have them either die or turn out not to be the person I thought they were. But most of all I was tired of hurting. I knew where I wanted to go, where I *would* go once I knew for sure that Emily was completely safe, that she and Alek would work out and he would look after her the way I would, and then I was gone. I had realized, on this ridiculous journey of self-discovery, that I loved Mikey, but it wasn't enough to make me stay and watch him die like everyone else I had ever loved. Because sooner or later, that's what would happen. So I would thank him for everything, and leave. He never had to know how I felt.

There were some things you couldn't come back from. And I wasn't talking about Mikey breaking my heart, or Nova killing zombie babies. It was trust. I had no trust in any of those people anymore. And for that reason, I didn't feel safe there. I didn't want to be around them anymore, any of them. My external injuries hurt much less than the bitter war that was raging inside me.

I had used Emily as a reason to escape the walled city, but that kid had stolen my heart and kept me sane. She had brought me back from the hateful person I had become, making me think about more than just myself, more than just surviving each day, but actually living. But it was still there at the back of my mind, my reason for really going with her.

I had wanted to escape, I had wanted to continue on the journey that my husband and I had intended on going on all along. He had talked about his parents' home out in the sticks, where he believed it would be safe, and that's where I was going to go. Because after all these years, and all the pain that had come to pass, I still trusted Ben—my dead husband—way more than anyone else in this godforsaken world.

He was the only one who had never let me down, who had made me believe my own worth. The only one to ever make me see that I was truly important and worth going through anything for. I trusted his judgment, and he had always trusted mine, and he still held my heart after all these years.

A small part of me still niggled for Mikey, but Mikey didn't want me, and he certainly didn't trust me. He also didn't love me, and how could he? How could anyone love a woman like me? I was broken, and I didn't think there would ever be any fixing for me. And I was okay with that. Really. I had come to terms with myself, with the way I was now. I could never be the old Nina, the one before the infection. She was long gone, dead alongside her husband. This new Nina was flourishing now, and maybe she wasn't as tough as I thought she was, maybe she wasn't as soft as the old me, but she was strong and capable of surviving this world on her own terms.

So I was leaving, no matter what, and I would find Ben's parents' cabin, and I would make it safe enough to live in. I had no belief that his parents would be alive, and I was accepting of the fact that they would be deaders themselves now, and it would be up to me to finish them off and put them at peace finally. But it would be safer there than anywhere else, and at least on my own I would only have to worry about me. And that was a far better bet than loving and losing more people I cared for.

Because I would prefer to be alone in this world than continue to go through this emotional torture.

TWENTY-EIGHT

We had driven in silence for several hours, the night passing us by in a blur. Nova had refuted any attempts at me taking over the driving, no matter how much I had bitched at her. Really, I knew that she wanted the distraction of driving; her thoughts were clearly as dark as my own, but she kept them to herself.

"I need to pull over," she said with a loud yawn.

"I can drive," I offered again, but knew there was no real point in asking—she wouldn't let me.

"No, we can just pull over and sleep for the night. We're high up, we'll be fine."

"What about Joan?" I asked, giving a loud yawn myself. I downed a couple of the painkillers that Nova had given me earlier, washing them down with water from my flask.

They were marvelous little white pills that numbed not just the pain in my shoulder and stomach but helped with my flu also. Thankfully, my flu was definitely on its way out. I was still snotty, but nothing like

I had been three days ago. I had to agree that it probably wasn't the flu after all and just a crappy cold, but I wasn't going to admit that to Nova anytime soon.

Nova pulled the truck to the side of the road and switched off the lights. "I'll go check on her. It's going to get cold out with the engine off. She'd be safer and warmer sitting up here with us."

"Sure, want me to come?"

"No, stay here, no point both of us getting cold. I'll be right back."

"There were blankets we packed from the city?" I asked, not remembering packing anything like that. She nodded and climbed down, closing her door behind her.

I listened to the soft voices coming from the back of the truck for a minute of two and then the sound of things being moved around. I shivered, the cold already seeping into the truck now that the engine was off. I'd be glad when summer arrived and it wasn't so damn cold all the time. Saying that, by summer I would be in warmer climates anyway. Ben's parents' cabin had been far south, and it was almost always warm there. That was bad news for deaders, since they tended to smell worse in the sun and the cold helped to slow them down, but it was good news that I wouldn't have to worry about being frozen to death all the time.

Besides, I never was one for snow and rain; I was always much more of a beach girl. God, what I'd have given to be sunbathing on a beach right then instead of freezing my ass off inside a filthy truck in the middle of nowhere surrounded by deaders.

The apocalypse sucked.

My door opened, making me jump, and Joan's face peered up at me.

"Room for a little one?" she said cheerily.

"Sure." I grinned and moved over to allow her room.

She climbed up, carrying several blankets with her, and a moment later I heard the door on the back of the truck slam closed and Nova opened the driver's door and climbed in, also carrying blankets.

She wiggled her eyebrows at me. "Time for a slumber party, ladies!"

Despite everything, I freaking chuckled. I was tired and achy and still sniffly, it felt like there was no hope in this world anymore—but really, there hadn't been for the past three years or so, so what was new? So I giggled.

"Are we going to be having a pillow fight?" I asked between laughs.

"Don't you fuckin' know it?" Nova laughed back.

I looked across at Nova and we both burst into unrestrained laughter. And damn, it felt good to laugh. I mean, it hurt my shoulder and stomach, but my heart lifted with each loud laugh that escaped my cracked lips. As if the heaviness that had been burdening me for the past week was finally letting go. I glanced back over to Joan and saw her grinning expectantly.

"Is that a yes?" she asked.

Joan snuggled into me, and her smell almost knocked me out. I choked and spluttered, coughing on bile that rose in my throat, and I cruelly and apologetically pushed her away.

"I'm sorry, we can't snuggle. You still smell too bad." I grimaced.

I could practically taste her stench on my tongue, and that was not a smell I wanted to taste! Why couldn't she smell like something yummy, like peaches and cream or ice cream? No, she smelled like piss and shit, raw sewage and zombie gore. It was vile and made my stomach twist painfully with the urge to purge itself of its contents. It coated my teeth, leaving a film of month-old piss and decay across them. Joan looked hurt—offended, even—but it couldn't be helped.

"Really, I am sorry, but no. Just no." I shuffled away, pulling my blanket up to cover my mouth and nose. I couldn't even try and be polite about this, and I'd like to shake hands with anyone that could.

She huffed out an annoyed breath and turned over, dragging her own blanket over herself and muttering something I didn't care to hear. I should have felt bad, but I didn't. It wasn't like we could even open a window to let fresh air in. For the first time in a week I was actually grateful for the cold/flu that I had. At least it blocked out some of her smell.

I snuggled further down in my seat, wrapping the blanket tightly around me, making sure it was pulled right up around my neck and covered my ears. It was ridiculous, but I'd always had this thing about bugs crawling in my ears while I slept. Even the zombie apocalypse couldn't shake that fear. I closed my eyes and listened to the wind howling outside the windows and let my thoughts drift to the monsters outside.

They didn't feel the cold, or the wind. They didn't care about snow or rain. They only cared about filling the unfillable hole in their stomach, feeding the insatiable craving they had. *What must that feel like to them?* I wondered. The anger and hatred that I saw every time in their eyes when they spotted new flesh. The hungry, painful groans they emitted because that feeling they have inside them persisted no matter what they did.

"Nina? Are you awake?" Nova whispered next to me.

I didn't open my eyes, but I was glad for the break in the silence. "Yes," I replied.

"I need to ask you something, it's really important."

"Sure, go ahead."

Silence followed and I started to wonder if she had actually fallen asleep, when she spoke again. "This is really important. I need the truth. No matter what."

"Okay," I replied hesitantly.

"I can take it."

"Dude, will you just ask already?" I snapped, beginning to feel nervous.

Joan had started to snore next to me, and I'd heard her snoring before. It didn't abate the deeper into sleep she got; it only worsened. I had hoped to fall asleep before her, but instead she was happy in the land of Nod and I was now wide awake, filled with worry and dread at what Nova was going to say next.

"Okay, I think I'm ready to ask," she whispered, and I listened to the ruffle of her blankets as she turned to face me.

I did the same, turning my head to look directly at her. In the darkness her eyes glistened, and I could just about see the apprehension on her face, the slight tremor in her words as she spoke.

"What is it?" I asked sincerely.

"I feel silly asking."

I groaned. "Seriously, you're killing me. Ask already!"

"Okay, okay." She cleared her throat and I waited anxiously, feeling like I was at the edge of the abyss ready to fall in. "Did you still want to spoon?"

It took me a second to comprehend what she was saying, and then I reached out of my covers and punched her in the arm.

"You're such an asshole!" I said loudly, not caring if I woke Joan up.

She chuckled, fending off my hits. I sat back down with a grumble of annoyance.

"Nina?"

"Whaaaat?" I groaned, exaggerating the word and simultaneously pulling the covers back up around me to cover my ears, but even though I groaned, a smile still sat on my face. "No, dude, no spooning," I added on, just to be clear on the subject.

She chuckled again, almost inaudibly this time. "I'm sorry I let you down."

She said it so quietly that I barely heard it, I turned my head to look at her again, but her eyes were closed. She wasn't asleep, but clearly she didn't want to talk about it anymore. And I was okay with that. Whatever I said always seemed to be the wrong thing anyway, and I knew that there was no way to make her feel any better.

She had lost her older sister, and I think she was hoping that I would be her surrogate one. With her recent actions she knew now that would never be possible. I loved Nova, truly I did, and I didn't judge her for what she had done. Like I'd said, I respected it in many ways. She did what was necessary, but I no longer trusted her, or anyone else at the base.

I was lonely. I was lonely surrounded by people, and I was lonely on my own. I had come to realize that I had merely traded one walled city for another. I was lonely behind them, and outside of them. Maybe it wasn't other people that were broken, maybe it was me. I was the one that was constantly struggling with my actions, with others' actions.

And if that were true, then I really was better off on my own in this world. Lonely or not.

TWENTY-NINE

The noise of deaders was what woke me—the hungry growls and the beating of hands on the truck. I woke with a start, shaking off nightmares of teeth and hands, nails being dragged down my back and carving my skin up like a cheese board.

I looked over and saw Joan and Nova still sleeping, and frowned in amazement that they could sleep through all the noise. The only good thing was that the truck was high up, and there was no chance of the deaders actually getting in to us. It was still damn unnerving, though. That and being trapped in this truck with Joan all night had only fermented her smell.

I rubbed the sleep away from my eyes and leaned forward, looking down into the mass of deaders with a grimace. They were gross. And by the looks of it they had been out there for a while. What were once men and women, and one child—because obviously seeing just zombie men and women isn't enough of a freaking nightmare to wake up to in itself, so we had to include a little girl with wonky pigtails into the mix—all converged around us. They went a little wild when they saw me looking down at them. Their jaws snapped hungrily, fat rotten tongues lolling out of their putrid decaying mouths. Their clothing hadn't fared well, and gaping holes revealed far too much sagging gray flesh hanging from decaying bodies.

I gagged and sat back, before reaching into my pocket and pulling out more pain meds. My nose was almost fully blocked thanks to the stupid cold, but I was somewhat grateful as I could practically *taste* the smell inside the truck. And it did not taste good.

I made showering my first priority when we got back to base—possibly even above getting my wounds treated properly, and maybe even above finding Jessica and letting her know that she needed to terminate her demon spawn. What was another hour of being pregnant and crushing her dreams against me being clean for the first time in over a week? Exactly. It was an undisputable argument.

Okay, so I was a bitch. But at least I'd be a clean bitch.

The sound of another vehicle in the distance had me sitting bolt upright again, and I looked out the window as another truck began moving closer to us. Several of the deaders turned, attracted by the new noise, and they began shambling toward it. I pushed Nova gently, but she didn't move and so I pushed her again, a little harder this time. Her head slid along the window in her door, yet she still continued to snore loudly.

I leaned in close to her ear and whispered, "Spiders."

She jumped alert almost immediately, pushing me so hard that I flew backwards and tripped over Joan's legs. Joan grumbled but continued snoring.

"Where?" Nova said, her eyes going to outside and widening when she saw the truck coming toward us. "Nina! There's other people, why didn't you wake me?" she yelled angrily.

I got up from my position and scowled. "I did," I said with irritation.

"No, you yelled 'spiders.' Other people are way more important than spiders, darlin—you should know this by now. What the hell is wrong with you?"

I stared incredulously at her, my brain working around a hundred different insults at once, until Nova broke out in a smile.

"I'm just fuckin' with you." She pulled out her guns, clicked off the safeties, and sat back down, waiting for the truck to get closer.

"Who is it?" I wondered out loud. I didn't expect her to know, but I voiced the question anyway.

Nova shrugged. "No idea, but I don't like them already."

"Me neither," I mumbled. "Shouldn't we do something?"

"Like?"

I shrugged. "I don't know. It feels kind of stupid to just sit here and wait for them, though. They could be anyone."

"They might just pass us by," she said unhelpfully, because we both knew that was unlikely.

I ignored her comment and watched the truck get closer, dread pooling in my gut. But really, what was new? I didn't want to be afraid. I wanted to be brave. But all I could feel was trepidation and worry.

The truck stopped, and I could make out two, possibly three people moving around inside it. They could be harmless, but my gut said otherwise, and I had learned to trust my gut in these situations.

We stared out the window in silence. The thing was, none of us were doing anything at the moment—not the people in the other truck and not us, not with all these deaders in the way. Before we could even reach each other, we would have to deal with them. I looked over at Joan, seeing that she was still sleeping soundly, and I almost laughed. Almost.

"So, what are you thinking?" Nova asked, her eyes searching my face for something when I turned to look at her. "You got a plan in that pretty little head of yours?"

I laughed then. A lot. Some of it was still the fear that was clogging my veins, and some of it was nerves, but most of it was just the simple amusement of her question.

"When do I ever have a plan?" I managed to say between breaths.

"True," she retorted. "So?"

"So?" I repeated.

"Lock and load?" she asked.

"Lock and load," I replied.

"Fuck yeah!" she laughed, in her true Nova style.

I dragged her bag over and unzipped it, pulling out guns and loading them, stashing knives in my pockets, and handing guns and weapons off to Nova. Not that she wasn't previously loaded up to hell, but as she always said, a girl can never carry enough guns.

I sat up and looked over at her. "Shit, I lost my katana back there," I said, referring to the place where I'd nearly become zombie chow.

Sometime between nearly hacking myself in half and running for my life, I must have dropped it. It was a damn shame, too, because I loved that sword. I was just getting good with it, and it reminded me of Mikey.

She smirked. "What about a good ol'-fashioned machete?"

"I could use that."

She reached behind her chair and dragged it out. It was sharp and deadly, and looked expertly kept—if there was ever a way to expertly keep a machete, anyway. My eyes appraised it and I gratefully took it.

"Don't lose that," she said dryly. I couldn't tell if she was joking because I was always losing my weapon, or if this thing was actually really important to her. Either way, I hoped to keep ahold of it for a long time to come.

We glanced back up at the other truck, finally making out three people, and all looked to be doing the same thing as us: gearing up for a fight.

"You ready for this?" I asked.

"What do you think?" she retorted, and without waiting for my reply, she opened her door and kicked out as the first deader reached in for her. It stumbled back a step and she aimed and shot it in the forehead. The gunshot sounded out loudly and then it echoed across from the other truck as they, too, made their move and began shooting their way to us.

Nova shot the next deader in the head as it trampled over its fallen brethren and then she jumped down, a gun in each hand, and she aimed at them, putting them out of their ungodly misery without a second thought. I followed her out, jumping down and landing feet first onto one of the dead deaders…re-dead deaders…completely and totally dead deaders. Whatever! It mushed under my boots and I slipped and then gagged, and maybe even vomited a little as his guts exploded around my feet. Because of course I couldn't even be cool about getting out of the truck, I had to go and look like an idiot right off the bat.

I moved out of the way of the door, pushing it shut with my elbow to keep Joan safe, because I was hoping to make it through this mess, and I did not want to find our truck full of the undead afterwards. And yeah, the crazy old broad had grown on me.

The zombie child lunged for me, its pigtails swinging as its mouth tried to take a chunk out of my kneecap, because that was as high as the little shit could reach. I felt the tiniest amount of guilt when I kicked it

223

away and danced circles around it until I was finally standing behind it and I squeezed my trigger. Nothing happened, and I squeezed again and again as the child deader lurched closer. I dropped the useless gun and reached for another gun. I was a terrible shot, but I didn't think I could go wrong with such a close-up kill.

Gunshots were going off all around us, and the growls of more deaders were escaping from the tree line as they came at us, attracted by all the noise. As quick as we were putting them down, more were coming. I didn't even have time to look up and check on Nova or the people from the other truck, but at least I knew that we were all fighting for our lives at the moment. And while we were fighting for our lives against the deaders, at least we were not trying to kill each other.

The zombie child had turned around to face me, and I got a full-on feature of what was once probably a very beautiful little blond girl, but was now anything but beautiful. She was worse than the stuff of nightmares. A vision to haunt your dreams. She opened her mouth, revealing broken, jagged milk teeth and a mouth full of horrors, and lunged for me again.

I jumped backwards, bumping into another deader that had been sneaking up behind me, and yes, I did realize that this was the second time this had happened to me in less than twenty-four hours. I ducked just before either of them grabbed me and made me their brunch, and they clashed together clumsily, not being able to stop their own forward momentum because they were stupid. *Ha! Score one for Nina*, I thought bitterly. They untangled themselves and turned toward me, their eyes wild with hunger and hatred.

"To hell with this," I mumbled to myself, withdrawing my newly acquired machete, and I took another step backwards to allow myself some space to swing. Luckily, the shoulder that had been stitched together was not the one with my machete-slashing hand. Now that was a statement I never thought I would hear myself saying.

I slashed through the air and took the first deader's head off, but I didn't get to cheer in victory as black gunk splattered my body and my shoulder throbbed painfully from the swift movement. In some sick and twisted way though, I was enjoying the thrill of the kill, the thrill of ending its life and preserving my own. I used to feel bad for every kill, guilt eating away at the death I was inflicting. Because even though these monsters would gladly kill me without batting a rotten eyelash, I was a human, and I did realize what I was doing. I guess that was the difference between monsters and men. Now, though, I felt delight as I watched the head of the deader roll under the truck, and the body slump to its knees before falling forward. Maybe I'd lost my humanity after all, or maybe I'd realized that there was no way to survive this but to kill. Because it really was a kill or be killed world.

The deader girl came for me once more, trampling over the fallen deader, and I swung and sliced through her scrawny, pale neck, watching as her head fell from her shoulders. Her body fell forward, but I didn't stop to see it come to its final rest as I was too busy jumping over the deader bodies and joining the thick of the fight again. Because this was where I felt alive—killing them, putting both them and me out of their misery. So maybe I wasn't a monster after all.

Nova was firing with both guns, her shots almost always accurate and dead center into each of their filthy rotting foreheads. I sliced and stabbed my way toward her, helping to finish off the last of the ones within our range. My eyes looked up to see that the three men were also coming to the last of their zombies, and I knew that our time was almost up.

We had fought the dead, now it was time to fight the living. And that was something I could never take delight from.

THIRTY

The groans were minimal, and generally coming from the random heads littered across the road—the ones that were still in their eternal torment, that hadn't had a bullet or blade through their brain and so continued to hunger on, despite their lack of bodies (and as such, stomachs to fill with flesh). It didn't seem to bother them. In fact, they kept on in much their usual way despite their lack of torso. It was both deeply disturbing and hilarious.

Nova had reloaded in the seconds it took for me to dispose of the last deader, and she now had both her guns trained on the men in front of us.

"It's okay, ladies, no need for any more killing today. We just thought you might need a little help is all," the first man drawled out. He watched us beneath the peak of his filthy red cap, his jaw twitching beneath a long beard. He lowered his gun, but he wasn't fooling anyone. Certainly not Nova.

"Well, thank you for your assistance, you can be on your way now," she said calmly.

Her words were steady, but I swear to God I could hear her heartbeat pounding furiously in her chest. I still had my machete in my hands, and that wasn't much good in a fight from this distance, but there also wasn't much I could do about it now. I also realized that with all the swinging and stabbing actions, despite it not being my fighting arm, my shoulder wound had eventually opened up, and I was seeping hot, sticky blood down my front and back.

"Looks like your friend there could use some help," red cap man said with a nod of his head toward me. "You all right there? Did a zed take a bite out of you?"

"Not today," I replied with as much calm as I could muster from my shaky vocal cords. And really, his words were appropriate—considering a deader had taken a bite out of me yesterday.

"Looks real bad from here," one of the other men said, and he must have thought I was as dumb as a bunch of rocks if he thought I'd missed the small grin on his face and the shifty look he'd given to his friends.

"Well, it's not so bad from over here, so you can get going now," Nova said.

We were at a stalemate, I realized. They weren't leaving without us, and we weren't leaving with them. Bodies were going to fall, hearts would stop beating, and blood was going to flow. This was the part I hated the most. Man against man. Why did we have to kill each other when there were already so many other things trying to kill us? Couldn't we just work as one happy freaking family, for God's sake?

"I think you should come back with us. We have people that can look after you, treat that wound," red cap man said, his finger on the trigger of his gun making it painfully obvious that this actually wasn't a question, but an order.

Well he was shit out of luck, because neither Nova nor I were very good at taking orders.

"What do you think, Nina? Do you want to go with these kind men and get all fixed up?" she asked, a playful lilt to her words while she kept her eyes fixed on her prize. And by "prize" I mean the bearded dude that was about to get his head blown apart the moment he made his move.

"No, ma'am, I'm just fine right here," I replied tartly.

I wasn't okay. Not even a little bit. Ignoring the fact that my shoulder was now bleeding heavily again and coating me in blood, I was about a minute away from turning psycho on their asses. Fear had worked its way through me and was now a tiger waiting to be unleashed. I was ready to unload my own special brand of crazy if they as much as *tried* to take me.

Because I would not—could not—go with them. Not only would they make my last days on earth very painful ones, but I would never get to see Emily again. I would never get to say how proud I was of her resilience, and how truly sorry I was for being such a total bitch to her when we first met…and for most of the time after that. I would also never get to tell Mikey that I loved him and explain what had happened with Rachael. I wouldn't get to say a proper goodbye to him or Emily. And that couldn't happen. I wouldn't allow it to. I had to make amends.

The third man—a slim white guy with shaggy hair that clung to his neck like a second collar—grinned, and I knew it was time. I cleared my throat and breathed, readying myself to run behind the truck as quickly as I could. I needed a gun, or close contact with my machete, and right then I had neither.

"We've got this, darlin'," Nova said quietly. And just like that I felt strong and ready.

A gunshot sounded out, making me jump into action, and I ran to the truck, dragging Nova with me. She fired several times as I pulled her away, until finally we were crouched beside our truck and a final gunshot rang out.

Nova quickly looked around the side of the truck and then moved over to me, and I glanced over at her and shook my head.

"You're smiling," I noted as calmly as I could.

I dropped to my belly and peeked underneath, not quite sure about what I was seeing—other than lots of dead zombies and someone walking around.

Nova lay down next to me, still grinning. "What are we looking at?"

I turned to her with my best "what the actual fuck" look. "Were you hit? Did you bang your head? I'm looking for the three men that were just shooting at us, asshole," I snapped, my voice rising when I knew I should have been keeping quiet.

"They weren't shooting at us, Nina," she replied with a grin.

I looked back under the truck, but all I could see was the bodies on the ground, a mass of limbs, both rotten and not, and someone walking in between them. The feet stopped and a second later another shot rang out and a zombie body shook from the force of the bullet entering its skull.

"Well who were they shooting at then?" I whisper-shouted, pulling out my gun.

I was a terrible shot, but maybe I could shoot a foot from here. That would definitely give me an advantage.

"They're dead," Nova said with a chuckle, and sat up. "That was your boy out there." She stood up, and like an asshole she pointed at me and laughed. "You look ridiculous—get your ass up of the ground."

I looked from her to the feet coming toward me, and then back to her before slowly standing. The footsteps came with a soft crunch of gravel underfoot, and then he was there.

Mikey.

His face as handsome as I remembered it and his gun poised. There was a small curve to his full lips as he took me in and his dark eyes soaked me up.

"Where there's trouble, there's Nina," he said playfully, but his words were thick with emotion.

"Ain't that the fuckin' truth," Nova laughed, and threw her arms around him. "You took your time," she mumbled against his neck.

I continued to stare in shock and amazement, and he, despite Nova having thrown herself at him, was still staring at me. She finally pulled back, slapped his cheek playfully, and flounced away, leaving Mikey and me alone.

My mouth opened, and then closed again. I wasn't sure what to say to him, now that it came down to it, so I said nothing. I stared, and the more I stared the more embarrassed I got by my own silence. It was Mikey who finally broke the silence.

"Are you okay?"

"Yes," I squeezed out through my tight throat.

"You're bleeding."

"Aren't I always?"

He chuckled. "Yeah."

Mikey took a hesitant step forward, one hand moving to the back of his neck, where he rubbed along his hairline—a gesture so familiar to me that my heart panged at the sight of it. I had missed him—his movements, his voice, his kind eyes that didn't stare at me like I was a horrible person. His beard was longer, his shoulders ever so slightly broader. He'd been working out more in our separation and it was paying off. Back at the base there was always something to do, but when your job was done, you were left with time on your hands.

"What are you doing here?" I asked incredulously.

The words came out harsh and mean, and I rushed to correct myself, because besides the fact that he'd just saved my life—again—I was ridiculously happy to see him, and the sappy female side of me, hoped that he had come for me.

"I'm sorry, I didn't mean it like that. I'm just in shock, I guess."

"I was just passing, saw there was trouble, and like the good Samaritan that I am, I stopped to help. I didn't even know it was you until Nova stood up," he said with amusement.

"Oh," I replied, my heart sinking.

"Nina?"

"What?"

"I was joking." He smiled at me.

"Oh!"

"I came for you, Nina."

Without another thought, I rushed forward and threw myself at him. I ignored the sarcastic eye-roll I wanted to give myself for being such a chick about it, and I ignored the pain in my shoulder and stomach, because the song playing in my heart just then was so much more important to listen to.

Vomit! Okay, okay, it's sappy, but it was my sappy, and I needed it—wanted it—and was grasping at it with both hands, desperate for more of it. So freaking sue me.

"I've missed you so much." He spoke against my neck, and I almost sobbed with relief at those words.

Holy shit, I was a walking, talking female cliché, but right then I didn't care. All I cared about was that he was here, he had come for me, despite everything that had happened, he cared enough to come and find me.

For the first time in so many years—since Ben had died—I finally felt that someone truly cared about me. Tears escaped my eyes no matter how much I tried to stem them, and I eventually relented and sobbed against his neck, needing him so desperately—needing his arms to support me, his kisses to make me feel whole again, and his words to soothe my broken soul.

His hands moved to my face and he pulled me away from his neck, giving himself just enough room to press his mouth against mine. He kissed me hungrily, as if we'd never kissed before, and I kissed him back with just as much ferocity, devouring his kisses and feeling constantly hungry for more of them and more of him. I would never have my fill of him, or such a profound feeling of relief like the one I had right then.

"I'm so sorry," I mumbled against his mouth.

And I was. I was sorry that I hadn't told him the truth, that I hadn't trusted him to keep that truth to himself, and I was sorry that I had been too stubborn to realize it. Trust went both ways, and while I had been deliriously angry with the fact that he hadn't trusted me, I equally hadn't trusted him.

"No, don't apologize, that's my job. I was a total dick to you. I know that, I know I ruined what we had. That's on me."

I shook my head, but he pulled away and looked carefully into my face, his eyes burning with intensity.

"None of us are perfect in this world, we're both far from it, but when you find someone worth dying for, you have to believe that they're worth living for too. You are worth living and dying for, and I'm sorry that I hurt you."

"I'm sorry too." I blinked away the tears and smiled at him. "I have so much to tell you. I want to tell you everything."

"I know it all—Rachael, the baby, everything. You were doing the right thing, I know that, and again, I'm so sorry." He pressed another rough kiss against my mouth and I clung to him with both hands. "God damn, woman, you've been driving me crazy. It's like you're living in my head. Everywhere I turned you were there—or at least the ghost of you." He laughed, but I could hear the strain in his laugh, and feel how desperately he meant those words and needed me to understand them. "I've been such an asshole." He shook his head and pulled me close again, his beard scratching against my neck once more.

"It was both of us," I relented. "Not just you and not just me."

I felt him nod. "Fine, I'll meet you halfway," he chuckled. "You never let up, do you?"

"Never," I replied, and hugged him tightly, my fingers digging into his sides. "Never."

THIRTY-ONE

Mikey took my hand and led me around to the front of the truck. We found Nova picking through the dead. It took the term pickpocketing to a whole new level, but it was a necessary task. She grabbed discarded weapons and anything useful from any of the many pockets, and looked up at us with a huge grin.

"You two good now?" she asked, checking one of the men's guns for bullets. "Because I can't stand any more of her sulky bullshit."

"I was not sulking." I turned to Mikey. "Seriously, I was not sulking."

"Yeah, we're good." He looked down at me with a soft smile that reached all the way up to his eyes, and then his face dropped into something darker. I could see the tension in his features.

"What is it? What's happened?" I asked numbly, my gut filling with dread.

Nova came toward us, looking as worried as I felt. "Spit it out, Mikey," she barked out bluntly.

"The base was attacked," he said just as abruptly, the words sounding painful to him.

"The Forgotten!" I snarled angrily. "They found us."

I had put them to the back of mind, refusing to think about Fallon and the evil scum he worked with. But suddenly it felt like my ignorance had gotten everyone killed. Because Alek had told me and Mikey that Fallon wouldn't stop looking for us. We had been warned and we had ignored the warning. We had hoped that we had escaped him, that we had put enough distance between us the Forgotten and, but we had been wrong.

Mikey shook his head quickly. "No, it wasn't them."

"Fallon?" I asked.

"No, it was the dead. A huge horde, by the looks of it." He swallowed loudly and looked away, taking a deep breath before looking back at me. "Nina, I don't know how to say this."

My world froze, my heart pausing on a beat as I waited in anticipation. He watched me, choosing his words as carefully as possible, and I knew it was bad—so bad that he couldn't say the treacherous words that he knew would break my heart. He shook his head, his nostrils flaring, and he opened his mouth to speak.

"So don't," I said abruptly, my eyes like fire. "Don't say it, don't tell me. Please."

Because I knew, I could see it in his face. I could already hear it in his tone. And it would break me, break every single part of me and everything I was. I couldn't face it—his words, the pain I knew they would bring me.

"Please, Mikey," I pleaded, my chest feeling tight and painful. I didn't want to listen. I wanted to run away from him and his words. He offered me no comfort now, because I knew he was about to crush me with his words.

Mikey shook his head and looked forlornly to the floor. "She's gone, Nina. I'm so sorry," he whispered, his words getting stuck in his throat. Because he knew that he had to say them, no matter how much I begged him not to, because if he didn't I would never accept it, I would never truly believe that she could be gone and I wouldn't get to see her ever again.

The words left his mouth and I heard them. Hell, I even felt them. Like tiny splinters, they cut me—small shards of fine yet deadly glass embedding themselves in my skin, burying deep inside my flesh and tearing me apart from the inside out. I heard his words and I saw his own pain, telling me that Alek was gone also, but I'd left, I'd checked out. I couldn't think about what he was saying. I couldn't think of the sweet girl that was now dead. The woman that she would never get to become, the future that she would no longer have. And the things that she would never experience.

Mikey's arms were around me before I collapsed to my knees, and he pulled me up against his body even while I thumped manically against his chest, blaming him for my loss, for her death, and for the fact that the world just sucked so much ass right then.

I cried, I wailed, and I sobbed. I ached because of the hole that her loss had already left inside of me. It made no sense that I'd never see her face or hear her sweet voice again. And then there was the crushing, soul-destroying guilt that I hadn't even bothered to say goodbye to her when I came on this stupid, pointless journey with Nova. That was what burned through every part of me. I could never make it up to her.

Somewhere in the fog I heard Nova asking about others from the base—her friends, Michael—and then I heard her join me in my misery at the loss of so many people. She'd lost just as much as me, perhaps more. She had lived with these people for months, grown close to them, defended and protected them, and now they were gone.

I looked up sluggishly through my tear-soaked lashes and saw her pull out her gun and march over to the deaders on the ground. It was senseless and pointless since they were already dead, but wasn't that the beauty of pain—that there was no understanding of it, no making sense of the way it ate you up like acid and ruined everything, blending it all into one giant blur of throbbing pain?

She shot at the deaders on the ground, turning them to rotten mush with each bullet. It was a waste of ammo and would draw more deaders to us—she knew it, and I knew it—but pain wasn't reasonable. It didn't let you think logically, it just was. And I understood it, and I felt her pain, and if I could find the strength, I would have done the same. I would hack and chop and stab and slice away at the dead, because the need to kill and destroy these things—these things that so freely take the lives of our loved ones—was suddenly so mind-consuming that I could hardly breathe from it.

Nova stopped abruptly and dropped to her knees, landing in the pile of sludge and gore that was once a deader. A deader that was once a human being just like her or me, but was now so very far removed from that. As she began to cry I finally found my strength and quickly went to her, falling to my knees in front of her shaking body. We leaned into one another, holding each other close as we cried, letting our misery add kindling to our already raging anger. Because someone, or something, would have to pay for our losses.

I hiccupped through another angry, retching sob and took a long swallow of water from my bottle before taking a steadying breath. I

felt dehydrated from all the crying, but it was needed, and I couldn't
have stopped myself even if I had wanted to. A part of me realized that
it wasn't just Emily-Rose I was crying over, though of course her loss
was the greatest loss of all. But it was the years that had gone by, the
hurt that had been building up inside me. My body was overflowing
with pain, but I felt ready now to take on whatever I needed to, to get
her some retribution. To get some vengeance for Emily.

Nova was carefully patching my bite back up, since all my machete-
swinging awesomeness had torn it back open. It stung to hell and
back, and I could see how worried Mikey was about it. After all, we
had both been witness to what bites did to people. I guess we just had
to be grateful that the zombie virus was brought on by death and not
fluid transference. And Nova had adamantly insisted that despite my
crying like a baby over how much she was hurting me, it was not life-
threatening.

"So, who else is left?" Nova asked sluggishly, her words sounding
rough and raw in her dry throat.

I held my water bottle out to her and she poured a little over her
hands to wash them clean of my blood before rubbing them along the
rough ground.

"Zee, but he's in really bad shape—no saying if he'll actually
survive. Michael and Melanie were with me, so they're okay. Matty
and Jessica…" Mikey looked up at me as Jessica's name fell from his
lips. "Did you find anything out? About the other woman?"

A deep shudder wracked my body and I shook my head. "No, it
was all pointless. She died, and…and…" I squeezed my eyes shut, the
words feeling too traumatic and dirty to leave my treacherous lips.

Mikey reached for my hand, giving it a squeeze of comfort, but it
brought none.

"They were both zombies by the time we got there," Nova explained darkly, and I listened as she lit another cigarette. She didn't bother to explain whether she meant Hilary and Deacon or Hilary and the baby, and I didn't care to explain either.

"Fuck," Mikey muttered. "Fuck!" he repeated, harsher this time. "How long has Jessica got?" he asked.

"Not long. We need to get back to her as soon as we can," Nova said.

I opened my eyes and looked over to her. "And then what?"

"Then we get that thing out of her." She took a long drag on her cigarette, staring at me as the smoke left her lips. "We get it out of her anyway we can," she said, enforcing the situation that we both knew must happen. "I won't let what happened to Hilary happen to Jessica."

"Ninety-nine bottles of beer on the wall, ninety-nine bottles of beer…"

Mikey jumped to his feet and pulled out his gun. In all the stress of the last hour I had completely forgotten about the crazy pants.

I grabbed his leg. "It's okay, she's okay. Well, she's not *okay*, but she's not a threat anyways." I quirked an eyebrow.

Joan jumped down from the truck and danced over to us, and Nova snorted out a dry, humorless laugh.

"Someone needs to actually get her 'Ninety-Nine Bottles of Beer' to shut her skinny ass up," she bit out, sounding almost angry.

I got up as she came closer and I offered her some small semblance of a smile. It wasn't much, but it was the best I could do, and given that my world had just crumbled, I was surprised I managed anything at all. "Hey, Crazy Pants, how are you doing?"

"I'm doing wonderful!" She twirled around in a circle happily, and I couldn't stop the small laugh that escaped my cracked lips.

She'd slept through everything—the attack of the deaders, the killing of the men, and the misery of us finding out we'd lost our loved ones. Her happiness seemed so out of place, yet it was welcome. Because I felt like I was drowning in unhappiness, it was engulfing me and pulling me under, and I could see the same thing happening to Nova.

"So, tell me, what's for breakfast?" Joan looked over at Mikey and whistled through her gums, because, well, there weren't a lot of teeth left in her mouth anymore. "Well, hello there, young man." She licked her lips and winked.

Mikey looked to me, his eyes wide in horror. "Nina?"

Nova laughed, a small sound that slowly built in a full-on crescendo. I joined her, and soon even Crazy Pants was joining in, though I was almost certain she had no idea what she was laughing about, but she laughed as if we were at a stand-up comedy show. Mikey was the only one who didn't laugh, instead choosing to look plain confused by the mass hysteria that had taken hold of the crazy women in this little group. I didn't even know why we were laughing, and as my laugh began to tail off, I let out another choking sob.

I got a grip on myself finally and introduced them. "Mikey, this is Joan, also known as Crazy Pants. Crazy Pants, this is Mikey."

"And is he…you know…single?" she asked from the side of her mouth as if he wasn't standing right in front of her and listening to everything that she was saying.

I smirked and looked at Mikey. "No, he's not. He's with me."

Mikey smiled back at me, and then I turned back to Joan.

"Besides, your husband would not be a happy man if you went and hooked up with someone new, now, would he?" Never mind the fact that her husband was dead…

Her eyes glistened mischievously. "No, he wouldn't. Real shame though."

"Is she for real?" Mikey asked with a bemused smile.

I smiled affectionately at her. "Yeah, she's for real."

Nova stood up. "We need to get our shit together and get going back to base. They're going to need some help securing the place. We're taking this truck, right?" she said, gesturing to the men's truck.

"Damn straight we are. It's the least they can do," I replied.

"We're not going back to the base. It's too badly compromised," Mikey said, and I think both Nova and I breathed out a sigh of relief at that. I was glad to see that I wasn't the only emotional wreck around there.

"Where are we going then?" Nova asked with a tight frown.

"We're going to the mall," he said, his grin wide and his dimples showing.

"The mall?" both Nova and I said in unison.

"Yeah. Instead of continuing to go back and forth for supplies, we're going to stay there. Everyone is already on their way there. Or at least they were getting their shit together to leave and head there when I left to find you." He smiled happily, and I guessed that the mall must have been Mikey's idea.

"I still don't see why we can't go back to the base," Nova said, though I knew she was relieved about it.

Mikey's smile dropped and he swallowed. "The base is too big for us to manage. There aren't enough of us now to keep watch. The gates were pulled down, and there were a lot of breaches." He paused before continuing. "Besides, I don't think anyone could stomach staying there now."

Now *that* I could understand and get behind. I wasn't sure the mall was a much better option than the base. I mean that was, after all, where Rachael had tried to kill me and I'd discovered the level of crazy I had been traveling with. But I knew it would be so much worse on Nova.

"Is that wise? Will it be safe enough?" I asked, but I didn't know why I bothered with the question, because it wouldn't have been decided upon if they didn't believe it to be safe. So I asked the real question I was pondering: "Nova, are you cool with this?"

Nova was like a machine, throwing items and things into the cab of her truck. She grabbed guns from the ground, prying them from cold, dead fingers without so much as a pained look. "I'm cool with it," she replied blankly, her voice washed clean of any and all emotion.

But I could tell from the sad look on her face that she wasn't cool with it, but I also knew that she would be fine no matter what, that she'd deal with it all regardless. She was a survivor, like me, and survivors picked themselves up and got on with the job. I felt exhausted from my meltdown, from the ache of losing Emily, but I felt stronger for releasing all the pent-up anxiety that had been building inside of me for weeks.

So I did what I always did, what I'll *always* do: I got up and dusted myself off, and I got ready to fight again. To survive again. And to make it through another day. Because that's all you could do, all you could really hope for in this life.

Just one more day.

THIRTY-TWO

"Nova, can I take our truck? I don't want to drive theirs." I pointed to the other men's truck, and Nova shrugged.

"Sure, whatever," she said while trying to scrape something that resembled a piece of brain off the side of her boot.

"Joan, are you riding with Nova?" I added quickly.

Nova abruptly looked up, but before she could shut me down, Joan leaned over and hugged her.

"We can sing songs!" She smiled happily as she skipped past me, and I patted her shoulder.

"You owe me," Nova groaned, and walked away to her newly acquired truck.

I smirked at how Joan would fit into the little group that was now on its way to the mall. I thought of Michael, and what a dick he was, and then I thought of how much Joan was going to piss him off and it brought me a small amount of sickly satisfaction.

"Will you be okay driving on your own?" Mikey asked, interrupting my thoughts. His posture was rigid, and I quirked an eyebrow as he hurried to correct himself. "What I meant was—" He rubbed a hand across the back of his neck and sighed. "I don't know what I'm saying. I guess I just don't want you anywhere but next to me, as ridiculous and chauvinistic as that sounds." He shrugged and took my hand in his. "It feels like I only just got you back."

I smiled the best I could, forcing my cheeks to rise and warmth to fill my eyes, even though I felt sad and empty. Because I did know what he meant, and now with Emily gone, it made him even more important to me. As if he was now under a microscope and all my attention was solely focused on him.

"I'm not going anywhere," I whispered to him, giving him my words, the ones I knew he desperately wanted to hear. The ones I meant from the bottom of my heart. "But don't start with all that male crap. I am perfectly capable of handling myself. You are not G.I. Joe, and I am in no way Barbie. So quit it."

He nodded before opening his mouth to say something, but I cut him off before the words even left him, because I knew exactly what was coming next.

"Maybe not perfectly capable, but I get by well enough."

Mikey grinned and nodded again. "Sorry."

"Well, I'm leaving, so make up or break up," Nova said, and climbed into her truck. She slammed her door and started the engine, and I watched as she turned to scowl at Joan, who must have started up her latest rendition of "Ninety-Nine Bottles of Beer" or some other equally annoying song.

"She's right," Mikey said. "We need to get out of here. There's a huge horde somewhere around here." At his words, a chill ran the full length of my spine.

It was never-ending, the constant running from someone or something. It was exhausting, and the pressure that I had finally released only half an hour ago was slowly beginning to fill back up—like an ever-dripping tap that you couldn't quite shut off all the way.

"Let's get going," I agreed on a heavy sigh, and started to walk to my truck. I turned back to ask Mikey where he had parked, only to find him less than a step behind me, and we almost head-butted each other from my sudden stopping. "Whoa, this is my dance space, Mikey, that's yours." I laughed and took a step back.

"Sorry, wasn't expecting you to suddenly stop walking like that." He laughed nervously. "I'm just around the bend. I'd stopped to piss when I heard all the talking and snuck up on you and those other dudes and found the Mexican standoff thing going on."

He grinned, and I realized how freaking lucky we were that he'd stopped to piss where he had. What would have happened if he would have decided to hold his bladder for a little longer? I had a feeling that things would have turned out a whole lot different.

"Can I grab a lift?" he asked.

"Sure." I climbed in the truck. "I guess I couldn't really make you walk could I after you helped us out with these guys, could I?" I smirked.

"Helped out? I saved your life."

I snorted out a dry laugh. "Don't be so dramatic, Mikey. We had them right where we wanted them."

He climbed in with a frown and I started the truck as he shut the door, choosing to ignore his pout. Up in the truck, I got a full view of the destruction—the bodies and blood, the death that seemed to follow me wherever I went. It looked worse from up high, the rivers of red and black blood mixing and coating the road like some crazy, messed-up abstract painting.

"God, will it ever end?" I asked, more to myself than to Mikey.

I started to drive, listening to the sickening crunch as bodies were driven over and bones were crushed under the heavy truck. It didn't get any less disturbing the more I had to do this sort of thing, and my stomach churned with the need to vomit. How does anyone get used to this—become so accepting of the way the world was now? I didn't think I would ever get to the point in my life of accepting it. It would be like giving up on life.

"Toast, potato chips, cookies," I muttered to myself to keep my mind off what I was really driving over. "Gravel, wood chips, autumn leaves." I gagged at a popping sound that was more than likely a skull cracking opening like a coconut.

"Teeth, skulls, limbs and backs," Mikey muttered back in amusement.

"Asshole!" I snapped back.

"That's me." He grinned.

I swallowed the lump in my throat and bit back my next nasty remark. See, I was really trying not to be a bitch anymore. I decided to ask the other question that I really didn't want to ask, but needed to know.

"Do you know what happened to her?"

He was silent for a long minute and I glanced sideways at him, seeing his face looking pale, and I know that it must have been bad, that he must have been feeling as sick and as sad as I was. I shook my head, deciding that I didn't want to know anymore. His expression alone summed up my very real fear for her. I'd rather remember her the way she was: working in the makeshift hospital and learning to heal people. I chose to remember her smiling and feeling loved and cared for by Alek, and by me. Whatever way she'd died, it wouldn't be the death that she deserved; to silently slip away painlessly in her sleep.

246

No, almost none of us get that luxury now.

"Actually, don't tell me. I don't want to know." I smudged away a stray tear that had escaped. "And Alek? Please tell me he went out with a fight." I really hoped that he hadn't turned into a deader. He had told me one night that it was his biggest fear. Of course, that was everyone's darkest fear, but still, I couldn't forget the horror in his eyes at the thought of becoming one of *them*.

"I promised him he would safe. I told him if he helped me get you and Emily out of there that we'd all be okay." Mikey shook his head, his shoulders slumping. "I'm a damn liar, Nina, because now he's dead."

Now I really felt shitty. I also didn't know what to say to that. It wasn't Mikey's fault that Alek had died, not any more than Emily's death could be on my conscience, yet her death would and always would be. So I knew that my words would be useless to him. What could I say—*no, it's not your fault?* He wouldn't believe that, and no amount of convincing from me would make him believe it. Not right then, not while his guilt was still so fresh and thick. So I kept quiet. Sometimes words are better left unsaid. Instead I reached over, finding his hand and interlocking our fingers, squeezing tightly to let him know that I felt his pain, and I understood it.

His truck came into view, and I pulled up behind it, knowing that Nova was just behind me in the other truck. Mikey unexpectedly reached over and gripped my face in his hands before pressing his mouth to mine. I took it, the brutality of his kiss, the force behind it, the feeling of love and anger that he put into it, and the feeling of sadness and guilt that he was trying to wash away. I took it, and I loved it. I embraced it, needing to take it as much as I needed to give it back. He finally pulled out of the kiss and stared at me for a long moment. I felt shaky and breathless, despite knowing that I really needed to get a grip because I was being ridiculously lame and girly just then.

"Not to be a sexist asshole, but do you think you could stay behind me?" he asked. "I'll take the lead on this."

I rolled my eyes, my mouth filling with a thousand reasons on why he was a sexist asshole and I how could manage perfectly well on my own without any of his overprotective bullshit, but instead of speaking it, I shrugged. Because I was beginning to understand that sometimes to show your true strength you had to let people take care of you. Even if that meant letting them be a sexist pig.

"Whatever," I mumbled.

He smiled, showing me his dimple, and climbed out of the truck. I watched as he walked to his own vehicle and climbed in. The roar of his engine started, and as a mini convoy we began to drive toward the mall, toward what was left of our small family. From where we were it should take around two days, and that was if we made it past the stupid road with all the assholes on it that like to play Whack-A-Human with our trucks.

I grimaced at the thought of what they might do this time. Last time they threw a women in front of the truck to get us to stop, and Rachael hadn't even batted an eyelid at it. *Could I do that?* I wondered. *Could I run down another person without remorse?* That poor woman had looked scared as she'd stood there waiting to die, and clearly she hadn't wanted to do it, but she was clearly coerced into doing it. Could I really kill someone in cold blood like that? Because surely that woman was an innocent as much as I was. I grinned and shook my head. Okay, so maybe not like me.

I decided not to think about that at the moment, and focus on the road in front. Since Mikey was driving lead, I guessed he'd be the one to take the brunt of whatever they did this time. Unless he knew another way around.

The hours ticked by as we drove, the wintery scenery passing by in a blur. It was the same everywhere: vehicles abandoned, deaders roaming the roads, and skeletal bodies littering the blacktop. Same images, different town. I was used to this being my life now, that all I saw at every turn was death and destruction, but it didn't mean that I didn't miss the old days when I had a job to go to, and simple things like housework. When a phone call to my mother used to make me roll my eyes because I knew I'd be on the phone for the next two hours, and my evening of soaking in a nice hot bath with a face mask on was not going to happen. God, I would do anything to hear my mother's voice one last time.

I knew it was stupid to think like that, to dream of my old life— but it was also good for the soul in some ways, to think about the past, to remember the people that I'd loved. I normally steered clear of thoughts like this, and point-blank refused to discuss my old life with anyone. But maybe I was wrong. Maybe I was pissing on the graves of my family's and friends' by refusing to acknowledge their loss—their very existence, even.

So I thought about them.

I thought about my mother and father and the way they still held hands after thirty years of marriage. The way my father still called me his little bean even though I was a grown woman. I thought about Ben, my dead husband. How he had loved jogging and hated DIY. I remember the feel of his kisses and the touch of his hands on my body. I thought about my old work friends, and I wondered if they had made it out alive and if any of them were still alive somewhere in this shithole of a world, surviving day to day like I was.

By the time night was falling and Mikey was pulling to a stop by the side of a small lake, I had tears streaming down my face. But they weren't just sad tears, they were happy tears, because for the first time in so long, the memory of those people didn't hurt anymore. It was bittersweet. My heart ached for them, ached over their loss, but it had felt good as well. I'd thought of the funny times we had shared, the sad times, the mad times, and the bad times. I pulled the truck to a stop and wiped my face on my sweater, trying to remove all signs of emotion from my face.

Mikey came to my door and tugged it open before climbing inside. He shut it, and the light dimmed and went out, and we both sat there in silence, staring at the tranquil lake. His hand found mine and squeezed, much like I had done to him earlier.

"We'll survive this," he said, his words filled with truth.

"I know we will," I replied.

Because we would. We had to. Because I refused to let the memory of my friends and family die. They had to live on no matter what the cost to me. I carefully stored Emily-Rose's beautiful face in the vault in my heart, mentally placing it next to Ben, where I knew she would be forever safe.

I said my goodbyes to her, the guilt still heavy inside me. She was happy now, living it up somewhere much better than here, and I was happy for her. Even though I would always miss her.

THIRTY-THREE

Dinner was a dining experience and a half. We had gotten supplies from Nova's old camp, but they had mainly consisted of weapons and clothing. Mikey had brought food—mainly ketchup which was weird, but I liked ketchup so I wasn't complaining too much. Especially since whoever those men had been, they had been traveling with a truck full of bottled water and what we decided was either human skin or beef jerky. Mikey finally drew the short straw and sampled it, deciding it was jerky, and we got to making a meal with it. Jerky and ketchup was my new favorite food, I decided. It was chewy and meaty and ketchupy goodness in my mouth, and I ate it until my stomach hurt. And then I ate some more.

The air was fresh and clean by the lake, a slow, cold breeze drifting over the calm waters. But I didn't mind the cold for once; in fact, it was a welcome respite in some ways. My cold had almost all dissipated, leaving behind only a small sniffle and a dry throat. The early evening was both peaceful and reflective as we thought quietly to ourselves while munching on our food, and for once there were no deaders around to ruin things.

"More?" Mikey asked, holding out more jerky.

I shook my head. "No, I'm so full I feel sick." I smiled, deciding that being full was a good thing to feel sick over, and obviously way better than feeling sick over the stench or sight of rotten bodies.

"This was hella good, but man, what I'd do for a backyard barbeque burger and a beer," Nova sighed wistfully. She glanced sideways at me, waiting for me to give her shit for bringing up things she missed again, but I didn't.

For the first time in years, I mourned the loss of the things I both loved and missed. It was my turn to sigh now, a deep, heartfelt sigh for all those selfish little things I used to take for granted.

"French fries." I looked over at Nova and she grinned. "I miss them so freaking much. I would possibly kill for them, or at least trade in a kidney or something for one more mouthful of that greasy, salty goodness." I blushed for some inexplicable reason.

"Laundry detergent," Mikey said after clearing his throat. He too, looked embarrassed by his small revelation when I quirked an eyebrow at him and Nova chuckled. He shrugged. "I like clean clothes." He shrugged again and looked away. "And I like to smell nice."

Nova snorted. "That ain't happening anytime soon."

"I know," he grumbled, picking at his clothes. As if to further emphasize his misery, he lifted up his arm and took a deep sniff of his armpit and then made a weird gagging sound in the back of his throat.

"Don't worry, we all stink," I said, and patted his knee obnoxiously while I laughed. But while I laughed about it, I was actually being truthful. His smell had gone from sexy, musky, and masculine, to dirty feet and something rotten.

"I honest to God miss laundry detergent, though, and the way my clothes always smelled so good after washing them. And fabric softener!" he groaned and looked off into the distance. "I'm so sick of my clothes feeling like cardboard and smelling like sewers. I guess it's kinda ridiculous that I care about this shit, but it can't all be killing and death." Mikey shrugged and tore open another ketchup packet before squeezing it into his mouth.

I couldn't agree with him more, but what was there to say? It was ridiculous to pine for things we couldn't have anymore. So many people were being torn apart by these walking abominations, and of course that was the worst thing ever, but that didn't mean we weren't human and didn't long for a little luxury every once in a while when we got to take a time-out from killing and surviving through each day. Even if that luxury was something as strange as laundry detergent.

I looked over at Joan curiously. She'd been perceptively quiet since getting out of the truck. Every once in a while she'd look up at Nova and frown while narrowing her eyes, and then turn to give me a jaw-splitting smile. It was hilarious, really. Nova had become the bad guy for a change, and I was the good one. This was definitely a first for me. I was guessing that Nova had given her shit for singing, her patience finally wearing thin after several hours of listening to Joan warble next to her.

"Joan?" I asked cautiously, trying to gauge how she was feeling.

She looked up with a small smile that reminded me of my grandma when she used to knit me sweaters and call me her "little sweet cheeks." My sweet, innocent grandma that had thankfully passed away long before the apocalypse, God rest her soul. Grandpa hadn't lasted more than a year after she had passed, and they were buried together in a cemetery back near my parents' house. It was sad, but at least they were still together.

"I miss new underwear," Joan said, and I nodded in agreement. I could totally get behind that. New underwear, or just *clean* underwear, would be amazing. "I loved putting on some sexy underwear for my husband," Joan continued wistfully, and we all grimaced at the thought. "He was a real goer, if you get me."

I stared dumbfounded for a moment and then did a full-on body shudder. The comment wouldn't have been half as bad if I hadn't just imagined her as my very own grandma.

"Sex. I miss sex as much as much as hamburgers." Nova looked over at me. "What? I was really good at it," she laughed. "What I'd give for one more hot night with my boyfriend." Her smile slipped, but not in a sad way—more in the way that she was getting lost to her own thoughts. "God, I miss his kisses, and he had the biggest hands." She held out her hands as if to emphasize her point. "Big hands to match his—"

I coughed to shut her up. I wasn't a prude, I just didn't want to hear that right then. Not with Mikey being so close. My hormones had gone into overdrive since we'd kissed.

I smirked and looked up at Mikey through my lashes, trying to be as casual as I could about it. Casual or not, he was full-on staring at me with a hungry look. And not hungry as in "I want to eat you up as a midnight snack like the deaders do," but hungry as in…well, I think you get the idea. I swallowed nervously and looked away, feeling my stomach grow warm with desire.

Mikey's truck had been almost out of gas by the time we'd pulled up at the lake, and after checking all the tanks, we'd decided that his truck would have to be left behind when we set off in the morning. I hated the idea of leaving a working vehicle behind, but there was no other option. We were miles from anywhere useful, with no way of siphoning gas from any abandoned vehicles. Plus, most of the stuff was starting to turn bad so there was no guarantee that the sludge we got out of an abandoned vehicle would be any good. Mikey had thought the same thing, insisting that it would most likely just blow the engine. My thoughts went again to how much longer we would be able to continue to drive anywhere, and what we would do when that was no longer an actual option for us. There would be no transporting food and water, no hightailing it out of somewhere when there was a horde of deaders or worse.

"Who's on first watch?" Nova asked with a stretch and a loud belch. "Please say you."

"Sure, I'll do it," I replied without even having to think about it. I always preferred first watch. I'd much rather stay awake for an extra couple of hours and then get one long chunk of hopefully uninterrupted sleep.

"Cool, then I'm off to bed. See you lovebirds in the morning. Joan, you're with me, come on." She held a hand out to Joan, who begrudgingly took it. "Don't look at me like that, you crazy broad. I'll spoon you if you want." She winked at me and then chuckled as they walked to their truck, and I couldn't stop the giggle that erupted from me.

I watched them grab blankets from the cab and drag them into the bed of the truck, and then the night fell into peace once more. I looked out across the lake again, watching the small ripples move across the surface. It was beginning to get cold again, the frigid winter air showing us that it was still there and hadn't forgotten that it could kill us as much as anything else in this cruel, hard world.

The air stirred as Mikey moved closer, his hand reaching for mine.

I looked over at him and smiled, nervous but glad to have him there, in that moment with me. I had so many things that I had wanted to say to him previously, wanting to get back to the base and tell him all my dark and dirty secrets, yet now my mind was blank, filled with nothing but static noise. Now he knew all of those secrets and he'd still chosen to come and find me. What could I say to that? He let go of my hand and wrapped his arm around my shoulder, pulling me close to him. I leaned in, feeling the warmth of his body heat wrapping around me and colliding with my own. I let out a shaky breath before I spoke, gaining a little composure.

"I'm sorry," I said as confidently as I could.

His lips brushed the top of my head and he tsked at me. "Well, now I have to apologize, don't I? Damn it, woman, I was hoping to come out of this thing looking totally cool and un-blameable for anything." He kissed the top of my head again and laughed before I could punch him in the ribs.

"You're such a dick," I laughed back.

"I know," he agreed, and I groaned in annoyance at him. "I'm sorry," he said more solemnly. "I'm really sorry."

"For being a dick? It's okay, I'll get over it." I stumbled over my words.

"No, I mean, I'm sorry for…wait, stop calling me a dick." Mikey pulled away from me and looked down with a frown, which quickly broke into a smile when he saw me laughing. "I've missed you," he said, leaning down and placing his lips gently on mine.

I kissed him back just as gently, my fingers reaching up and tangling themselves in his hair. I got lost inside his kiss, a kiss that I didn't quite realize how much I not only wanted but needed.

Moments passed, and I could have quite happily stayed in the moment for longer, forgetting all rational thoughts and consequences, but I reluctantly pulled out of it, knowing it wasn't safe to be this unaware of my surroundings. The lake seemed free of zombies, but you never knew when one could stumble upon you.

I smiled at him. "Just to be clear, are you sorry for being a dick or not?"

"Fuck off," he laughed, and pushed me away from him.

He quickly reached over and took my hand in his again, and I looked down at our intertwined fingers—his large, calloused ones, and my own too-thin ones with broken nails and showing signs of malnourishment. Looking at our hands, his large and mine small, my thoughts drifted to Emily-Rose and sadness engulfed me again.

"I can't believe she's gone," I choked out painfully, and then I started to sob quietly. It caught me by surprise. I thought I had put it to bed, I thought I had said my goodbyes to her earlier, but apparently my heart had decided that I hadn't.

Mikey pulled me back into his arms and I went to him willingly, needing his strength just then, since mine had left me a trembling wreck of a woman.

"She loved you," he murmured against my hair.

"Don't." I shook my head. "It hurts too much." I wiped furiously at my eyes.

I struggled to control myself, to tame my raging emotions. I felt anger that was different from anything I had ever felt before. It wasn't anger at the world, or people, or even the deaders that had likely killed my precious girl. It was anger at myself.

"I was supposed to protect her, Mikey. God, I'm so useless. I couldn't even keep a teenage girl alive. What kind of person am I?" I said angrily. My cheeks felt hot and my hands shook with sadness and rage.

Mikey stared at me the entire time, his eyes deep brown pools filled with concern. His forehead held that small knit of worry right between his eyebrows, the way it did when he was deep in thought. He rubbed a hand across the back of his neck, his full lips spreading into a small smile that made my heart ache. I was in so much pain, and I couldn't see a way out of it, a way to rid myself of the guilt I felt.

"Nina, you're a feisty, tactless woman. You speak without thinking, and nine times out of ten you act without any consideration for others."

I raised a distraught eyebrow. Seriously, if eyebrows could be distraught, this eyebrow was incredibly so. He realized his words were not having the desired affect and continued before I could slam my fist into his face.

"Wait that came out wrong! What I meant to say was, you're the kind of woman that would go on a suicide mission to find a woman that was impregnated with zombie sperm just to see if she could save her and another woman that was *also* impregnated with zombie sperm. And that's amazing—you're amazing." His hand cupped my face. "I love you, Nina, and I love the kind of person you are. Don't you dare feel shitty about who you are."

I stared dumbfounded at him, not sure what to see by his truthful statement. It was both sentimental and harsh, and I loved him even more for saying it—for saying something so sincere and not sugarcoating any of it. I wasn't perfect—far from it. I knew that, and so did he. But he didn't care.

"I love you too." The words rushed out and I waited for my treacherous heart to turn to stone at my words. I should have felt guilt for loving Mikey—I was still technically married to Ben, after all. My wonderful, long-dead husband. I'm sure that in a court of law the marriage would be considered null and void because of his demise, but in my heart I was still married. However, my heart stayed beating, it kept on despite my words, and I took that as a sign that this was okay. That being with

Mikey was the right choice, if it ever really was a choice.

Mikey smiled. "In hindsight, that was an incredibly weird way to tell you how much I loved you, wasn't it?"

I nodded and grinned, feeling the anger drain from me at his words. "Yeah, little bit," I laughed. "But I've come to expect that from you."

"It sounded way better in my head, if it's any consolation."

"I don't exactly say the most thoughtful of things," I sighed. "It's not like I can really say anything about your lack of tact and weird timing, is it, now?"

He shook his head and grinned. "Not really."

His hand moved to the back of my neck and he leaned over and kissed me, his mouth feeling hot and needy on mine. I kissed him back, loving the dance our mouths made together, the way his rough beard scraped against my face, making me feel raw and loved. I always felt so connected to him, like this had always been—just me and him. Feeling breathless, I finally pulled away, quickly doing a scan of our surroundings and checking for deaders.

"You need to go get some sleep. You're on watch after me."

He raised an eyebrow at me. "I'm not leaving you out here on your own."

"Are you really being a sexist jerk again right now? Because your good looks will only get you so far. I will kick your ass if you don't stop pulling this shit on me."

I raised an eyebrow right back at him, and neither of us said anything for a long while, before Mikey finally relented.

"Okay, okay, I'm sorry. I know you can handle yourself. I'll go get some beauty sleep." He winked and stood up. "I'll be in the back of my truck when your shift is over." He stared at me for another long moment and then walked away.

I watched after him, knowing there was no way I was going to his truck later. Our makeup sex would not be in the back of a truck. Besides, I totally had the heebie-jeebies after the last time we did it in the back of a van and we had woken up surrounded by hundreds of deaders. That was, after all, when everything seemed to really go downhill—ending with the death of pretty much all of our friends. And that was not something I wanted to experience again—mainly because I was drastically running out of people, and people dying was a shitty way to end a hookup.

I shuddered at the memory and continued to stare off into the distance.

THIRTY-FOUR

I swapped shifts with Nova around midnight—or what I assumed to be around midnight. The moon was fat and round in the night sky, not a cloud in sight, making it both cold and strangely bright out.

Either way, I was glad to be finally getting some sleep. The thing about staying up on watch when everyone else went to sleep was that it was boring—I mean like mind-numbingly boring. Either that or you sunk into a depression that had you wanting to blow your own brains out by the time your shift was over, because all you had during those long, lonesome hours were your thoughts and memories. So it was boredom that made me sleepy as I waited for Nova to come and relieve me. I longed for stupid things like my iPad to play some ridiculous game on to help me pass the time. Of course that wasn't going to happen anytime soon, though, since all electronic devices had become some of the most pointless objects known to man. All that information, trapped inside these silly little gadgets with no way to retrieve any of it. It was so depressing, it was funny.

261

I bid goodnight to Nova, climbed into the front of my truck, and grabbed my blanket before wrapping it up around my ears. It was freezing outside, and I longed to turn on the engine and start the heaters, but it would be a total waste of fuel and the noise would attract deaders for miles, and Deaders in the Dark was never a fun game to play. At least that's what I kept telling myself. Around an hour into shivering my ass off, I wasn't so sure if it wouldn't be worth wasting a little fuel. I could feel myself on the brink of sleep, only I just needed a little more warmth to send me over.

I peeked my eyes open and rubbed my hands together, blowing into them to generate some hot air. I stared out of the windshield and watched Nova jogging in place and doing jumping jacks for several long minutes. I was guessing it was to keep warm just as much as it was to keep her fit. My door cracked open, the light coming on and startling me, and I jumped before grabbing for my gun and swinging it in the direction of the now-open door.

Mikey stared in at me, his brown eyes almost black in the dark. "Easy." He held his hands up. "I thought you were coming to…you know, after your shift."

I was cold, tired, and cranky, and I couldn't stop the irritation from lacing my words. "You presumed wrong then, didn't you?" I looked away, not wanting him to see how much he had spooked me, or irritated me in his presumptions that I would just jump into bed with him.

"Whoa, what did I do?" he asked, climbing all the way in and shutting the door behind him.

The truck instantly fell back into darkness, and I was glad of the sanctuary that it provided. I wasn't really angry at him, though, even if his presumptions *were* irritating, and I forced myself to apologize.

"I'm just tired," I said. Okay, so not quite an apology, but I was thinking it in my head so it was almost the same thing. "I don't sleep much these days, and when I do, I wake in a shitty mood." No need to tell him I'd been waking from my dreams screaming—nightmares, torture, and zombies plaguing my sleep.

"It's okay," he said softly. "Am I okay being here? I can go, leave you to sleep." He turned to go and I reached out automatically, grabbing his arm to stop him from leaving.

"No, please stay." The words rushed out of me before I could stop them, and I knew I sounded ridiculously lame, but I couldn't help it. Now that he was there, I did want him to stay. I didn't want to be alone. I inwardly groaned at myself. "It'll be warmer if you stay, and I'm freezing," I tacked onto the end to save myself from sounding completely pathetic.

"Sure sure," he said, sitting back down. If it was possible to hear a smirk, then I could definitely heard his.

We lapsed into silence, both of us staring out into the darkness, trapped in our own dark thoughts. I thought of our losses and of our gains, of how much the world had changed, and of the scary things that moved in the night, and I assumed he was thinking the same. And then I thought of Mikey, of his kisses, and his arms around me. I thought of how much I had missed him, missed the physical contact of a man.

"All that ketchup gave me killer heartburn," Mikey said, breaking the silence.

Okay, so clearly just I was thinking about those things, then. I sighed heavily.

"I'm tired, I need to sleep," I said, not wanting to talk anymore.

I felt him shuffle around, and I was getting ready to snap at him again when he spoke.

"Come here. Body heat and all that," he said, holding his arms out to me.

I moved over to him right away, not needing to be asked twice, and he wrapped his blanket over my legs while I wrapped my blanket around the top half of us. I slouched into him, his arm coming to rest around the top of my shoulder, and I laid my head on his chest. The soft *thud-thud* of his heart made me sleepy, the sound so very human and so very reassuring. Our body heat mingled together and I felt drowsiness tugging at me. It was strange, being this close to him after everything we had been through. I felt both comfortable and uncomfortable. But it also felt right.

His arm traced a pattern on the top of my arm, and I waited for him to try something with me, but he made no move to do anything. Every once in a while he kissed the top of my head, and something akin to pleasure bloomed in me. I relaxed even more and closed my eyes, welcoming the nothingness behind my lids.

I never would have believed that I would find this again. I assumed I would be alone forever, doomed to die a horrible death at the hands of a madman or the teeth of a deader. Of course either of those options was still a possibility, but was nice to know that I wouldn't be totally alone, and someone would mourn my tragic death afterwards.

I sighed, feeling both sad and happy, but mainly content there in his arms, and then I cringed because obviously I hadn't mean to sigh and make it obvious that I was somewhat happy and content. Mikey's hand stopped stroking my arm and I felt his head move a fraction, as if he were trying to see my face and decide if I were asleep or not.

"It was a yawn," I said quietly. "I'm trying to sleep."

"A yawn?" he asked.

"Yes, a yawn. I told you, I'm tired."

"Sure, sure. That was what I thought. Nina is really tired, she often sighs and then yawns." His tone was ridiculously smug, but I didn't have the energy to argue with him.

"Whatever," I replied instead, the hint of amusement in my tone. "Just go to sleep, will you?"

I actually did yawn then, and I felt him chuckle, and I couldn't stop myself from laughing back. "Just shut up," I snorted on a soft laugh.

I draped an arm across his middle and I tugged him closer, wanting more of his heat, feeling greedy for it. My fingers danced around the edges of his sweater unintentionally, fingering the hem of it, until they slipped underneath. I grinned in the dark when he froze, his body going tense as my fingers touched his heated skin and made small circles on it. I was about to giggle again, and tease him about garnering some self-control, when his hands abruptly moved from around me and I almost slumped sideways.

"Whoa," I called out.

He turned his body toward me, and his hands clasped either side of my face without any hesitation. He tugged my face up to meet his, and his lips pressed firmly against mine, his tongue pushing between my lips greedily. I really wanted to say no, to tell him I needed to sleep, and that I wanted our makeup sex to be more than this. But I couldn't stop him, or me.

Our hands moved restlessly under each other's clothing, almost frantically, finding skin both hot and sweaty under the blankets, and chilled out of them. We moved clothing and covers aside to reach the parts we were both so eager for—a breast, a thigh, a hard stomach, firm shoulders. Mikey was careful with my fresh wounds; the stitches on my stomach and shoulder were tight and sore and he avoided them as best he could. My hands were on his belt, unbuckling and lowering his jeans before I even realized what I was doing, and then like a woman possessed I was straddling him, tugging the blanket up and around my shoulders to keep us both warm and lowering myself down onto his lap.

We both sighed as he pushed slowly inside of me, and I gasped at the feel of him both hot and hard inside my softness. Our mouths connected and our teeth clashed as I moved on him over and over, eager for this feeling to last, to never have to think about anything outside of this cab again. I wanted to be trapped in this bubble with him, in that moment, for as long as I could, and deny that the world was what it was just outside the window. Because outside the window were nightmares and demons, the very things that went bump in the night and frightened small children. There was loss and death and sadness, and I hated it all. I hated everything about the world, and needed to make it vanish from existence if just for a few moments. I was hungry for it, starving for freedom from this terrifying nightmare that was life.

And so I kissed him hard and soft, and gently and feverishly. I moved on him, my hips bucking and grinding against him, loving the feel of his mouth on my skin, his hands gripping me and tugging me harder and closer to him, until we were almost one. And I clung to him and this moment, refusing the tears that wanted to escape and begging for obliteration.

Here I wasn't a bitch, and I wasn't hard and broken. I wasn't sad with loss and grief. I was a woman, and like all women do, I too needed to feel wanted and desired. I needed to know that I was more than just a killer of the dead, but that I was also me. Nina. After all this time, I was still me, and I could still be soft and feminine when I needed to be. Because here I didn't have to be tough. Here, wrapped around him, I could be me with no pretense.

But like the inevitability of the sun rising, I knew this moment wouldn't last—couldn't last. His hands gripped my ass, pulling me against him harder and harder until I was panting and mewling, sweat trickling down my spine as I bit down on my lip and swallowed back my cry of pleasure. Lights burst behind my eyes, my muscles and nerve endings tingling and tense with longing as we rode the wave, and I clung to the feeling for as long as I could.

I gripped onto Mikey, burying my face in his neck as I caught my breath. Even then I was reluctant to leave his closeness, wanting to keep this soft, feminine part of me for a little longer. Mikey made no move either, his hands trailing up and down my back, his mouth placing soft kisses on my neck as he caught his breath.

It was hot in the truck, the air almost sticky and thick with heat—our heat—and I felt something akin to satisfaction. Sleep began to suck me under and I decided it that it actually was time to move now. I pulled back, looking into his shadowed face. A small frown puckered between his eyebrows and I traced a finger across it, smoothing out the frown. His dark eyes looked seriously into mine with unflinching resolve and I leaned in, meeting him halfway as we kissed again.

"You're such a sweet-talker, Mikey," I said jokingly, my voice still throaty with lust.

He grinned at me. "It was the sexy ketchup talk wasn't it?" He kissed me again, all the while trying to stop himself from laughing. "That wasn't what I came in here for, you know," he said quietly, his voice serious.

"Really? I'm pretty much certain that was what you asked me to meet you in the back of your truck for." I stared down at him with a raised eyebrow.

"I just wanted to hold you."

"Because you're such a gentlemen?"

He laughed again. "No, I'm not, but I did just intend to hold you. I missed you. I've hardly slept since I fucked everything up. I can't sleep properly without you."

I knew exactly what he meant, because I had been suffering through the same thing: every night waking up screaming and covered in sweat as I dreamt of zombies; their blackened teeth and clawing hands.

"Obviously if things had progressed this way, I wouldn't have complained, either." He grinned at me.

I rolled my eyes but smiled. "Asshole."

He grinned back and watched as I climbed from his lap, feeling a little embarrassed at how I had basically just attacked him and used him—his body—for my own satisfaction.

We dressed and resumed our pre-makeup sex positions, with me leaning against him, my arm draped comfortably across his middle, though now I felt no tension between us, no feeling that I was on the edge of a precipice waiting for something, and both of us felt a little more relieved that maybe things were back on track. It wasn't just the sex, or the fact that we had both finally admitted how we felt about one another. It was the meaning beyond all of that—the knowing that no matter what happened, we had shared something special. We had found our light in such dark times, because we had found one another. Both of us were ridiculously imperfect, and yet perfect for one another.

THIRTY-FIVE

I woke gently, for the first time in weeks. No screams tearing their way up my throat, no panicked sweats. I woke with a stretch and a yawn, and I blinked against the sunlight streaming in through the window. A small bird sat on the hood of the truck, and I watched it in fascination for several moments before it flew away, as if somehow sensing that it was being watched.

I pushed the blanket off me and looked around the truck, making sure that the coast was clear before I opened the door and jumped down. Mikey was sitting with Joan by a small fire near the shore of the lake, and I made my way over to them. He turned at the sound of steps and smiled when he saw it was me.

His face looked younger and less stressed than it had yesterday, though he still looked light-years older than what I knew him to be. His dark hair was choppy and messy, sticking out at odd angles, and his beard was so long I could probably braid it—not that he would let me, of course. His skin was dirty, and small lines caught at the corners of his eyes and mouth. I smiled at him as I sat down, leaning over to press a small kiss to his cheek. It caught both of us by surprise. I wasn't normally one to show such affection, but the loss of Emily had made me realize more about myself than I wanted to. I didn't want to waste another minute of this life being closed off and cold with anyone.

"We're making breakfast," Joan said, her eyes shining with happiness. "I wanted to do a big breakfast—bacon, eggs, sausages, the works—but Mikey said we would have to make do with oatmeal and berries." Her eyes slid to Mikey and she frowned. "I'm not keen on oatmeal, but he said he makes the best oatmeal ever. That he used to win awards for his oatmeal-making skills! Can you believe it?" Her frown transformed back into a smile.

"No, I can't quite believe it." I smirked at Mikey, who shrugged sheepishly. "Awards?"

"Yep, awards. I don't want to go into it too much and toot my own horn, so let's just leave it there," he said hurriedly.

I grinned and shook my head. "Whatever," I replied softly, and leaned back on my haunches.

It was cold out again but it was definitely starting to heat up, and we hadn't had any rain for a couple of days, so I was taking it as a good sign that winter was over and spring was well underway. At least I hoped so. I didn't know why, but I felt that maybe things would be better when spring arrived—that maybe with the new season, things might be different. Easier somehow. Things sure as hell couldn't get harder.

"Nothing happening this morning?" I asked Mikey.

It felt strange that we hadn't seen a deader for almost twenty-four hours. The area seemed to be clear of them, which was bizarre. But then we were in the middle of nowhere, I guess, so there wasn't much to attract them. Staring out onto the lake, I thought again of Ben's parents and their small log cabin. They had lived close to the shore, with almost nothing around them for miles, and there had been a small island that they used to take a small fishing boat over to so they could do bird-watching. At the time, Ben and I had teased them about it. It had seemed so random—bird-watching. But Ben had been right when he'd said that getting to them, or at least their cabin, could be the answer to our prayers until this whole mess died down. Unfortunately, he hadn't been right about the last part, since the zombie infection had never died down, but spread.

I looked over at Mikey, who was stirring a small package of oatmeal into boiling water with considerable concentration. He did, after all, have a reputation to live up to now, and lumpy oatmeal would not be winning any awards.

I had decided yesterday that I wasn't going to stay with the group, but would help get everything back to the mall and make sure everyone was settled there before leaving, and I hadn't changed my mind. Now, though, I hoped that Mikey would come with me. I didn't want to be on my own, but at the same time I didn't want to stay in a group anymore. There were too many complications, too many losses for my heart to take, and too many things that could go wrong. Add that to the fact that I had severe trust issues and this group had done nothing but prove time and time again that I couldn't trust them, and well, you get my drift.

Mikey looked up and smiled. "Everything okay?"

I knew his question implied more than what he was saying, but right then wasn't the time to discuss my future running away plans. Because yeah, I was running away, but I was good with that decision. I'd rather run away and live like a hermit than watch any more people

I cared about die.

"As well as things can be in an apocalypse," I said instead.

"Ain't that the truth," he replied, and turned back to his oats.

"Where'd the oats come from?" I asked.

"I dug around in the truck, found a whole sack of oats in the other truck." He shrugged and smiled at the same time.

I noticed the small pile of berries next to him, blackberries and raspberries, and my mouth began to water instantly. Suddenly Mikey's award-winning oatmeal-and-berry breakfast didn't seem so bad after all. Though I severely doubted it would win awards.

He poured me some oatmeal into an old tin can that was now a makeshift bowl, and dropped a handful of berries into it. We didn't have spoons, so it was hands in, which was fine by me, apart from the scalded fingertips. The breakfast was amazing, and I could almost forget our current shitty situation. Or maybe not forget, but certainly I could live with it at the moment. Of course, that was always easy to say when there were no deaders chasing you.

"We need to get going soon. I'll go wake Nova up." I stood up, feeling satisfied in so many ways. My stomach felt full and warm, and I'd had the best night's sleep in weeks. Certainly it was the first time in a while that I hadn't awoken sweaty and wanting to scream in fear.

I hated to leave this little sanctuary. It was almost like we had put the world on pause since pulling up, and I wasn't quite sure I was ready to press play again, but I knew we had to at some point. Besides, now that we knew the outcome of Hilary, we needed to get back to Jessica as quickly as we could if we wanted to save her.

"Oh, let me!" Joan stood up and I saw the mischievous twinkle in her eye.

She ran off before I could stop her, heading straight to Nova's cab. She opened the door as quietly as she could and climbed inside, and I watched in strange fixation as she moved closer and closer to Nova's sleeping form, until they were almost a centimeter apart and then licked her from her chin right to her forehead. Nova yelped and pulled away before pulling a gun on a cackling Joan and pushing her hard enough for her to fall off the seat. I stood up wondering if Nova would shoot her—I knew I sure as hell would if she licked my face—but Joan couldn't have been too concerned, since I could still hear her laughing loudly.

She climbed out of the truck and skipped toward us, flopping down next to me with a huge, exaggerated sigh. Mikey busied himself on stirring Nova's porridge as she stomped her way over to us, looking furious. And I tried not to grin too hard. It was difficult. Really really difficult.

"What the fuck, Joan? You never wake someone up with a lick to the face!" Nova yelled down at her with a scowl.

"Or with telling someone there are spiders," I piped in obnoxiously.

Nova turned her scowl on me. "Yes, or that."

"Even if they are a ninja," I replied without looking at her.

Mikey burst out laughing and then so did I. When I looked up, Nova wasn't even grinning so I swallowed the rest of my laugh down.

"Mikey made his award-winning oatmeal-and-berries breakfast," I said helpfully.

Mikey handed over the final serving of breakfast and Nova took it with a huff before sitting herself down and ignoring us all. She wasn't really a morning person, but once she'd eaten, I knew she'd be her cheerful self again. It seemed that this trip had us switching personalities, and if I were truthful, I didn't want to give this one back. It was much better being more easygoing instead of weighed down by terror and hate. Almost like I could breathe properly for the first time in years.

Nova lit a cigarette right after finishing her oatmeal, and she stared silently into the dying flames of the fire. By the time her cigarette was finished, she was her usual happy-go-lucky self again.

"I can't believe how quiet it is here," she commented, and I had to agree. It was, but I didn't want to say it out loud and jinx it so I merely nodded in agreement. "Last night I didn't see one zombie. Not one. That's almost never happened."

"I wonder why," Mikey said with a finger stuck in his mouth as he chewed on his nails. "Not that I'm complaining. It just feels a little weird, and weird tends to make me uncomfortable."

"Like you said, there's nothing around for miles. Probably just that." I finally joined in the conversation. "Anyway, let's just enjoy the peace and quiet instead of questioning it. Maybe it was just our turn for a break. After all, we do seem to have extremely shitty luck."

No one challenged me on it, so I guessed they agreed.

"How far are we from the mall now?" I had no sense of direction, or distance. Some things never change, I guess.

"Another day. Maybe we could get there before nightfall if we put our foot down and don't run into any trouble," Mikey said, his hands hovering precariously close to the flames of the small fire. "But you never know what you'll find out there on the roads. Shit changes all the time."

"Speaking of trouble, we're going to have some at the road of the damned," Nova said. "Not that I ever worry about those fuckwits, but in the sense of bringing everything to the table, it's something we should discuss. What new treat will they have for us today?"

I rolled my eyes. I had already been thinking the same thing. The distressing thing was that there was more than enough in this world to be worrying about—deaders hunting us day and night, lack of food and water, the elements getting to us—and then you have to go and add psychos and nutcases into the mix for good measure. I would be glad when I was tucked away in my little corner of the world, not having to worry about any of this shit.

"We don't need to worry about them anymore." Mikey lowered his hands until they were millimeters away from the flames and I stared transfixed, willing him to move his hands before he hurt himself but not wanting to voice my concerns out loud. "The deaders got them."

He surprised me by actually sounding sad. But that couldn't be right; those people were murderers—the worst kind of murderers because they had no beliefs or convictions behind their murders, just the very simple and illogical reasoning that they wanted what you had, and would try and get it by any means possible.

"What do you mean? How do you know that?" Nova asked, her voice sounding as frustrated as I felt.

I leaned over and slapped Mikey's hands away from the fire, not being able to watch him almost burn himself any longer, and he looked up at me sheepishly while rubbing his hands together.

"The horde that took out base, it took out them too," he said matter-of-factly.

"Shit," Nova said on a breath. "How fuckin' big is that horde?"

I knew she wasn't really asking for an answer, but I couldn't stop myself from replying anyway.

"Too big," I said darkly.

Joan leaned into my side then, obviously sensing my sadness. She was a crazy old bat, but I was beginning to really care for her. In many ways she was like an animal: she could sense fear and anger, sadness and more, and she reacted to those emotions. I think it probably stemmed from her living feral for so long, but I had no real way of knowing. For all I knew, she could have been this crazy long before the apocalypse. Either way, there was no changing her. She was how she was; all we could do was accept her and comfort her the best we could when the real world sucked too much. I placed an arm around her shoulders and pulled her close. She still smelled awful, but at least out in the open it wasn't so bad. She looked up and smiled at me, revealing her broken and browning teeth, and I grimaced, my oats threatening to make a reappearance.

"Do you think we should all try to wash today—you know, while we have a chance? After all, the area seems clear," I said while smiling down at Joan. "All of us," I emphasized, so she didn't get offended.

"That's not a bad idea, actually. I love cold water." Nova stood up, took a quick look around us to be certain no deaders were sneaking up, and then she began to undress as she stalked toward the edge of the lake.

I hadn't actually meant a full-on strip wash, and when Nova walked straight into the water buck naked, barely flinching as the freezing water lapped her thighs, I was stunned. She submerged herself, head and all, and then popped her head out of the water and smiled.

"God damn that's good," she yelled over to me. "Get your asses in here."

Mikey, being a typical man, followed her every curve and every glisten of water on her bare skin, regardless of the fact I was seated right next to him. Not that I really cared too much. I wasn't the jealous type—and besides, she had an awesome body, considering we were all so malnourished. I punched him in the shoulder as Joan left my side, ran to the edge of the lake, and began to undress.

"You going to watch Joan do a strip show for you now?" I teased with a small laugh. Because no, I wasn't a jealous woman, but there was appreciating and then there was just plain perverseness.

His face flooded red and he averted his eyes. "Sorry, I um, I was just…"

"You're a dude, I get it. Whatever. But give her a little privacy, pervert." I stood up with a grin and made my own way to the water.

There was no way I was getting naked here, not with all of my wounds just starting to heal; plus there was my bruised ego at Mikey staring so transfixed to Nova's ass, of course. I crouched down and touched the water, feeling the iciness of it on my fingertips, and shivered, staring up at Nova in shock.

"How are you not freezing to death?" I asked incredulously.

Nova grinned, and it was then that I noticed her teeth clenched tightly, her jaw set hard. She nodded and swam toward me before climbing out and putting back on her filthy clothes. Her teeth chattered violently.

"God, that was good," she said before hurrying off to the fire that Mike had now built up.

I shook my head. That woman was completely crazy—maybe more than Joan in some ways. I looked over at Joan as she silently kneeled down at the edge of the lake. The water lapped around her as she stared down at something. I stood up and moved across to her.

"Everything okay?" I asked cautiously, not sure on whether I should be worried or not.

She didn't look up at me as she spoke. "What happened to me?" she whispered. Her words sounding painful. "I used to be so beautiful, and now…"

She looked up at me, her eyes brimming with tears. But I was lost for what to say to her. The apocalypse had destroyed us all, both inside and out, that was for sure. But it wasn't often that we tended to look at the outside damage. What was the point? When you were running for your life or killing for your loved ones, the external stuff didn't matter. My body was evidence of this. It was only in moments like this that you really considered the damage done to you.

Joan's hands tentatively touched her face, and she stared down again at what I now realized was her own reflection. Her fingers worked their way around her eyes and forehead, over hollowed cheekbones and thin lips, sunken eyes and rotten teeth, and then there was the nest of hair on her head, which was no doubt swarming with lice. I wanted to tell her she was beautiful still, but that it didn't matter what she looked like—the fact that she was still alive and breathing was a more beautiful and amazing thing than anything. But my words got lost before they left my throat, and I ended up standing with my mouth open in and a silent o like the cruel-hearted bitch that I was.

"Leave me," she said quietly, and I knew my moment had passed to comfort her, and I felt awful for it.

"Sure, take your time," I said, and backed away, never having gotten to wash myself, but not really caring so much anymore.

I walked back to the fire and sat down opposite Mikey and Nova, who both looked at me expectantly. I shrugged and looked down into the fire without saying anything, my guilt eating away at me. That was exactly why I wanted to leave and be on my own: I was a shitty friend, I was a shitty partner, and I had been a shitty surrogate mother to Emily. I was just plain old shitty.

"What's eating her?" Nova asked. "Sorry, bad choice of words," she added on at the end.

I finally looked up, feeling full of sorrow. "She just realized that she isn't what she thought she was anymore."

"What does that even mean?" Nova asked, her eyes looking toward

Joan, who was still staring at her own reflection.

"She thought she was Joan, the wife of her dead husband, and she just saw the damage the apocalypse has done to her. She's just realized that she can't be that person anymore," I said sadly.

We all went through it to some degree—that moment when we realized that the person we were needed to be laid to rest if we wanted to survive this fucked-up world. You couldn't be who you previously were and survive. It just wasn't possible. Not unless the person you were previously was a cold-hearted killer to start with anyway. Good people, kind people, they were the ones that really lost everything. Because they lost not only family and friends, but they lost themselves somewhere also.

"What did you say to her?" Nova asked quietly, finally understanding what I was saying.

I shook my head. "Nothing. I said nothing."

"Jesus, Nina." Nova stood up and walked over to Joan, but I turned away, not being able to watch as she gave her the comfort that I couldn't.

"What's going on?" Mikey asked, getting straight to the point. "I know something's up, so give it to me straight."

"I'm leaving the group. I'm going off on my own," I replied, looking up at his face. I couldn't keep it from him anymore, and this seemed like the perfect time for him to know the truth. He had told me he loved me yesterday, all of me, but I wasn't sure how truthful that really was. Because how could anyone love someone as cruel as me?

"Why?" he asked, his features scrunched in frustration and confusion.

"Because watching people die is killing me. Because I'm a horrible person." I gestured over to Joan and Nova. "So I'd rather be alone with nothing to lose than *with* people and lose everything."

THIRTY-SIX

"**Y**ou're moods are fucking killing me!" Mikey snapped and stood up. He glared down at me and I huffed in defiance. "Seriously, you're giving me whiplash with your back and forth. Happy, sad, angry—make your mind up, but know this." He pointed down at me, and I stood up abruptly, surprised and taken aback by his anger and hostility toward me.

"What?" I snapped back.

"You're not leaving me again. Wherever you go, I'm going too. So get that in your head, woman! You don't get to get rid of me so easily."

We stared at each other for a long moment and then he yelled over to Nova and Joan that we needed to get back on the road. He looked back at me, a deep scowl etched across his face, before turning and storming toward the truck.

Annoyance and happiness rolled into one inside me. He was annoyed that I wanted to leave, yet had told me in no uncertain terms that he was coming with me. It was sweet and beautiful, even if his delivery was ridiculously shitty.

I stamped out the dying fire and waited for Nova and Joan to make it back up to me. Okay, so I was delaying getting in the truck with Mikey. So sue me. Maybe he had spoken a lot of truth—I *was* flitting from one emotion to another—but it was hardly something that I'd planned. And shit, if I couldn't get depressed in a zombie apocalypse, when could I?

"Seems you're charming everyone today," Nova snarked, looking at Mikey as he started the truck. Even from our distance, you could see how furious he was.

"Whatever," I snapped back.

I climbed into the truck, not acknowledging Mikey or the chilly mood between us, and after watching Nova and Joan get in their truck we turned in a circle and headed back out onto the highway.

There were no deaders as we drove, and the longer we drove with none in sight, the more freaked out I was becoming about it. I wanted to broach the subject with Mikey, but stubbornness and the fact that I didn't want him to bite my head off again stopped me. So instead I slumped in my seat and stared out the window, watching the world go by in a blur.

I must have drifted off at some point, and when I woke it was raining—only lightly, but the squeak of the windshield wipers jerked me awake and I abruptly sat up and rubbed at my eyes.

"Everything okay?" I asked cautiously, feeling out his mood.

"Fine," he replied sharply.

"Can I get you anything? Do you want to swap? I can drive for a little bit."

"Nope, I'm good," he responded sourly with a small snort.

"Well, clearly not. You're obviously still pissed at me." I folded my

281

arms over my chest. This was getting ridiculous now. His moods were getting to be as bad as mine.

"Pissed doesn't even begin to explain it," he muttered.

I turned to face him, forcing my words to come out calm and clear and not pissy. I didn't want an argument with him. In fact, I wasn't exactly sure why he was being such a total dick about it. So I wanted to leave. Surely he had to understand why—especially now that he knew everything that had happened with Rachael and this crazy zombie baby shit. The loss of Emily was just the final nail in the coffin.

"What exactly is your problem, Mikey?" I asked, feeling exasperated.

"You were going to leave, again!" he snapped. "And after everything, after everything I did to find you, to show you. Do you not forgive me, is that it? Because I've said I'm sorry, I can't say it again and make it mean anything more."

"Mikey," I began, but then the rain died off and the truck seemed quieter than the moment before. I took a deep breath and went on. "My leaving isn't about you."

"Then what is it about?"

"It's about me. I can't live through another loss. And I can't live with those people. I don't trust them, but most of all, I don't trust me." This was all so ridiculous when there was so much else to be worrying about. But the smallest of things meant the greatest of changes in this world. "I'm leaving for me, because I need to, because it's what's best for me."

He didn't say anything for a long time. His teeth found his lower lip as he started to chew on it thoughtfully. I began to think I had wasted my words on him when he finally found his voice again.

"But you trust me?"

I glanced over at him to find him staring straight ahead.

Did I trust him? Did I believe that he would do whatever it took to survive this world? Did I believe that he was a good person and that he would protect me as much as I would protect him?

"I do," I replied.

"Then I'm definitely coming with you," he said, still without looking at me. His jaw was still tight with tension, his shoulders stiff. "We're not arguing about it."

I rolled my eyes. "Fine, whatever." I played it nonchalantly, but I was glad he wanted to come. I didn't want to lose him either, and all my talk of leaving everyone behind so I didn't witness anyone else die was true, but I truly believed it would be just as painful to leave him behind and never see him again as it would be for him to die.

He smiled, the anger falling from him like snow cascading down a mountainside. Relief swallowed his features and he reached a hand out to me, and I placed my palm inside of his.

"Good, because I was going to follow you anyway."

I rolled my eyes at him.

"So, is there somewhere you want to go?" he asked, sounding a little excited about the prospect of a mini road trip with me.

Unfortunately this road trip would be filled with fighting our way for survival and killing zombies, not visiting town highlights and having dirty sex in seedy motels. Well, it more than likely wouldn't, but I wouldn't cancel out the dirty sex if I had my way.

"I do. I want to go to my parents-in-laws' home." I rushed out the words, not sure what his reaction would be.

I mean, things were very different from what they used to be. I'm pretty sure that somewhere in the *New Boyfriend Rulebook* there was a particular rule about not taking your current boyfriend to visit with your dead husband's parents. I watched him frown, the corners of his eyes crinkling before he smoothed them out and spoke.

"So, I'm guessing that they lived somewhere pretty secure then? For you to believe that wherever they are would be safer than the mall?"

Good reply was all I could think. "Yes, they retired to a small town in the South. They lived in a little cabin by the edge of the lake there, and used to go bird-watching over on this little island."

"Aaah, so you're thinking the island will be safe?" He looked over at me, making sure that he was following me correctly, and I nodded. "Okay, well that seems as good a place as any. Do you know exactly where?"

I shook my head and felt a blush creep up my cheeks.

And he frowned and shook his head. "But you now roughly, right?"

I shook my head again, and he slammed the palm of his hand on the steering wheel and yelled something incomprehensible.

"What?" I yelled back.

He glanced at me quickly. "So you were just going to drive off into the distance and hope that you stumbled across this place? Have you not learned anything? Do you not live in the same fucking world as the rest of us, Nina? It's dangerous out there. This is not a time for a road trip into the unknown."

I opened my mouth to say something but he abruptly cut me off. "Don't. Just don't, because you'll say something stupid and piss me off more, and then we'll argue, and I don't want to argue with you anymore. It's not like you fucking listen to me anyway!"

I rolled my eyes and looked away from him, feeling my temper flare but having no outlet for it. Because he was right, and I had no argument.

Mikey dragged a hand over his beard. "God damn it, Nina," he grumbled and shook his head. "I can't believe that you were just going to drive off into the unknown." He huffed again, and this time I couldn't keep my mouth shut. But instead of arguing with him over a point that he was totally right on—because it was a stupid idea to just drive off with no idea where I was going—I decided to calm the situation down.

"I knew it was in the fucking South!" I snapped. "I could probably find it on a map."

"And you have a map to hand, do you." He snorted out a laugh of utter disbelief as I shook my head. "When we get to the mall we'll grab a map and you can show me properly where it is."

It was my turn to chew on my bottom lip. "I'm sorry."

Mikey shook his head again. "I'm sorry too," he grumbled. "We'll figure it out."

We didn't stop to eat until much later that day. A small garage was coming up, and it seemed like the perfect place to check in with Nova and Joan. The fuel situation was an obvious worry—these trucks didn't get much mileage to the gallon—but I was hoping that there might be some good fuel still left to get us where we needed to go.

We pulled the truck to a stop, and shortly after, Nova pulled up beside us, looking happy with herself. Even Joan looked pleased. Nova opened her door and, standing on the doorframe, looked out to us.

"Whatsup bitches?" She grinned and blew a huge pink bubble before letting it pop.

She began chewing manically again while I frowned at her. Things definitely seemed to be getting back to how they should have been: me cranky, and her as cheery as a rooster in the morning.

Joan poked her head out and smiled. "Yes, whatsup bitches?" she cackled loudly, and Mikey burst out laughing.

"Joan, what've I told you about the cackling?" Nova snapped, and Joan stopped with the creepy laugh.

I shook my head at them both, and glared at Mikey for playing along with them. He grinned back at me, not in the slightest bit put out by my scowl. Which was good. I didn't really want him to be a total sap with me.

"Just checking on your gas situation. Everything okay?" Mikey asked, a finger lodged in his mouth while he chewed on a nail. I wanted to tell him to quit that shit, but decided he was pissed enough at me right then.

"Oh. No, then, we're pretty low. We could use something to keep us on the road. Unless you want us all to shack up in the one truck?" Joan wiggled her eyebrows at me and Mikey, and I had the distinct feeling that she had seen us last night. I mean, we weren't exactly discreet, but I hadn't planned on giving a peepshow to anyone, of course. Why she had chosen now to let it be known she had seen us, I had no clue.

"Let's see what's here then." Mikey jumped down from the truck and shut his door. His light-hearted, soft side fell away, and he turned serious as he pulled out a sharpened machete.

"Joan, you wait with the trucks. If there's any trouble whistle three times," Nova said, coaxing Joan back inside the truck despite the pouting that she got in return.

We started walking toward the doors of the small gas station, trying our best to ignore the blood stains and dried-out limbs scattered by a car with its door hanging wide open. The door to the gas station pushed open easily, and I stuck my head inside and waited a beat to see if I heard movement within. When I didn't, I slapped my palm on the door loudly. Tension was coiled in the pit of my stomach as we waited for a long minute with several more slaps on the glass to draw any deaders out to us.

My hackles raised even higher as I heard the distinct sound of a groan coming from inside, and I let out a quiet breath and steeled myself for a fight. It was dark inside, the light not penetrating the inside of the store too well, years of built-up dirt and grime blocking out what should have been the first glorious day in a long while. The shadows moved, and I waited for the deader—or deaders—to reveal themselves.

A deader came slinking out of the shadows, its face drawn and sallow. Its cold, fogged-over eyes fixed on me as it let out another groan of hunger and frustration and forced itself to move quicker. It was then that I, and then Nova and Mikey as they came up beside me, saw what was hindering its steps.

Another deader was attached by handcuffs to the first deader's ankle. And every step the first deader made dragged the face of the second deader along the cold linoleum with an uncomfortable squeak. It looked up at us, its skin hanging rotten and putrid from its bones, is fingers trying to clasp onto something so that it could get up and get us itself, but then the walking deader took another step and its face hit the floor again with a sickening *crunch*.

Shadows fell away and we realized that this deader was a crawler anyway, and wouldn't be able to stand up in any capacity since it had no legs. No lower torso in fact. Its body ending at its torn away waist line.

"Fuck, that's gross," Nova said from next to me, and stepped inside, the dimness blanketing her.

She took out a blade, stepped forward, and rammed it into the forehead of the first one, ignoring the scratching the second one was doing to her boot. As she pulled out her blade and let the deader fall to the floor, she crouched down and thrust the blade into the back of the crawler deader's skull. She wiped the blade down the back of one of them, cleaning it free of the purification, and stood up.

"If you find some smokes, they're mine," she said as she moved off into the darkness.

Mikey brushed past me, looking back over his shoulder. "If you find any cherry Jolly Ranchers, they're mine." He winked and continued inside.

I snorted out a laugh, thinking of the first time we met and our fight over my favorite bag of candy. And then my face fell and I stared after him in horror.

"Hell no, they're mine!" I yelled and ran inside.

THIRTY-SEVEN

The place had been ransacked to within an inch of its life. Not even crumbs remained, which didn't entirely surprise me, but it did depress the shit out of me more than it should have. We checked under racks and behind the counter, even cautiously checking the storeroom, but found nothing but bones and empty boxes.

"Well, this was a total waste," Nova bit out angrily. I saw the light turn on in her eyes and she turned and headed for the two deaders by the doorway.

Rooting through their pockets, she found a lighter and a half-empty pack of cigarettes. She smiled and lit one up before standing up with a long, drawn-out sigh.

"I found a map." Mikey said, handing it to me. "Find it, circle it, and I'll work out the rest. Let's check for gas and get going. I want to reach the mall by nightfall, if possible," Mikey said.

"Okay." I rolled my eyes at him. "Do you really think we can make it before then?"

He shrugged. "Don't know till we try."

After checking the pumps and finding them bone dry, we climbed back inside and continued on our way. It was still only mid-afternoon, but the sky was darkening for a storm. I looked up at the dark gray clouds that were slowly but surely filling the sky, and I let out a heavy sigh. Winter had never been my favorite time of year, but now it was definitely my most hated time of the year. I was only grateful that the snow had melted in the last week or two and it was rain that was coming down. We were falling into spring, which was at least livable.

The rain worried me. It made it almost impossible to hear any deaders or other humans creeping up on you. I sighed again, feeling nostalgic for happier times—times when I didn't have to be on alert twenty-four seven, and times when I could snuggle up in front of my fireplace back home, with a hot chocolate and marshmallows and a good book. Those days were long gone, and it was hard to believe that they had ever really existed, that I didn't just make them up. I certainly couldn't see them happening again—not in my lifetime anyway.

The rain finally exploded from the clouds and came hammering down on the truck, and Mikey slowed the vehicle and whacked on the wipers. Visibility was poor with how heavy it was, but I trusted him to keep us safe.

We came upon a small wreckage of three or four cars, and Mikey slowed down even more as we passed, checking for any survivors. I rolled my window down, my face getting lashed from the rain as I checked out the vehicle. Hands banged on the inside of the windows and jaws snapped against the glass, letting us know that there wasn't anything alive inside, and I quickly put up my window.

After that we didn't see anything for miles—just miles and miles of open road. There were abandoned cars and old wreckages, but nothing that made any of us want or need to check for survivors. As time wore on, it was becoming more and more apparent that the population was dwindling—or at the very least safely tucked away somewhere.

The rain beat down harder, and the wipers were on as fast as they could go. Mikey was leaned right over the steering wheel, staring into the haze, and I knew he was trying to find somewhere for us to stop for the night. If we didn't, we were going to have an accident at this rate.

Finally, about two miles later, we saw a sign for a motel and he took the next exit, searching out the run-down little motel and pulling up out front. We waited several minutes for Nova and Joan to pull up and discussed through open windows our plan of action.

The walls were smeared with blood and empty suitcases littered the parking lot, and it was obvious that there had been fights to the death there at some point or another. One of the motel doors hung on one remaining hinge, and even over the lashing rain you could hear the screech of the wooden door on the ground as the wind moved it back and forth. But the thing that struck me the most was the caved-in roofs of two of the rooms. It was as if something had fallen from the sky and crashed through the ceiling.

"I say we get to the main office and find keys, and then all bunk in one room for the night. One of us stay on guard at all times and keep an eye out for looters," Mikey suggested.

"We should park around back. This isn't our truck, after all. We wouldn't want anyone to think we're someone we're not, now, would we?" Nova replied dryly.

Mikey thought it over before nodding. "Okay, let's look for keys first, and then move the trucks afterwards."

We all agreed and loaded up with weapons, advising Joan to once again stay in the truck, for both her safety and ours. She was sweet, but she was a walking, talking, and singing liability. Not to mention that she cha-cha'd at the most inopportune moments.

We climbed out of our respective trucks and were soaked to the bone within seconds. I kept my grip on my machete tight as we moved hurriedly toward the little office. Nova tried the handle and it turned easily under her hand. She let the door swing open and then thumped on the side wall twice. We waited for deaders to appear, but after a few seconds of nothing we all moved inside, glad to be out of the rain. We held our weapons high just in case, though, since it had been almost impossible to hear anything with the rain pelting us.

The air stilled as we waited for our eyes to adjust to the dimness. I stamped my foot on the rickety floorboards and we continued to patiently wait for any sign of a deader.

"I guess it's clear," Nova said happily just as we heard a loud bang from one of the back rooms. "Or not," she added with a roll of her eyes.

We moved behind the counter, keeping our eyes alert for any movement. There was a door that led to a back office, and Nova knocked loudly on it, receiving a loud thump and a groan in return from a zombie on the other side. She turned to look at us with a raised eyebrow.

"Leave it" I said. "No point in putting ourselves at risk unless we need to."

I pointed to the wall of keys next to us, indicating that we had everything we needed right there. There were a lot of keys—way more than what there had seemed from the front of the motel—and I had to assume that it stretched around the back quite a bit. That freaked me out, because we couldn't see back there, yet it was possibly the safest place to bunk for the night since it was out of sight.

We each grabbed a selection of keys before rooting through the drawers and shelves in the small space behind the counter for anything of use, but as usual, there wasn't much. I looked outside at the pouring rain and steeled myself to go back out into the frigid cold.

We moved briskly past our trucks and around toward the back of the motel, finding a parking lot full of deaders all staring intently into the sky, their hands reaching for the thing that was hitting them. Thankfully, the rain was also masking our scent, and we quickly retreated around to the front to discuss our options.

"This really isn't a choice. We need to fight them and take shelter inside," Nova said.

"I don't like it," I replied. And I didn't. It was a shitty plan, and I didn't want to do it. But I knew it was completely pointless to disagree, since we needed to take shelter from the storm somewhere. Nova was still staring at me, and I relented. "Fine. But I don't like it. I just want that to be clear."

"I'll add it to the list of other shit you don't like, darlin'," Nova replied.

"I'm not that bad," I grumbled.

"Yeah, you are," Nova chuckled.

I looked sideways at Mikey, who automatically held his hands up. "I didn't say anything."

I narrowed my eyes at him and then turned and scowled at Nova. "What-the-fuck-ever. Let's just get this over with, please," I huffed out in annoyance and worry.

Nova pulled out her two guns and grinned. "The rain will mask the sound." She wriggled her eyebrows up and down and moved around the corner.

I was a terrible shot and the first to admit it, but nine times out of ten guns were typically useless, the only exception that of an emergency situation. Guns were loud; they signaled your whereabouts to anyone and everything within a ten-mile radius, and that made them just as deadly to the user as they were to their intended victim. But some days, like today, I found myself jealous of Nova's experience and accuracy.

I checked behind us one last time before following her around. The deaders were still staring up at the sky, making the weird, throaty sounds they make, when Nova began shooting at them. Their bodies fell to the ground in crumpled heaps one at a time as I looked on, impressed.

I marveled as she moved forward, shooting over and over, and the zombies dropped like flies. Those that she missed, either Mikey or I took out with our machetes. They turned to us like babies reaching for their mamas, their gummy, rotten mouths snapping for a breast or a bottle. Within five minutes the lot was clear of their deadly mouths, and they remained prone and completely dead on the ground.

Nova swung around to face me, grinning from ear to ear, and actually looked happy. She stuck her tongue out to catch the raindrops on it and shook her head from side to side like a dog shaking water from its fur.

I remembered her looking that happy right before we went on our first scavenging mission together. I smiled, wishing I could still see her as the woman I had then, instead of the woman I saw now. She was still Nova, but now I could see her cracks, and I could see her brokenness. Things were always easier when you didn't know each other's secrets.

"I hate the rain," I replied with contempt. My clothes were beginning to stick to me as the rain soaked me to the bone, and my hair, though tied back and away from my face, clung around my neck, making me feel choked and claustrophobic.

"Let's clear some rooms," Mikey said, and patted my shoulder comfortingly.

Nova tilted her face back up to the sky and opened her mouth, letting the rain fall inside. I turned and followed Mikey over to one of the closed doors, his hand first trying the door handle and when it didn't open, he moved to the next one along.

"We'll check the locked rooms afterwards. The unlocked ones are the ones for concern right now," he explained, and I nodded in agreement.

I was cold and soaked to the bone, and wanted nothing more than to climb into one of those beds—beds that previously I would have looked down my nose at, since I wouldn't have been caught dead staying at such a gritty little motel—but now it was a dream come true. Beds, and duvets, and pillows! After sleeping in the truck for a couple of days, I was more than ready for a real bed to sleep in.

Mikey tried the next handle. The door opened up easily, and I readied myself just in case something dead was inside and waiting to attack us. A set of eyes stared back at me, and I raised my gore-covered machete higher, flinching when a scream broke free from the mouth of the person inside.

Because the one thing deaders don't do…is scream.

THIRTY-EIGHT

I stared into the dark, unsure of what I was seeing and hearing, and of what to do. Nova pushed past me and ran into the room like a bull in a china shop, and the screaming increased for a second before abruptly stopping.

Mikey was at my shoulder staring in, and when the screaming stopped he stepped out of the rain and inside the foul-smelling room. My eyes adjusted and I saw Nova sat on the end of the bed with her hand firmly clamped over the mouth of a child who couldn't have been more than ten or eleven. The kid was thrashing wildly in Nova's arms, eyes wild, and still screaming behind her hand, but she didn't let go.

Mikey and I quickly checked out the rest of the room—declaring it clear, if not disgusting—before coming back to Nova and the child. I knelt down in front of them, glancing briefly at Nova who looked as helpless as I felt. At first the slender frame and long hair of the child led me to believe it was a girl, but on closer inspection I knew it was a little boy. My eyes met his as he continued to pant and claw at Nova's hand, tears streaming from his wild sunken eyes.

I placed a gentle hand on his knee. "It's okay, we're alive, and we won't hurt you."

He stopped thrashing for a moment and I smiled, leaning in a little closer. Seconds later, his legs kicked out, catching me in the right boob, and I fell back with a howl of pain, clutching at my injured breast. This only seemed to rile him up further and he screamed wildly behind Nova's hand. She let go with a scream of her own, and he darted from her lap and straight out the door.

"He bit me. He fuckin' bit me!" Nova held up her hand, and sure enough there was a crescent mark of a mouth on her palm. A little blood ringed it, but thankfully for her, he hadn't done any real damage.

"Welcome to my world," I said quietly, my hand tentatively reaching for the bite mark on my shoulder that Nova had stitched back together.

She stood up sharply and ran to the door. "You little punk, I'll fuckin' find you!" she called out after him.

"Nova!" Mikey yelled, pushing her out of the way to see where the kid had gone. "We need to find him. He's just scared."

"He fuckin' should be," she snarled.

I stood up, feeling winded and sore from the breast kick, and I rubbed at my aching chest as I came to stand next to them.

"Shut up," I snapped at her. "He was frightened."

She glared at me, and I met her glare with a raised eyebrow until she relented. "Leave the little shit, we need to clear this place," she said through gritted teeth and left the room.

"Where did he come from?" Mikey asked.

I shook my head. "No clue." I looked back around the room, seeing the mess and the haphazardness of everything. "Where is his family?"

297

Mikey turned to look. "I think he's alone," he replied, sounding angry and helpless.

I glanced up at him, unsure of what to do. I didn't want to leave that kid running around on his own like that, but I also didn't want to go looking for him in the torrential rain. Besides, who knows where he could have run off to? If he'd survived this long with either a group or on his own, I had to trust my gut instinct that he would be okay out there. If he was on his own, I wondered how long he had been like that. How long had he been surviving like this? He was young, he couldn't fight zombies—shit, *I* could barely fight zombies, and I was a grown-assed woman.

The sound of a gunshot next door made me jump, and I left the filthy room to follow after Nova, deciding that once we knew this place was clear I could figure out what to do about the kid. Hell, maybe he'd come back all on his own and I wouldn't need to go looking for him.

Next door, Nova had put down a deader that looked incredibly old—possibly from the original outbreak. We didn't see many of those anymore. Or if you did, they were bones in a heap with a snapping mouth. Just as dangerous if you got close to them, but at least they couldn't really chase you. She came back out from the bathroom looking frustrated.

"Two down," she said, and left the room.

We cleared all twenty rooms of deaders, thankfully finding only a handful trapped inside, leaving us with plenty of relatively clean rooms to choose from. There were family rooms that interconnected with a room next door, and we chose one of these to be our base for the night. We could all have a little privacy from each other if need be, but we'd also be close enough that if shit went down, we would all be there to clear out at the same time.

I dragged the top cover off the bed and shook it out outside, letting the dust fly up. The rain dampened it, but it was also a way of refreshing the musty fabric. I placed it back on the bed and climbed on top, pulling it around me, greedy for its warmth. Now that I was inside, the chill was really getting into my bones and my teeth began to chatter.

"Do you want me to take first watch?" Joan asked with sincerity.

I almost laughed, but managed to refrain. While it was kind of her to offer, there was no way in hell that I would get any sleep if she were on lookout for us. We all declined, and I offered to go first, which she seemed incredibly grateful for. Her eyes had a faraway look, and kept swimming out of focus with tiredness. After a quick meal of something indescribable and incredibly salty and chewy from the stash of food from the stolen truck, Nova and Joan bunkered down.

I clicked their door closed once I heard both of them begin to snore incredibly loudly. Being awake was one thing, but being awake listening to other people sleeping was another.

"You should get some sleep," I said to Mikey.

He was on middle watch after me, and that totally sucked for him, because that was the worst one in my eyes. He had pulled another blanket from one of the other vacant rooms and had it wrapped around his shoulders. He was shaking as much as I was from the cold, and I hoped that the room would heat up soon. Neither of us wanted to start a fire since we'd have to then open the door to let the smoke out, and also the light would give an indication that someone was there. And in the dead of night we did not want anyone sneaking up on us, even if we were heavily armed and willing to kill for our survival.

"I'm too cold to sleep," he chattered. "I'm going to change. I found some clothes in the suitcase in the bathroom. They're not mine, but they're dry."

I made a face and he nodded in agreement but shambled off to change anyway. It was always creepy wearing someone else's clothes, especially knowing that person was more than likely dead, or worse: the walking dead. But it was always worth it when you got to peel away your old gore- and grime-soaked clothes and dress in something relatively clean. A few minutes later he came back, still shivering but not as much as before, and he sat on the edge of the bed with his blanket around his shoulders.

"There's more clothes. You should probably change too," he murmured, a chill running through his body and making him do a weird body tremble. "You don't want to catch a cold."

In the grand scheme of things, a cold seemed the least of my worries, but then realizing I had only just gotten rid of a cold, I had to agree. I stood up, moved into the small bathroom, and bent to look through the small suitcase of clothes. It was hard to see anything in the dark and I instinctively went to turn on the light switch but stopped myself at the last moment with a sigh.

I rooted through the clothes, picking out what I could between the brief flashes of lightning that lit up the small window. There really wasn't anything useful other than the actual clothing itself, and I quickly picked out a vest top and blouse, plus a long cardigan to go over the whole thing. Jeans which were way too long for me but could be rolled up, made it into my keep pile, but I was almost heartbroken to see no clean socks. I would never wear a dead person's panties, but socks I had no problem with.

Reluctantly I dropped my blanket and peeled my dirty, ripped clothing away from my equally dirty and beat-up body, and I redressed as quickly as I could. I fingered the large hole in my old T-shirt, the bite mark from the deader and the slash across the middle making it abundantly clear how close I had come to being zombie food.

Cold covered my arms, goose bumps blanketed my flesh, and my teeth chattered even louder than previously as I struggled with still slightly damp skin to get my foot in the jeans. I took off my socks and wrung them out, not wanting to put them on, but not wanting to go barefoot, either.

I grabbed the blanket from the floor and wrapped it back around my shoulders, my toes going numb as I pilfered through the clothing hunting for I wasn't really sure what. I came up with a short-sleeved T-shirt, which I tried to tie around one of my feet to keep it from getting too cold. It was uncomfortable, and I looked ridiculous, but heat began to claw back into my numb toes, so I grabbed another T-shirt and gave my other foot the same treatment. I took one of the smaller towels in the room and wrapped it around my wet hair and then stared at my reflection.

I was skin and bones, as pale as snow, and with dark rings under my eyes; the new clothes hung from my skinny frame and I looked forlornly into the face of someone I barely recognized anymore. I wondered sadly where she had gone, and if I would ever find that woman again. Or if she really had died so many years ago, along with her husband, leaving behind just this empty shell. I tipped my head to one side and pulled the towel from my hair, roughly rubbing it over my dark locks until they were just damp and not sopping wet anymore.

I ran my fingers through the dark waves, tugging at the knots and tangles until I was satisfied that it was the best I could do. I felt lost inside and I looked dead on the outside, haunted and vacant, and I wondered how long it would be before my body finally joined my soul in hell.

THIRTY-NINE

A soft tap on the door made me jump, and I looked away from my deathly morbid reflection and opened the door. Mikey was standing there looking confused. His dark eyes found mine and he crossed his arms over his broad chest.

"Does Joan…sing in her sleep?" he asked.

I grinned. "More than likely. What song is it?"

He shrugged. "I'm not sure, I can't make it out." He looked down at my new clothes, eyeing my choice of footwear with a tilt of his head and a smirk. "Sexy."

"Not trying to be," I said haughtily, shouldering past him, already feeling like enough of a dork in my getup without him confirming it any more for me.

I went to the joining door and pressed my ear against it, grinning even more. Mikey joined me, pressing his ear to the door also, and we stared into each other's faces as we listened to Joan singing quietly in her sleep.

"Ninety-nine bottles of beer," I said quietly, getting lost in Mikey's intense gaze.

"Make it ninety-eight. I haven't had a beer in far too long." He grinned back.

His tongue ran along his lower lip, and I wasn't sure if it was a subconscious move or if he had done it on purpose, but the sight of that one small movement had my stomach tensing and I swallowed loudly. I pulled away from the door.

"You need to get some rest," I said quietly, my words holding no conviction.

"I do," he replied, but made no attempt to go lie down.

"I'll stay by the window," I said, making the decision for both of us.

I slipped past him and stood by the window, pulling the curtain back a crack, and stared out into the rain. It was still quiet outside, barring the deluge of rain, of course, which continued to beat down on the world in heavy sheets. No shadows moved promising us the threat of a deader attack. The bodies of the dead that littered the ground remained still and silent. They were finally dead and at peace, and I was insanely grateful for that, though I was worried about the little boy that had run off, wondering what his story was and if he was somewhere safe and dry for the night. But for the time being we had no choice but to wait out the storm.

"Nina," Mikey's gravelly voice rasped from behind me.

I turned to look.

"I'm not tired," he continued, watching me unfalteringly.

There was so much longing and heat in that look that I found myself taking a steadying breath. I knew exactly what he meant. The tension was coiled around us like vines, and I couldn't tear my eyes away from his. That was a lie; I could have, if I'd wanted to. But I didn't want to. I wanted this—him. I liked the way he made me feel—the way he seemed to recognize the stranger I was becoming to myself—and I needed it. I needed to know who I was now, to be reminded of this very thing by his confident touch and sinful stare. I gave him the smallest of smiles and he moved forward, his hands encircling my waist and tugging me harshly against his body. He stared down at me with a craving that seemed to be buried deep down inside of him.

I tipped my chin up, raising my mouth to meet his, and he leaned down, pressing his lips against mine. I opened up to him, taking each forceful, experienced kiss, and giving my own back full of even more heated desire. Our tongues moved together and we took small steps backwards, our moves never leaving each other's until the back of his knees bumped the bed and he spun me around abruptly, laying me flat upon the old mattress, and then lowered his body over mine.

Trapped under him, his arms a protective cage on either side of my head, I felt safe and away from the cruel, hard world that we lived in. The room was darkening, the storm building to its full crescendo as lightning streaked across the sky and the room flashed brilliantly before draping us back into darkness again. It was perfect—a combination of mystery and shyness swallowing me whole. His mouth found my neck, placing soft kisses along my collarbone and then back up to my mouth, sending tingles across my body. I was breathless and we hadn't even done anything yet. His hands moved under my clothes, finding a soft breast and hard nipple, my skin still chilled to the bone but heating up with every second that passed.

My own hands moved over his neck and then down to his back, feeling muscles and strength where I was only skin and bone, and I couldn't help the small amount of jealousy that raised inside of me. I was wasting away yet he seemed to be thriving. His hands found my belt buckle, and moments later the sound of my zipper interrupted our heavy breathing. My own hands worked the three buttons of his fly, and once they were undone, he stood and deftly slid the pants down his legs, and then removed mine. A chill ran through me from the cold, but then he was back on top of me, arms on either side of me, wrapping me in the heat from his body in moments, his kisses hungrier and more urgent than before.

Mikey stopped kissing and looked down at me with a smile, his eyes shining in the moonlight. Even with his now thick beard I could see his pronounced dimple, and I smiled back at him. I nodded and he gripped my thighs, parting my legs more as he gripped my hips with experienced hands and pushed himself inside me. I gasped loudly before he swallowed both my gasp and his own groan with a forceful kiss. Mikey closed his eyes as he rocked into me, and I moved my hips to meet his every demanding thrust.

Our skin was slick with a light sheen of sweat despite the cold. My hands slid from his shoulders, his beard rough against my face and neck as he ruthlessly kissed me. His tongue flicking against mine in familiarity, as if we had been doing this for months and he recognized every part of my mouth and body. I lost myself in time, thinking only of the moment, because really, when did we ever get to be lost in a moment anymore? When was it okay to think only of the moment, the singular, unfaltering process of desiring pleasure from something or someone? I needed this, I was famished for it—for him and the attention that he showed my body and my soul.

He rocked into me over and over, our bodies slapping together as I fought to stay in control and not let my orgasm escape. I wasn't ready for it to end yet, but it did, and I turned my head to the side, pressing my mouth to his forearm as my knees squeezed his waist and my body trembled. His movement slowed to something tenderer and he leaned down and nudged my cheek with his nose, nuzzling me until I turned to face him again. I looked up at him through lust-filled eyes, and his mouth turned up in a smile right before his muscles tensed and he thrust into me over and over, pulling out of me as he found his own ending.

Mikey moved off me, lying down at my side before pulling the blanket over the top of us. I moved into him, resting my head against his chest, and listened to the sound of his heart beating frantically in his chest, eventually slowing to a more steady rhythm. Neither of us moved for a long time, both of us trapped in the moment, and both of us willing participants in the capture.

There weren't enough times like that, where you could appreciate your life and the fact that you were still breathing. Every day was a battle to survive, a new obstacle and new threat that promised its vengeance upon you. So I clung to this moment—clung to Mikey— letting the peacefulness absorb into my flesh and soak into my memory. Because who really knew when we would have this time again?

Life was short and precious, and while I didn't know when my end would come, I knew for certain that I wouldn't make it to the end. I wanted the tough, bitchy me to come back, but she was gone. She had left me when I had first remembered that not everyone left in the world was bad. She had begun to ebb away when I had met Emily. Emily, who had restored my faith in other humans and shown me that there was still innocence out there, that there was still hope to be had. Mikey had put the final nail in my coffin with his unapologetic feelings for me. He had sealed my fate with his smile and his warm eyes, and his strength that rolled off him in heavy waves, forcing me to look inside myself and begin to heal.

Soft snores left his mouth, and I leaned up on one arm to look down into his face. He was relaxed, his mouth open a little as the snore left his throat. I slid out from under the covers and dressed, feeling ridiculously embarrassed when I realized that I'd worn the T-shirts wrapped around my feet the entire time.

I took my seat by the window and stared out into the night, wondering what the time was, what month it was, and what day it was, but knowing that I probably wouldn't ever find out. Time used to rule my life, and in some ways, even after all this time, I was still getting used to the fact that it didn't anymore. It had been a long time since the initial outbreak, but it was only now that I felt I was back in the fight. Being behind the walls had been scary, but nothing like what it was like outside of them. Yet I thrived on it, enjoying each sunrise for what it was…the real possibility that each day could be my last.

FORTY

Morning came, light streaming in through the small gap I'd allowed in the curtains. I had been staring through it for hours, but it was as quiet outside as it was inside. I had left them all to sleep, my mind still too active to drift off when it had been Mikey's time to take over watch, and by the time it was Nova's turn I still hadn't been ready to sleep. As if I'd been guzzling on cans of Red Bull all night, I felt pent up with energy and ready to face today.

The joining door suddenly swung open and Nova stood in the doorway looking dazed and bewildered, and, if I'm honest, slightly hilarious. Harsh red pillow lines were etched down one side of her face, and her hair jutted out at bizarre angles. She stared at me bleary-eyed as she tried to vocalize her thoughts. She moved over to the chair facing me, took one long look at Mikey lying on his side still snoring, a blanket wrapped over his large frame, and hefted her feet onto the table. She pulled her cigarettes out of her pocket and lit one, taking a deep lungful before finally remembering how to speak.

"You didn't wake me," she observed, her throat sounding dry.

"I tried to, but you wouldn't wake," I said.

She stared at me, her eyes wide in disbelief. "You lie!" But I could tell she wasn't so sure about that. "I have never not woken up for a shift."

I put her out of her misery with a small smile. "I do—lie, that is. I wasn't sleepy, so I left you to it."

"I think I needed that," she said, pulling a hand through her ratting red locks.

I nodded. "You all did."

"What about you?" she asked, taking another drag.

"I'll sleep when I'm dead," I replied, turning my attentions back out the window.

"You shouldn't tempt fate."

"You're right." I laughed darkly. "I'll sleep later today."

It was still raining, but sunshine was gleaming through the clouds, fighting its way for space in the sky. It was also warmer than yesterday, and I was more than happy about that. A small figure flitted at the edge of the tree line, and my body tensed and froze as I stared intensely at it. There was a small waist-high fence surrounding the entire parking lot, and beyond that, trees. I saw the movement again, and even though it was some ways off, I gripped my machete tightly.

Nova dropped her feet from the table and pulled the edge of the curtain back before peering out. We both stared in silence, and as a small child's face came into view, Nova jumped up from her seat. Her feet stomped across the room, startling Mikey awake.

"What the hell?" he mumbled, scratching at his beard and staring around the room accusingly. "What time is it?" He glared over at me. "What day is it?"

"That little brat is out there," Nova whisper-shouted, standing

309

behind the door and peering out through the peephole.

I watched from the window as the kid made his way across the parking lot, avoiding the dead bodies all around him. His eyes skittered across all the windows, checking for movement, before he ran to the side of the building.

Nova cracked the door open quietly and slipped outside, and I was pulling on my still-damp socks and pushing my feet into my boots as quickly as I could. Mikey stood up, his towel dropping to reveal his nakedness, and for a moment we both just stared at his morning… presentation…both of us a little embarrassed about the surprise entrance. It wasn't until Joan wolf-whistled in the doorway that Mikey hurried to hide himself and I snorted out a laugh.

"I'll be right back," I said, and quickly left, clicking the door quietly shut behind me.

I'm sure Mikey yelled not to go at my retreating back—either that or he was begging me not to leave him alone with Joan—but I was already out of the door and moving along the side of the building in search of Nova and the little boy.

A scuffle back around the front of the building had me running faster, and I rounded the corner, my front hitting Nova's back with an "oomph." She had the little boy in her grip again, and while he kicked out, his mouth snapping at her hands, he never made a sound. I wasn't entirely sure why. Yesterday he had been vocal about our presence, but today it was like he sensed to keep the noise down—though the light drizzle would drown out any small noises he might make anyway.

I moved around the front of Nova, grabbing the kid's ankles as he tried to kick me like he had yesterday, and I laughed in his face.

"Not this time," I bit out, keeping ahold of his ankles as he thrashed around. "Will you chill out? We're not deaders, you're safe."

He stopped fighting, his lips pulled back into a snarl, his eyes cold and lifeless. "What's a deader?"

His voice made him sound younger, and where I had initially thought ten or eleven I now thought maybe eight or nine. He looked cold, and I realized guiltily that he must have spent the night outside. His dark hair was plastered to his forehead, and though his face was still covered in dirt, I knew it was much better than it had been last night.

"A zombie," I stated, watching the fear cross his face.

"The biters," he stated, his words devoid of emotion.

I nodded. "Yes, the biters. I call them deaders, because they're... dead, but biters works to."

"Because they bite," he whispered, his voice hollow.

I nodded again. "Yeah. Because they bite."

We fell into silence, and I think even Nova was confused about what to do now that she had him. Obviously she didn't intend on harming him, never mind killing him. Her grip, however, stayed firm and tight on him. Now we were just three people, standing in the rain, getting wet and cold once again. I hated winter.

"Why are you here?" he asked bluntly.

"We have a group of friends that are hidden and safe, we're going to find them," I said, trying to keep my story short and to the point. "Are you alone?" I asked, because that was what I was the most curious about.

He hesitated a fraction of a second before nodding once, but he didn't look the smallest bit sad by that fact. His gaze stayed locked on mine, devoid of any emotion now that the anger and fear were ebbing away.

"How long have you been alone?" Nova asked, almost reading my mind at my next question yet to be voiced.

The boy didn't answer the question, but instead answered another question I hadn't yet voiced.

"My name's Adam." He said it almost proudly.

I looked over at Nova, who raised an eyebrow. "Hi, Adam. My name's Nina," I replied.

"Nina's a bitch," Nova snorted out.

I scowled. "Takes a bitch to know a bitch." I scowled at her and then looked back at Adam. "That's Nova. She's also a bitch. But you're safe with us. We won't hurt you."

He blinked once and then again, his small forehead puckering in frustration. "You shouldn't say the B word," he said, and I couldn't help but let out a small laugh at the sweetness of his words. Adam, however, sounded offended by my laugh. "It's not funny. That's a bad word."

"I'm sorry, you're right. It is a bad word."

"My birthday party was no fun. Mommy and Daddy were scared of the bad people knocking at the door. Daddy used the B word lots of times."

My throat closed up and I struggled to breathe, much less get words out to reply to his sad statement. Luckily Nova filled in for me.

"How old were you at your birthday party?" she asked carefully.

"I don't know." He blinked again, his big brown eyes burning into me with sadness.

I looked up at Nova again, who only shrugged at me. "How old are you now, Adam?" I asked.

"I don't know," he said with such innocent earnest that it hurt me like a physical lash to my heart.

"How long have you been on your own?" I asked cautiously, not sure if he was going to lash out angrily again, or perhaps even burst into tears. But he did neither. Instead he answered me in his calm little voice.

"A really long time. Mommy said to wait for her, but I don't think she's coming back. Daddy was hurt, she said she was taking him into the woods for a rest and she would be right back." Adam looked away, his dirty shoes snagging his attention. "But she never came back. I waited and waited for her, but then I got hungry."

I had heard many sad stories since this all began, but this was the one that I found the most heartbreaking. He was just a kid—a little boy. I put the missing pieces of the story together in my head. His father must have died, and the mother was taking him into the woods so as not to upset Adam. I was guessing that the father—once dead—had turned, and attacked the mother, and neither had ever come back for Adam. How the hell had he survived all this time on his own? How had he kept himself fed and watered, and safe? It was mind-boggling.

I shook my head sadly. "Nova is going to let you go now, but please don't run. I promise that we won't hurt you."

I looked up at Nova and gestured for her to let him go, and she did without question. I could tell from the look on her face that his story had cut her deep, too. Adam was short, and his long, scraggly hair looked almost black—but that could have been due to the fact that it was thick with dirt and grease from years of being unwashed, or that it was soaking wet from the rain. His face was thin and pale but his cheeks still held that cherub look that all kids had. But his eyes were far too grown up for his young face. They told too many dark tales for a boy his age.

"Let's get back to our room and get you something to eat, Adam." I spoke as if I knew what the hell I was doing.

I wasn't a mother, and I had never aspired to be one previously. Certainly in this lifetime I never wanted to be one—not with the way things were. What would be the point? This world was not for children. I could only hope and pray that someone at the mall would take him under their wing and care for him, because I really didn't want it to be my job. I thought about Jessica, realizing that this little boy might be the perfect solution for her. That is if we could get that demon spawn out of her and keep her alive long enough to be his new mother. It was almost the perfect solution for both him and her, and I knew I had to get him back there to her as soon as I could. I had been worrying about whether Jessica would believe me about Hilary and the zombie baby and be willing to get rid of the thing growing inside her, because she was so desperate to be a mother again—even if it meant to something that wasn't quite human, or the possibility of it taking her own life. But with Adam there, motherless and alone in the world, she would have a reason to keep on living, she would have a reason to give up on that monster inside her. At least that was what I hoped. I certainly had a better shot at convincing her with Adam by my side.

I reached down to take his hand and he stared at it uncertainly, blinking and then looking back up at me. I thought I heard my heart crack at the fact that he didn't know what to do, that the simple gesture of holding someone's hand was now so foreign to him. He was as lost as all of us in this crazy, horrible world, and I prayed that we could find him some peace and love. Because every child deserves that. Every child deserves to be loved and to feel safe.

FORTY-ONE

Back at the room, Mikey was dressed and looking uncomfortable. I raised an eyebrow at him as I came inside, Adam at my side. The kid clung to my legs at the sight of Mikey, and I bent down and pried his hands away so that I could look him in the eye.

"Adam, this is Mikey. He's a good guy too. You can trust Mikey," I said as calmly as I could.

Adam stared back at me, his eyes skittish and his desire to run away evident. He looked over my shoulder at Mikey and then Joan and then back to me.

"Do you trust him?" he asked innocently.

I looked Mikey in the eye. "I do." I nodded, agreeing right away. My own words took me by surprise, because I wasn't lying. I did trust Mikey, only I hadn't realized how completely I trusted him until just then. I turned to look at Mikey, who was staring down at me, his expression blank but his eyes soft.

"Okay," Adam replied. "Can we eat now?"

I sat Adam at the table and Mikey made us some oatmeal as the rain continued to pour down outside. There was no fresh fruit this time, but the oatmeal was good and filling regardless, if not bland. But bland food was still amazing food when you thought about how many times we had come close to starvation.

Adam ate his by tipping the bowl to his lips and slurping it down. He stared at my food longingly as he placed his own bowl back on the table, white, sticky oats surrounding his mouth like a milk moustache.

"Still hungry?" I asked.

He nodded and I pushed my bowl toward him. He snatched the bowl up quickly and tipped the food down his throat without another word, and I smirked as he slurped loudly.

Mikey offered me his oatmeal but I refused, opting for some jerky and ketchup, though it wasn't long before Adam had that in his hand also. He burped loudly and looked at us all blankly, and I saw the familiar look of exhaustion on his face. It was almost identical to Joan's the previous night.

"Do you want to sleep?" I pointed to the bed. "There are three of us to keep guard and make sure nothing happens while you do."

"Four!" Joan said loudly, making him jump.

"Sorry, four of us."

Adam nodded and I walked him over to the bed. He climbed on it and placed his head on the pillow, and I draped the blanket across his small body, watching as he flinched at the unfamiliar motion of someone tucking him into bed. He was small—probably due to the malnutrition, though some, I would suspect was just bad genes. I went to move away from the bed, but his dirty hand shot out and grabbed mine before I could go.

"Don't go," he whispered, sounding frightened.

I pushed the hair back from his face and smiled at him, seeing the panic and fear that maybe I would disappear, or that perhaps this was a dream to him. That when he awoke we would be gone and he would be all alone again.

"Scoot over," I said, climbing onto the bed.

Adam shuffled backwards and I lay down next to him, pulling the blanket over us both. His big round eyes stared up at me with unfaltering innocence, his chin trembling, and I panicked that he would cry. Crying kids were so far out of my comfort zone, I worried that I would freak out if he did. So I placed a hand on his cheek and stroked it while shushing him. His chin slowly stopped trembling and his eyelids began to close, and then exhaustion finally took over as he fell into a deep sleep.

None of us spoke for a long time, all afraid to wake the poor kid up. He seemed so lost and frightened, yet he was obviously clever and strong to have survived on his own. Or at the very least, a really fucking quick runner. What that must have been like, I wondered, for a small child waiting for their parents to come back? For the thing of nightmares to be knocking at your door? To be starving, cold, and alone?

I eventually slid off the bed and we all moved next door, keeping the interconnecting door open so we could check on him. I sat down on the edge of the bed feeling sad and tired.

"Is anyone thinking what I'm thinking?" Joan asked seriously. "Because it's pretty obvious to me what needs to be done."

I stared at her, dreading would come out of her mouth next. She eyed us all carefully, making sure that we were all listening to her, completely rapt to her.

"Spit it out," Nova said while lighting a cigarette.

"I think we need to make some mojitos." She grinned and nodded. "Right?"

I blinked and then began to laugh quietly. Joan was no help when it came to survival of the body. I doubted she could fend off a bunny, let alone a zombie attack, but her random musings always seemed to lighten the mood, and in turn lighten our souls. She would annoy the living heck out of Michael, but I'd be damned if she wasn't the sort of person that he needed around him.

"Mojitos would be amazing," Nova sighed. "But I think we need to decide what to do with the kid before we make those."

"He's coming with us," I said automatically.

"I know that," Nova huffed. "That shit goes without sayin', but someone needs to be looking out for him, and while he's cute an' all, I don't want that to be me." She made smoke rings into the air and then poked her finger through the center of one. "I'm not really the motherly type."

"You can say that again," Mikey muttered.

"I will cut you," Nova snarled.

"You can try," he snapped back. He looked up to me. "You seem to have a good rapport with him." He shrugged.

I held my hands up. "Whoa there, I'm not going to be anyone's surrogate mother. I'm more the Lone Ranger type than a mama bear."

"The Lone Ranger? Really?" Nova raised an eyebrow at me.

"Yes," I replied, sticking to my own self-analysis. "Whatever, I think I have the perfect solution."

Nova stopped blowing rings and leaned forward in her chair, listening intently.

"Wait," Joan butted in. "Is this before or after the mojitos?"

I snorted out a laugh. "After, waaaaay after." I turned my attention back to Mikey and Nova. "So I was thinking Jessica could look after him." I held out my hands, waiting for the praise of my genius plan.

"That is if she's not dead yet?" Nova said darkly.

"Or she doesn't die while we try and get that thing out of her," Mikey said equally darkly.

"Yeah, yeah, semantics." I brushed off both of their worries, even though they were very real concerns of my own. Because I didn't want to worry about that right then. My head and heart could only take so much drama at one time, and at the moment it was getting to the safety of the mall and keeping this little boy safe.

Mikey sat down on the edge of the bed and looked down at his feet in thought. He clasped his hands together under his chin and didn't say anything for a long time. When he finally looked back up, he was in agreement that it would be a great solution for both Adam and for Jessica. Not that I ever actually doubted my plan, or needed his or Nova's approval, but it was always good when people agreed with your genius! After all, a child was what got Jessica into all this trouble in the first place, maybe a child could be what got her out of it.

"So now we need to decide what to do about traveling. This storm is still bad. Personally, I think that we should wait it out for twenty-four hours, but if you both want to travel, then I'll go along with it," Nova said, screwing up her empty cigarette pack. She looked at it forlornly.

"I agree. I think we need to stay put for another day. I don't want to risk having an accident out there. We already have enough shit to worry about as it is," I said before looking around the door to check on Adam. He was still sleeping soundly. Poor kid hadn't moved since he'd closed his eyes and I wondered how many uninterrupted sleeps he'd had since the world ended. "Besides, it will be good for the kid to get to know us before we ask him to come with us."

"It's too dangerous to travel in this storm. We can barely see in front of us. Let's sit tight and hope it passes over. We can check these rooms for anything important and get some much-needed rest before traveling tomorrow. We'll be at the mall by tomorrow night easily." Mikey turned to me. "Which means that you need to get some rest today. No one should take a full nightshift on their own." He pointed at me with annoyance.

"Whatever." I rolled my eyes.

"No, not whatever. That shit's not cool. The sleep was appreciated, of course, but we're a team, and we work as a team. None of this Lone Ranger crap anymore," he said with a low growl of authority.

I rolled my eyes again. "Fine," I snapped out. "Teamwork."

I hated teamwork. I was not a team player in any way, shape, or form, but if it could get him to stop being so freaking grumpy then I'd relent. At least for the time being, because we were all sardined into this stupid little motel with no escape from one another.

"Nina, can I have a quick word with you?" Mikey stood up and moved to the small bathroom, once inside he shut the door and pulled out the map we had found in the gas station and a pen. "Where was the Island? I want to start preparing."

I took the pen he offered, and looked the map over. He had folded it to the right section and was surprised with myself when I managed to find the exact place I had been talking about. Fond memories flowed through me. Summer vacations with Ben's parents, barbeques and beer, and kissing Ben as we stayed up to watch the stars. I may not know the exact directions to get there, but I could never forget that place.

"You okay?" Mikey asked.

I nodded and circled the cabin and Island, though on the map it

320

was barely a dot. "Yeah, I'm fine." I handed the map back over to him and he looked it over with his own little nod as if he were memorizing the journey.

We came back out of the bathroom to wolf whistles from Nova and I almost blushed. Almost. Instead I chose to give her the finger and roll my eyes.

"Nina, you wait here with the kid, and Nova and I will go look for any supplies." Mikey stood up, and I glowered at him.

"And why am I not allowed to go?" I snapped defensively.

"Because you're the only one he trusts, and if he runs off again, we won't be waiting around to find him. We leave tomorrow morning, rain or no rain. Kid or no kid." He moved toward the door and I stared angrily at his back, knowing he was right. About everything.

I hated being wrong.

"Fine," I snapped again, wanting to get the last word in as he left the room.

He didn't reply, but it didn't make me feel any better. Nova looked back at me with a grin.

"Fuck off," I snapped at her and she left with a snicker, clicking the door closed as she went.

Joan looked across at me expectantly. "So, what now?"

I rolled my eyes. "I don't know, maybe we could make mojitos," I said sarcastically.

She looked pleased, and clapped here hands together. "Yay!"

FORTY-TWO

Mikey and Nova returned from their scavenge of the seedy motel with mixed emotions. Mikey was grumpy as hell that there wasn't anything useful left. He did manage to find some more clothes and drag them back in a suitcase, but there was nothing in the way of food or drink.

Nova, on the other hand, was extremely happy after finding a shit-ton of cigarettes, and even some alcohol. This had me wondering why only those things had been left behind. All the food had been taken—not that we were expecting much, but there was always nearly something left behind: a health bar or some gum, half a bottle of juice…something.

Adam was still sleeping and we set about putting some sort of meal together. Between what was in the stolen truck and what we had left from both Mikey's and our supplies, we got a good meal of beans, rice, and peas. It wouldn't be the tastiest thing we'd ever eaten, but it would be filling. And sometimes, you just needed that hole filled with something—anything to stop the ache that you would feel all the way through to your bones. Hunger was the worst. Sometimes when it got so bad, you could hardly talk, never mind walking, but talking and fighting for your life were out as well.

We made a small fire in one of the hotel trashcans and used another to cook the water and rice in. At least with all the rain we wouldn't go thirsty, and we had set about collecting and salvaging as much of the water as possible. Joan had picked some herbs she had seen at the fence line when she and Nova had gone to pick the pockets of the deaders, insisting that they were edible and tasted amazing cooked with rabbit or duck—not that we had either of those things, but we took a great big bunch of them and I prayed that we found either a rabbit or duck on the way back to the mall. She chopped them up and added them to the dish, and Adam began to stir as we served up the food.

"Nina," Mikey said quietly, nodding over to the doorway.

I turned around and looked over to find the waif of a boy standing in the doorway, looking lost and a little bewildered. He blinked at me, and I had the strangest urge to reach over and smooth down his disheveled bed hair.

"Hey," I said, softly, giving him a small smile that turned into a weird half yawn and possibly freaked the little tyke out. I reached out a hand and he quickly scooted to my side. "Are you hungry?"

He nodded rapidly, and Nova served up a large portion for him.

"It's hot. Don't burn yourself on it," she said as he snatched the food from her and sat on the floor next to me.

Adam dove into the food with gusto, grunting greedily, licking his fingers, and smacking his lips together noisily. And if the food was too hot for him, he didn't show it at all. I watched him with a small, satisfied smile before I let it fall as a realization set in. We had fed him and let him get hours of uninterrupted sleep, and I was almost certain that it was probably the best food and sleep he'd had in years, but now what? I didn't know what to do with a kid—let alone a kid in an apocalypse. It wasn't like we could exactly go on a bike ride or play soccer.

He finished eating and looked up at me eagerly. I asked Nova to give him the remaining food, and he took it gratefully but didn't bother to acknowledge her with a thanks. In fact, he hadn't really made note of anyone else but me.

"You went away," he whispered after he finished his second portion, as if he was finally able to strike up a conversation now that he had food in him.

I looked down at him, staring into his big dark eyes, and guilt flowed through me. "I'm sorry. I was only next door—here. We didn't want to wake you." I reached over to ruffle his hair, and then changed my mind at the last minute, letting my hand fall away.

He looked back down at his empty plate and began smearing his fingers around it, wiping up any leftover grains. I wasn't sure if he was totally satisfied by my answer or not, but at least he had stopped with the guilt trip and I could finish my own food in peace. I scooped the remaining rice into my mouth, appreciating the herbs Joan had put in, because they really did taste good. Good…my meal tasted good and it was hot and filling. I smiled without thinking—a sleepy, vaguely satisfied smile, but a smile all the same.

"She smiles," Nova commented, and I rolled my eyes even though I didn't bother to look up at her.

After eating, there really wasn't any question about what I would do next because my eyeballs were beginning to feel like there was sand stuck to them. I yawned, feeling like my jaw was going to dislocate.

"I need to sleep," I mumbled, stumbling to my feet. The

combination of food and sweaty body heat in the small room was making me drowsy. I yawned again, making my eyes tear up. "I'm gonna go lay down. Someone keep guard and shit."

"That's a bad word," Adam said quietly behind me.

"Sorry, kid," I replied unapologetically.

I made my way into the next room and climbed onto the bed, finding the space where Adam had slept only an hour ago. It smelled of him, and not in a good way. That kid hadn't washed in years, in his stench was pungent on the pillow. I flipped the pillow over and gripped the edge of the blanket before pulling it up over myself, and then I closed my eyes and let myself be sucked into a deep sleep.

I wasn't sure how long I had been asleep, but I felt the bed stir and I sluggishly opened my eyes. I blinked to clear the sleep from my head, but I was still too tired to wake up properly. A small form was tucked against the front of my body. Adam. I smiled and wrapped an arm over him, holding him close as we both drifted off back to sleep.

I woke several hours later, feeling stiff and sore from being still for so long. The room was getting dark, and when I listened hard, I realized the rain had finally stopped. I sat up at the sound of laughter—not the deep, gruff sound of Mikey or the loud guffaw of Nova, and definitely not the horrendous cackle of Joan. This laugh was light and innocent, a natural sound that came from a child. I sat up, seeing that Adam wasn't with me now, and I stumbled off the bed and through the door.

Mikey, Nova, Joan, and little Adam were sitting on the bed playing cards. The curtain was pulled about halfway across to let in some of the waning light from the day, but it was still quite dark. I yawned and stretched, and Mikey looked over at me with a wink just as Adam turned around and gave me a toothy smile. I hadn't realized before that his two lower front teeth were missing. Or maybe it was just that he hadn't smiled so big before.

"It stopped raining," Nova said.

"So I heard." I yawned again. "God, what I'd do for a coffee," I said, and moved to sit down on the edge of the bed closest to Mikey. He put an arm around me and I leaned into him, the gesture feeling completely natural.

"My mom drank coffee," Adam said. "It made her breath smell funny."

"Yeah, it gave me bad breath too," I sighed. "Still miss it though."

They resumed their game of cards and I went and sat by the window. I pulled the chair out from under the little wooden table. It was cheap and old-looking, scratched and stained through years of abuse, much like myself. I pulled the musty curtains back a little further and stared out at the parking lot. The deader bodies were still there—not that I expected them to have moved, but you never knew what was going to stay dead anymore.

FORTY-THREE

The chair opposite me slipped out from under the table, and Nova sat herself down in it. She clasped her hands in front of herself and stared at me silently.

"What?" I snapped, still cranky from waking up and my severe lack of caffeine.

"Nothin', I was just sitting with you. What's up your ass?" she bit out.

I rubbed a hand down my face and then looked at her apologetically. "Sorry, I'm still waking up. I never was much of a morning person."

Nova snorted out a dry laugh. "You're not much of a day person, either. Or a night person, or a—"

"All right!" I snapped again. "I get it." I turned away from her, slinking back into my own thoughts. I couldn't help how hurt I felt at her assessment of me. I felt different inside, and thought that meant maybe I wasn't as toxic as I used to be. That maybe I was turning over a new leaf and heading into "not a *total* bitch" land.

"I thought I had changed," I mumbled out, keeping my eyes

looking out the window so as to avoid her stare. "At least a little."

"You have," she replied automatically. "But you're still you."

I finally tore my gaze away from the rotting bodies and met her stare.

"So what are you telling me? That there's no hope for me? That I'm destined to be the bitch that everyone hates no matter what I do?" I huffed out an annoyed breath and tried to calm myself. I was taking this way too personally, and I wasn't quite sure how we had gotten to this standoff.

Mikey cleared his throat from across the room, and I glanced across to him to see that both Joan and Adam were staring at me open-mouthed. Heat traveled up my neck and embarrassment flooded me.

"You said the B word again," Adam said with a shake of his head. "But it's okay, I can tell that you're upset. Mom used to use bad words when she was upset."

I looked away from his big round eyes, resting my gaze on the wooden table. I fought for something to change the subject, anything to draw the attention away from my stupid, overly dramatic outburst.

"Stop being so melodramatic." Nova rolled her eyes at me. "Seriously, chew some bubble gum and lighten the fuck up." She slid a fresh piece of gum across to me.

"When are we leaving?" I asked, clearing my throat. "It's stopped raining."

"That's what I said," Nova replied.

"We'll leave soon," Mikey said, still looking at me with concern in his eyes.

I hated that look. It made me feel weak and pathetic. And there was one thing I knew after all this time out here: I was not weak. Even when I felt I was really weak, when I didn't think I had the strength to fight through another day, I did, because I was strong.

"If we leave now we might not get there in time for nightfall, and I hate driving at night. It attracts too much attention."

I nodded and turned away. Nova was still staring at me, and I had an unnatural urge to scream really loudly in her face just to scare the shit out of her.

I pushed my chair back and stood up. "I'm going out," I said, moving toward the door.

"I'll come with you," Nova said, standing up.

"No, I want some space. I need some space," I replied sharply, emphasizing the need.

"No one goes out on their own. You know that, Nina," Mikey said calmly. "Calm down and sit down."

His words had the opposite effect on me and instead incensed me to leave this stuffy little room even more. I could hardly breathe with everyone's stare, with their condescending, judgmental looks. I hated it. And I hated the thought that I would always be seen as this snippy bitch. And my attitude at the moment wasn't helping me win anyone over. But I couldn't help it.

"I'm just stepping outside. I'll be fine. I won't go from right outside," I pleaded.

I stared at Mikey and he stared right back. Of course if I wanted to go, I damn well could, but we were a team, and we worked as a team, and I was trying really hard to be a part of it. I swallowed, feeling the suffocating, stale air make its way down my throat and into my lungs.

"You stay where we can see you, and I'll be at the window watching," he said, his words gruff.

I really wanted to tell him to stop acting like an over protective boyfriend, but in reality, I knew he'd do this if it were anyone and I wasn't getting any special treatment. Still, it pissed me off. A lot.

"Fine," I snapped. I pulled on the handle and opened the door, already starting to feel better when the fresh air hit my face.

"Nina!" Mikey barked, out making me jump.

"What?"

"Machete?" he asked with a raised eyebrow.

I patted my opposite hip and he nodded unhappily, and I finally stepped out into the fresh air.

I clicked the door shut softly, ignoring the little voice inside me that wanted to slam it hard enough to make pictures fall off the walls, and then I began to pace. I moved out from under the small canopy that covered the motel room door and let the heat of the day soak into my skin.

It wasn't exactly warm, but it was warmer than it had been in a long time—as if the storm of the past couple of days had blown away the last of winter, and spring was now well underway. That thought put things into perspective and made me smile. I had made it through another winter—my first winter outside the walls. I had come so far, learned so much, and yes, I had lost a lot, but each loss had made me stronger, and I truly felt ready to take on anything and anyone.

I walked, listening to the sound of my boots crunching the stones underfoot. I stepped around the corpses and tried my best to see the beauty of the day: the trees that were beginning to bud with leaves, the color of flowers ready to open, the fact that the sky was freaking blue! Blue…it had been gray or white for so long, I had almost forgotten that it could be blue.

I sat down on the hood of an old, beat-up Mustang, pulling myself up until I was comfy and then I took in the motel. It was rusted and falling apart from years of weather abuse and neglect, and I wished I could have seen it in its previous state. Sure, it was a shitty place and one I wouldn't have ever been seen dead in, but there was also a hidden beauty to it. If you looked past the cheapness, it was also quaint. Or maybe it had never been cheap and broken; maybe it had always been pretty and quaint but I hadn't taken the time to see it properly.

In many ways, nothing was what it seemed anymore, and nothing was to be truly trusted. People, things, places—there was always another side to them, and not always bad. There could be good in the world…if you took the time to look.

I thought of where I had come from, and how far I had come, and then my thoughts drifted to the other people from behind the walls— the many people that were still being forced to live under somebody's rule. People that were starving and dying, and being sentenced to death because of the people running those places.

And then I thought of the Forgotten.

I squeezed my eyes shut, hating that they were still inside my head, haunting me. The memories of what they did to me and what they forced Mikey to do were suddenly fresh. For a while I had put them aside, but now I felt angry—not just for me, but because they could do so much good. They could help other people if they wanted to. If they knew the truth, they could save those people.

I slid off the hood and made my way back to the motel, standing outside the door, knowing that Mikey was at the window watching me and knowing that Nova thought I couldn't truly change, that I was selfish and always would be selfish. And then there was Adam, the little boy inside, an orphan who'd survived out here on his own for all this time, despite all the odds stacked against him.

But we'd made it this far, and as much as I wanted to run and hide at Ben's parents' cabin, there would be a time for that, but right then I knew what we needed to do. Because Emily had said it to me months ago, and yet somewhere along the road we had forgotten—I had forgotten. Or maybe not forgotten, but I'd been too afraid to do it. But now that Emily was gone, now that I didn't have her to worry about, I knew that now was the time.

I opened the door and all eyes turned to me. No one said anything, and after several long, tense moments I broke the silence. "Sorry, that was a little dramatic. But then, what I have to say is pretty dramatic." I swallowed, my throat feeling dry. "I have a plan. But I'll need some help."

"A plan?" Nova asked, lighting a cigarette.

"Well, not a plan, more of an idea." I rolled my eyes.

"An idea?" Mikey said, coming toward me.

"Well," I shrugged, "I guess it's more of a vague, very loose concept."

Mikey smirked. "Well, go on then. Tell us this vague, loose concept of a plan that you've just thought of." He folded his arms across his chest and waited.

"Yeah, get on with it," Nova said through a mouth full of smoke. "The suspense is killing me," she added drolly.

Joan raised her hand in the air.

"What?" I asked.

"Did you find it?" she asked with a smile.

"Did I find what?"

"Nova said you were going to find yourself, did you find it? If you find yourself, maybe there's hope for me! I lost myself a long time ago and haven't been able to find myself since," she said with hope.

"Oh," I replied. "Well, yeah, I guess I did find myself, in a way."

"So your plan?" Mikey asked, ignoring Joan completely. "Or your vague concept. Because I thought we had a plan that was more solid than whatever thing you've just thought up."

Nova frowned. "You two thought up plans without me? What am

I, a fuckin' leper?"

"Bad word," Adam mumbled.

Nova scowled at him. "The world full of bad words, bad people, and bad things, kid."

"I'm leaving," I said to her, drawing her attention back to me.

"Correction, we're leaving," Mikey interjected.

"When? What do you mean you're leaving?" Nova stood up, her scowl growing by the second.

"Once we get back to the mall, I want to go out on my own." I rushed out the words, feeling like a traitor for saying them.

"Is this because of what I did? Because I killed the zombie kid? I thought we'd sorted that shit out?" Her nostrils flared in anger, and I sensed Mikey staring at both me and her in confusion. We hadn't ever really told him what had happened when we found Deacon and the baby—just that the whole trip had been a waste since Hilary was dead—and I realized that I probably should have told him the full story.

"No, it's not because of that, and in some ways yeah, it's everything to do with that. And more." I held up my hands when she tried to interrupt me. "This is all beside the point."

"Like fuck it is," she snapped angrily.

"Bad word," Adam said again, placing his hands over his ears.

I pinched between my brows. "No, it really is, because I don't want to leave now—at least not yet." I hurried out before she could yell at me again. "I'm not leaving."

"We're not?" Mikey asked, looking thoroughly confused. "And please start including me in the whole 'are we or aren't we leaving' thing," he said with an edge of pissiness solely directed at me.

I rolled my eyes at him dramatically before speaking. "No, we're not."

"Why not?" he asked, still sounding pissy enough that I wanted to shake him. I guess I hadn't realized how much he had been looking forward to going off the grid with me.

I looked down at my feet, knowing the next thing out of my mouth would cause the most arguments, but it had to come out regardless. I took a deep breath before looking up. "Emily said that she wanted to kill the Forgotten for what they did, and I want to live out that wish."

"Nina!" both Mikey and Nova said at the same time.

I hushed them both and hurried on. "Not all of them. Just Fallon. If we can kill him, then I think we could get the others to listen to us." *Because obviously killing people is my thing now,* I thought sourly.

"Listen to what, though?" Nova asked, still looking angry but curiosity winning her over now. "What do you want to say to any of them?"

"We're not going back there," Mikey said.

I glanced over, seeing his body rippling with tension.

"I want to help the people behind the walls, and to do that we need an army. We need the Forgotten," I said, mumbling the last part because really, I wasn't so sure of my loose concept of a plan now that I had said it out loud. It was clearly a death sentence…just hopefully not for us.

Silence had descended upon the group, and Adam finally took his hands down from his ears and continued shuffling the cards.

Joan looked up at me, her expression soft. "I'm in." She smiled, her chin high.

"Umm, thanks," I replied, not bothering to tell her that there was no way in hell that she was coming with me, and yet feeling equally pleased that someone was on my side.

"Where are we going?" She smiled again, looking from me to Mikey, and then over to Nova. "Will they have mojitos?"

FORTY-FOUR

The mood was somber in the truck the following morning. Mikey had barely said a word to me since the previous night's discussion, and I couldn't entirely blame him, I guess. Well, I could—of course I could—but I was choosing to be a responsible adult for once and lay the blame at my own feet. It sucked.

Nova had briefly spoken to me, and had apologized over and over for killing Deacon and "the thing," as she referred to it, begging me not to leave. The whole thing just made me all the more frustrated, because she was missing the entire point. I wasn't fucking leaving! At least not quite yet, and only if I made it out alive.

Which I had every intention of doing.

Now that my own strength had been proven to me, I knew I could survive anything. Well, almost anything. Some things would just make a girl dead no matter how strong you were. Like a bullet to the brain, for instance, which I'm sure Fallon—the leader of the Forgotten and his band of merry psychos—would have no problem in doing.

But God, if we could just kill him—again with the whole killing thing being second nature to me—and get the others to listen to what I had to say, things could work out. Mikey had said that a lot of the Forgotten didn't agree with the way things were being done, but did it because they wanted to live. Surely if we took out the threat to their lives, or at least the major one, they would be willing?

I had to believe that there were some good people left in the world. I had to, or I would just curl up and die right then. Emily couldn't have been the last good person in the world. I looked over at Adam, his face pressed against the window as he watched the world pass by, and I knew then that there was at least one other good person in the world.

We rounded the corner and the mall loomed in front of us. It seemed just the same as the last time I was there, and yet so much had changed. Deaders loitered in the parking lot, surrounded by their murdered brethren. *Same old, same old,* I thought with a heavy heart.

They turned at the sound of the truck, and began their slow shamble toward us. Mikey and Nova steered between the rotting bodies as best they could, but some hits were inevitable. Adam curled up in the footwell of the truck with his hands over his ears, blocking out the destruction, and I kind of wanted to join him. I didn't want to see that, the bodies breaking apart as our trucks hit them, their flesh splitting open and releasing dead maggots and rotten guts. We zipped passed a female deader, her coat whipping up around her as the air briskly moved. She spun and almost fell, and then her feet must have got confused with which was doing what because she collapsed to her knees, and even with the noise from our engine, I heard her kneecaps crunch.

We pulled around the back of the mall, Mikey jumped out to open the service entrance, and I slipped into his seat and eased the truck inside. When the gate was secure in place, I cut the engine and climbed out. Adam followed me out, his hand slipping easily into mine.

The air smelled stale, with not even a breeze to move the smell along. Everything seemed quiet, yet we could see several of our trucks from base camp, and so knew that our group—or what little of it remained—was here, and we collectively breathed a sigh of relief.

"Are you okay?" I asked Mikey as we walked to the small employee door.

He looked down at Adam and then back at me. "I think your plan is stupid."

"It's not a plan, it's a vague concept," I replied with a smirk, hoping to win him over with my wit and charm. It didn't work.

"We'll all be killed," he said, his words heavy with worry.

"They'll listen to you."

"No, they won't." He looked away from me, as if the very sight of me annoyed him. "And you'll die, and it will be my fault." His words were somber and painful.

Maybe it was a stupid idea that would get us all killed. And maybe I should just have just left it and been on my way, but at that point it felt like I'd been running for years, and I didn't want to run anymore. I wanted to stand and fight. I want to protect and I want to survive, not just live day to day. And currently, my nightmares were filled with the threat of the Forgotten and the horror of life behind the walls. Living with those horrors was no way to live, and the only way I knew to make them go away was to destroy them.

"No, it will be my fault. Now get a fucking grip, Mikey. We can do this."

At my words he jerked his face back to mine, a small curve starting on his lips. "I love it when you talk dirty."

"Shut up." I laughed lightly and pushed his shoulder.

"You two bitches done?" Nova said, pushing past me. She scowled down at Adam, who closed his mouth before he said anything about her swearing.

The hallway was like I remembered, though now it felt used—as if I could hear the movement of feet echoing along it. We hurried along, eager to see everyone, our friends, our family, or what little was left of them. I wondered how they were all settling in; it was, after all, their new home. At the end of the corridor, Nova pushed the door wide open, stepping into the bright hub of the mall. A loud *crack* rang out and she stumbled backwards with a cry of pain.

I looked at her flailing body stumbling backwards, trying to work out what the hell had just happened, and then I looked to Mikey, confused. Another *crack* sounded out, and Joan yelped and quickly slammed the door shut and we were plunged back into semi-darkness again.

"Nova!" I yelled, before Mikey's hand clasped tightly over my mouth.

"I'm here," Nova panted out. "I'm alive. Fuck, that hurts," she gasped, and I felt the air shifting around us.

I followed the sound of her voice, watched for the subtle shadow of her body on the floor, and I knelt down at her side. "What happened?" I asked, still confused.

"Gunshot," Mikey said, his ear pressed to the door.

I looked at the place where Nova was clutching her stomach, noticing the dark patch seeping around her hands, and realization finally hit me.

"Oh shit, oh shit, oh shit." I tore off my blouse and pressed it against the wound.

Nova hissed but clutched at the blouse, stemming her own blood flow. "I'm okay, I'm a tough bitch," she said through clenched teeth.

"Who's in there, Mikey?" I asked. My voice sounded too loud and panicky, and I knew that any second, whoever was in there was going to come out and kill us all. In theory we should have been running, dragging Nova, Adam, and Joan out of the danger. Yet there we were, frozen to the spot in fear.

"Fallon," he said, turning to face me. "It's Fallon in there, I'd know his voice anywhere."

"Shut the fuck up!" both Nova and I said in total disbelief at the same time.

"What are the fuckin' chances of that?" Nova looked over at me, her jaw hanging slack from both the revelation and the pain.

Tears of anger and frustration burned my eyes. Why wouldn't he just let us go—let Mikey go? How could one person be so intent on slaughtering so many innocent people? It was then that I realized that Fallon would never let Mikey go, or me.

"They came to end this, end all of you." Mikey pulled out his gun.

I could hardly see him in the dark, but I heard him—heard his gun. I heard the safety click off, and I heard the thump of his heart, heavy and foreboding in the dark.

"Nina, take Adam and Joan, and you and Nova get the hell out of here."

I watched his shadow turn away from me and I stood up abruptly. "No, don't you dare go in there, Mikey. Don't you fucking dare!"

Adam had begun to whimper next to me, and his little hands were tight around my leg, his small fingers digging into to my skin. Joan was off whimpering somewhere else in the dark, but God knew where because I couldn't see her.

I dragged Mikey back away from the door, knowing we only had seconds before they came to find us. The only reason they were hesitating was because they didn't know how many of us there were out here. Clearly, we had taken them by surprise, and they were taking it cautiously because of that. They hadn't expected someone to just walk right in like that, but we wouldn't be so lucky a second time. We needed to go. Now.

Mikey pulled out of my grip. "He'll kill you, Nina, and it will all have been for nothing. I can't let him get you again—I can't watch what he did…"

"We'll do this together, we'll take him together," I pleaded, gripping his arms roughly.

"And the kid? What happens to him if you die?" Mikey said flatly, stepping backwards.

"I can barely keep myself alive. What are the chances he'll be safe with me?" I bit out angrily.

"It's better this way. I'll kill myself before he makes me hurt anyone else, I promise, but I can't do that if he has you." His voice was tinged with deep desperation, and I felt sorrow and loss like I hadn't experienced before. It cut worse than Emily-Rose, and worse than Ben. Because I had let him in, I had let him have my heart. I wouldn't ever get this chance again; our time was over. "I love you, Nina."

A shadow moved behind Mikey, and I realized that Nova had stood up and was limping back toward the door. My heart froze when I thought of her life-threatening injuries, and what would happen to her when she died from them.

"Nova?" I whispered, almost too scared to say her name in case she growled in response and lunged for us. Because if she were dead and had just turned, then she was about to take a bite out of one of us unless we took her out first.

"Take care, darlin'. It was worth the crazy ride, I promise you that… now fuckin' run, all of you!"

I saw the space around us light up as she lit a cigarette and then, holding it between her lips, she turned and charged at the door.

She shoulder-barged it open, and as the light flooded in I saw her two guns in her hands. I saw the flash of them as she fired them over and over, and I saw firsthand as her body shook while bullet after bullet pounded into her flesh. She fired back at the threat beyond those doors, her body blocking any bullets that tried to make it past her. And whoever was there continued to shoot back at her, riddling her already-damaged body with bullets. She dropped to her knees and her guns rang empty, and then she fell face forward just short of the door.

The door swung back closed, and we were embraced back into the darkness, trapped with the sounds of crying and whimpering from Joan and Adam. Yells and shouts rang out loudly from behind the closed door, and I realized that I was gasping for air. I was panting, the room going dizzy and spinning as I struggled to suck the oxygen into my lungs. Because it was all too much, too goddamn much. How could it be happening now, after what we had done to get back there, to save Jessica, to give Adam some sort of peace?

"Nina?" Mikey whispered, his voice close to my ear. "We need to go. She's bought us time, she may even have killed him, but we can't risk sticking around to find out."

"What about everyone else?" I whispered back, warm tears bleeding from my eyes. "All the people from the base?" But I was already moving, already backing out of the hallway as quietly as I could while still staring at the place that Nova had just been.

"They're dead. Fallon wouldn't let them live if he knew they were with us," Mikey replied darkly, and I knew he was right.

The shock of that simple statement broke me, and fresh misery erupted within my warring mind. Because of me all of my friends were now dead. Because of me. I couldn't do it. I couldn't carry on. I couldn't live with the guilt.

Adam clung to my leg tighter, his cries sounding muffled as he buried his face in my pants. And I realized that I *had* to carry on. I had no choice. Because I had Adam to look after now, and somewhere else in that godforsaken corridor, I had Joan.

"We need to go," Mikey said again, his words more urgent.

He gripped my hand and began tugging at me, pulling me along the hallway until we were back outside and the sunlight was blinding me. I turned to see Joan stumbling out of the darkness too, her face crippled in pain and sadness. She avoided things like this, she hid, and so to see it, to be a part of it, was soul-destroying for her. Even her alter ego couldn't take this much stress.

Mikey pulled us toward the truck, and I pushed Adam and Joan inside while Mikey dragged open the gate. I looked back toward the staff entrance one last time, thinking how only moments ago Nova had walked in there with us, alive and looking forward to seeing her brother and her friends. Of how she had bought us precious moments by going back through that door and hopefully killing some of Fallon's men.

I thought of how I had wanted to go after Fallon and kill him, how I had wanted to use the Forgotten to take down the people of the walled cities. To help free those people trapped in misery behind their walls.

Now it all seemed so ridiculous. Pointless, and so impossible. Yet beyond that, I felt angry and frustrated. Because for every step forward, there seemed to be so many more backwards. And I couldn't do it anymore. Because men like Fallon needed to die, they needed to be ended—finished—if there was ever going to be hope for anyone again.

"Nina!" Mikey urged, climbing inside the truck. "Come on, quickly, they'll be coming."

I looked in at him—seeing him, and Adam, and Joan, and knowing I would never see Emily or Nova or so many other people that I held dear to me, ever again. My mouth tightened into a thin line. Because I knew what I had to do—what I wanted to do to protect the people I cared about. Because I couldn't lose another person I loved. I couldn't let another innocent person go through the suffering that those men were subjecting people to.

I understood Nova's actions now. It wasn't just about giving in and sacrificing yourself. It was about protecting those you cared about. No matter what. That little boy needed someone to look after him, and it couldn't be me, because I only ever got people killed.

"Don't." Mikey breathed out the words, his eyes filling with terror, like he'd read my mind. Adam began to cry, his quiet sobs turning to wails.

"I'm sorry," I said to both of them. "Look after him, Mikey." And then I slammed the door of the truck shut. I mouthed *I love you* as Mikey reached for his door handle, and then I turned and ran.

I ran away from Mikey, away from our truck, and away from my freedom. I ran back through the employee entrance, ignoring the sound of Mikey shouting and begging me to come back, knowing that he wouldn't—couldn't—come after me because he had to look after Adam. Adam who was wailing loudly.

I ran back down the dark and death-filled hallway toward the main mall entrance. I pushed open the door, stepping over Nova's bloody body with my gun raised high, hoping to take them by surprise, hoping I wouldn't die, but knowing I possibly would. But it would be worth it. Because no matter what, Fallon would continue to kill innocent people that didn't deserve his judgment, and someone had to stop him—someone had to try. Because it wasn't fair, it was cruel and wrong, and life was hard enough as it was.

So I stood up for every innocent person that he had harmed, because I wasn't running from it anymore. I wasn't running and hiding, I was facing up to him, and be damned the consequences. Because those innocents didn't have a voice, and like Mikey had said, I did. So let my voice ring out nice and clear that I wouldn't stand by anymore, that I wouldn't let those people die for nothing.

And if I died? So be it. Like Mikey had said, 'your loved ones are worth both living and dying for.' And Mikey was worth every beat of my heart and every drop of my blood. I'd protect him, the way I failed Emily, the way I failed Ben. They all died, and though it was illogical, I blamed myself. So I would protect Mikey the only way I knew how.

Because I knew I'd see him again one day, in this life or the next.

READ ON FOR A SNEAK PEAK OF ODIUM IV..

ONE

MIKEY

The truck rumbles along with as much gusto as it had previously, yet now it feels empty. Everything feels empty. Nina went back inside. She left me with Adam and Joan, knowing I wouldn't be able to leave them. She had wanted her vengeance no matter what the cost to herself or anyone else.

I hate her.

My shoulders shake as I try to contain my sadness, as I try to ignore the ache of despair that bubbles away in my stomach. Adam cried himself to sleep at some point in the last hour, and Joan is still staring numbly out the window like she has been for several hours. It's the quietest she's been since I met her, and I wonder how much of her so-called craziness is actually real. Because the look on her face makes it clear that she fully understands the importance of what just happened.

We won't get much further before the gas runs out. We'll need to stop soon, find somewhere safe to spend the night. But nowhere is safe. I can't run away from my past anymore. It's all caught up with me, and

346

now I've lost everything and everyone. How many more times can I do this? Run from it and them? Hide and hope that I can escape the memories of friends and family that have died because of my selfishness and stupidity? I slow the truck, wanting to turn around—and not for the first time—but then I think of Adam and Joan, and how they rely on me now, how Nina has put their safety in my hands.

I hate her.

Rubbing away the tears that have trailed down my dirty cheeks, I grit my teeth. My anger will be my fuel—my anger at her and at them, but mostly at myself. I look in my rearview mirror, seeing the setting sun behind me, slipping below the tree line and buildings that we're passing, and I panic again.

We'll need to stop. They need to eat, and I'm pretty sure one or both of them has pissed themselves. I can't care for them; I can barely care for myself. Damn her! My hands grip the steering wheel tighter, my calloused knuckles going white.

I hate her.

All she had wanted was to help people. Even in her bitchiest moments, that was all she had wanted. She covered her kindness with attitude, but she wanted the world back to how it was, when we helped one another, when we cared, and felt, and loved, and we survived as a human race and not as selfish individuals.

I have never regretted anything in life, not until this moment. Even my fucked up past I haven't regretted, because to regret it was to change it, and if I changed one damn thing, I may never have met her. And to never have met her would have been my biggest regret yet.

I love her.

And now she's gone. She went back to do what I had been running from—what I had been hiding from. She went back to end this fight.

And it cost her everything, it cost me everything. She was brave and beautiful, and I lost her.

What the hell am I going to do now?

ABOUT THE AUTHOR

Claire C. Riley is USA Today and International bestselling author. Eclectic writer of all things apocalyptic and romance, she enjoys hiking, movie marathon, & old school board games. Claire lives in Manchester England with her husband, three daughters and naughty rescue beagle.

She writes under C. Riley for her thrillers and suspense.

She can be found on Facebook, Instagram, TikTok and more!

For a full list of her works, head over to her Amazon author page.

CONTACT LINKS

Website: www.clairecriley.com

FB page: https://www.facebook.com/ClaireCRileyAuthor/

Amazon: http://amzn.to/1GDpF3I

Reader Group: Riley's Rebels: https://www.facebook.com/groups/

ClaireCRileyFansGroup/

Newsletter Sign-up: http://bit.ly/2xTY2bx

IG: https://www.instagram.com/redheadapocalypse/

Twitter: @ClaireCRiley

Tik Tok: @redheadapocolypse

Made in the USA
Monee, IL
06 July 2024

61329075R00208